BURNING
SKIES

St. Martin's Paperbacks Titles by
Caris Roane

ASCENSION

BURNING SKIES

BURNING SKIES

CARIS ROANE

St. Martin's Paperbacks

BURNING SKIES

Copyright © 2011 by Caris Roane.

All rights reserved.

For information address St. Martin's Press, 175 Fifth Avenue, New York, NY 10010.

ISBN: 978-0-312-53372-4

Printed in the United States of America

St. Martin's Paperbacks edition / May 2011

St. Martin's Paperbacks are published by St. Martin's Press, 175 Fifth Avenue, New York, NY 10010.

10 9 8 7 6 5 4 3 2 1

ACKNOWLEDGMENTS

Many thanks to my agent, Jennifer Schober, for all the ongoing conversations about the Guardians of Ascension. Yes, Endelle rocks!

To Rose Hilliard, whose constant stream of encouragement has made writing this series a pleasure.

To Danielle Fiorella—I didn't think the cover to *Ascension* could be topped but somehow you did it. *Burning Skies* is a visual feast.

As for Laurie Henderson and Laura Jorstad, do you keep diamond "files" in those beautiful brains of yours? The production and copyedits are absolute perfection.

I am once again so very grateful to Anne Marie Tallberg, Eileen Rothschild, and Brittney Kleinfelter for working so diligently to create that critical link between author and reader.

And as always, many thanks to Matthew Shear and Jen Enderlin who have created an extraordinary team at SMP.

Go, team!

Let go . . .

The undead.
A state of being.
Not of vampires
But of the lost and lonely.
Oh, heart that cries,
Live and
Be satisfied.

—*Collected Poems,* Beatrice of Fourth

CHAPTER 1

Got a death wish, handsome?

Marcus heard the woman's voice in his head, but the sound was like gears grinding. He refused to respond.

He hit the gas harder on his Harley, leaned, took the curve in the road with ease, felt the vibration up both arms and smiled.

He wore sunglasses on a sunless Pacific Northwest day. Even in June, the weather could pile up overhead. It did today, so he took the mist and occasional rain in his face and still he smiled.

The retro Harley had arrived a week ago, and he'd finally left his boardrooms long enough to take the hog over to the Olympic Peninsula. He cruised the coastal route, preferring views of the wild ocean waters to the depths of forest, at least today. Sometimes he liked disappearing into the narrow inland roads where the conifers towered overhead and an entire world lived in shadow.

Hey, slow down, gorgeous. You aren't that immortal.

Go home, he sent, his mind to her mind. *The answer is the same . . . no.*

Endelle, the Supreme High Administrator of Second Earth, was in his head again as she had been off and on for weeks now. He was tired of the same old, same old—*Come back to Second Earth, return to the Warriors of the Blood, take up your sword, serve my sorry ass.*

She might not have said *serve my sorry ass.* Those were his words and like hell he was going to do that.

He'd cut off his left nut first.

Aw, Warrior, don't be like that.

Yeah, the bitch was back, somehow watching him, somehow reading his mind, somehow talking straight into his head and making another run at his sanity. She was one powerful vampire.

She was also a piece of work. Endelle had served Second Earth as Supreme High Administrator for most of her nine thousand years and she'd lost her subtlety her first day on the job. He loved her and hated her. Right now she was a gnat in his head and he didn't have the means to swat her away. He sighed. There was no way he'd be getting rid of her until she'd had her say.

Whatever.

He went faster, twisting the accelerator, pushing the bike to its limit, to that place where the wheels almost broke loose and threw him into a deadly spin. Almost.

He used his preternatural senses to gauge the trajectory of each dip and turn in the wet road. He extended his hearing so he could determine what cars or trucks were headed in his direction and just how soon they'd pose a threat. See, he was being safe. Sort of.

Endelle had one thing right: He wasn't *that* immortal. No vampire was completely immune to death. If he slammed hard enough into a wall of rock, or got his head cut off in a sword fight, yeah he'd be dead.

So just how much of a death wish was this?

He wore black leather, the only time he did. Leather kept the cold out, the moisture out. As he pushed along the coast, he was on a high. He felt *good,* a sensation that escaped him most days . . . and nights. For a man with billions, God his life sucked.

"I'll ask you again," Endelle said, only this time her breath was in his ear. "You got a death wish or what, Warrior?"

"Endelle, what the fuck?" he shouted into the wind. Her body was now plastered against him from behind. "What are you doing here?" One slip of his control and the bike would slide away from him, do a few flips, send him barreling into oblivion.

"You must be going eighty, ninety miles an hour. What gives?"

He gritted his teeth. Words punched out of his mouth. "Get off my bike."

"Mm." She wiggled her hips. "This feels *good*. And those vibrations . . . straight up my ass. I might just have to get me one of these."

"What the hell do you want?" he cried.

"You know why I'm here." She cuddled closer, her arms around his waist.

"I'm not going back," he cried.

She fingered his hair. *Who do you think you're kidding?* she responded, sending the words straight into his head. *You've been letting your hair grow and we both know what that means. A few more months and you'll have warrior hair.*

The hell I will and get out of my head. He didn't ease back on the speed.

He felt her sigh as she hugged him hard. "I need a man," she shouted.

"Not gonna be me," he shouted back, dipping the bike as the road curved to the left.

"Wasn't asking, asshole."

The arms disappeared. The warm press of body as well. Thank God.

The next second, however, she materialized on his handlebars, her knees in his face. He had to lean a little to see the stretch of road in front of him. It was somewhat straight for at least a few hundred yards. Shit.

"Dammit, Endelle! Get off my fucking bike!"

She was dressed in black leather from head to foot except for the small red feathers that trimmed the V of her vest. *Come back to us,* she sent. *We need you, Warrior.*

She leaned close and now he really couldn't see the road, just the depth of her cleavage above a really low-cut leather vest, trimmed with red feathers. Her bare arms were wet from the rain and mist.

Fuck.

He had one of two choices—cliff leading to the ocean or mountain wall.

Yeah, fuck.

He swung to the right and went over the cliff. "You are such a bitch," he shouted, hitting airspace.

With preternatural speed and a bit of levitation, he folded off his black leather jacket and black T-shirt and, at almost the same time, mounted his wings midair. He turned into the wind and headed . . . down. He had power and he was fast, goddamn fast, but not faster than the gravity that took his bike down a slope of seaside cliff. His Harley bounced off a couple of trees, slid over stone outcroppings, then landed in a huge-ass fucking pile of driftwood about thirty yards from the surf.

He let the obscenities fly.

The gasoline in the tank did a nice pop-and-flare that turned to a pitiful stream of black smoke under the drenching mist and rain.

He trained his wings into the offshore breeze so that he

didn't roll. He hovered above the wreck, his mouth still a tumble of profanity.

"Aw. Too bad." Endelle now stood on the largest water-stripped log, looking down at the wreck, her arms folded over her leather-feather chest. She didn't smile as she lifted her gaze to him. She just stared. Damn, her eyes looked ancient. He always forgot that about her. Vampire life gave longevity to muscle, skin, and bone, youth returned and savored, but the eyes never lied.

She smiled. "You ready to stop playing spoiled-little-rich-boy? You ready to do some man's work again?"

He flipped her off as he drew in his wings, supporting himself in the air with old-fashioned levitation. As soon as the last of the feathers and connecting mesh support disappeared into his back, he folded to his house on Bainbridge Island, straight to the master bedroom. He thumped his way to the bathroom, shoulders hunched, fists so tight that both arms hurt. He stripped, got seven showerheads to steaming, then stepped into his shower.

"Damn, Marcus, how much you been working out? You have the ass of a god."

He turned to face her, and naturally her gaze fell to his jewels. She shook her head and sighed. "You warriors are so fucking hung and I really do need a man."

"Get the hell out of my bathroom. Get the hell out of my house and get the hell out of my life." He turned to face the water, grabbed soap and lathered.

"You don't have a choice on this one."

"The hell I don't. You had one favor. You called it in. I served. We're done."

"That was four months ago. I've decided I get another one. You do a lot of squat-thrusts? Hey, what's with the mist? And do you really think I can't see through that shit?" She snorted. "But if you're feeling modest, mist away."

Mist. He should have known better than to try. Mist was designed to confuse the mind, and a powerful mist could confuse the mind of mortals and ascenders alike—just not the leader of Second Earth. Endelle was too damn powerful. Still, it was his bathroom. Privacy would have been nice.

He stopped talking. There was no point. Endelle was as stubborn as the rotation of the earth. But then, so was he. She ought to know that. He wasn't four millennia for nothing.

"Morgan's not sleeping very well," she said.

At that, he stopped moving the soap around his chest. Endelle rarely called Havily by her first name.

Havily Morgan.

Oh. God. Havily. The woman meant for him. The one he craved. The one he fantasized about making love to every goddamn night.

So the fuck what? he sent, the soap moving again.

"She told me about the fennel, vampire."

"What fennel?"

"She smells you, Warrior. You know what that means."

"Don't call me *Warrior*. I'm a businessman and I'm not going back. Not for you. Not for Havily. Not for anyone. I belong here. I'm happy here." Sort of. Besides, he'd made one helluva life for himself on Mortal Earth and after seeing the war up close and personal again, he wasn't having it, not any part of it.

"Morgan drags in to work every morning now. You know anything about that?"

He rinsed off, left the shower, pushed past her and grabbed a towel. He dried his hair first then worked his way down his body. Yeah, he knew something about why Havily might not be sleeping very well. It was his dirty little secret and the hell if he was going to share it with Endelle. What was going on between them was private, a word Endelle respected about as much as she respected his mental shields.

"That's what I thought," she murmured. "You've been getting into her pants with no one the wiser. You enthralling her or what?"

At that he rose up and glared, straight into her brown

eyes. "You think so little of me that you believe I would *enthrall* her?"

"No. I don't. I just can't figure out what's going on because that little twat of yours has shields I have one helluva time bypassing."

He glared a little more, then his gaze dropped to the red feathers. They were small, crimson, beautiful. "What are they and where are you getting them?" One of his corporations operated in the fashion industry. Yeah, he was a businessman first.

"A little import shop on Central Two. They come from Mortal Earth. Someone's raising cardinals in Tucson. Don't worry. It's organic. The feathers are collected *after* the birds are slaughtered."

"You're a walking PETA nightmare."

"You gone vegan on me, or what?"

"No. I still eat steak."

She looked him up and down. "I know what you mean. Still prefer meat myself."

He rolled his eyes, swung the towel around his hips, and strolled into his bedroom. Apparently he wasn't getting rid of the bitch until Labor Day . . . maybe. And here it was only June.

"Spill it, Endelle. I have meetings this evening until ten."

He heard her sigh as he worked his way through his sock drawer. He glanced at her and frowned a little. Sighing wasn't high on Endelle's list. He straightened up. "You worried about hurting my feelings?"

"No. It's just one more fucking thing I can't control. So here it is. I've been getting this *feeling* lately that something's going on with Morgan, something big. And . . . I'm worried. I know you've been seeing her, somehow, though I haven't got the *how* of it figured out yet, but just be careful, would you? And if something out of the ordinary happens, be prepared."

"You never liked her."

She jerked her arms at him, her fingers spread cat-like, then shouted, "What the fuck does that have to do with anything? The truth is, I never gave a shit about Havily Morgan one way or the other except that she's been just one big fucking disappointment from the day she ascended. You wouldn't know about that because you've been here tickling your balls for the last two centuries, but her rite of ascension was a BFD with no payoff. The future streams were all lit up about her, that she needed protection, lots of it, that she would make this huge contribution to the war.

"So of course I gave her Luken as her Guardian of Ascension. I'm rubbing my hands together thinking now we've got something, now we'll see some real shit. Then she ascends and all she's got are some super-powerful mental shields that make it hard to get into her head. That's it. *Shields*. What the fuck good are shields to the war effort?"

He couldn't help but smile. She probably wasn't even aware that she was now standing on the arms of the leather club chair near the window.

She looked down at her stilettos. "Shit. I just punched holes in your chair. Ooooh. I feel sooo bad."

He wagged his head back and forth then moved to the side of his bed. With a pair of socks in one hand and the towel snug around his waist, he sat down. "You're too impatient," he said. "You always were. Some powers emerge over time. Look at Kerrick. He can fold now, right? He had all that power but until he completed the *breh-hedden* with Alison, he couldn't fold. Now he can. I couldn't fucking levitate for the first thousand years. Havily's only a hundred years on Second Earth. Give her time."

Thoughts of the *breh-hedden* stopped his mind for a moment. He still couldn't believe that the *breh-hedden* had actually touched his life. For centuries this extreme form of ritual mate-bonding between Warriors of the Blood and powerful women was believed to be nothing more than a myth. Then it had hit Warrior Kerrick when his *breh*, Alison

Wells, began her rite of ascension four months ago. Shortly after, Marcus had been struck down as well.

"Listen up, asshole," Endelle cried, "because you may have just made both my points. First, I don't think she's got time because I have this sinking pit of a feeling in my chest about her. Do you hear me?"

He stared at her, the hair on the nape of his neck rising, but he said, "You're screeching like a bad off-Broadway actress. Why the drama?"

She narrowed her eyes. "And my second point, asshole, is that I think Havily needs you to get her where she needs to go. She's holding back. Big time. I think she's more powerful than she knows, but she can't let go. You could help with that. You've got a lot of vampire years under your belt." She smiled. "By the way, that float-and-mount you did, watching your wings come while you just hung midair, that was some powerful shit."

Whatever, he sent. He tossed the pair of socks into the air then caught them. He did this again and again.

"Not coming back," he stated. Maybe if he said it often enough, she'd take the hint. "But . . . I will watch out for Havily." He couldn't help that. It was in his nature and, yeah, the *breh-hedden* had struck hard four months ago when he'd been back on Second Earth to help out for a few days. It had started with catching the scent of honeysuckle and ended with a kiss that almost turned into full-on sex—in less than a minute. Jesus, when he thought of what he'd almost done to Havily that last night and what she'd almost let him do . . . Christ.

None of it mattered, though. Havily lived on Second Earth. He lived on Mortal Earth.

Except at night. She came to him in his dreams—that weren't dreams—every night.

Endelle sighed. Again. "Whatever, asshole. But if something happens to her because you can't be bothered, then that shit's on your head." She lifted her hand and was gone. Finally.

He sat with the towel around his hips, his socks once more in his hand, his feet flat on the floor.

Endelle was right. Something was going on with Havily, because from the first night that he'd folded back to Mortal Earth, she'd been coming to him while he slept. And as much as he wanted to believe it was just a dream or some kind of weird-ass ascended fantasy, she was real. She was also *really* naked.

He would wake up with her either balanced on his hips or in the act of impaling herself on his rigid cock. She just wasn't aware of what she was doing, at least not initially, because she appeared to be caught in a dream.

The trouble was—and his conscience beat the shit out of him for this—he couldn't seem to bring himself to stop this nightly ritual or whatever the hell it was. Partly because he couldn't quite make sense of what was happening between them or even where they were . . . exactly. His bed remained the same, but the room faded to a line of very dark shadows all around the edge as though he were someplace other than his house on Bainbridge.

When it had first happened, he really had believed he'd been caught up in some kind of freak-shit preternatural dreamscape so he'd helped himself to the experience, savoring her body. Unfortunately, his enthusiasm as he grabbed her forced her to awaken, and she fled, dematerializing from his arms. So it had been real, but not real, a dream, but not a dream. All he knew was that his skin carried her honeysuckle scent until he showered the next morning. The experience was *real,* even though he couldn't explain *how* it was real.

So help him God, he hadn't turned her away once, but he should have.

God help him, he should have.

Havily Morgan *craved* and she despised herself for it.

She sat on the side of her bed, the sheet and comforter drawn back. She wore a soft cream negligee, and boy did she need her sleep. Her mind and body were exhausted from another day of service to Madame Endelle. The woman put the *b* in *bitch* as well as the *i* and the *t* and whatever.

She leaned forward slightly, releasing a heavy sigh. But it wasn't Endelle that weighed her heart down now, that spiraled her daytime exhaustion into a dark cavern of despair. No, it was Warrior Marcus and her complete inability even in her dreams to stay away from him.

She stared out the window, which overlooked her small patio and a good portion of Camelback Mountain. The hillside was nothing but a black monolith this late at night, a dark presence of ancient volcanic rock burnished by the desert sun, dotted with prickly pear and scattered oily creosote shrubs. Lizards lived back there. Scorpions. Rabbits. Coyotes.

She'd like to crawl among the rocks and maybe disappear. Maybe then she'd get a good night's rest.

She turned and put her hand on the sheets, smoothing the wrinkles out of the black silk. She'd purchased the sheets a week after the dreams began because they were the same sheets that were on *the bed*, the ones in *the dreams*, the dreams where she encountered Warrior Marcus—*every night*.

A sigh caught her again. The chances she would find a good night's sleep in this bed were slim-to-good-luck-with-that.

Ever since she'd met Warrior Marcus, she'd been stuck in an in-between place, neither here nor there. She was Marcus's lover, but she wasn't his lover; what happened between them was real but it wasn't real.

She just didn't understand what was going on and worse, she didn't know how to stop what happened between them *every night*. Worse and worse, it was always the same. She would fall asleep and somehow in her dreams she would strip out of her nightgown, search for him and find him and be with him.

He would by lying in bed on black silk sheets and very

much asleep. She would draw the covers back and he would be naked. She always looked at him, a long lingering look down the length of his powerful warrior body as though she couldn't get enough of the sight of him.

She would engage with him in a very sensual way. She would put her nose to his body and take in his extremely erotic scent, a blend of earthy grasses and licorice, like fennel. Arousal would seep into her until the vein at her neck throbbed. She would then let her fantasy take flight and she would mount him. At some point he would awaken, or perhaps he never was asleep, she just didn't know. His desire for her took many forms, the answering buck of his hips, the way his arms would skate up and down hers, the way he lunged for her throat with his fangs.

But as she drew close to that sweet place of ecstasy, she would always, always, *always* wake up to absolute horror at what she was doing. She had come to believe that he was doing this to her, that somehow, being the powerful vampire he was, he was summoning her to his bed and seducing her in her dreams.

For that she despised him almost as much as she despised herself for going to him every night.

What followed was also the same. She would draw away from him and out of the dream-like state in a strange swishing glide that would return her to her bed, on her knees staring at the wall above her headboard. Being *returned* to her bed made her think the experience had to be real yet she just didn't know the *how* of it.

Lately, however, when she would return from being in this dream-fantasy, she would fall on her face and sob her heart out. That the fantasy left her sexually frustrated was half the difficulty. The other half belonged to the cravings that had gripped her heart, her body, her veins for the past four months. She was in a constant state of torment and had been from the moment she had met Warrior Marcus.

Once the tears ceased, however, the real frustration began, because it was Warrior Marcus's scent that lingered on her body. For hours afterward, as she tossed on her bed, she would smell his rich erotic fennel scent and her body would tremble. Cravings for him came in waves and she couldn't make them stop. The *breh-hedden* had her cornered and trapped with nowhere to go but to wait for the dawn and for her next workday to begin all over again.

Would to God that she had never met him.

So she sat on the edge of her bed, exhausted, in need of rest but knowing that the night would play out as all the others and once more she would be deprived of rest.

She closed her eyes. She wrapped her arms around her chest. Surely she could choose differently this night. Surely just once she could avoid seeking him out in her dreams, holding his sex deep inside her, waking up frightened and unfulfilled then falling away from him to return to her bedroom.

She hated this ritual yet she craved and couldn't seem to stop it.

Something needed to change, but what?

As she finally climbed between the sheets, she vowed that she would alter the future, no matter what it took. There had to be some way to stop the dreaming.

With a commitment made, she closed her eyes and began drifting toward sleep. She mentally sent out the affirmation, *I will change this.*

She released a heavy sigh.

I will change this.

At last, sleep came.

Tend to Havily's dreams.

Alison Wells awoke uncertain what had disturbed her sleep. She was alone in bed, her usual state since her warrior, Kerrick, was out battling, and would be through the night, not returning until dawn. She wore one of his black T-shirts and lifted the hem, pulling it up to her nose. She smiled. The shirt smelled like Kerrick, the warm scent of cardamom-and-man combined, the telltale scent being the most remarkable aspect of the *breh-hedden*. According to Kerrick, she smelled of lavender, while from the first moment she had met him, his spicy cardamom had filled her with the deepest cravings.

She craved even now, but she'd have to wait until dawn to find the relief she needed when Kerrick finally tumbled into bed.

During her ascension four months ago, she'd endured three of the most frightening, challenging days of her life when she'd left Mortal Earth to ascend to Second Earth. The process had been extraordinary; she'd answered her call to ascension by demonstrating power at one of the dimensional Borderlands, she'd battled death vampires to stay alive, she'd fought the fierce and powerful General Leto in an arena battle and won. When the three-day period drew to a close, she underwent a ceremony at Madame Endelle's palace. Endelle had imbued her with the relative immortality of Second Earth and with the vampire traits of fangs.

But what had awakened her?

Tend to Havily's dreams.

The familiar voice spoke inside her head, a masculine voice, which belonged to a Sixth Earth ascender known simply as James. From the time of her ascension some four months ago, James had communicated telepathically with her several times. She couldn't explain why, but she had developed a fondness for the vampire, sensing in his presence great warmth of spirit and certainly a desire to help Madame Endelle and the war effort.

James had become her occasional guide as she moved through her new duties on Second Earth. Originally, Alison thought Endelle was to contact James, but he had made it clear that for now Alison was to be the go-between, the one he used to offer what limited help he could to Endelle's faction.

She closed her eyes and concentrated. *What's up, James?* she sent.

Haven't got much time, he responded. *You need to keep*

tabs on Havily, stick close for the next few days and encourage her in her dreams, which are not dreams, and do what you can to give her a push in Warrior Marcus's direction. Do you understand?

Sort of, she sent. Now, why couldn't James speak in less cryptic sentences? Dreams that aren't really dreams?

She heard a soft masculine chuckle inside her head. *Now, what would the fun be in that,* he sent, which also meant he had *read* her thoughts.

Alison was so new to the world of dimensions, yet so heavily burdened with responsibility, that she couldn't quite find the same humor in the situation. *James, I wish I could laugh about this as you do, but do you have any idea how badly the war is going for Madame Endelle? How close Commander Greaves is to world domination?*

A long pause followed. *Yes,* he murmured. *I do, which is why I'm here.*

You're from Sixth Earth and have all this power, she sent, *so why don't you just fold your ass to our world and take care of business?*

She heard James sigh before he sent, *My dear, you don't know how tempting that would be, but it simply isn't allowed, it isn't the way life is meant to unfold. If higher powers solved the problems, then mortals and ascenders alike would just sleep away their existence. We're meant to strive, to grow strong, to overcome. It is the way of the world, immortal and mortal alike.*

Must you give me a reasonable answer?

He chuckled again, a soft breeze-like sound that made her feel homesick for something she didn't understand. She had been living on Second Earth for such a short time, but these four months had been the happiest, most fulfilling of her life.

He sent, *Just tend to Havily's dreams.*

Dreams that aren't really dreams?

Precisely. Then he was gone.

Avoidance springs a trap.

—*Collected Proverbs,* Beatrice of Fourth

CHAPTER 2

Havily awoke screaming because in this dream, that wasn't a dream, the sky was on fire all around her. She sat in her nightgown on the hard desert ground, except that she wasn't in the desert. Blackness rimmed where she sat, though the sky above was lit up with giant grotesque flames in strange shades of pink mixed with blue and green, like something at a spectacle. And Warrior Luken flailed in the air, his wings on fire. *On fire!*

"Luken!" she screamed.

She rose to her feet and turned in a circle. She recognized the Superstitions, one of the entry points to Mortal Earth, one of the places the Warriors of the Blood battled death vampires.

Her heart pounded in her chest. She didn't understand what was happening. Was she really seeing Luken? His cries ripped through the air.

Once more she screamed. "Luken!" She reached her hands toward him. She tried to move in his direction but couldn't. The space that enclosed her, while protecting her from the flames, also prevented her from reaching the warrior.

His back arched and suddenly he fell twenty feet to earth. She heard the terrible thud, saw him roll and writhe in the dirt.

She had to do something, but she wasn't effective in this strange nowhere space. So she closed her eyes, relaxed her body, and swished out of the desert-that-wasn't-a-desert. She opened her eyes. She now stood beside her bed.

She grabbed her iPhone from her nightstand and with shaking fingers called Central. Jeannie would know what to do. Jeannie had worked at Central Command on Second Earth for decades, as long as Havily had ascended, which meant probably longer. The woman served the Warriors of the Blood, routing calls from their leader, Thorne, keeping all the lines of communication open warrior-to-warrior. If anyone could help in this situation, Jeannie could.

"Central. How can I help?"

"Jeannie," she cried. "This is Havily. I've just had some kind of . . . vision. I think Luken's at the Superstitions and he's been burned. His wings have been burned. There was some kind of fire in the sky. Can you get someone out there? Maybe I'm wrong, but . . . can you get someone out there?"

"I'll get Thorne on the com. Stay close." How calm she sounded—but then Jeannie had no doubt seen and heard it all.

Havily kept her iPhone pressed to her ear. Her chest grew damp and she brushed the annoying sensation away only to realize tears were falling onto her breasts.

She knew, *she knew,* Warrior Luken had been hurt, maybe killed. The minutes passed and more tears fell.

At last, Jeannie came back on the line. "Sorry it took so long, Havily. Thorne folded to Luken and it was exactly as you described but he couldn't get back to me until just now.

When he arrived on the scene, a squad of death vampires showed up. He took care of them, of course, but Luken . . . oh, God . . . Luken's in bad shape. Thorne wants to know how you knew."

Havily shook her head as though Jeannie could see her. "I don't know. It was some kind of dream or vision or something but I watched him fall from the sky."

"Thorne will want to patch in, so, hold on a little longer. Okay?"

"Of course."

Havily choked on a sob. At least Thorne was with him. He was the leader of the warriors. He was also very powerful; if anyone could get Luken through this, it was Thorne.

Jesus . . . Luken. Havily had a fondness for all of the Warriors of the Blood, but Luken had been her own personal Guardian of Ascension. He'd been assigned to protect her when she entered her rite of ascension all those decades ago. He was good and kind and had a huge heart to match his huge warrior body. Havily knew he had a thing for her, and though she maintained a platonic relationship with him, she was fully aware of Luken's affection, even his love, for her.

Thorne's gravel voice hit her ear. "So you had a vision?"

"Yes. Something like that. I'm . . . I'm not really sure. I think I'd just fallen asleep."

"Hold on."

Havily waited a little more, then Jeannie came back on. "Thorne wants you to come to the Superstitions because he knows you mean a lot to Luken, but he said only to come if you think you can handle it. It's pretty bad out there. Horace is on the way, too, but he said Luken could really use your support. I can do the fold from here. Just let me know if you think you're up to it."

"Give me a sec," she said. She set her phone down. Of course she would go. The Warriors of the Blood battled death vampires every night on behalf of all of Second Society. The least she could do was support one of the brothers when he was down.

She folded her nightgown off and with a second preternatural thought, folded a pair of jeans and a yellow T-shirt on. She didn't bother with her long, layered red hair as she brought socks and Nikes onto her feet. She grabbed her phone and cried, "*Fold* me."

"That's my girl," Jeannie said.

The journey between was a short ride, only a second, maybe two, a dark trip through nether-space then a touching-down of feet on solid earth.

When she materialized, she found Thorne kneeling beside Luken. Thorne was all business as he said, "Jeannie's going to do a cleanup. Close your eyes."

Havily obeyed, and a blinding flash of light tore over her eyelids. She opened her eyes. The horrible battle debris, all those parts of dead vampires, blood, and feathers, had disappeared, thank you, God. What wasn't gone, however, was the stench in the air of burned feathers and the harsh chemical smell of the fire.

Thorne bent over Luken's massive shape and spoke quietly to him, his deep rough voice a profound reassurance in the still night air. Luken lay on his side, shaking, his eyes open but his expression not exactly present. His wings . . . were gone. His skin was burned badly on his legs, thighs, arms, and back. His long thick warrior hair, hanging from the tight *cadroen,* lay over his shoulder untouched, which seemed like some kind of miracle.

Havily dropped down beside Thorne and swallowed the bile that rose in her throat. She was not going to lose it, not when the mightiest of the warriors lay shaking and burned. He tilted his head and his gaze skated to hers, his eyes rolling. "Havily," he whispered.

She glanced at Luken's hand. She checked to make sure the skin wasn't burned before she drew his fingers into her palm, holding him oh-so-gently. "I'm here. We'll get you through this, Luken."

"Good," he whispered then coughed. "I . . . I thought I heard you call my name." He coughed some more.

"I did call your name."

His eyes closed and his body quieted, his fingers now limp.

Havily gripped his hand hard, but there was no answering response. She glanced at Thorne as tears stung her eyes. "Is he dead?"

Thorne put a hand on Luken's chest. He folded away the leather weapons harness. "No. His heart beats. But . . . shit. Of all the warriors, he had the most beautiful wings. They were the color of his eyes."

"I know." Luken's wings were as massive as his muscular body was large. He had the broadest wingspan of all the warriors, and the color was an exquisite powder blue. Was it possible his wings were gone forever? Havily had never seen this kind of damage before.

A vibration behind Havily had Thorne spinning and leaping to his feet, a sword in his hand where one hadn't been before. Thorne was the consummate warrior, heavily muscled, all man, ready to go.

The arrival, fortunately, was just Horace. The healer took one look at Luken and drew in a sharp breath. He pulled a slim phone from his pocket and barked a brisk string of words, essentially commanding a squad of healers to the Superstitions. "Don't argue with me" came as a last gunshot into the receiver. A pause. "Then get them here as fast as you can." He thumbed his phone and slid it into the loose white pants he wore, his expression grim. He met Thorne's gaze. "My team will be here in ten minutes."

The next moment he was behind Luken, both hands over his wing-locks, fingers spread, eyes closed. The glow that emanated from his hands forced Havily to blink then look away. She had seen Horace at work before, but never had a glow been as bright as this one, which meant the injuries, even from a healer's perspective, were serious.

She shielded her eyes then glanced down at Luken. His whole body relaxed visibly, as though Horace imparted a sedative with the healing.

"We'll have an ambulance here in about twenty minutes," Thorne said.

Havily wished Central could have just folded Luken straight to the hospital on Second Earth, but injuries fared badly during dematerialization and the resulting increased pain would have been a form of torture. For that reason, Endelle had set up emergency facilities near each of the Borderlands on Mortal Earth. They were rarely used, since most healing could be done by Horace and his team on-site. But at times like these, the clinics were critical.

Horace nodded. "Good. We'll be able to work better in a hospital environment." He was a lean man, with wavy brown hair to his shoulders. He wore a loose V-neck pullover shirt of white cotton with navy embroidery that followed the neckline. He reminded Havily of the hippies on Mortal Earth during the 1960s.

Thorne rose to his feet and moved away from Luken a couple of yards. He called Central and spoke to Jeannie. Not long afterward, the rest of the warriors started showing up. A few minutes later the six men, including Thorne, stood in a half circle next to her. Except for Warrior Medichi, they all wore black leather kilts, black weapons harnesses that allowed for wing-mounts, black gladiator-style sandals with shin guards, and silver-studded wrist guards also in black leather. They were a powerful brotherhood, all spattered in blood from fighting, all bearing swords in hand. Santiago flipped his jewel-encrusted dagger in his free hand.

Warrior Medichi never mounted his wings and wore his version of battle gear: black cargoes, black tee, steel-toed boots. He did, however, wear the same weapons harness, the silver hilt of a dagger protruding from the central angled slot.

As a group they stared down at Luken, but no one said a word, five warrior souls exhausted from the recent months of accelerated battling. Commander Greaves had been importing an increasing number of death vampires from all over the world to fight the Warriors of the Blood on a nightly basis, a strategy that had culminated here tonight with the use of some kind of incendiary bomb that had burned Luken while he was in flight.

Santiago slid his dagger into his weapons harness, a slot just lower than his heart. He drew close and put his hand on her shoulder. "Thanks, Hav. *Madre de dios,* his beautiful wings." He withdrew his hand and vanished.

The men couldn't be gone from the various Borderlands for long. The death vamps arrived in waves, and any that slid unchecked down the Trough, that nether-space between dimensions, would claim victims on Mortal Earth tonight.

Kerrick came forward and also put his hand on her shoulder. She looked into his green eyes. "We'll take care of him," she said. She still held Luken's hand.

He nodded as he dematerialized.

Jean-Pierre came next. *"Merci, soeurette."* The term was affectionate and meant "little sister." His eyes were wet as he followed Kerrick's lead and was simply gone.

Zacharius approached next. He bent low and kissed her on the cheek. He stroked the back of Luken's hand with a finger; then he, too, folded away.

Medichi knelt beside her, and she felt the strength and comfort of his powerful arm as he squeezed her shoulder. "We will never forget that you were here for him when we couldn't be." A movement of air, a little breeze at her back, told her he was gone.

For some reason, as she gazed at Luken, the fact that he lay with his head near the base of a tall stand of ocotillo, that he didn't even have a scrap of cloth to separate his fine blond warrior hair from the dirt, made the tears come and they just wouldn't stop.

A few minutes more and the healers began to arrive so that there were five in all, each with hands poised above Luken's skin.

After what felt like hours instead of a dozen more minutes, the ambulance pounded across the open desert terrain. Only then did she release her hold on Luken's hand. But because Horace insisted that her touch was as vital as any of their healing efforts, she rode in the ambulance all the way to the emergency clinic, her fingers once more wrapped around Luken's.

She only let him go when the burn specialists arrived and he was hooked up to an IV.

She was reminded, yet again, that even the most powerful of vampires could die.

Marcus woke up with a headache. He opened his eyes and glanced at the low dresser across from his bed. The sleek chrome clock pulsed the hour in bold annoying red numbers—one in the morning.

He sat up, straight up.

Something was wrong. He could feel it. But what?

He pushed his hair back with both hands and breathed hard through his nose. He stared out the expansive picture window that made up the northern wall of his master bedroom and met a dark night sky dotted with stars.

Most of Bainbridge Island was hidden beneath a wilderness of trees, but he'd built his house at the water's edge for the view of Seattle across Puget Sound.

He took a deep breath. Why did his head hurt?

Again, something was wrong.

He drew his knees up, the black silk sheet forming a dip between his legs. He circled his forearms around his knees and clasped his hands together. His thoughts turned in exactly the direction that troubled him.

Havily.

Endelle's warnings poured through his head.

Havily hadn't come to him tonight, and she always came to him. In all these months, she hadn't missed one night, so, yeah, something was wrong. But just how worried should he be? The hell if he knew.

He slid from bed and crossed to the bathroom. His vampire-warrior body always seemed to run a little hot so he never wore pajamas, which made late June and the start of summer almost time to crank up the air-conditioning. Few homes in this part of the world had forced air, but then few residents of Mortal Earth were vampires.

Relieving himself took the length of two or three serious yawns. He had a mountain of work tomorrow and he needed his sleep, dammit.

He washed his hands in the dark, or the semi-dark as it was for him. His ascended vision could see quite well. He dried his hands then stood up straight and let his gaze rove the lean muscled lines of his body. He worked out with weights every day, and sparred at least twice a week, sword in hand, with his second-in-command, Farrell Ennis. Ennis was also an ascender who had chosen exile on Mortal Earth. They were practically blood brothers.

His gaze fell to his heavy cock, partially stiff from sleep and from thoughts of Havily. Even a quick image of her flashing through his mind brought desire streaking the entire length. He flicked the tip in punishment since he couldn't get Havily off his mind. But the sharp jolt made him hiss. These days it took so little to make him come. One or two thoughts about the redheaded ascender, a few tugs, and he was gone. So, shit.

His gaze ran upward to his hair. Endelle was right. He'd been letting his hair grow. Because he'd had a corporate cut for at least the last century, he'd forgotten that his hair curled at the tips. Would Havily like his hair longer?

Then he chastised himself for wondering anything so useless.

He left the bathroom and moved to the windows. He pushed open the far-right pane and heard the soft lap of the sound's water hitting the sandy beach below. A rush of cool damp air followed.

So why hadn't Havily come to him?

He turned back and looked at his bed, a nice big bed to accommodate his warrior body. Funny thing was, he never brought any of his dates here. He had never wanted to.

Now, every other minute, he pictured Havily right there, on her back, on his bed, her body writhing. His cock responded all over again. He glanced in the direction of his groin. "Down, boy. She's not here. Won't be here. Get used to it."

His thoughts traveled back and hooked on the last time he'd truly been with Havily, four months ago, at Endelle's palace. He'd been so consumed by her, by her honeysuckle scent, that he'd kissed her.

But that wasn't all that had happened. The craving he'd been feeling for her swamped him, caught him in a heavy undertow, and pulled him down. He'd been 100 percent out of his mind with his need to be with her, to take her sexually, to partake of her blood, to get inside her head in deep mind-engagement. He'd pushed her into an adjoining room of the palace and pinned her against the wall. She in turn had been equally as lost and had been an oh-so-willing, whimpering, moaning participant. There had been no doubt in his mind that had they not been interrupted, he would have taken her then and there and she would have been with him all the way.

But Luken, thank God, had stopped him. He'd peeled him off Havily, beaten the shit out of him, and essentially knocked some sense into his head.

Marcus had never been so out of control as that last night on Second Earth. Afterward, he'd apologized to the Warriors of the Blood then folded back to Mortal Earth, back here to his home on Bainbridge. He'd considered apologizing to Havily as well, but he hadn't trusted himself to be anywhere near her.

Now he stood by an open window, in the early hours of the morning, knowing that something had happened to her tonight and wondering what the hell to do about it. His protective urges rose, a line of restless stallions, ready to gallop but nowhere to go.

He thought about calling her; then his rational mind stepped up to the gate and shut him down but good. He had nothing to offer Havily, and to be calling her and asking if she was all right would suggest that he had some kind of intention of getting involved in her life and he sure as hell wasn't going to do that.

Havily lived on Second Earth, one whole dimension away. Most of his nineteen corporations had dealings with Second Earth but he never went there himself, not for business, not for any reason. He had plenty of support staff, self-exiled vampires who made regular dimensional trips to Second Earth, all by legal permit, to conduct and foster his various businesses.

No, he had no real reason to call Havily, not now, not ever.

There was, however, someone he could call who could give him information—and she would definitely be up this time of night.

He crossed the room to his nightstand. Picking up his interdimensional iPhone, he thumbed the screen.

"This is Jeannie. How can I help?"

"Hey, Jeannie." Would she recognize his voice?

"Warrior Marcus," she shrieked, then toned it down immediately. "That is, good evening, Warrior Marcus, how can I help?"

Marcus laughed. He'd known Jeannie a very long time, long before his departure from Second Earth two hundred years ago. She worked at Central Command, manning the communications night after night between Thorne and all the Warriors of the Blood. She'd been a good friend to him through the centuries; she was one reason he'd hated to leave. "I need to know if Havily Morgan is all right."

A pause followed as well as a sigh. "You know I'm not allowed to discuss warrior business. Even if my channels are secure, your phone isn't."

"I'm not asking about the warriors. I just need to know if Havily was involved in any of the activities this evening?"

"Yes." But she volunteered no other information.

Marcus put a hand to his chest. Shit, he was struggling to breathe. "Was she . . . injured?"

"No, not at all. I can promise you that. She is perfectly well." A pause, then more stridently, "But I really can't say anything more."

"I understand." He released a sigh. "Thank you, Jeannie. You've helped a lot."

"You're welcome."

"I'll say good night."

"Marcus?"

"Yeah?"

"You were always my favorite."

"Back atcha."

"Coming back anytime soon?"

In the dark and in the comfort of his bedroom on Bainbridge Island, he smiled. "Don't think so."

"Too fucking bad, Warrior. Thorne's calling. Gotta go."

He thumbed his iPhone and set it back on the table.

Good. Havily was all right but Jeannie's unspoken words indicated there had been some problem tonight in which Havily had been involved.

He climbed back into bed, stretched out, then laced his hands behind his head. What was he supposed to do with the conundrum that had become Havily Morgan?

Tonight? Nothing.

Tomorrow he'd head back to his office building, the one he owned in downtown Seattle. Business was a perfect distraction from a situation he needed to ignore anyway.

He worked hard keeping his empire in line. Lately he'd been dealing with a couple of strikes on different continents and some serious competition from a Chinese firm looking to move in on his Mortal Earth European operations.

Tomorrow he had two board meetings. One corporation exported PCs to Second Earth; the other was a highly specialized company designed to serve the horticulture industry. So yeah, he needed his rest.

He yawned, closed his eyes.

Okay. There was just way too much here he couldn't control.

Whatever.

Endelle, Supreme High Administrator of Second Earth, reclined on her chaise longue. She wore a soft purple linen gown for comfort since she would be on duty all through the night, just as her Warriors of the Blood were on duty, however different their assigned tasks.

Instead of battling with a sword, Endelle hunted her prey in the midst of the darkening, that piece of nether-space she inhabited during her meditations. While in a state of meditation, she was able to split-self, to become two separate corporeal forms—one that reclined on the chaise, the other that slipped into the nether-space of the darkening, free to move around and act within that space in a second physical body.

What her second split-self couldn't do was leave the darkening, except to return to, and rejoin, her first corporeal self—all very third-dimensional preternatural shit that no one else on Second Earth, not even Greaves himself, could do.

So here she was, her primary self reclining in meditation and her second self, her split-self, chasing that bastard, Darian Greaves, from one end of the planet to the other, at least while in the darkening.

She had one job to perform during her nightly vigils—to keep Greaves from increasing the size of his army of death vampires here in Phoenix.

In the past decade he'd taken to shipping death vamps from all over the world to the metropolitan area in an ongoing effort to destroy the Warriors of the Blood, to wear them down so that they made mistakes and got themselves killed. It was a clever, subtle strategy that did not in any way alert the authorities to his machinations.

COPASS was the committee that governed the process

of ascension to Second Earth and which had also established several critical rules for how each faction could conduct its war efforts. Basically, she and Greaves weren't allowed to engage in open warfare for the simple reason that they were each too powerful. Engagement had atomic implications, and both she and the Commander had agreed not to do battle personally.

But Greaves could ship death vampires to Phoenix Two and Endelle could chase his sorry ass through the darkening and stop him.

At least, thank God, Greaves wasn't omnipotent. Yes, she could thank the Creator for small favors.

As she moved in her split-self, she drew close, so close to her prey. Silver tendrils appeared, small beacons of light that belonged exclusively to Greaves. His light trails never ceased to surprise her because evil ought to be represented by red flames and black smoke, not silver streams of light, for Christ's sake.

His voice came to her next, full of persuasive resonance, as he addressed his minions. "A place, my brother ascenders, has been prepared for you, of great honor for your service to my cause. In return, being stationed in Metro Phoenix will provide all the opportunity you need to sate your appetites, since the Sonoran Desert has five access points to Mortal Earth."

An interpreter spoke rapidly in a language she didn't know, but something that sounded like East Indian. This last statement mentioning five access points, once flushed through the interpreter, was met with a round of lifted fists and war cries. Funny how Greaves failed to note that the access points were guarded by Warriors of the Blood.

A moment more and she skidded into Greaves's arena, thinning the line between real-space and nether-space, so that she could see her prey. He was absurdly attractive, with his bald head and muscular warrior build. He had large, round dark eyes and carried himself like a cultured gentleman. He wore what he always wore, a fine-pressed wool suit.

He preferred Hugo Boss. He was a fucking hypocrite and she loathed him.

Given his level of power, no doubt he would see her as fully formed. She didn't know. She'd never bothered nor cared to ask him. The others, in their limited abilities, would only be able to perceive her as an apparition, a ghost.

Greaves stood before three squads of death vampires, *three,* and yeah, they had dark skin, growing lighter because of dying blood, and so beautiful, each one with glittering black eyes. She'd arrived just in time.

She cleared her throat and everyone turned in her direction. Of course they knew who she was. Every government institution in the capital city of each Territory had either a statue of her or an enormous oil painting in her likeness. And yes, she could be found on Second's version of the Internet.

However, since the time that Greaves had begun his serious campaign fifteen years ago, when he had persuaded the first of her Territorial High Administrators to align with him, these Territories had been provided with new statues of the Commander, new portraits, new posters, new COMING ORDER buttons, coffee mugs, and mouse pads, the bastard. She didn't even have mouse pads. What became of those edifices and paintings made in her image, she really didn't want to know.

She cast a locked-down shield around the twelve night-feeders. She had control of them now. Greaves, thank you God, could not bust through these shields.

But for just a moment, as her gaze swept over the pretty-boys, she was struck again by their extraordinary beauty. What fucking irony that something so deadly would be so beautiful—but then that was the point, that a mortal would meet a death vampire and not comprehend the danger. The dark eyes, the porcelain, almost bluish skin, the features worthy of worship, all served to enthrall the mortal victim. A pair of fangs would strike, seeking one thing—the empowering effects that came only from dying blood.

"You're early tonight," he said. "How delightful." But he didn't wait to converse; he merely lifted an arm and vanished, on to his next appointment. Where he intended to go, however, was not something she could trace. It might take her three hours to discover, or three minutes. Hunting Greaves in the darkening was one long exercise in sheer luck combined with hours of mind-numbing effort.

Whatever.

The death vampires blinked. The interpreter wet himself and disappeared. The death vamps lifted arms to dematerialize but she had them pinned. She would keep the shield in place until the local Indian Militia Warriors arrived to finish off this group of bloodsucking bastards.

She called Central. "Hey, Jeannie. I'm transmitting the coordinates of twelve more assholes."

"You go, girl," Jeannie said. Endelle's phone had GPS but even though she could call from nether-space, for whatever reason, she couldn't get the GPS unit on the phone to transmit. So she sent the coordinates via telepathy, which Jeannie had no trouble receiving. At the same time, she heard tapping on the computer. A moment later Jeannie said, "That would be Mumbai. I'll alert the local Chief Militia Officer that there are twelve to dispose of."

"He'll be celebrating for days on this one."

"No shit."

Endelle laughed. She actually liked Jeannie, but then she'd known her a goddamn long time. "Later."

"Good hunting, Madame Supreme High Administrator."

Endelle touched the phone then replaced it in the pocket of her meditation gown.

She was ready to continue on, to keep searching the world over for the silver tendrils of light, for the whisper of breathing that meant she was closing in on Greaves's ass, but at that moment Thorne cut in. He was her second-in-command and shared a telepathic link with her, the only vampire on Second Earth to do so.

Come home now, his gravel voice rippled through her head.

She cursed the disruption. Once begun, she didn't like to be distracted from her darkening duties. However, Thorne never intruded unless there was some kind of fucking crisis at home. So, yeah . . . shit.

She pulled away from India and began the long slide through the darkening all the way back to her meditation chamber. Once she arrived, she relaxed her mind, letting it pull down deep until all she saw was a well of darkness. Step by step she moved out of nether-space and back into her primary self. She took deep breaths.

After a minute, she opened her eyes. Despite the desperate nature of Thorne's call, she smiled. For just this moment, during this small speck of time she had to herself, she looked up at the ceiling of her private retreat deep within her palace on the side of the McDowell Mountains. She was safe here. Even when Greaves and his death vampires had attacked four months ago, they had been unable to penetrate the layers of shields that kept her in complete safety in her womb-like meditation space.

Two dozen four-inch candles, all in white, sat at precise intervals on matching shelves all around the room. The shelves were set four feet above the floor and lit the small rotunda in a warm glow. Burgundy velvet drapes hung at intervals between the shelves, ceiling-to-floor, for no other purpose than to soften and color her space.

The meditations that kept her moving at light speed through nether-space always left her logy for a minute or two afterward, her mind too loose to function at top level. But Thorne needed her and she needed to get her ass moving.

She slid her legs over the side of the chaise longue. She leaned forward and took deep breaths. Dammit, she was too dizzy to move. She'd have to wait a few minutes. She had a lot of power, but even she had limits.

Thorne stood in Luken's treatment room at the emergency clinic shaking his head back and forth. Havily was next to him but neither of them spoke, which was a good thing. As the leader of the Warriors of the Blood, *the man in charge,* the man who was supposed to have *all the answers,* he was shocked and having trouble concentrating. He'd been Endelle's second-in-command for too many centuries to count. To say he was feeling it was to say red was red. He couldn't remember the last time he'd slept two hours straight and right now he wanted his Ketel One neat and to-the-fucking-rim.

Jesus H. Christ.

What a big fucking nightmare. Incendiary bombs? At the Superstition Borderland? On Mortal Earth?

How was he supposed to deal with that? And he really didn't want to think about what would have happened if Havily hadn't called Central to warn him about Luken, which begged another big fucking mysterious question.

"I just don't understand, Hav," he said. "How did you know he'd been hurt?"

Luken was suspended in the air, facedown, in a contraption that looked like it had come from a circus. There was rhyme to the reason, however. The healers surrounded his back and were working on his wing-locks. Christ, what a mess.

Havily pressed her fingers to her lips, and her lovely light green eyes flooded with tears. She stared at the hospital bed across the room. "I guess I had some kind of vision." Her voice trembled, new leaves shaking in a breeze. "I somehow found myself sitting in the desert looking up at him. I saw flames in the dark night sky and his wings on fire." She rasped a breath. "Oh, God."

Thorne put his arm around her and pulled her hard against him. She looked so vulnerable in her yellow T-shirt and rumpled red hair. Her jeans were dirty from having sat on the ground beside Luken. She was young by Second Earth standards, only a hundred years old. She certainly wasn't used to seeing the violence he and his brother warriors saw every night of their fucking lives. He felt her relax against him and gave her shoulder a squeeze.

She had a right to be upset. Luken was the largest of the Warriors of the Blood, wearing muscle like a breeding bull. If Luken could get hurt, then they all could. The symbolism sliced deep.

Jesus. An incendiary bomb on Second Earth.

And Luken's wings were *gone*. In addition, there was a lingering smell of burned feathers in the air.

Thank the Creator he was still unconscious as Horace and his team worked over every part of his skin. He looked better but it would be a few days before he recovered. The real question surfaced—would his wings renew or would scar tissue form over the apertures and make it impossible for him to fly again?

Such accidents were known to happen, especially among the flight-performance artists who worked the spectacle circuits. Disability insurance for these entities, which made liberal use of extensive and exotic fireworks displays, was exorbitant, like medical malpractice insurance on Mortal Earth.

Thorne shuddered, and Havily looked up at him. "Are you okay, Warrior Thorne? This has to be hard on you as well."

He nodded, but damn his throat was tight. Havily shifted slightly and slipped her arm around his waist. In the past few months, ever since Warrior Marcus had blasted through their warrior world for his three days of service, Havily had drawn closer to all the Warriors of the Blood. She'd always been a favorite, but the events surrounding Alison Wells's ascension, in which Havily had served as the woman's Liaison Officer, had brought the ascender closer to them all. Lately, she'd been performing a wonderful kindness for them. At dawn, at the end of the warriors' shifts, she'd meet with them at the Cave, the warriors' private rec room.

She brought hot Starbucks and a couple of dozen maple scones and buttermilk doughnuts, which got devoured within minutes. But it was her presence that eased them all, her earnest expressions, her desire to help, and the knowledge that for the past several months she had made some really useful changes at Endelle's administrative headquarters. Her enthusiasm and her service helped all of them, dammit. And tonight she'd just saved Luken's life.

Yeah, his eyes burned and then some.

"Will he be all right?" she asked. She had a lovely voice, light, melodic, except when she got particularly adamant on a point. Then the tone evened out to something approaching strident—a necessary effect since she worked every day within twenty yards of Endelle.

"Of course he'll be all right," Thorne said, wondering if she could gauge the lack of truth in his voice.

"What about his wings?" she asked, her voice little more than a whisper.

"I don't know. I've never seen anything like this."

She was silent for a moment. "I wish Endelle would get here. She has healing abilities. Maybe she can help. Are you sure she's on her way?"

"She's coming." He'd contacted her through their shared telepathic link, interrupting her meditations. He knew it would take her a few minutes to shake off the effects of doing her split-self moves through nether-space. The truth was he couldn't have kept her away. She played her tough-bitch role really well, but he knew her heart, he knew how much she loved her men.

The air shimmered. Thorne slid away from Havily as gently as he could while at the same time drawing his sword into his hand, but thank fuck it was only Endelle. Speak of the devil. She wore a purple gown, something like a Grecian robe, which he knew she wore when she did her darkening work.

"Holy shit," Endelle cried, her loud voice drawing the attention of all five healers in her direction. "Why the fuck does this room smell like someone's been lighting chickens on fire?"

Havily burst into tears and moved to the window.

Thorne just stared at Her Supremeness. For being the

ruler of all of Second Earth, the damn woman was as tact-
ful as death vampires at a prayer meeting. "The enemy used
some kind of firebomb, Endelle. Apparently, the sky all
around Luken exploded. His wings were burned well into
his back and he fell to earth . . . hard."

Endelle whistled. "Well, shit, that's gotta hurt."

Understatement of the century, he sent, but aloud he said,
"He passed out on-site."

"Thank fuck for that. Is he on opiates?"

"Yes. Even Horace thought it was a good thing, and you
know how he hates drugs of any kind."

"So what is *she* doing here?" She jerked her chin in Havily's direction, disapproval in her tone.

Thorne knew of Endelle's disappointment in Havily, so
he smiled a little as he said, "She saved Luken's life. Now
what do you say?"

"I say I find that fucking hard to believe."

He rolled his eyes and told her the story even though he
still didn't understand how Havily had known what was
going on. Her explanation of having had some kind of vision
just didn't fit into his current understanding of the usual ascender's preternatural powers.

Endelle grimaced. "Morgan, get over here."

Havily wiped her face before she turned around. To her
credit, she stiffened her back and straightened her shoulders before rejoining them.

In her usual take-no-prisoners manner, Her Supremeness said, "What Thorne has told me doesn't make a lot of
sense and I want some answers. You say you had some kind
of vision and saw Luken fall from the sky?"

"Yes. I watched him. I can't exactly explain how it happened. But I woke up and the next thing I knew I was sitting
in the desert, on the ground, and I could tell from the geog-
raphy that I was at the Superstitions. I saw the sky on fire,
then Luken—" She put her fingers once more to her lips, and
her gaze skated back to the bed. The rest of the story came
out almost in a whisper.

"Well, it sounds like you have some kind of link with Luken, maybe left over from his guardianship when you ascended." She shook her head back and forth, scowling in disapproval. "These visions of yours? They ever happened before?"

Thorne watched color invade Havily's creamy white cheeks, but she didn't answer the question.

Endelle scowled all over again and glared at her. "Why the fuck did you just tighten your shields, Morgan? You hiding something from me?"

"It's . . . it's a little personal, but yes, I've had these visions before."

"Anything I can use against the Commander?"

Havily shook her head. "No."

"That's what I thought. Well, if you happen to get any useful visions anytime in the next ten millennia, you'll let me know, *right*?" Her sarcastic tone fried the air between the women.

"Of course," Havily responded evenly. Thorne was fucking proud of her tonight. It took balls to stand up to Endelle or at the very least not to crumple into a faint.

"Then if the pair of you will excuse me, I've got a bastard to chase around the world." She gritted her teeth. "And tomorrow I'm going to have to take this firebomb attack before COPASS, or at least request a hearing. An incendiary weapon works both ways. They start burning us, we'll start setting all those glossy black wings on fire. Whatever. Havily, I'll see you at the office tomorrow."

"Yes, Madame Endelle."

But Thorne waylaid her with a hand on her arm. He jerked his head toward Luken. "Can you do anything for him?"

Endelle glanced in the direction of the bed then sighed. "My healing powers don't exceed Horace here. What can be done for him, Horace will do." With that, she lifted her arm and was gone.

"God, I hate her sometimes," he muttered.

Havily drew close once more, but a small chuckle left her lips. "You lie."

Thorne laughed. "Yeah, I guess I do. I'd give my life for her, but you'd think she could try a little harder sometimes. And she sure has it in for you."

"She's just really frustrated right now." Havily slipped her arm around Thorne's and gave him a squeeze. "Alison tries to make headway with Endelle but even she loses it now and then, which is amazing because I swear Alison is a saint. Do you know what she said last week?"

Thorne looked down into light green eyes that actually showed some humor. Havily was a beautiful woman, and some of that beauty pierced his heart. He was so grateful for her presence among his warriors. "Tell me," he said.

"She called Endelle a mule, an 'ornery, ill-tempered, incorrigible mule!' I smiled for days."

Thorne chuckled. "Kerrick found himself one helluva mate."

"And that door swings both ways."

"I'll say an amen, Havily Morgan." His heart swelled. Yeah, she'd become a bright spot in their dark days and nights.

What the soul craves, the dream reveals.

—*Collected Proverbs*, Beatrice of Fourth

CHAPTER 3

At two in the morning Havily got a fold through the dimension back to Mortal Earth. Bless Jeannie. What would any of them do without her and the rest of the support staff at Central? Havily had some power; she could fold anywhere on Second Earth. But she still couldn't fold between dimensions.

She was now back at her condo at the base of Camelback Mountain. She stripped off her socks and Nikes, jeans and T-shirt, bra and thong. She slid the cream-colored nightgown over her head, adjusted the lace straps, then climbed into bed. She fell face-first onto the pillows and groaned. Yep, exhausted.

Thorne would remain at the clinic through the night, standing guard, just in case any death vampires got the clever idea to attack Luken when he was out cold. Come morning, he would contact the Chief Militia Warrior for Metro

Phoenix Two and have a detail assigned to the room, but not an ordinary detail. With death vamps around, at least a score would be needed to keep watch. Death vampires were considerably more powerful than the average Militia Warrior. To bring down a death vampire, a minimum of four Militia Warriors were required.

Havily rolled onto her back, took the edge of the top sheet in her fingers, and rubbed back and forth, the motion soothing. She stared at the multitude of paper butterflies she had hanging from the ceiling, all decorated with colored ink and glitter, each one a miniature work of art. Each butterfly was different in design and suspended so that when she looked up she could see the wingspans. From every angle they were beautiful.

She often counted them when she couldn't sleep.

She had stayed at the clinic until the medical staff had entered the room to turn the massive warrior onto his back. The sight of the rest of Luken's burned flesh brought on a serious gag reflex, which she had only barely controlled. When she started weeping again, Thorne ordered her to go home. She protested, of course, but he added very gently that he would appreciate it if she would still come to the Cave at seven to bring the warriors their usual coffee and doughnuts.

It was the least she could do when the Warriors of the Blood were all that stood between Endelle and her administration and a monster bent on taking over two worlds. Darian Greaves had been positioning himself for decades to do just that, building an army comprising both death vampires and regular Militia Warriors, seducing High Administrators around the globe into his camp, and generally winning an overall public relations war.

Havily loved Second Earth with a passion that went beyond comprehension—but then part of ascending to a new dimension involved a great deal of yearning and longing, the call of a new world, of a new experience, of a new everything.

She touched her incisors and felt her vampire fangs throb in response. She even loved being a vampire, having the ability to take blood, to give potions, as weird as it was. Except that it wasn't weird once the ascension process was complete. Then being a vampire just felt *right*.

Her thoughts turned to her long-deceased fiancé, her beloved Eric. She had shared blood with him, and the act had been one of the finest experiences of her life. But she rarely allowed herself to think of him, because she was still sad, even after fifteen years. He had been a decorated Militia Warrior and had died battling death vampires. Once more the tears began to flow.

She folded a tissue into her hand and wiped her face. A rough sigh tumbled out of her exhausted body. She never stayed up this late. Working for Endelle during the day was an incredible challenge and she needed to be on her toes, all ten of them, to keep up with Her Supremeness and to not let the spiteful, ill-tempered scorpion-woman ruin her day.

Her gaze drifted from butterfly to butterfly. Her eyelids grew heavy. Maybe given the level of her fatigue she wouldn't be drawn into the bizarre sexual fantasy-dream she usually experienced. Surely just this once she would be spared the horror of waking up while engaged in full-on sex with Warrior Marcus.

Whatever. She was too tired to fuss anymore.

She heaved one last sigh. As her head rolled on the pillow, sleep claimed her.

Marcus drifted from deep sleep into a half-waking state because he felt *her* again, the weight of her on his hips, her knees pressed into the mattress on each side of him, her body moving against his profound arousal. He wasn't buried in her, not yet, but oh . . . my . . . God.

Then he awoke the rest of the way. Havily was here and she was safe and she was with him.

He resisted the urge to grab her arms and make certain she was whole and unharmed. Despite Jeannie's earlier reassurances, he was worried for her safety. However, any brusque movement on his part would awaken her from what he knew was still a dream state. And if nothing else, his four months' experience had taught him that the moment she awakened, she'd recoil from him in horror and slip away.

That he didn't have the power to stop her from disappearing when she woke up still fried him.

So for the last four months he had experimented, testing her limits to see what he could do, or not do as was the case, to see how long he could keep her in a half-dreaming state so that she stayed with him.

He glanced around his bedroom, which was not quite his bedroom, but a dream-like place that included his bed, okay, *a* bed, and *felt* like his home on Bainbridge Island, but wasn't, even though he could hear wind rattling the windows. He was in his bedroom . . . but not . . . so where the hell was he?—which was the same question he'd been asking himself since this whole madness began.

The room was dark, especially around the perimeter, as though fading to a blackness that had no end. The symbolism wasn't lost on him—the only way he could have what he most wanted, what he craved, was in some kind of dream state.

Weird.

Whatever.

As she moved against his cock, he suppressed a moan. No loud noises. Her eyes as usual were closed, and he knew she wasn't awake, yet not quite asleep, or not very deeply.

He still didn't get what was happening. For one thing, Havily detested him because he'd quit the Warriors of the Blood two hundred years ago. She saw him as a deserter.

Yet despite her dislike of him, she came every night to his bedroom that was not his bedroom, in this peculiar aberration of power and dreaming. He had never heard of anyone on Second Earth possessing this kind of ability, yet here Havily was moaning in that sweet melodic voice of hers as her honeysuckle scent infused the air of his *somewhere* bedroom.

Marcus, she whispered over his mind, her hips undulating, the sweet wetness of her flesh stroking his cock.

Havily, he responded, his telepathic voice low and dark. Yeah, he'd learned a lot in all these weeks—no jarring movements, no sharp commands, no fangs in her neck when oh, God, he ached to taste her blood.

If he did any of these things, she would awaken. Then she'd take one horrified look at him, no matter the level of her passion, and drift away from him like a dream he couldn't recapture no matter how hard he tried.

Once she left, he would experience a sliding sensation, a blink of unconsciousness like he was folding or being folded. He would reappear in his bed painfully aroused and in need of release. He sure as hell had taken a lot of cold showers over what had been a very long spring and had the appearance of turning into an equally long summer.

But Havily was here now, in his nowhere bed, and he had another shot at taking their nightly ritual to a *more productive* level. He was nothing if not a problem solver and he hadn't been idle in pondering their current conundrum, as in how to keep her with him long enough to consummate the relationship. She obviously desired him, which meant that each time she left without experiencing release, she must have been as frustrated as he was.

Tonight, though, he had a plan, something he hadn't tried before. Maybe tonight everything would change.

He drew a slow deep breath. He slid an arm around her waist very gently to support her. A soft moan followed.

Her breasts, and God they were beautiful, were almost at eye level, the weight of them heavy in front since she leaned forward. She had large deep-rose areolas, which were as familiar to him now as the hand he used to cup those breasts. He curved his hand around her right breast and withheld a groan but Havily mewled. He drew his hand the length of her breast and lightly rubbed the nipple. Her sweet voice mewled again.

He wanted to suckle but the times he'd tried, the sensation had been too powerful for her and she'd shied away, awakening fully and disappearing beneath his touch. But he wanted her breast in his mouth. He wanted to suck hard until she was screaming.

First, though, he had to figure this out, how to do this, to connect physically without waking her, how to give her pleasure without having her fade from his arms.

God how he wanted that, as though his life depended upon making her happy. The drive he felt toward her burned in his chest and had been burning since he'd first met her.

He put both hands on her waist, holding her. He throbbed now, hard as granite. He lifted her and very slowly impaled her on his cock. This, miraculously, she would allow. She even arched in his hands and flung her head back, crying out. It always surprised him that she didn't awaken, one more sign that she needed this as much as he did.

Come for me, he whispered again within her mind, her sweet honeysuckle scent strafing his nostrils and piercing his brain.

I can't. Her voice was a whimper in his head. Yeah, she was frustrated as well.

If only he could get her under him, he could use his magic and work her into a frenzy. But he'd tried that maneuver more than once, and each time she'd awakened.

His gaze fell to her throat. His breathing quickened as a growl rattled around in his chest and his fangs emerged. Saliva flooded his mouth. He wanted her beneath him, writhing. He wanted his fangs sunk into her vein and drawing her nectar into his mouth, down his throat. *Havily,* he whispered again. God, how he wanted her. Could she feel the depth of his longing?

She rose up and down his column now, her body clenching and unclenching. But as she drew closer to orgasm, he knew what would happen. She would come to consciousness, frightened, bewildered, embarrassed, then in the space of a second disappear, a specter caught in a breeze.

How to keep her here? He thought he might have a clue and tried it now. *Stay with me,* he murmured within the depths of her mind. If he spoke aloud, she'd disappear. But he could converse telepathically and keep her with him. *Stay with me this time. Let me give you satisfaction.*

I want to, she sent, whimpering all over again.

Let me take care of you.

Yes.

Then sleep, Havily, more deeply now. Sleep.

Her body responded and grew slack, her hips now quiet on his.

Hello. This was new.

Shit, maybe this time it would work. His heart hammered a few ecstatic beats. He took over and worked his hips up and down, sliding his cock in and out of her willing body. Her moans increased, but only within his mind. This was good. This was very good. He worked her slowly and slid his hand down her buttocks. God, she felt so good. Her buttocks were so smooth, firm, so squeezable. Her honeysuckle scent poured out of her. He couldn't be imagining that. He *smelled* her.

Sleep, Havily, he whispered again over her mind.

She stretched out on top of him, her breasts against his chest, and damn did that feel good. He surrounded her with his arms. His heart was now a jackhammer in his chest. He was close to victory. He could feel it. This time. Hell, this time, it might just work.

He kept the rhythm slow and steady. He closed his eyes as well. He put his lips to her forehead and kissed her. She arched her neck. He dipped low and found her mouth. *Sleep,* he whispered again as he kissed her. But he wasn't demanding. He just drifted his lips over hers as the moans inside his head came in little gasps now.

He felt her grow very tight. His heart raced a little more. He increased the speed steadily, thrusting in and out. Damn she was tight. Oh, yeah, this was good. Very good. Damn good.

Sleep, he sent once again, his lips still plucking gently at hers.

He wouldn't be able to hold back much longer. He increased the pace. *Yes,* she whispered through his mind.

She broke the contact with his mouth.

Yes, from her mind again. She repeated the word over and over. *Yes, yes, yes.*

Her body pulled on him. The small of his back tightened, his thighs trembled, oh, shit, he was coming. But at the same time, she opened her mouth wide and cried out over and over. He erupted in a long brilliant ejaculation that caused his head to roll back. He kept pumping into her body until he jettisoned every drop, his hands squeezing her waist, keeping her planted on top of him.

Then he looked at her. Her eyes were closed and she was smiling. Her hips worked him oh-so-gently, as though she was savoring the feel of him. She cooed, a soft pretty warble, exactly the sound he had expected her to make. She gave a little gasp, sighed, then sank back down on his chest.

He held her for a long time. He cradled her in his arms, and stunned tears broke over his eyes. A man could get used to this, holding a woman in his arms in the middle of the night, so deeply content because he'd given her satisfaction.

God. *His woman.*

Wake for me now, he sent. He released the tight hold he had on her, his hands gliding down her arms. He craned his neck to look at her face.

Her eyes opened slowly. She blinked at him. "Marcus?" she murmured. "That was . . . so good . . . but . . . what is this . . . where am I . . . where did you take me?" She looked around, and the innocence and confusion on her face tore at his heart and his conscience. He became painfully aware that what he had just done to her, which was similar to enthralling a woman, might not be viewed by her in a positive light.

Then her eyes opened all the way, a wide stare of light green eyes that locked onto his as she came fully awake. "You seem so real." She blinked again.

In that instant she was here, now, with him, and he wanted to keep her with him, hold her, wherever the hell they were together. Dammit, he wanted her to stay.

He slid his arms around her once more. "Stay with me," he cried, his panic rising. "Don't go. We should talk about this. Please, Havily—" But he was losing her, he could feel it in the stiffening of her muscles and in the horror that replaced her look of satisfaction, her contentment, her fulfillment.

You bastard! she shouted within his mind.

He froze. He was always shocked by how much she despised him. And there was nothing he could do, nothing he could say. She would leave him.

"Fine," he retorted. "Run away like you always do. But I don't think you'll soon forget how I just made you feel." He released her and folded his hands behind his head. She was still connected to him, still one with his body. Her disgust with him had pissed him off, scraped his nerves raw once more, and frankly he wasn't going to make the disengagement easy, not when she came to him at night, not when she teased him by sliding against his cock *every damn night*. This time, she could do the work.

She shifted her hips and he bucked hard to let her feel the connection once more, that his cock was buried deep inside her, that *she* had come to him for this purpose. She brought him to this place every goddamn night. Well, fuck her for looking at him as though he lived on the underbelly of a slug.

She gasped then lifted and glided off him. "I hate you for doing this to me," she cried. She covered her breasts with her arm, rose up, then faded away toward the dark edges of the room. Because she left, his departure from this nowhere place occurred at the same time. Once again, he felt that strange rush-and-glide as pitch darkness surrounded him.

He blinked, straining to see, but one more blink and he was lying on his bed in exactly the same position, with his hands folded behind his head. He was on top of the sheet now and as before completely naked.

For a moment he thought about folding to Second Earth and hunting her down. He knew where she lived, her little condo at the foot of Camelback Mountain. He wanted to get in her face and gloat. He wanted her to know that whatever game this was, for all her distaste of him personally, she wanted him, she pursued him, and he'd pleasured her.

Hah.

Well, at least in that he found a measure of contentment in their little war. At least in that he could smile at the ceiling, settling his shoulders deeper into the mattress. He'd done the very thing he'd been trying to do for four months now, since Alison's ascension, since his return to his life on Mortal Earth—he'd brought his woman to a screaming climax.

His smile broadened, at least for a time, then it dimmed. Who was he kidding? This would never be enough, these encounters that had no more substance than if he'd awakened in the middle of a wet dream.

Still, he'd kept her with him until the end this time, and he would take satisfaction from that. Sort of.

He'd come inside her, which made him wonder. He looked down at his partially thickened cock still weeping his fluids. He blinked. He felt over his abdomen and chest, but there was nothing of his come present on his body. He felt only a thin sheen of sweat.

If this had been a wet dream, he would have been covered in his seed.

So where was the unmistakable evidence that he'd just had one helluva fine orgasm?

He was pretty sure he knew and once more he smiled at the ceiling. If he was right about all of this, Havily Morgan had one big-ass shock coming to her.

Good.

Havily knew the encounter was just a dream, like all the others she'd experienced, *endured,* over the past weeks. Of course it was just a dream, except that in this dream she'd actually had an orgasm. And somewhere in the course of the dream, she'd stripped off her nightgown . . . as usual.

She lay in bed, staring at her ceiling, at the collection of glittery butterflies. The air conditioner came on, and the large flock moved as though in flight.

She smiled. She didn't know exactly what this was she had been doing at night, but she could feel the ease of hormones that drifted through her veins now, those beautiful hormones that gave her such a light peaceful feeling.

She had to admit one thing—her fantasies *rocked*! She could even laugh at herself now. She had given Marcus such form, such shape that when she'd awakened from the fantasy-dream, for a moment she'd actually believed he was real.

Her smile faded. She believed he was real in the same way she had believed the fiery attack on Luken had been real . . . because the attack *had been real*.

She shuddered and squeezed her eyes shut. Of course the attack on Luken had been real. She'd made a phone call, and Thorne had confirmed the tragedy.

But this *thing* with Warrior Marcus was not real, never had been real, *couldn't* be real. Oh, God, it really couldn't.

She took several deep breaths and calmed the feelings of panic that constricted her chest. Of course it wasn't real. But . . . and here she closed her eyes . . . in the dream-fantasy, Marcus had smelled so wonderful.

She touched her fingers to her lips. She smelled all his delicious fennel scent and smiled. In her fantasy he had kissed her—and what had he kept saying to her? *Sleep.* So she had, and then she'd orgasmed. He was such a big, power-ful man and his hips had pistoned hard. And his cock, like a baseball bat.

Desire swept over her once more and her hips rocked as she let all the incredible sensations sweep over her, which in turn caused her back to arch off the mattress. That's when she felt the oozing between her legs.

She had just finished her period. What the hell?

She sat up carefully and flipped on the light. She grabbed a handful of tissues and pressed between her legs. She looked down at the tissues certain she'd see blood. However, what came out of her wasn't red.

What came out of her smelled richly of . . . oh, God . . . *fennel*.

This was a man's essence, his seed.

Marcus?

No.

Impossible!

So what was this? What had happened? She hadn't been with a man. She'd just had a sexy dream, a hot sexy dream, that's all.

Really.

Her heart rate increased. Had she been drugged? En-thralled? Raped?

Was someone in her house?

She glanced around at the shadows. She reached out with her senses but she knew her home was safe. No one else was present.

She stared down between her thighs, at the white tis-sues below her peachy-red pubic hair. Once more that deep, musky fennel scent, like grasses in summer, spiraled up to her.

There could be only one answer. Somehow Warrior Marcus had gotten to her. He'd found a way to penetrate her dreams then penetrate her.

Marcus.

That bastard. What had he done to her? *How* had he done this to her?

Antony Medichi, out of Italy in the late Roman era, sat next to Havily on the ratty brown leather couch. The hour was early, not yet seven, and given Luken's accident and her role in the near-tragedy, she couldn't have gotten much sleep.

There was a haunted look about her lovely light green eyes this morning.

"You sure you're okay?" he asked. The night's fighting, thank God, was over and as usual the brothers were together at the Cave, one last bonding before heading to bed for the day.

Havily sat next to him, a venti iced coffee held between her hands. "Of course I'm okay. I mean I could use a little sleep, but all that matters is that Luken is doing so well." She stared down at her cup and twirled the straw.

"That's all that matters."

Thorne had just given a report on how well Luken was recovering; a team of healers was with him and would remain working on him until Horace was satisfied. The warrior had even awakened for a few minutes and conversed with Thorne. He wasn't in too much pain. Horace had seen to that. As for Luken's wings, it was a wait-and-see.

Still, Havily wasn't used to seeing that kind of horror, and he couldn't help being concerned about her. She'd become important to the Warriors of the Blood, sort of a mascot, a beloved mascot.

He held a café mocha in one hand and a buttermilk doughnut in the other. He took a sip, then a bite. He loved that she sat next to him. He'd forgotten how soothing the presence of a woman could be, especially in the off-hours like this, after a night of battling when a warrior's nerves were still standing up straight and screaming, his body bruised and hurting. Havily was like sliding into a warm bath, an ease, a comfort. He treasured her.

She was dressed to kill this morning as well, which always helped. She wore a short skirt in light blue that showed off her bare tanned legs. She had on elegant heeled sandals with sapphire-like gems on the front straps. Her blouse was cream silk, and around her neck hung a large piece of jewelry on a chain that sparkled in black and gold with small light blue crystals. The blouse had a perfect V-cut, and because she was leaning forward on the couch, her arms on her knees, she showed a nice line of cleavage. Dynamite.

But her hair was her finest feature. It floated all around her shoulders, a cloud of red, and a beautiful red at that, dark, lustrous. A man could sink his hands into that kind of hair. Her skin was very creamy. She was beautiful.

On her Liaison Officer salary Havily could have afforded a much larger home than her modest condo. Instead, he suspected she spent most of her money on clothes—or at least she looked like she did. She liked the labels. Her Gucci sunglasses hung over the edge of her Marc Jacobs bag, and he had talked with her enough over the years to know that she preferred Ralph Lauren to other designers. Endelle might still dress up in her animal skins, but Havily now set a tone in the admin offices that had all the women fussing with makeup and hair and clothes.

Yeah, the office was improved, and maybe that was something about her he'd never really understood until now. Wherever she went, the environment improved. That may not have been a preternatural power, but it was a certain kind of magic at headquarters.

Even here at the Cave, her magic had been spreading. She'd recently seen to the repair of the TV for them and now it ran on CNN, set up to be activated by a motion detector. As soon as anyone entered the room, the news flared up, not too loud, just a steady background drone full of Mortal Earth info. That, too, had a strange soothing quality.

Okay. He was half in love with her but then they all were.

Lately however, whenever he was around her, he'd started feeling an ache in the center of his chest, a longing he didn't quite get. He wasn't foolish enough to think she could ever have feelings for him, not after the *breh-hedden* in the form of Warrior Marcus had hunted her down in March and shot her full of intense lust for the bastard.

No, he'd lived too long on earth, either dimension, to think there could ever be anything between himself and Havily Morgan. But for the strangest moment he wished he could take her home, make love to her, then fall asleep curled up around her body.

With such a vivid thought, his body reacted and the coffee slid from his hand. With vampire speed he caught it before it hit the floor, splashed, and made a mess.

"Careful," she murmured.

"Long night," he said, his voice a hoarse whisper. He kept his gaze away from her.

He felt her hand on his shoulder. She rubbed back and forth, a real comfort, and it was all he could do to keep from either flinching or grabbing both of her arms and hauling her against his chest. Shit. He wondered if this was the way Luken felt around her.

Luken of course had been on his mind, on all the brothers' minds. Havily's, too, no doubt. She had a connection to Luken. He'd been her guardian during her ascension but he'd also had the worst crush on her since.

Medichi still didn't quite get, though, how Havily had found Luken in a vision. She had related as best she could what had happened to her, that she had somehow *seen* the sky on fire and Luken fall to the earth.

Warning bells had gone off at her description of having a vision. The whole thing smacked not of a Second Earth power but of a third-dimension ability—and if that was the case, she could be in trouble. If, after a century as a vampire, she was now developing new powers, powers that would finally explain why the Seers a hundred years ago had insisted she needed a warrior guardian during her three-day rite of ascension, then she could be in danger all over again. Third abilities were rare on Second Earth, and Greaves would not want anyone with that level of power aligned with Madame Endelle, simple as that.

A tremor went through him when he thought of her alone in her small condo. To his knowledge the place had a mediocre security system. Also, he didn't think she had the ability to make mist, and she certainly had no skills with a sword or even a modest ability to defend herself.

He felt uneasy. He'd have to think about her situation. Maybe there was something he could do.

"Hey," he said softly. "I plan on visiting Luken this morning. Want to come with?"

Havily nodded. "What time?"

Medichi shrugged. "Later. About eleven I think. Given what he's been through, he'll need to sleep for a few hours."

"I would really like that."

"Then I'll see you at the clinic at eleven."

"Perfect."

Yes, she was.

He was beloved,
But I could not take him to my bed.
He brought the rays of the sun to the earth
And the stars were named for his exploits.
He was as gentle as a soft rain.
But the door of my house remained closed.
I was not for him.
I belonged to the tempest.

—*Collected Poems,* Beatrice of Fourth

CHAPTER 4

"She saved your life, brother." Antony Medichi's deep voice filled the small clinic room.

Havily stood in the doorway and suppressed a sigh. The Warriors of the Blood were one gorgeous lot.

Medichi leaned close to the bed, his elbow resting on the top of the mattress since Luken was sitting up all the way, the automatic bed raised to support him. Luken looked deathly pale, which was so unusual for the largest of the warriors. His complexion was normally a beautiful golden color. His thick blond hair, having been protected by the *cadroen,* hung in waves over his shoulders and down his chest. He was naked to the waist, a thin white sheet covering his thighs. He actually looked vulnerable, despite the massive size of his pecs, his arms, and his shoulders.

Thanks to the work of the healers, his skin had lost its

fiery blistered appearance. Except for his pallor, he was amazingly recovered.

He caught sight of her and smiled, his blue eyes lighting up. "Havily. Come in. Please."

"Hey," Medichi called to her softly. "The dragon actually let you out of her lair?"

Havily laughed as she moved into the room. She loved both of these men so much, but she found herself biting back tears.

"Don't you look pretty in your blue skirt," Luken said.

"Thank you." She drew close to the bed. He extended a hand and she took it. He squeezed gently, his obvious affection for her shining in his eyes. How many times had she wished she could feel more for him than she did?

"I don't remember much about last night—only that you were there. How did you find me?"

"Well, I'm still not sure. I think I had a vision, or something. Although right now it's kind of a blur." A lump formed in her throat. "I've never been more frightened."

"Both Medichi and Thorne say I owe my life to you, but what I want to know is how the hell I'm ever going to repay you."

"I was just glad to be of use," she said, but her voice had dropped almost to a whisper. "Tell me you're feeling better."

"A thousand percent. You know Horace. Man of miracles."

All Havily could do was nod. Her mind had filled once again with the horror of the night before and finding him in the Superstitions so . . . burned. She wanted to ask about his wings but was afraid to bring the subject up. Luken loved to fly. She couldn't imagine him living out his life on Second without his wings.

"You know, Hav, Medichi and I have been talking about the vision you had and we can't help but wonder if there's something more going on here. With you, I mean. All these years, we've all wondered why you needed a guardian to protect you."

"I know. Believe me, I know. I'm reminded of my failings daily."

Luken smiled, a crooked curve of his lips. "Well, Endelle isn't very subtle, is she?"

"As subtle as a rattlesnake . . . *coiling* and *striking*."

Luken laughed then stopped. He drew in a ragged breath.

"You okay?" she asked.

He nodded. "Smoke got to me last night as well." He nodded, cleared his throat, then continued. "The thing is, Medichi and I have been wondering if maybe what you experienced last night isn't an onset of a new power or something. We all develop our powers at different paces. I had a bitch of a time with telepathy for the first two hundred years.

"Anyway, because you saved the life of a Warrior of the Blood"—here he jerked his thumb at Medichi then back at himself—"we're concerned that your contribution will be noticed by, well, the enemy."

Havily had for so long known what a disappointment she was to Madame Endelle that she couldn't quite comprehend what these powerful warriors were saying to her. "Are you worried for my safety?" she asked, astonished.

Both men nodded.

"Exactly," Medichi said.

"Really?" She just couldn't fathom it.

Luken gave her hand a squeeze. "We want you set up with a telepathic link, and I think Medichi would be best to do it. That way, if you ever got in trouble, you could contact him right away and he could get to you."

"A link? You mean like the one Endelle and Thorne share?"

"Yes," Medichi said. "Just in case. What we know about Greaves is that he leaves no stone unturned. If he either fears you could threaten him or sees you as an asset, he'll make an attempt to get control of you."

"You're serious," she stated. She glanced at each of them in turn. She was so darn used to being the least significant person in her small group of powerful ascenders that she was having a hard time not laughing at their concern. However, they both appeared so grim, each brow furrowed, each pair of eyes staring hard at her, that a shiver traveled straight down her spine and agitated her wing-locks.

She drew in a quick breath. The decision wasn't hard to make. These were warriors, and they'd been battling this particular enemy for centuries. If they said she was in danger, she was taking them at their word. "I'm in," she said quietly. "But exactly how would it work?"

"When the link is set up," Medichi explained, "all you have to do is concentrate on me then telepathically speak my name."

You mean, like this? she sent.

He nodded. "Except that we don't have to be in the same room." At that he smiled. "We know you have powerful shields, which is a good indication that you can permit someone inside your head and the other way around. Have you ever gone mind-diving?"

"You mean deep mind-engagement?"

"Yes," Medichi said. "Moving within another person's mind."

"I attempted it once with unhappy results." She thought of Eric. She had once dived inside his head, a really careless maneuver, and he'd doubled over in pain. The poor man had been left with a terrible headache for three days. That a power of hers had caused him so much suffering had crushed her to no end. This was one of the major differences between Militia Warriors and Warriors of the Blood: Most Militia Warriors lacked advanced powers. Havily shifted her gaze to Luken then back to Medichi. She was struck all over again by the sheer size of these men, the Warriors of the Blood. All of them had exceptional preternatural abilities, which, coupled with their physical strength, allowed each warrior to battle a number of death vampires at any given time. They were Second Earth's elite fighting unit. There were a total of only seven known warriors of this stature in the world, eight including Marcus.

"I knew it," Medichi cried. "You're untapped. I've been thinking it for a long time."

"What do you mean?"

"You have major powers that haven't emerged yet. It sure as hell would explain what happened four months ago."

She wished more than anything that he hadn't brought the subject up. She felt the blush begin and was completely incapable of stopping it. He referred, of course, to Warrior Marcus and what all the warriors knew to be the onset of the *breh-hedden* between them.

What they couldn't know was that in some inexplicable way, she had just had sex with Marcus this very morning.

"I didn't mean to make you uncomfortable."

"No. No, of course not. It's just that . . . I've had visions of him, as well." Once again she was overwhelmed with the probability that they weren't visions but actual experiences.

Oh. God.

Which would mean, of course, that she'd been having sex with him for four months now!

Oh, dear God.

She squeezed her eyes shut and pushed all those unsettling thoughts out of her head. When she opened her eyes, she straightened her shoulders and turned to Medichi. She took a deep breath, "If the link involves mind-engagement, I think I'd be fine."

Medichi frowned slightly. "I want to assure you, Hav, that this is a fairly superficial level of mind-engagement. Nothing deep. One level below telepathy. I won't be able to see your memories or anything like that, which can occur with deeper levels of mind-diving."

For a brief moment she felt really uncomfortable with the arrangement. She couldn't explain why, exactly, but the thought of allowing this kind of link with Medichi felt as though she was being unfaithful to Marcus. Which was utterly and completely ridiculous. So ridiculous in fact that she nodded in a swift dip of her chin and said, "Let's do it. You've convinced me. What do you need me to do?"

Medichi moved to stand in front of her then put his hand on her forehead. "Just relax."

It wasn't easy to be close to so much lean muscled warrior. Medichi was the tallest of the brothers and very handsome in his Italian way. He had high strong cheekbones, dark brown eyes, and long straight black hair. She forced her shoulders to settle down and worked to unknot her stomach. Finally she gave up and closed her eyes.

"You're doing fine."

At first his hand just felt warm, but a moment later she felt his mind slide against hers then dip inside. A tingling followed, along with something that felt like a solid clamp on her brain, which made her smile.

Do you feel that? he sent.

She opened her eyes. She grinned. "It's the oddest sensation."

He nodded. "I'm going to fold to the Cave then reach out to you, as a test. That will put a dimension between us. We'll see how well this works."

"Okay. Good. Do it."

He smiled at her first. "You know, that's what I like best about you. You're so game." He lifted his hand and was gone.

She shifted her gaze to Luken. "It really is weird." She tilted her head sideways. "It's like that feeling when you've gone swimming and water ends up in your ears and won't come out. I want to shake my head."

Luken just looked at her, his expression warm, affectionate.

Havily. You there?

She heard Medichi as plain as day. "Yes," she said aloud,

then laughed at her stupidity. *I mean, yes,* she sent mind-to-mind. *I said it aloud as soon as I heard you . . . in my head, I mean.*

Yep, you've got powers. And I'm not hurting you?

Not even a little.

A moment later he materialized in front of her, smiling.

"How do I call you?" she asked. "I mean how did you reach out to me? Does this mean you can hear my thoughts?"

"Only if you direct them at me. It's a link. I'm not in your head. It's telepathic. Think of it as long-distance tele-pathy."

"Oh, okay. I guess that makes sense. All I know is that I'd hate to subject you to the ongoing chaos of my thoughts. Sometimes it's like a lettuce spinner in there."

He laughed. "Don't worry. The link is nothing like that." He grew sober for a moment, his expression inscrutable. He then cleared his throat. He glanced at Luken. Havily's gaze followed. The warrior's eyes were closed.

"He must be exhausted," she whispered.

"Yeah," Medichi said, his voice low as well. "I guess I'd better hunt down my bed. I'll be battling by eight." He turned to her. "I'm always here for you, Hav, you know that, right?"

She nodded. "You're the best, Antony."

Eldon Crace, High Administrator of Chicago Two, minion to his deity, Commander Darian Greaves, had muscles on his muscles now. Oh . . . yeah.

And, shit yes, sweat poured off him in streams, but not because of fear like it used to. Now he sweat because he pumped iron several hours a day and because he'd built him-self a goddamn righteous forge, the old-fashioned kind, deep in the heart of Greaves's compound. He never wore a shirt, just a black leather kilt and warrior battle sandals.

Decades ago, before his ascension to Second Earth, he had worked for a smithy in rural Indiana. He had always enjoyed the nature of the work, taking metal, heating it up until it glowed red, then pounding it into whatever shape he wanted. The metaphor pleased him immensely.

Horseshoes then.

Manacles now.

A few months ago, shortly after he'd been introduced to the exquisite properties of dying blood, he'd constructed the forge deep within the Commander's compound, well into the belly of the earth, on the lowest level not far from the vast room used to test all manner of weaponry, including incendiary bombs.

He had labored hard over the forge. The ventilation alone had been one bitch of a challenge. Because the compound existed beneath the Commander's famous peach orchard, the ducting had to be routed a good mile from his current position.

But he'd gotten it done and now he had a proper workstation.

Sometimes life's simplest pleasures were the best.

He could think in the space he'd created for himself. Right now he pounded the hell out of a strip of glowing red metal the old-fashioned way, on an anvil, beating it so that it would fit the small wrist of a woman. Yes, his newly emerging death vampire nature had strong appetites and by God he indulged them.

For one thing, he really liked keeping his blood donors close at hand.

He glanced to his right, and desire flowed down his chest and into his abdomen, then low into his groin. A mortal woman hung from her manacled wrists, her dark eyes blank now from her new reality, her body a sagging weight barely supported by watery knees. He liked his donors weakened through the trauma and sheer fatigue of hanging from manacles. He liked his women worn out when he was ready to take what he'd earned. He also liked them draped in white gauze, a sacrificial symbol that pleased his vampire soul.

He laid a message over the mortal's mind: *Your life gives me life and for that you are blessed.*

He enjoyed delivering false hope. Her gaze flickered toward him, despair giving way to possibilities. But his sudden burst of laughter drew the blank stare once more as she looked away, her body sagging a little more.

She would feed not only him this night but also several of his personal attendants, those death vampires he'd recruited to serve as his guards and general lackeys.

He often did the hunting for his blood donors by himself, slipping quickly down to Mortal Earth before Central's grids could happen upon his powerful signature. Other times, he would take his squad with him. He had sufficient advanced power to fold them straight to Mortal Earth, which would keep them off Endelle's Central grid for a good long while.

He knew how the grids worked. They scanned back and forth looking for the signature of the death vampire, but Metro Phoenix took in a vast section of real estate and so far, in the past four months, he and his squad hadn't been caught once.

God, he loved his life, a new life, the life his master had given him when he'd insisted that Crace drink a small goblet of dying blood. The thought of that first experience still aroused him, every damn time.

But it was the months that followed that had fulfilled him, the increasing physical strength, the clarity of mind, of purpose, the incremental bursts of expanding power.

Power was the real drug, the real erotic pressure on the pleasure points of his brain.

He'd never been happier.

He'd never been more powerful.

He'd also left his former life behind.

He rarely traveled to Chicago Two and he no longer had contact with his wife, Julianna. How odd to think that at one time she had been everything to him, the center of his world and his ambitions. But dying blood had changed all that. Now she was a fly in the ointment, and every text he received from her made him want to destroy his fucking BlackBerry. The woman needed to move on. Rumors had it she was screwing everything in sight, no doubt to try to attract his attention.

Whatever.

A muffled noise struck his ear. With his newly improved preternatural hearing, he detected movement beyond the steel door of his forge.

"This had better be good," he shouted, the ring of metal on metal a seductive rhythm in his ears. The blood donor actually jumped.

He glanced at the steel door to his right, rivets gleaming.

The door opened and a fellow war-maker appeared, a relatively short vampire by the name of Rith. The bastard also took dying blood but he clearly made use of the antidote immediately afterward since he showed none of the hallmarks of the ordinary death vamp: no porcelain skin, no faint bluish tint to his complexion, no increased physical strength, no blackening of the wings, no beautifying of the features.

Rith was odd looking. He had short straight black hair, a wide forehead, and a broad nose. His eyes were black and deep-set. There had to be something of the Orient in his DNA. He stood maybe five-seven in his bare feet.

Unimpressive.

The idiot would be improved a thousandfold if he gave up the antidote.

"I do have news," Rith called to him from across the space, "and I think you'll be interested in this."

"The mortal-with-wings?" Crace asked. Four months ago, when the fiasco involving ascender Wells drew to a close, Greaves had shared with him intriguing if highly improbable info from the future streams about a mortal-with-wings.

At the time, Crace hadn't believed it was possible. The

only mortal ever to have wings before an ascension was the original ascender herself, the famous Luchianne. When nothing came of the Seers' rumors, Crace had thought it a hoax. Had it proven otherwise, had there really been such a mortal, Crace would have been at the head of the line to go in pursuit. Such a mortal would have had enormous power.

"No. Sorry," Rith replied. "Still no follow-up on the original report. But I do think you might prefer this one." Rith even smiled.

At that Crace stopped striking the strip of metal. Rith intrigued Crace for the simple reason that he didn't know the man's thoughts. He had fucking powerful shields. In addition to that, Rith cloaked every facial expression, every tell his body might provide as to a clue to the bastard's mind. In this Rith was a genius. For all Crace knew the vampire could be happy as sin or in a dry riverbed of despair. There was no way of knowing.

Rith waved a piece of paper in his direction. The forge was probably 130 degrees. Rith remained near the door and held it open with his foot, no doubt enjoying the cool air from the hallway beyond.

"Bring it to me," Crace stated. He smiled. He liked to think Rith suffered.

Rith didn't hesitate, though. He moved forward and the door slammed behind him. Nor did he pay the smallest heed to the woman hanging not far from the door, even though she whimpered, hoping to attract his attention. Good thing the bastard walked quickly or Crace would have felt the need to punish.

He shoved the metal back into the coals and took the dispatch. He read the contents in a quick sweep then frowned. The communication indicated that an ascender, Havily Morgan, had just appeared in the future streams as a threat to the Commander's plans for world domination.

"What do we know of her?" Crace asked.

"She's a warrior pet, as in Warriors of the Blood, which could mean trouble. She works directly for Madame Endelle as some sort of administrative coordinator, an executive I think. She's in charge of the Ambassadors Reception as well as the Festival."

"Really." Now, that was interesting.

"She used to be a Liaison Officer. She may still serve in that capacity. Her status seems ambiguous at this time. It is well known Madame Endelle dislikes ascender Morgan."

Crace frowned at the dispatch. "This doesn't make sense. If she is such a threat, why haven't we had reports about her? Why now?"

Rith shook his head. "I'm really not certain, although the Seer report on the third page uses the word *emergence*. She may just be coming into her powers."

Crace lifted a brow. He knew what that felt like.

Rith continued, "Even Warrior Kerrick only recently developed the power to dematerialize, his new power having emerged after his ritual *breh-hedden* with Guardian Wells."

Crace didn't like to think about Alison Wells. She was one of his stellar failures, which still rankled. The bitch.

Crace continued to read then paused on something else he didn't get. "What does this mean that her blood mimics dying blood? I've never heard of such a thing. You know, these Seers Fortresses are so full of shit."

"I happen to agree with you about that."

Crace glared at Rith. "Do you?"

Rith inclined a brow. "Yes. Most function at an accuracy rate of sixty-seven percent. That's a lot of noise in an orchestra."

Well, the bastard actually made sense. He turned his attention back to the dispatch. "So, essentially, the Commander wants us looking for this Morgan female, a Liaison Officer of questionable status but whose powers might be emerging and whose blood might mimic dying blood."

"Yes, master."

Crace glanced at Rith. This part of Rith's careful manners Crace approved of, that he called him *master*.

"The Commander wishes me to request that you make a special effort to apprehend ascender Morgan."

Crace lifted a brow. "*Just* apprehend her? So he wants the woman brought in?"

Rith smiled. "His words were colorful. He actually said to bring her in *dead or alive,* at your discretion."

At that, Crace laughed. "Very Old West of him."

"Yes, master."

Havily tilted her laptop just a little as she read through the committee reports on the state of preparations for the Ambassadors Reception and Festival. She had persuaded Madame Endelle to hold the combined event in order to boost her administration's image around the world. Endelle clearly lacked those aspects of political instinctive skill that would sustain the support of her allied Territorial High Administrators.

In this respect, in the war of propaganda, Greaves was winning. So far, 53 of 167 High Administrators had switched allegiance to the Commander, 3 of them in the past four months. If Endelle didn't find a way to connect more effectively with her Territory governments, she would lose them to the Commander one by one.

From Havily's dedicated research into the history of the most effective administrations throughout the centuries, those that employed a certain degree of ceremony and ritual tended to endure the longest. The human mind, whether ascended vampire or mortal in nature, bonded through ritual.

Bringing the Territorial ambassadors to White Lake and honoring them with a reception one night and a major spectacle the next was an important step toward binding Madame Endelle's government. Of course, Her Supremeness had come to the idea kicking and screaming. But once committed, she made no further protests. Havily was saddled with the complete responsibility for the affair. Not that she minded. Event coordinating seemed to be in her blood.

The response to the initial invitations had been positive—and overwhelming. All of the Territories still aligned with Endelle were sending ambassadors to the Festival, a gesture of goodwill that would have strong payoffs in the future.

In a couple of hours Havily would be meeting with her head of security, Colonel Seriffe, a Militia Warrior. He was in charge of securing fifteen miles of lake, desert, and mountain, no small task, but his plans were so thorough she had every confidence in him.

Her final meeting with all of the team leaders wouldn't take place until tomorrow. As things stood she was very satisfied. All but a handful of the ambassadors had arrived at the White Lake spectacle site, and the numerous hotels that flanked both the east and west sides of the lake were humming with activity.

Her teams had arranged numerous small, private events from boating to teas to guided tours through the famous White Lake gardens for each of the representatives. With a hundred world-class gardens and an equal number of massive hotels, White Lake was the perfect location for every aspect of such a large event.

The Ambassadors Reception would be a formal affair and would be held in three days' time in the largest ballroom of the Bredstone Hotel, probably the finest hotel in the world. All attending ambassadors would be formally presented to Endelle at that time. The Festival, on the other hand, was open to the public and would include one of the most massive displays of spectacle Second Earth had ever seen. Half a million ascenders were expected to attend the event. Security alone involved ten thousand Militia Warriors and an overall security system, along with a Central Command, the likes of which had never been employed at an event before.

No expense had been spared.

Every potential breach of security had been evaluated by Colonel Seriffe.

A knock sounded. Havily looked up and saw that Alison

was in the doorway, smiling. Her bump barely showed behind a loose blouse in lavender silk. She wore soft black pants and flats. Her blond hair was straight and loose, held away from her face with a narrow black velvet band. She was pregnant with Warrior Kerrick's child, a little girl, and she glowed.

"Do you have a minute?"

"For you? Always." She closed her laptop.

Alison moved into the room and shut the door behind her. Havily felt a slight rush to her head at this gesture. Alison always left the door open unless the topic was personal . . . and serious.

"I just returned from seeing Warrior Luken," she said. "I thought I'd update you. The doctors feel very hopeful about his wings. Did you know they can regenerate in less than a week?"

Havily put a hand to her chest and closed her eyes. "I am so thankful. But are they certain?"

Alison shrugged. "Eighty percent at this point. Thanks to Horace, the scarring on the wing-locks was minimal."

"That's very encouraging."

"Yes." Alison approached the desk. "In a similar vein, Warrior Medichi asked me to check on you. He said you were at the Superstitions last night."

"I was. It was . . . horrible." A mess, burned feathers everywhere, blood and death. "I tried not to pay too much attention to anything except Luken. He's such a powerful man but lying there shaking, his eyes wild with pain—"

Alison rounded the desk and put her hand on Havily's shoulder. Waves of warmth flowed through her and eased her heart.

"Thank you," she murmured, covering Alison's hand with her own.

"I'm always here for you," she said. "I need you to know that. You were a tremendous comfort to me during and after my ascension."

Havily looked up at her and saw the sincerity in her eyes.

She recalled the two of them sitting on Havily's bedroom floor, weeping together. Alison had thought she would never see Kerrick again, and Havily had wept because Warrior Marcus had left Second Earth with no intention of returning. She shouldn't have been so upset that he left when he did, since it had been for the best, but the *breh-hedden* had taken its toll and so she had wept. The women had bonded because of it.

She smiled. "I try not to burden you since you have enough on your plate with Madame Endelle."

Alison served as Endelle's executive assistant, a job nobody wanted. She had the good grace to grimace and shake her head. Generally, she was a model of discretion and composure, something she had to be since her boss was a foulmouthed she-devil. But it helped to know that Havily was not the only one suffering at the executive end of the building.

"Regardless," Alison said, "anytime you need me, I'm here for you." She then took a deep breath, and her hand slid off Havily's shoulder. "Now there are a couple of things I've been commissioned to ask you." She moved back to the front of the desk and took up a chair opposite Havily so that they were eye-to-eye.

"Sure," Havily said, but her heart rate rose.

Alison smiled then tilted her head as though she was nervous as well. "I need to ask you about your dreams."

Havily blinked. More than once. She felt a wave of heat climb her cheeks. "My dreams?"

"Yes, but I can see that I've already embarrassed you and for that I'm so sorry."

Havily laughed because she didn't know where to begin except to wonder what had brought her to ask the question in the first place. "Why do you need to know about my dreams?"

At that, Alison looked away from her. Her shoulders sagged just a little, and she sighed. "I can't explain exactly except that I *know* your dreams have great significance and I was asked to *tend to them*."

"You're to tend to my dreams? Madame Endelle wants you to tend to my dreams."

Alison shook her head. "Not Her Supremeness, but more I can't say. So let me ask you this: Have you been having unusual dreams lately?"

Havily laughed again but she didn't know what to say. "Well, it turns out the dreams that I thought were dreams aren't really dreams."

Alison nodded and released a strange, knowing noise, "Ah. That actually sounds about right. Do you want to explain?"

There was something in Alison's tone that once more set Havily at ease, and for some reason the whole story just poured out of her—the tale of the last four months, and of Marcus.

To Alison's great credit, she listened intently and nodded her reassurance several times. She never once gasped or expressed disgust, despite the content of Havily's admission. But then Alison had been a therapist on Mortal Earth and had probably heard everything, especially since the Commander had actually used Alison as his personal therapist for the entire year preceding Alison's ascension. Now, there was a bizarre story.

When she finished her dream history, Alison sat back in her chair. "There can be no question that this is the *breh-hedden*."

Havily nodded. "I completely agree."

"And you're certain these aren't normal dreams or fantasies."

Havily sighed. "I had physical proof this morning when I 'returned' from what I had thought was a dreaming experience. Trust me, the events of the past four months *happened*."

When Alison fell silent, Havily asked, "What are you thinking?"

"I'm trying to connect the experience you had of your vision of Warrior Luken with those you had with Warrior

Marcus. Do you believe there's a connection? Or can you see a connection?"

"I don't know exactly except in one aspect in particular. On both occasions I ended up in a place that darkened around the edges and blocked me from going into the place that was real. Does that make sense?"

"Not exactly."

"So you haven't experienced anything like this?"

"No. Not at all." Alison was silent for a moment then said, "Well, I would just like to impress you with my belief that for some reason, this ability of yours to dream and yet have very real experiences is critical. Obviously, because of this ability you saved Warrior Luken's life. So my suggestion to you is that you be careful of this power, treat it with great respect, and be on your guard."

Havily nodded. "I will." She then told her that both Warrior Luken and Medichi had been so concerned for her safety because of what they believed to be her emerging power that she now had a telepathic link with Medichi.

"I think that's excellent. Something is going on here of great significance. I can feel it. I suspect you can as well."

"You know, I've been so busy with the Festival that I haven't stopped to think about anything else. But you said you had two things to discuss with me?"

Alison rose to her feet and rolled her eyes. "Endelle told me I was to yell at you until you agreed to go to Mortal Earth and persuade Warrior Marcus to come back to Second Earth and resume his duties as a Warrior of the Blood."

At that Havily chuckled. "Does she even know Warrior Marcus?"

"I know. That's what I thought. My impression of him is that he's going to do what he damn well pleases and she can just, you know, stuff it."

"*Hello.* Exactly."

Alison laughed. "You know, the only thing I would recommend is that you go to Mortal Earth and talk to Marcus about what's been going on between you two. I can sense how distressed you are, and I suspect these strange dreaming episodes will only continue unless you confront him. But I refuse to say more than that." She straightened her shoulders and added in a sharp voice, "Well, then, now that I've *yelled* at you about Warrior Marcus, I can tell Madame Endelle that I have hereby discharged my duty."

She smiled a conspiratorial smile and turned on her heel. She gave a little wave as she left the room.

Havily sat back in her tall executive chair and spun it around to look out at the expanse of desert to the east. The sun was high overhead, and there wasn't a cloud anywhere—typical June weather. Beneath the glare of the sun, the desert had a washed-out appearance this time of year, as though the baking effects of the constant sunshine stripped all the plants of color.

The monsoon storms and rain would change all that in a month or so, green things up a little, help the desert plants to bloom once more before the arid fall and winter set in.

Second Earth was an amazing blend of nature left to its own devices and the creation of extraordinary gardens. Horticulture was greatly prized in the dimension of the vampire, a very strange juxtaposition. She smiled. Who would've thought—vampires and gardens? But then the strange mythos of the vampire on Mortal Earth did have a basis in the reality of Second Earth. Death vampires epitomized Dracula's nature.

As Havily considered Alison's suggestion, she knew in her bones that she was right. She did need to talk to Marcus, and not about returning as a Warrior of the Blood. She had at least two hours before her meeting with Colonel Seriffe. That ought to be sufficient time to set a few things straight with her would-be vampire lover.

At the same moment that Marcus heard the buzz of the intercom, he felt *her* presence.

Holy shit. Havily was in the building. He knew it, *felt it,* as though she stood right next to him.

On the back of that sensation, he experienced an overwhelming need to get to her immediately, to make certain she was safe.

He lifted an arm, the universal signal that he was about to dematerialize, then remembered where the hell he was. He was on Mortal Earth, so he lowered his arm and forced himself to calm the fuck down. He took deep breaths, a whole string of them, one after the other.

The intercom buzzed again. He went over to his desk, still tingling from the near-fold, then touched the button on his desk phone. "Yes, Jane."

"Security has a Miss Morgan to see you. She does not have an appointment."

"Thank you." He paused, then spoke the words that would make history in his corporation. "I'll go down myself."

Jane didn't respond. He smiled. He could just see her face in the next room, her large brown eyes popped wide. He'd never in the course of their twenty years together left his office for the purpose of meeting anyone in the lobby. Why the hell was he changing protocol for Havily?

So why was he?

He had two reasons. The second reason he ignored because it involved their lovemaking last night. The first reason was that his instinct to get to her and to protect her was so profound that if he'd had any doubts the *brehhedden* still had hold of him, he didn't anymore.

Finally, Jane said, "Very good, sir. I'll tell security you're on your way."

He released the button.

As he moved toward the door, his brain fired off in a dozen different directions, reminding him of his immediate schedule. He had a meeting in fifteen minutes. Legal had sent contracts up to sign. One of his boards would be here in half an hour.

Fuck.

He passed by Jane's desk, her fingers rat-a-tatting the keyboard, but her thoughts shot at him before he remembered to cast a mental shield.

Gorgeous. Why did I have to have the most gorgeous boss in the world and the man never ages but wow that new Tom Ford looks sculpted . . . positively sculpted to his wrestling shoulders. Speaking of wrestling, I'd like to wrestle his ass to the . . .

Marcus turned in the direction of his administrative assistant, who looked perfectly innocent as she typed away. She glanced up, her brown eyes wide. "Was there something you needed?"

He blinked. "Please cancel my next appointment and put the board off for another thirty minutes."

"Right away, Mr. Amargi."

He was known on Mortal Earth as Marcus Amargi, his last name chosen from the ancient Sumerian vocabulary. He hadn't used a surname in thousands of years. *Warrior* Marcus had sufficed until two hundred years ago.

She shifted in the direction of her phone, punched a button, lifted the receiver, and began reworking his schedule. Having heard her thoughts reminded him that he'd have to make a change soon. He needed a younger executive assistant, because Jane was aging and he wasn't. So, shit. She was the best assistant he'd ever had. She could finish his breaths. Of all the ways he'd been forced to deal with his immortality on Mortal Earth, this one proved the trickiest.

As the years passed, as all the mortals he dealt with in business aged and he didn't, he had often had to dissolve entire corporations and create new ones to deflect the inevitable questions. In the end, one of his best strategies had proven to be the hiring of self-exiled ascenders, like himself. That way age never mattered and strategies became a group effort.

He headed to the elevators, and once he was on board he shored up his shields. He rode down to the ground floor of the building knowing he was making history, knowing that this one act, meeting a woman in the lobby, would be speculated upon for years to come.

He didn't care.

What he cared about was if anyone had followed Havily to Mortal Earth or into the building and whether or not a war would erupt around her.

He remained outwardly cool, unmoving, unflinching. But his wing-locks thrummed, his fangs pounded in his gums, and he prepared to make a shitload of mist if necessary. He kept flexing his fingers in case he needed to draw his sword from his locked weapons locker on Bainbridge Island. Or a gun. Vampires were allowed to use guns on Mortal Earth.

Whatever.

Havily stood near the security desk. Now that she was here, doubts of varying sorts pummeled her mind. Why had she come? Dear Creator, why had she come? Would he be angry that she was here? Would she take one look at him and forget all that she needed to say to him?

Alison had been right to nudge her in the direction of this visit. It was long overdue; this nightly dreaming nonsense had to stop. In particular, Marcus needed to stop coming to her and seducing her, or whatever it was he was doing.

Also . . . she had a few things she wanted to say to him about his service as a Warrior of the Blood.

For all these reasons, she was nervous when normally she wouldn't have been, even though she was fully aware that nearly everyone in the lobby was staring at her.

But then again, she'd come armed wearing her favorite Ralph Lauren. She had her hair in a tight professional twist. She wore serious closed-toed heels, which put her at six-two, taller no doubt than most of the women in the building.

Slung over her shoulder was a Marc Jacobs, her favorite.

She wore simple pearl studs and a Rolex watch, the latter her only real splurge of the last few years.

Glancing around, she approved of the building. Good

security. She suspected that billions in transactions, floor upon floor, passed through these walls.

Whatever she thought of Warrior Marcus, she had to admit she liked the general *feel* of the place. The decor was high-end but there were a great many plants all around the lobby, indicating that the owner spent money on the working environment as well as the financial future of his empire.

Oh, great. She hadn't wanted to approve of anything about him, but right off the bat she did.

She blinked.

Fennel.

Her heart rate started to climb.

Warrior Marcus had not even come into view, but his scent preceded him. She closed her eyes and weaved on her feet. Whatever her nightly encounters with him had been, the actual presence of his smell, *the real deal,* sent line drives straight up her thighs.

As usual, the well of her body clenched and she reached for the edge of the security desk to support her buckling knees.

"Havily." The word shot across the space between what she knew was the warrior she'd been avoiding for four months and her tender ears. His voice, speaking her name, forced her lips apart. She had no words as she turned in his direction, just myriad sensations that ignited a familiar fire.

Her gaze found him and drifted over his dark brown hair, which was no longer corporate short and straight but long to his chin and curling at the ends. *He's letting his hair grow, his warrior hair.* Otherwise, he was as she remembered him, his beautiful olive skin, his fierce expression, and his dark brows that were perpetually slashed over light brown eyes. He wore a tailored suit, although *tailored* seemed like an inadequate word to describe what she saw. He remained immobile as her gaze traveled in a slow, lethargic drift down his massive warrior body, clothed in fine-pressed black wool with a narrow pinstripe.

Again she approved and she didn't want to.

She reminded herself that despite his accomplishments and his excellent wardrobe, whatever he was in this world had cost lives on Second Earth. He should have been battling; instead he had made a lot of money and bought suits and hired security personnel. She knew without having to be told that he owned the whole damn building.

Even though she was drawn to him like cream to strawberries, and wanted to get a fold straight back to Second Earth . . . like now . . . she moved forward and extended her hand. "Hello, Marcus." How strange it felt not to address him more formally as *Warrior* Marcus.

She watched his shoulders rise as he drew in a breath and took her hand in his. His clasp was warm and strong, the pads of his fingers fleshy, but she already knew that since she'd felt him in her dreams.

The reminder of what they had shared brought a warm flush to her cheeks. She drew her hand out of his. "I've come on behalf of . . . certain parties of interest to you." She could hardly say *Madame Supreme High Administrator of Second Earth* in front of a dozen inquisitive sets of Mortal Earth ears.

He nodded. "Won't you come up?"

"Yes, of course."

He guided her to the elevators, his hand never far from the small of her back. She had a strong sense that if an attack came, he would pull her against him with one hand and with the other draw a weapon.

That she was the object of such protective instincts sent ripples of pleasure through her abdomen. Again, her body clenched even when she didn't want it to. She wished just this once, while in his presence, she could *calm the hell down.*

As the elevator doors closed and they were the only ones in it, she heard him grunt strangely, a sound followed by a very faint grinding. Teeth upon teeth?

A moment later the small space flooded with a cloud of

fennel. She listed sideways, falling against the wall of the elevator. Worse followed when he clamped his arm around her waist to support her.

She gave a squeak and pushed his hand away. She took a step forward trying to create distance, a hopeless venture inside the stainless-steel box.

"Are you all right?" he asked, his voice low, husky, one resonant seductive thrall.

"Please don't touch me again, Warrior."

He backed away. In the shiny metal that surrounded the elevator buttons, she saw that he had moved into the far corner and stared at her from beneath hooded eyes. More fennel wafted around her.

Oh, God. Coming to Seattle was a serious mistake.

*The wheel came from the land of Sumer as did
the first vampire, Luchianne.*

—From *Treatise on Ascension*, by Philippe Reynard

CHAPTER 5

Marcus had never suffered in quite this way before. When
he knew, when he had sensed that Havily was in the building, his building, the building he owned, he had experienced
desire, confusion, urgency. He had not thought much beyond his need to make sure she was safe and that his building remained secure.

However, the moment he saw her, the moment he *smelled*
her, the molecules in his body had realigned and sent every
instinct in the direction of his groin and his need to bond
with her. That absurd imperative had swamped him, screaming at him to get inside her, to release his seed into her, to
take her blood, to penetrate her mind, all at the same time, to
make her his, now and forever.

He knew she watched him from the reflection of the
chrome plate around the elevator buttons, but did she have

any idea how her honeysuckle scent now filled the shared space and worked his cock into a state of hard readiness?

He had a couch in his office. Hell, he had two. Fuck that. He had a glass desk the size of a small barge. He'd clear it with a sweep of his arm and throw her on her back. He'd . . .

He closed his eyes, flared his nostrils, and dragged her scent into his nose. One stroke, he'd come. Fucking *breh-hedden*.

"Why the hell are you here?" left his throat in a hoarse mess.

"We . . . we have matters to discuss. You know we do and I want this . . . *thing* between us settled once and for all."

And exactly how did she plan to do that? The image of her on her back and him on top made the only kind of sense.

When the doors opened he moved up behind her. He knew he crowded her but he couldn't help it. His protective instinct was firing off missiles. He had his arm around her waist as he moved to the door to his suite.

He opened the door for her. He barely saw Jane as he ushered Havily into his office. He barked over his shoulder to his assistant, "We're not to be disturbed. For any reason."

"Yes, sir. Of course, sir," returned in a sharp stunned whisper.

He shut the door and wasn't surprised when Havily hurried past his desk to the opposite corner of the office near the windows. He watched her shoulders rise and fall rapidly.

Goddamn the *breh-hedden*. They were both held in a tight grip. Worse, the dreams had revealed exactly what she looked like naked, and that's all he saw as he looked her up and down. He'd cupped her ass in his hands. She may be wearing a tailored navy wool suit, but he knew what her breasts looked like, felt like.

His scrutiny stopped at *tailored* and *wool*. She'd come from Phoenix in late June where it was hotter than Hades right now. So she must have dressed for . . . Seattle.

Something about that made him smile, a little smugly

perhaps. "Did you have a nice trip?" he asked, shocked again at the hoarse quality of his voice.

"Would you stop that," she cried as she turned back to him.

"Stop what?"

"This whole room smells like a licorice factory."

Ah, yes, the one defining quality of the *breh-hedden*, the giving of specific scents, male and female, meant only for the other, detected only by the other. She was, for him, *the other*.

"All I'm smelling is honeysuckle, Havily. When I'm around you, that's all I smell. Fucking honeysuckle. Clouds of honeysuckle. A rain forest of honeysuckle."

She shook her head and frowned. "You mean you don't smell this sharp fennel scent?" She waved an arm about to encompass the room.

"No, not at all. Just *you*."

He crossed the room to stand near the window. He looked down at the view below, as he often did, but drew no closer to her than six feet. Less separation and he'd take her in his arms, he'd kiss her, he'd force himself on her as he'd tried to do that last night at Endelle's palace. Given her scent, she'd probably succumb, so shit.

He turned slowly to watch her. She faced the window now as well and was beautiful in profile, her nose a lovely curve, her lips parted. Her hair was an exquisite auburn; her complexion, a delicate cream enhanced with peach blush over her cheekbones. Her eyes were a light green like translucent jade. So beautiful. Once more, his groin responded. Okay, so maybe looking at her wasn't a good idea, either. "So, again, why have you come?"

"I need you to stop the dreaming," she blurted, her gaze skating to him then returning to look well beyond downtown, far out into Puget Sound.

Of all the things he had expected to hear, that wasn't one of them. How the hell had she construed their nocturnal engagements as something *he* instigated? "You're kidding, right?"

Her porcelain cheeks developed bright spots of color as she once more turned toward him, her shoulders pulled back, her chin high. "What does that mean?"

"I think you know what it means. *You* come to *me* in *my* dreams, vampire, not the other way around."

Confusion once more flitted over her eyes, her beautiful light green eyes, the same color . . . yeah . . . as the banding on his wings, just as Medichi had once observed. She shook her head back and forth. "That's not the way it is. *You* summon *me* and I can't seem to resist. I'm here to beg you to stop calling me to your bed."

His jaw shifted back and forth. He narrowed his eyes. "You've got the wrong end of the stick. I awake and *you* are riding *me* . . . every damn time. Think about it, Havily. Isn't that the way it always happens?"

She took a step back and dropped her purse as her hand flew to her chest. Her cheeks now flooded with color. "Warrior, please. The whole thing is distasteful and very *wrong*. I came to ask you to stop, not to have you throw the experience in my face. You have no idea how hard this is for me, to come to you, to ask this of you. I never wanted to see you again."

"Of course not," he muttered. "Not for perfect Havily Morgan to engage with a hedonistic captain of industry. You do know that my corporations provide millions of jobs around the world, don't you?" Why the hell had he gone down this road, as though he needed to defend his choices? What did he care what she thought of him?

Her nostrils flared and her chin rose higher still. "You deserted your brothers-in-arms. I will never forgive you for that! How many ascenders, how many *mortals* have died because you couldn't bear the war any longer? How many, Warrior Marcus? I swear I don't know how you sleep at night."

He crossed his arms over his chest. "Well, I haven't been sleeping very much lately, now have I, not when I'm awakened by a dream-nymph making use of my body." He was such a bastard.

"A dream-nymph?" she cried. "Oh, how I hate you for saying that."

Well, at least she'd started showing some sense.

"I don't *summon* you, Havily. When I wake up, you're with me, in my bed . . . sort of. You come to me, though I have no idea how you do it, or even where we are when we're together."

She shook her head. "I can't believe you're putting this on me. But it really doesn't matter how it's happening, I just know it has to end and I've come here to ask you to stop doing what you're doing."

"All I'm doing is responding to you."

"But why have you done it all this time? That's what I don't understand."

Because I loved having you in my bed, on top of me, your scent flooding my nostrils. "I could ask the same of you."

"I thought it was some kind of weird dream state, a kind of fantasy. I thought my subconscious was living out what I refused to do in my conscious life."

At that he smiled, but not kindly. "So this was your fantasy? You on top?"

She covered her face with her hands. More pink showed between her splayed fingers and crept toward her chin. He was pushing her, but that's what a man did when a woman held up a mirror and the man saw his reflection but disliked what he saw. And yes, it made him a bastard.

His conscience kicked in. He hadn't always been such a prick.

He ran a hand through his hair. "Look, why don't you sit down and we'll talk this through. We'll figure this out together. And I'll . . . try not to be so abrasive. This whole thing has kicked me out of stride." He gestured to the black leather sofa flanking the long wall to the left of the door.

She nodded. "Fine." She picked up her purse and crossed in front of him.

He noticed her immaculate makeup, the careful striation of eye shadow, eyeliner, the tweezed, arched brows. She carried Marc Jacobs. She looked sleek, fit, stylish. He would have gone for her in any dimension.

She set her purse beside the sofa and sat down at the end nearest the windows, her gaze once more settled outside. "You have a lovely view of the sound."

"I have a house on Bainbridge. It's kind of rustic over there. Most of the island is very wooded but my house is on a spur of beachfront." So why was he telling her this? He didn't sit down but stood very still in front of her, watching her, savoring her beauty.

Her brow wrinkled. "Is that the place . . . where I come to you? In your bedroom on Bainbridge?"

He nodded. "Yes."

Havily watched him. She felt exhausted, and she'd only been in his presence a few minutes. Her emotions were all over the place, as though she'd been dumped in a washing machine and set on the agitation cycle.

She was embarrassed and humiliated by the conversation. It had never occurred to her, not once, that she might be responsible for what had been happening between them, which in turn meant that he had every right to gloat and punish.

She wanted to disappear and for a moment thought about dematerializing . . . anywhere. Instead she murmured, "I used to live in this part of the world, on Mortal Earth."

He glanced out the window then back. "You did? Here in Seattle?"

She shook her head. "North. Vancouver Island. My husband and I had a farm outside Victoria, a few miles from present-day Butchart Gardens."

"You were married then?"

"Yes. A long time ago. Nineteen hundred two."

He chuckled.

"Why do you laugh?" she asked. Couldn't she even say that she'd been married without him laughing or smirking? "You know, you bug the hell out of me."

He closed his eyes for a brief moment. When he opened them, his gaze was kinder. "I didn't mean to offend you. But 1902 just doesn't seem that long ago."

"Right."

He nodded. "Believe me, a hundred years is a flash of lightning in the scheme of things."

He seemed tired suddenly as he moved to the window and looked down again, always looking down.

She knew he was four thousand years old. She tried to process that much time but couldn't. She put her hand to her forehead. She was tired and her neck ached. The fact that she hadn't gotten much sleep was getting to her. "Look. We don't need to drag this out. The truth is, I don't understand what's happening at night . . . in my or maybe *our* dreams. I can't seem to control what's happening, but I do know that every night I come to a place of consciousness in which I'm very awake, very aware of what we're doing. Can you tell me when that happens for you? When you become fully awake and aware?"

He looked uncomfortable as he shifted on his feet.

She gasped. "Are you telling me that you're awake earlier than I am?"

He shrugged and looked at her over his shoulder. "Sorry, but I'm not about to shove a beautiful woman out of my bed when she wakes me up the way you do. No man of sense would. I just didn't realize how serious this was until last night, when . . ."

She caught his gist and her cheeks flamed hot all over again. She knew exactly what he was referring to. She shaded her eyes with her hand. She couldn't even look at him. At the very least, the evidence of a man's orgasm was *messy*, but to be talking about it, referring to it, made her want to disappear from the face of the earth. The truth in this situation really distressed her—she didn't know this man and yet here they were discussing his . . . *seed*.

He moved to the chair set at a right angle to the couch. She heard the leather creak as he sat down. "Havily . . . I'm sorry. Shit, I'd undo this if I could. But you're right. We need to press on, get through this, and end it.

"As I was saying, I really wasn't sure what was going on between us. It felt real and yet there was a rim of darkness all around the space we shared. Did you notice that?"

She let her hand drop away and leaned back. "Yes, I did."

He nodded, and the sincerity in his face eased her embarrassment. She said, "What I'm asking is this: If I come to you again, will you awaken me early on so that we can try to end this impossible situation, not let it happen again?"

His gaze was considering, as though he weighed her words, held them in his hands, judged them. Finally, he said, "I will awaken you early on and I promise I won't attempt to draw you farther into sleep or to seduce you ever again."

She released a deep sigh. "Thank you for that. I'm truly . . . grateful." She rose to her feet. "There is one more thing. I was commissioned to ask you to return to service as a Warrior of the Blood. What can I tell my boss?"

He stood up as well. "You mean, Endelle sent you to beg on her behalf?"

Havily nodded.

"She expected you to *persuade* me?"

Havily smiled suddenly. "I don't think she knows you very well for all her nine thousand years. Even I understand how mulish you are. For that matter, the two of you have a lot in common. Still, she did know what happened at the palace between us, our *attraction* to each other, so she assumed I had some sort of power over you. But I can think of few things less likely than you returning to Second Earth. Tell me I am mistaken."

"You are not mistaken. I will not return."

Later that night Havily lay in bed, watching the bounce and spin of the glittery paper butterflies that hung suspended from the ceiling. The air-conditioning had come on, and the artificial breeze put the small winged creatures in flight. There were probably a hundred of them.

She had started with twelve, then kept adding to the collection over the years, as inspiration struck. The whole thing was one large piece of whimsy in what was otherwise a dull room of white walls, a green comforter, and black sheets, a room that never enjoyed any activity other than sleep.

She sighed. She had spent the last several hours reviewing her visit to Mortal Earth and her conversation with Marcus. She still couldn't believe that *she,* and not he, had been the creator of their nightly engagements.

She thought back to her vision of Luken and his wings on fire as he fell to the earth. Her vision of him had saved his life, since she had acted on what she had seen.

But how had she *seen* him? That's what didn't make sense to her, which led her once more back to Marcus. How had she engaged him in that nowhere kind of space, some alternate version of his bedroom in his house on Bainbridge? And when her vision of Luken had come to her, she had been sitting *in the desert,* yet not in the desert. Where was this place she went to when she had her visions?

Could she get there again without having an erotic dream of Marcus or without seeing someone she loved caught in a burning sky?

She closed her eyes. She concentrated very hard. She tightened every muscle in her body. She thought about different places and willed herself to move there. She even thought about Marcus's bed on Bainbridge Island, but nothing happened.

She sighed. She was so tired. She needed sleep badly.

The trouble was she feared waking up on top of Marcus again.

She put a hand to her chest and pressed hard. She needed to let him go. She really did. They could never have a life together. Her loyalty was to the Warriors of the Blood and he had betrayed them by leaving Second Earth and exiling himself in Seattle One.

But the mere thought of him, of being with him, of being engaged sexually with him, sent her fatigue flying away from her brain.

She groaned and rolled out of bed. She wore another cream lace nightgown, this one with a pleat down the center just below a high bodice. She wondered if Marcus would like it. Of course he would. He wore Tom Ford and looked like he stepped from the pages of *GQ*. And she loved his hair longer. She was used to warrior hair, which she thought extremely sexy.

So what did it mean that she and Marcus had been brought together like this? Some horrible trick of fate? He was so the last man she would have chosen for herself—except in physical essentials, of course. What red-blooded female wouldn't want Warrior Marcus? He was built like a Greek god, or in this case a Sumerian deity.

She paced her bedroom, the soft fabric of her long nightgown brushing between her legs, the silky texture a sensual glide over her skin. Even her nightgown made her wish for things she shouldn't be wishing for.

She paced to the windows and felt a vibration of air behind her. She whirled around, her heart flying upward. "Marcus?" she whispered. Had he come to her? Had he needed further talk? Oh, would he take her to bed? Hope soared. "Marcus?"

A man emerged—a very large muscled man with pale, bluish skin. "Not exactly."

She took a step backward. "Who are you?" She didn't know the vampire but he was huge, warrior huge. He was muscular and fighting-lean but he didn't have a sword in his hand; nor did he wear a weapons harness. He didn't even have on a shirt, just a black leather kilt and battle sandals. His complexion was very pale and he was unearthly beautiful. Oh, dear God.

"My name is Crace," he said quietly, his voice a seductive lure.

She was about to lift her hand and dematerialize but his

hand shot up into the air and she felt the field, a powerful one, fall around her. Panicked, she tried again to dematerialize but couldn't. She couldn't even move.

"What do you want?" she cried.

His gaze drifted down her body, paused at her breasts, then fell the length of her. He blinked and brought his eyes back to meet hers. "First, your blood, at least some of it. Then we'll just have to see."

Oh, God, oh, God.

She had only one recourse. She drew inward mentally and sent a cry for help straight to Warrior Medichi. *Death vampire,* she sent. *In my bedroom.*

"Shit," the death vampire cried out. "You've got a fucking link. Well, he won't get here in time, my dear."

Then the big body, bearing fangs, descended on her. Behind him she saw four additional death vampires, waiting, more beautiful unearthly creatures that moved like fog into her bedroom, apparently ready and willing to watch the fun and wait for turns.

As sharp fangs punctured her skin, she cried out in pain. The monster tore her neck open. Oh, God. Her mind spun. Would the link work? God help her if it didn't.

Deep within Medichi's mind, Havily's cry for help sounded like the shriek of a hawk. When her words pierced his brain, he cried out in agony because he couldn't stop what he was doing to fold to her position. Three death vamps had him fully engaged on Mortal Earth, at the White Tanks Dimensional Borderland.

He had to get to her.

Time to get fucking serious. He dipped his chin and pulled his dagger from his weapons harness. While clanging swords with his right hand he let the dagger fly and caught the pretty-boy to his left straight in the eye. The bastard flew backward screaming.

Behind him, he felt the air move. He spun, ducked, and shoved his sword deep into the belly of the second vampire. At almost the same moment, as he moved with pre-ternatural speed, he whirled back and his sword rasped against metal once more.

His last opponent was skilled, a Japanese warrior who knew how to wield a sword. A battle, blade upon blade, would take too fucking long. Medichi dematerialized and re-formed behind the bastard, catching him straight through the spine.

He didn't wait to see if more came; nor did he call Jeannie at Central for cleanup. He had to get to Camelback Mountain. Now.

He folded to Havily's patio. Behind the master bedroom window he saw an enormous warrior framed in the moonlight, bending her flailing body backward as he drank from her. She screamed and beat at him with her fists, but what chance did she have with that much raw muscle? Her movements slowed until her arms fell to her sides.

Even in the dim light, Medichi saw red.

He extended his hand, set up a field, and shattered the window, drawing it toward him, away from Havily.

The warrior drinking from her throat lifted his head. Medichi watched in slow motion as his fangs left the white throat. A smile formed on the bastard's face. A look of euphoria hit him as he dropped Havily, letting her fall to the floor. Her eyes were closed, her body limp.

Medichi lowered his chin and went for him, sword in hand, but even before he reached the low windowsill the warrior lifted his hand. He dematerialized and four death vamps came into view. Medichi stepped over the threshold, ready to engage, but they disappeared as well, which meant the first bastard possessed enough power to take them along for the ride. Holy shit. Who was this ascender with the brawn of the Warriors of the Blood and power that came close to echoing the Commander?

Whatever.

Right now, Havily came first.

He folded his sword to his villa, fell to his knees, and

examined her. Sweet Jesus, her throat was a mess. He lifted Havily into his arms, but she started fighting him and shouting, which was a good thing, except her nails bit into his arms.

"Hey, hey, hey," he whispered. "Havily. It's me. Antony. I'm here. I'm here. He's gone."

She stilled, gasped, then cried out, a hand clutching her bloody neck. "Is he gone?"

"Yes. He's gone. You're safe now."

He held her close then reached out with his senses into the rest of the house, searching for the enemy. But he found only a welcome stillness to the air. He carried her into the living room and laid her down on the couch. She sat up immediately as though afraid they would return, her hand still at her neck. Blood oozed between her fingers, and her legs shook. Shit.

She met his gaze, leaned forward, elbows on knees, then burst into tears. He watched her for a moment, his gaze drifting to the rivulets of blood that dripped down her chest and stained the lace of her nightgown. Fury filled him. He wanted that bastard's blood on his sword and on the ground, pints of it until the death vampire was good and dead.

Her sobs increased in volume. He resisted taking her back in his arms, offering her that kind of comfort. He was already too vulnerable where she was concerned. Havily had somehow broken through his defenses and begun arousing something very tender, yet very primal within him. Not a good thing for so many reasons.

Because he knew the wound at her throat would heal, he was more worried about her mental state. She'd been attacked. She'd faced her death tonight, and he wasn't exactly equipped to handle this kind of trauma.

He drew his card-like warrior phone into his hand from the narrow pocket of his black cargoes. As he dropped to kneel in front of her, he thumbed the card. With his free hand he rubbed her arm very gently back and forth.

"Central."

"Hey, Jeannie."

"What's doin', Medichi?" Always cheerful.

Medichi would have smiled if his heart hadn't been gripped by the sobs coming from Havily. "I need Alison. Can you get her for me? Tell her it's urgent."

"Of course. One sec." The phone fell silent.

Less than a minute later Alison's voice, thick with sleep, drifted through the line. "Hello, Antony. What's wrong? What's going on? I have the worst feeling. Is Kerrick okay?"

"This isn't about your man. I'm calling about Havily. She was attacked in her home. Death vampires. Do you think you can come to us?"

She didn't respond and the phone went dead. He stared at it, wondering what the hell to do and why she had hung up on him.

He was about to thumb Central's number again when suddenly he felt the air vibrate beside him. Shit. He was on his feet, sword in hand once more, but . . . okay, he took a breath . . . Alison stood in front of him. Of course she'd come.

She glanced at his sword then at the woman on the couch. He felt a wave of empathic concern flow over him as she turned and drew close to the sofa. "Havily, what happened?" she murmured.

Medichi took several steps away from both women. Jesus, his chest hurt. He stumbled in the direction of the window overlooking a large central fountain. He rubbed between his pecs and took deep breaths. This had been happening to him a lot lately, ever since Alison had bonded with Kerrick and Havily had been out of her mind when the *breh-hedden* hit her hard at Endelle's palace.

He had forgotten what it was to have women like this in his life. Mothers, sisters, lovers, the warmth of family, something he hadn't had for such a long time. Something he hadn't allowed himself from the day he ascended, from the time he had slaughtered those who had raped and killed his pregnant wife.

He weaved on his feet at the swell of empathy that filled the room. Sweet Jesus, Alison had power. Sometimes he even thought she exceeded Endelle, which had to be impossible. Although certainly not when it came to empathy.

He looked back in the direction of the couch. Yes, the concern, the pure love that radiated from the woman who was now holding Havily in her arms most certainly exceeded Endelle.

Within a few minutes Havily had stilled in Alison's arms, and her complexion took on more color. She blinked several times and even folded a tissue into her hand to wipe her cheeks.

Alison turned to him. "Antony, would you please see if Horace could come to us for a few minutes? I'd like him to tend to Havily's throat."

These words tensed his stomach and he was ready to fight all over again. He glanced at his sword. He folded the damn thing back to his vault deep within his villa.

He nodded to Alison and brought his phone back up to his ear.

Jeannie's voice came back on the line. "How's our girl?"

"We need Horace here." He heard the gasp, so he said, "Just a small repair . . . at her throat."

Jeannie never cursed, but the string of profanity that now left her mouth shocked even Medichi. "You okay?" he asked.

"There are some things that just get to me. I'll have Horace over there in five. He's been with Santiago at the Awatukee Borderland. Don't worry, the brother's okay. Just a skin burn."

Medichi laughed. *Skin burn* was code for a cut deep enough to slice through layers of muscle but not so deep that an artery had been hit. "Thanks," he murmured. "When you've relayed the message to Horace, I'll need Thorne to call. I'll be at this location probably through the night."

"No prob, *duhuro*."

"Jeannie, why the hell are you calling us that again?"

"Just showin' the love." She giggled as the phone went dead. He sure liked the girls at Central. Nothing fazed them . . . thank you, God. But the use of the word *duhuro,* an old-language word of deep, almost reverential respect—whose literal meaning was a combination of "servant" and "master"—still chapped his hide. He was a warrior who took lives every night of his life. The violent war he made didn't deserve that kind of accolade, as necessary as the nightly battling was.

Alison met his gaze. She had an arm around Havily, who in turn had her head pressed into Alison's shoulder. "I think we need Endelle in on this," she said. "I'm sensing something malevolent here, purposeful, unfinished. And you?"

"The same. Jeannie's contacting Thorne."

"Good. We need them both."

He nodded his agreement.

Havily shifted slightly to meet his gaze as well, and for just a moment he couldn't breathe. Even with both women in no makeup, and hair standing every which way, they were beauty personified, something that always hit his brain hard. His chest started to hurt all over again. He cleared his throat.

"I intend to stay here in case Hav receives another visit. Do you want to call Endelle or shall I?"

Medichi stared at her and she stared back. Now there was a duty filled with a thousand poisonous snakes.

But Alison laughed. "I can see how this is going to go for the next millennium. I've become cupbearer to the queen, haven't I? The messenger who usually gets shot?"

Medichi smiled, and some of his tension dissipated. "You're the one who said you were a Guardian of Ascension. I heard it with my own ears. I'm sorry, Alison, but some shit-jobs just come with the territory."

She responded with another laugh. "No doubt it would

be best if I went to her." But she turned to Havily and gave her shoulder a squeeze at the same time. "You okay with that?"

Havily pulled out of her arms and nodded. "Thank you, Lissy. I am. You've been a great help. Antony will take care of me."

Alison's gaze returned to him, and once more she smiled. "There is no finer warrior than Medichi. Just don't tell Kerrick I said that. He gets a little . . . *jealous*."

Medichi laughed. "Sorry. Can't guarantee that. Your *breh* is so damn powerful that it's always good to take him down a peg or two." Kerrick had been to hell and back when Alison had showed up a few months ago. Medichi had watched him suffer unimaginable torment beneath the pull of the *breh-hedden*. But Alison had been worth it. She had become a source of great comfort to all of them, a piece of a puzzle that had been missing so long they hadn't even known of their need for her. And she had fulfilled their brother, given him a daily refuge, her love, and the child in her womb. She represented hope in a hopeless situation. Medichi loved her but dammit, his chest was on fire.

Alison rose to her feet. She folded a brush and some kind of ruffled thing into her hands. She took a few swipes at her long blond hair with the brush, swept the mass into a ponytail, and used the ruffled thing to hold it in place. Without another word, she lifted a hand and disappeared. He took a step backward, almost stumbling. Because she had lifted her hand, he'd had a view of her swelling stomach.

He'd known of her pregnancy, but seeing it now made it real for the first time, knocking his consciousness sideways. Her emergence as a part of their team, as one critical member of the whole, had changed the dynamics of the Warriors of the Blood as well as the relationship between the Warriors and Endelle. Alison had changed so much and yet in the scheme of the war, very little. In fact the war had ramped up, but she'd somehow become a soothing oil between a lot of grating edges.

And she carried Kerrick's child.

Medichi's mind flashed with images of his long-deceased wife and her swollen belly. Pain slashed through him all over again, as real as if a dagger had been plunged into his heart. He drew air into his lungs as his throat tightened. He hadn't thought of *her* in a long, long time, at least not in this way, not in a way that reminded him of their child. And now he'd been reminded of her twice in one evening. Shit.

"What is it, Antony?" Havily asked.

He turned to stare at her, uncertain what she'd said.

"You look really upset. Are you all right? Are you worried about me?" She put a hand to her throat and winced. "I'm okay. Really."

He sucked in a deep breath and forced the phantoms away. Havily came into sharp focus. "Endelle will give us some kind of direction concerning this attack. We'll figure out what to do next."

But what the hell could they do? Havily had been attacked in her home by a powerful vampire he knew nothing about. So who was this bastard who had just turned their world upside down?

He approached her again and once more knelt beside the couch. "Can you tell me anything about the death vampire who attacked you? I've never seen him before but he was big, warrior-big."

"His name was Crace. He called himself Crace."

Sleep. What would that be like?

—Kerrick, Warrior of the Blood, Second Earth

CHAPTER 6

Endelle swam in the clear waters off the Great Barrier Reef.
She streamed power in the same way that her hair flowed
behind her. Even great whites didn't dare come close.

The ocean was her solace, a place of rebirth and regeneration, of soothing fingers all over her skin, easing her tensions.

And yet something about the waters didn't seem quite
right. She needed to surface soon. Her lungs had started
to ache for air. With long sure strokes, she swam for the
surface.

How much could a vampire take?

She'd asked herself that question a lot lately.

She could see the surface and pulled toward the break
between the water and deep blue sky beyond. She needed
air now, desperately, but the harder she swam the farther the
blue sky receded.

She was going to drown. Why?

She pushed, thrashed toward the surface. She dug down deep, into the most powerful reserves she had. She tried to fold a scuba tank to her, but failed. She tried to dematerialize back to her administrative offices, but couldn't. Instead the waters sucked at her ankles, pulling her deeper. What the hell was going on?

Endelle. Wake up.

Wake up? She was awake and she was fucking drowning.

Endelle!

With a hard jerk, the water disappeared and her marble desktop, hot beneath her cheek, appeared, along with the laptop. She blinked. Her office. She was in her office. She wasn't underwater. She wasn't drowning. She was safe. She sucked in air.

"Madame Endelle," a soft feminine voice called to her, a lovely melodic sound now as familiar to her as the marble of the desk. Alison. Kerrick's *breh,* his bonded mate. What the fuck was she doing here? It had to be the middle of the night. She glanced at her clock. It was only eleven.

Endelle was so tired. Shit, she'd been dreaming. Dreaming and drowning in the waters off the coast of Australia. She slurped a long stream of saliva back into her mouth and swallowed.

Charming. But then who the fuck cared?

She was drenched as well, and she'd perspired all over her brand-new cream ferret halter. Aw, shit. Her red leather pants were stuck in her crack. She shifted and made the adjustment.

She needed to get to her meditation chamber. She needed to pursue Greaves around the globe, prevent more death vampires from reaching Phoenix Two and continuing the assault on her Warriors of the Blood.

She sat up and blinked several times in loopy weaving swags of her eyelids. Alison was across the room in the doorway.

"What the hell are you doing here?" Her gaze flicked once more to the clock on the wall to her right above the never-used fireplace, then back to the blond goddess. "You should be home asleep, getting ready for Kerrick to return at dawn."

Her gaze dropped to the faint bulge at Alison's waist, made more prominent by hands folded in front of her. Warrior Kerrick had gotten his *breh* pregnant before she'd even ascended to Second. Talk about one hot *virile* vampire.

"Warrior Medichi summoned me, and I'll always come when the warriors need me." Alison was very composed. That was one thing about the woman Endelle could count on, *composure*. She had a boatload of that, thank you, God.

Her gaze dipped once more to the clasp of the woman's hands. The knuckles were tight and bleached through the skin. Something was going on. Oh, fuck.

She reached out to read her but Alison had shields, fucking powerful shields . . . and, again, thank you, God. In the past four months the newly arrived ascender had learned to protect her thoughts, and though it had taken some time for Endelle to get used to this reality—that she couldn't enter Alison's head at will—she had come to feel immense gratitude that at least one vampire in her realm could keep her goddamn thoughts to herself.

"So why did Medichi summon you and where the fuck is he?"

"With Havily. There was an attack at her condo. He didn't want to leave her. I said I would consult with you."

Endelle got that feeling, the one that felt like an enormous spider doing a break dance down her spine. A second impression followed, of that pansy-ass freak, Commander Greaves, and his sticky hands all over one of her execs. *Why,* was the question. What the hell did he want with such an underperformer as Havily Morgan?

She drew in a deep breath, then another. She sat back in her chair. She wiped her mouth with the back of her hand. More important, why did she have to slobber when she slept?

Alison wore jeans and a long light green T-shirt. Sandals. June was hot in Phoenix, even at midnight. Her hair
was pulled back in a ponytail. Damn, the woman was beautiful even without makeup: high cheekbones, light blue eyes
rimmed with gold. No wonder Kerrick had fallen so hard
for the powerful ascender, recently anointed Guardian of
Ascension.

She always saw the future in this woman. Change. Hope.

But had anything really changed? Yeah, for the worse.
The war was rolling along and one of her warriors was
in an emergency clinic recovering from burns, goddamn
fucking burns.

And now this.

So the Commander had either attacked Morgan or sent
someone after her. Terrific.

Endelle closed her eyes then reached out. She sent her
thoughts in Havily's direction, hunting, searching. It didn't
take long. The woman's emotions were a shriek through the
universe.

Havily sat in complete silence on her sofa in her living
room even though tears streaked down her cheeks. Medichi knelt in front of her, his long fingers resting on her
shoulder. No sex there, just profound compassion. So who
the hell had attacked her?

She had to work hard to push past Havily's shields, but
after about a minute she broke through. She replayed the
recent event. She knew the attacker well, a vampire by the
name of Crace, Eldon Crace, the current High Administrator of Chicago Two, allied with Greaves.

But damn, Crace was warrior-sized, a big motherfucker
now, the muscles across his back enhanced by the fact that
he was shirtless, one holy-hell range of meat. Christ, he
was almost as big as Luken. He never used to be this big,
which meant only one thing: *death vampire,* a condition
confirmed by his now extremely pale complexion and the
fact that he'd grown much prettier since the last time she'd
seen him.

Four months ago he had been a well-built, handsome administrator with a beautiful polished wife, Julianna. He had also been Greaves's favorite.

She knew Greaves had a policy of turning his subjects, encouraging them to partake of dying blood, then providing an antidote to keep the outward signs of the addiction from manifesting. Looked like Crace enjoyed the experience too much and had failed to make use of the mitigating serum.

Taking in his size and his new nature, Endelle knew one truth right now—if Medichi hadn't shown up when he did, Havily would be dead.

She searched a little more through Havily's mind and found the telepathic link between the warrior and Morgan. Jesus. Who the hell had come up with that and why? A little more searching revealed another truth, that Luken and Medichi had become concerned about Havily because of her recent vision of Luken, which had in turn saved Luken's life.

Sudden anxiety whipped Endelle's wing-locks into a mounting state, as though the sight of this newly created death vampire had jolted all of her self-preservation instincts to action. Within seconds she withdrew from Havily's mind and rose to her feet. Her wing-locks itched, a familiar sensation when shit went down.

She breathed in, felt the muscles of her back flex and twitch. The wet lubricant shed from her wing-locks and with another deep breath, she let her wings fly from her body, a swift ease of movement that lifted her onto her toes and felt like heaven. She always had this sudden sensation of tears and of joy when her wings emerged, fluffed and formed, feathers attached to an intricate mesh-like superstructure all at the same time, one fucking miracle of ascended power.

From thought to thought her wings changed color. They began as red then shifted to purple, to blue. The ability to change wing color was a Third ability and for Endelle usually reflected her emotional state.

She felt the accompanying hit of both adrenaline and dopamine, her brows rising in response. Only sex was better than this.

Alison had remained by the doorway, giving Endelle plenty of room to pace. "What the fuck is this powerful vampire doing with Havily Morgan?" She plunged both hands through her hair at her temples, gliding them all the way through her long black locks as she half walked, half flew the length of the room, twirling at the plate-glass windows, the tips of her feathers, red again, brushing against the cool, air-conditioned double-paned glass.

She loped the opposite direction, flying, touching down, walk, fly, repeat. She could feel Alison's empathy searching the airstreams, the intent focus of her therapist's mind, her desire to understand, her constant willingness to help, to be of use, to serve, to soothe, to ease. Kerrick must be in heaven with this woman.

And now a huge vampire had gone after Havily, which meant that Greaves had sent him, which in turn meant that he'd had some kind of Seer information that had prompted the attack, which also meant that Havily was worth something to him, that the future streams had coughed up a lot of information about her.

Rage boiled now, full-on vision-altering, hand-trembling rage as her thoughts pivoted toward the east, toward the Superstition Mountains and her useless fucking Seers Fortress. The one element she had relied on in past centuries for direction had been systematically stripped from her, and all because of rulings by COPASS.

The Committee to Oversee the Process of Ascension to Second Society had caved to Greaves's pressure over the years. Bottom line? No one could enter the Superstition Seers Fortress without permission from its High Administrator, and—surprise, surprise—the High Administrator *never* allowed Endelle admittance. She was fucking blind because of it.

The result? Critical information from the future streams,

information she had always relied on to keep her administration moving forward, had been reduced to a frog's stream of piss.

Whatever.

Which led her straight back to the conundrum of Havily Morgan. There could be only one reason why Morgan had been attacked—the future streams had revealed something of value about her.

She turned to Alison. "Do you think it's possible that Morgan has emerging powers?"

Alison nodded. "I do. She saved a warrior's life last night, the most physically powerful warrior in your arsenal, so yeah, I think she has emerging powers."

Endelle stared at her and nodded. "It's just that I've always been so disappointed in her. And now . . . shit . . . to have one of Greaves's most powerful minions after her just seems bizarre. Well . . . I suppose I have to assign a guardian now . . . which means—" She laughed suddenly and slapped her hand on her thigh. "Well, I'll be damned. There's a silver lining after all and Marcus is sooo not gonna like what I have to tell him. Oh, this is awesome! Just too awesome!"

At seven in the morning Marcus stepped out of the shower and nearly fell on his ass. He grabbed the stone half wall and caught his balance. "What the fuck are you doing here . . . again? And couldn't you have at least waited until I was dressed? What the fuck!"

Endelle looked smug as she leaned her ass against the sink counter. She wore red leather pants, black stilettos, and some kind of light-colored animal fur halter. Her gaze, as usual, settled on his groin. Her brows rose and she huffed a sigh. She folded her arms over her chest.

"Oh, for Christ's sake." He grabbed a towel and covered himself. "You already have my answer. Not coming back."

"You might just change your tune once you hear what I have to say."

"There isn't anything you could say that would—"

She cut him off. "Havily was attacked last night. Big motherfucker took her vein right here." She tilted her head and tapped two fingers over the left side of her neck. "*Folded* straight into her town house, death vampire by the name of Crace. He's also the High Administrator of the Chicago Territory aligned with Greaves. Crace brought four of his buddies with him supposedly to enjoy a snack as well. Hey, but don't worry. Medichi got there in time. Her nightgown was still in one piece and the only blood spilled was what came from her neck."

At first he didn't get the sensation that came over him, but his nostrils flared, his wing-locks thrummed, and sweat broke out over his entire body.

Endelle waxed on. "Havily said he had shoulders like Luken's. And Marcus, you're not gonna like this, but I think he meant to drink her dead. I think he brought the pretty-boys to feast."

Time stopped. He could no longer see. For some reason his mind dove into the past, to that moment when he had seen Havily for the first time in the Cave, where the Warriors of the Blood hung out after battle. He'd been seated on that piece-of-shit, torn-up leather couch smelling her scent, her sweet honeysuckle, and his body had reacted like he'd been doing lines of Viagra.

The warriors had been grouped around Havily and parted suddenly to reveal her like a moment on a Broadway stage. The heavens had all but parted to reveal a choir of angels singing the "Hallelujah" chorus. His groin sure had. He'd gone from mildly hard to steel with a dedicated throb.

Her beauty had made his head swim, his heart ache; every longing he'd ever known had strangled his chest. Like the vampire he was, he'd *craved* her.

And now some death vampire had drunk from her *with intent,* which may or may not have been of a sexual nature. But that didn't matter. The bastard had punctured her throat with his fangs. That was sexual enough.

His own fangs emerged to sharp pulsing points. He couldn't seem to get enough air, but that was because he was breathing like a monster, in deep heaving gulps. His cock had taken the shape of a missile pulling hard at the towel around his waist.

The need he felt split him into two equal parts. The first flooded the muscles of his shoulders, arms, and fists with preternatural power in search of the ascended enemy; his wing-locks were flooded with moisture, ready to release. The second part was pure sex, pure need to stake and claim what he knew by every burning cell of his body was his, belonged *to him,* not to any other vampire ascender or mortal in any other fucking dimension.

A single thought dominated his head: *Nobody drinks from Havily but me.*

Endelle had just effectively ended his two-hundred-year retreat from events on Second Earth. It was one thing to meet Havily in his dreams—or whatever the hell that was—and quite another to learn she'd been attacked, in her home, by a death vampire.

Dammit, she could have died. She probably would have if Medichi hadn't arrived to scare the bastard out of her house.

Yet even the thought of Medichi being in Havily's home— to come to her aid or not—sent shards of jealous rage slicing through his veins, bunching the muscles of his arms and curling his fingers into rock-solid fists.

The *breh-hedden* had him in a tight grip and there wasn't a damn thing he could do about it. He couldn't go back to his simple corporate life, to his dedicated pursuit of more and more.

And just like that, the axis of his life shifted.

When he glanced at Endelle, she still had one brow up but she was examining her fingernails. "I need a manicure." She blinked once. Twice. Three times. "There, that's much better." Her nails were now neon pink.

She was the most absurd woman he'd ever known. "So you happy about this or what?" he asked.

She turned to him, her wooded eyes settling on him in unexpected compassion. "Welcome back, asshole. Do what you have to do, then get your butt over to Havily's and for God's sake take care of business. Don't be the idiot Kerrick was and wait to complete the *breh-hedden*. Apparently—" She paused to roll her eyes. "—your woman is valuable to the enemy."

She lifted a hand and vanished.

Oh, shit. This couldn't be happening but it was, and he was done trying to feel differently about *his woman*. He was already half in love with her for many reasons, but the *breh-hedden*'s call was as much on his soul as it was in his body and he simply needed to be with Havily. He didn't try to look into the future. That she was in danger and needed him was enough.

Enough.

He got dressed the old-fashioned way, one sock, one pant leg, one shirtsleeve at a time, slowly, carefully, because he had to think about what to do with his empire at least for the next few days until he figured out what to do about Havily.

Once dressed, he continued functioning in mortal time and making use of mortal ways. He set the security alarm and locked up his house. He settled into his Jaguar and drove to the ferry, heading to Seattle.

An hour later, he was in his office. He went to his safe and withdrew several documents to sign over limited power of attorney to his second-in-command.

He pressed the button on his phone that connected him to his exec assist.

"Yes, Mr. Amargi."

"I need Ennis here. He's in the building. Find him for me. Tell him I need him ASAP."

"Certainly."

Everything he'd just said was a code, or rather several codes. *ASAP* was code for "Now or die, motherfucker." And *in the building* had been designed for the benefit of his executive assistant, leading her to believe Ennis was close by when in reality he could be on either Mortal or Second Earth or halfway around the world either dimension.

Farrell Ennis, his fellow ascender-in-exile, was one powerful vampire and about a hairbreadth from warrior size.

A moment later, a knock and a shove on the door brought the man into his office.

"Marcus, you bastard," Ennis cried as he slammed the door behind him. The wall rattled its displeasure. "What the fuck are you doing calling me back at this hour?"

Marcus laughed. Ennis had one fine sheen of sweat on his tanned face and the frustrated look of a man who'd gotten pulled from a bed he'd not been sleeping in. He was dressed, as befitted his second-in-command, in a black Valentino, but his tie was really lopsided. "She pretty?"

He groaned. "Chocolate skin, large green eyes, and breasts the size of . . ." He closed his eyes and cupped his hands in front of him. "I hope to hell this won't take long."

Ennis stood almost as tall as Marcus. He'd been one of several right-hand men he'd had at Sumer Industries for the last two centuries. Marcus had met him in a bar brawl in the Mediterranean, when one of his shipments headed for Rome had been attacked by Barbary pirates off the coast of Sicily. That was a long time ago, a lot of bar fights ago, a lot of stories told over swirling brandy. Ennis was an old-fashioned drinking buddy, a rogue ascender, an honorable vampire, and one of his best friends.

Marcus trusted the bastard with his life.

"So what's the emergency, asshole?"

Marcus took a deep breath. "Nothing much. I need you to take over . . . for a while."

Ennis's eyes lit up and he planted his cantaloupe-forming hands on his hips. "It's that fucking Liaison Officer, isn't it? Well, what do you know."

Marcus didn't blink, couldn't blink. His entire being hit a wall of paralysis. His chin lowered slowly, his arms stiffened, the hairs on his neck bristled. His nostrils flared as a low growl formed at the back of his throat, a resonant sound that slowly rippled up and out and filled the room.

Ennis lifted a brow then another. "What the fuck?" slipped from between his teeth, a whisper really, but the bastard grinned. "So the goddamn rumors are true?"

"Take it back," Marcus said.

"So the *breh-hedden* is real."

Marcus growled again.

Ennis lifted both hands. "Okay, okay. I apologize for saying *fucking* Liaison Officer."

Marcus watched his behavior from the side of his brain still capable of rational thought. He was astonished at the intense physical reaction he'd had to the disparaging comment. He tried to talk sense to his other self, the one standing like a caveman, feet planted more than a foot apart, knees bent, thighs flexed and twitching as he lowered his body. Give him a sword and a dagger and he'd be content to chop Ennis up into a few dozen packages of prime fillets.

Despite the apology, Marcus had a hard time easing up from his fighting crouch. He breathed hard, and his winglocks were a mess of weeping. He'd need to change his shirt after this.

"Shit, Marcus," Ennis whispered.

Now there was a fucking understatement. With what was left of his normal vampire brain, Marcus forced himself to relax, to stand down, to breathe. Sweet Jesus.

"You okay?"

Marcus glared. He didn't want to, but he was acting as though he'd already bonded with Havily, already completed the *breh-hedden,* like she'd become the sun, moon, and stars to him when all he'd done was meet her in his dreams.

The memory, of Havily riding him and screaming, swooped down on him, condor-like, and grabbed his mind with both talons. *That* had been the beginning of this current nightmare. From the point that he'd finally succeeded in doing what he'd wanted to do with Havily for months, his whole life had been taking one giant plunge down the mountainside, just the way his hog had gone over the Olympic cliff.

Aw . . . *fuck.*

He closed his eyes and drew himself upright, shoulders back, spine straight for God's sake. He flared his nostrils again but this time to draw in a long deep breath. After about a minute, he opened his eyes.

Ennis shook his head but a new grin quirked his lips. "Get going, asshole," he said, buddy-like. "I'll hold the fucking fort. Take care of your woman. Make her safe and, for fuck's sake, do all of us a favor and *make her yours.*"

"You sure you got this?"

"Yep. Now get the hell out."

Marcus turned back to his desk and pressed the Jane button.

"Yes, Mr. Amargi?"

"I'll be leaving town for a few days. Ennis is taking the helm. Please bring him up to speed."

"Of course, Mr. Amargi." He released the button.

"There's just one thing I want you to tell me before you go. What does your name mean? Amargi. You told me you'd tell me one of these days. Today looks like a damn good day for a revelation."

Marcus looked at him and somehow knew that there was great irony in what he was about to reveal. " 'Freedom.' In Sumerian, *amargi* means 'freedom.' "

That Ennis shook his head, grinned, then laughed, told Marcus he thought the same damn thing. Just how much freedom was Marcus going to have in the next few days, months, years? Hell, millennia . . . shit.

I don't know what to do.

Havily paced beneath the ficus trees on her small patio at the back of her town house. She rubbed her arms. Even though the June morning was hot and she wore a long-sleeved gray silk shirt and black leggings, she was cold.

She glanced at the window of her bedroom. At least it had been repaired already. Medichi had arranged for it, calling in a couple of favors to make sure that her home was safe once more. Safe. Now, there was a joke.

Militia Warriors swarmed the property, at least two dozen of them, some in front of her town house, some in her patio, a few more in the yard to the east of her home, a couple within her house, and another bunch traipsing along the exposed west side of her property. Behind the enclosed patio, Camelback Mountain climbed in a steep rocky incline to its twelve hundred feet.

The Militia Warriors treated her like a delicate orchid because she'd once been engaged to one of their own, her beloved Eric. Even though that had been fifteen years ago, the Militia Warrior family looked after her. The fact that she'd been attacked in her home had telegraphed through the ranks like lightning, and the assignment to protect her had been picked up by several of Eric's good friends, a testament to his character and their loyalty.

However, not a single Militia Warrior was a match for even the weakest death vampire, which was part of the reason Second Earth was in such desperate straits these days. Knowing that these men were at risk had her pacing the patio and even rubbing her arms, though the June temp had already climbed past a hundred and it was maybe ten in the morning. What distressed her the most was that she didn't want to be the cause of a Militia Warrior's death. Should the enemy attack, men would die, good men, some of them with families, and all because of her.

She put her hand on her throat. The fangs in her neck had been savage but, because of her quick healing, and Horace's help, she didn't even show a bruise. She paced and shook her head. The death vampire who had attacked her, Crace, had intended to do damage, to hurt her, to make her scream. She had fought his hold on her because the pain had been excruciating.

She felt nauseated by the thought. She put her fist to her mouth and bit her thumb to keep from screaming.

How had this happened? *Why* had this happened? She didn't have advanced powers, not like Alison, not like any of the Warriors of the Blood. Why on earth had Crace targeted her? It made no sense.

She had always felt inadequate that her ascension, which had required a warrior guardian, had been such a fierce disappointment to Madame Endelle and probably to the brothers as well. The side of right desperately needed powerful ascenders, but here she was putting so many in jeopardy—and for what?

Her eyes burned. The only remotely powerful thing she'd done was to have an inexplicable vision and arrange for Thorne to get over to the Superstitions and save Luken's life. Everyone kept saying that she had saved Luken but Thorne had killed the death vampires, Thorne had gotten Horace and an ambulance to the Superstitions, Thorne, Thorne, Thorne.

She brushed her tears away and slapped at a few low-hanging ficus leaves as she whirled and paced the other direction. The three Militia Warriors in the patio looked anywhere but at her.

At least the attack last night had prevented a recurrence of the dreams she somehow shared with Warrior Marcus.

"Havily."

A deep, warm masculine voice called to her from the sliders that led to her kitchen. She whirled and gave an odd wave as she caught sight of Medichi. Then she did the worst thing she could. She burst into a bout of really embarrassing girlish tears.

"Hey," he called out. The Militia Warriors each took a step away from him in deference as he crossed the patio. He was so tall, so heavy with muscle that he seemed to take up the entire small space. He gathered her against him and held her close. "Hey," he murmured again, petting her hair. She relaxed into his warm body.

"You didn't have to come by," she mumbled against his chest. "Shouldn't you be sleeping?" The Warriors of the Blood fought all night and needed to rest during the day.

She felt him sigh. "I can always sleep," he said. "So how you doin', although I think I can guess." He had a very deep voice and his chest rumbled against her face as he spoke.

"I don't want anyone to get hurt," she whispered.

"Not one of these men gives a rat's ass about that. We're here for you. We'll die for you and you're worth every damn molecule of effort. Look at me."

She drew back about half an inch and craned her neck to look up at him.

She heard a soft intake of breath as he blinked down at her. She saw his throat move in a rippling wave as he swallowed. He squeezed his eyes shut for a moment and seemed to gather himself. When he opened his eyes he said gently, "Call him back. We need him and you need him."

She didn't pretend she didn't know he was talking about Marcus. And maybe she should call him back. Maybe it was the only sensible thing to do.

She was about to reassure him that she would think about it when another deep masculine voice called out, this one with more resonance and punch to his words. "How about you take your hands off her, asshole."

Havily gasped as Medichi's hands fell away. The three Militia Warriors stationed in the patio turned in his direction, swords drawn, but each almost immediately pointed his sword toward the ground. "Sorry, sir," flowed from mouth to mouth.

Medichi shifted and turned, which afforded Havily a perfect view of . . . Marcus. He didn't look at her but glared at Medichi. His muscled shoulders were up around his ears and his hands were knotted into a pair of heavy fists.

Marcus was here? At her home? On Second?

Medichi took a step away from Havily, then another. He lifted his hands, palms facing Marcus. "I was just leaving," he said, and before Havily could protest, the flutter of air near her told her he was dematerializing.

She lifted a hand in Medichi's direction, not wanting him to leave her alone with Marcus, but too late.

She turned to settle a scathing glance on him. "Why are you here?" she cried, lifting an imperious brow and crossing her arms over her chest. She may *crave* him, she may even have thought she should *consider* asking him to come back for her sake, but ultimately, she still thought he was a horrible deserter and wanted nothing to do with him.

The terrible bond of the breh-hedden,
Breaks down walls.

—*Collected Proverbs,* Beatrice of Fourth

CHAPTER 7

Marcus stared at Havily. The decision to come to her had cost him so much and now all he could do was stare at her and wonder. He drew in a long drag of air through his nostrils, letting the honeysuckle scent of her scrape his nose raw. He loved every millisecond of it, every flare of nerve ending as his brain pounded with the certain knowledge that he had come home. At long last, he was home.

He had told Ennis that he would be gone a few days, to sort this out, but he knew, *he knew,* he wouldn't be going back. He'd returned to Second Earth, to this house, to Havily, to the goddamn fucking war.

He belonged here.

When he'd folded to the front door of her condo, he hadn't thought he was making such a final decision, but he was. There'd be no going back even though he also knew to a certainty that whatever this was between himself and Havily, *breh-hedden* or not, wasn't permanent, either.

His sister, Helena, had died because she'd married a Warrior of the Blood, and Marcus had every intention of picking up his sword and dagger again. Which meant that he wouldn't take a wife, or in this case a *breh*. He wouldn't do that to Havily—or any woman for that matter. Besides, what kind of hypocrite would that make him if he were to marry where he had once begged Kerrick not to?

Havily was so beautiful and even in casual dress she looked stylish. She wore snug black leggings and a loose, flowing gray silk shirt almost to her knees, reminiscent of Vera Wang, the latter a perfect complement to her peachy-red waves. She stood in the June heat looking crisp and fresh, her long, layered hair sparkling in the sun.

But her expression was all Havily, her brow raised, her lips curled in a soft, oh-so-pretty sneer. Her opinion of his character wouldn't exactly encourage a permanent connection, and that could only work to his advantage in the long term.

For whatever reason, though, in this moment in time, they were connected. They might even have something they needed to accomplish together. He was here now with his first duty already laid out for him by the call of the *breh-hedden*—to protect this woman. The warriors knew it. He knew it. He'd get to the bottom of the recent attack on her life, see her through this current crisis, then once more take up his place with the Warriors of the Blood.

For a moment, however, the past caught up with him, a particular memory that almost knocked him flat. He wasn't sure why he was thinking of his sister, of Helena, right now, but a vision of her came to him.

It was her wedding day, the day she had married Kerrick. She was the only family he had left on Second Earth, and he had begged her many times not to marry a Warrior of the Blood. Anyone connected to those who battled death vampires every night would be targeted by the Commander.

He had stood beside her at the top of the long walkway beneath an arch of honeysuckle. At the end of that archway, Kerrick waited for his bride. On either side of the archway, a hundred guests had all turned to watch Helena, but Marcus had stayed her with a hand on her arm.

Telepathically, he sent, *Please don't do this. Surely, you know what the end will be?*

She had sighed, smiled, patted his cheek. "Stop worrying," she had whispered. "This is what I want." How beautiful she had looked, her lovely light brown eyes, the same color as his, full of hope, compassion, and finally wisdom, for she had said, "Life is for the living, dear brother, and I love him."

Marcus had walked her down that long, difficult path beneath the archway of honeysuckle but all his fear became fixed on his brother warrior, his soon-to-be brother-in-law.

Kerrick had glowed with his love for Helena. Marcus had never doubted the man's love, but he questioned his selfishness. Marcus knew that if anything ever happened to Helena because of this marriage, he would never forgive Kerrick. Never.

When Helena had been killed, her children with her, something inside Marcus had gone wild with rage. His grief had transformed into a hatred so virulent that he knew he would have taken Kerrick's life. So instead of killing his brother warrior, he'd exiled himself to Mortal Earth. He had never thought to return.

Now he was here, staring at Havily.

He still wanted to beat the shit out of Kerrick for having married his sister, for having been the cause of her death, but even these powerful impulses dimmed in the face of the overwhelming need he had to be with Havily, spread his wings over her, make sure she was safe.

He strode toward her now, long confident steps, sure steps. She backed away from him in small shuffles since a bank of shrubs was directly behind her. He caught her by the arms and held her in a rough grip.

"Tell me," he cried. "Tell me. Are you all right? Are you hurt? Has your neck healed? Were you frightened? Did he touch you otherwise? Are you all right? Tell me."

She gave a little gasp, a small cry, then flung herself into his arms. He wrapped his arms around her, engulfing her, holding her tight. He closed his eyes, his throat knotted, his eyes burning.

"I just don't understand why he came after me," she said. "That death vampire, Crace, was so big, like Luken, and he had a squad with him. They . . . they were going to take turns drinking from me. But why me? It makes no sense."

Her voice was muffled against his shirt. He stroked her hair, his fingers drifting down her back. He felt the faint ridges of her wing-locks through her shirt, and his body heated up when it shouldn't have. He knew she needed comfort but the damn *breh-hedden* was taking over.

She moaned softly. Wing-locks were extremely sensitive to the touch, and he could feel her quick response to the light flutters over her back. He wanted his tongue on them as he took her from behind. She pressed her hips against him and a wave of honeysuckle rose up to knock him senseless all over again. He glanced at the Militia Warriors, each of whom had turned away, allowing for some privacy.

Once more his protective urges took over.

He let his arms fall away from her but at the same moment he shifted and caught her around the waist with his right arm. He drew her to his side. As she melted against him, he addressed the men within the confines of the patio. "Who's in charge here?"

"I am." The Militia Warrior nearest the street-side fence stepped forward.

"You may leave. Take your men. All of them."

"Of course, Warrior Marcus." So they knew who he was. Good. The last thing he could handle right now was another man questioning his authority. He'd lose it and someone would get hurt.

Within seconds the property was empty, but Marcus

wasn't taking chances. He moved Havily in front of him and with his body shielded her as he urged her back into her home. Once he had her within the cool, air-conditioned house, the slider locked, he created a deep covering of mist over the entire property.

Now that the house was securely hidden, the fact that he was holed up with Havily sent a wave of heat over his body. "I'm not going to be able to keep away from you," he said. "Tell me you know that. Tell me you understand."

Her eyelids fell to half-mast as she released a deep sigh. Another wave of honeysuckle hit him square in the chest. "No one is asking you to, Warrior."

The dam broke and he grabbed her hard, dragging her into his arms and kissing her full on the mouth, punching at her lips with his tongue until she parted and he slid inside. He moaned at the intimate connection. He pushed his hips against hers, letting her feel the hard length of him. He ground against her and was rewarded with a deep moan.

Her arms went around his back and he tensed, breathing hard as she slid her fingers in long glides between his wing-locks. Holy shit. Maybe it was the *breh-hedden,* but her touch was like fire, an intense burning that went straight to his groin.

He pushed her away in a sudden burst. He caught sight of her passion-drenched face, her swollen lips parted in surprise, the wrinkling of her brow. The cry of protest that broke from her throat put fire on his fire. He dipped, slung an arm behind her knees and picked her up. Another cry erupted from her throat, this time of pleasure, as her arms slid around his neck.

"Which way to your bedroom?" He needed room to maneuver and only a bed would do. This could take a while.

She leaned back, throwing an arm and pointing to the left. He swept her into the hall. She pointed again to the left. A moment later and he was at her bedroom door, which he shoved open with his foot.

The room had a vaulted ceiling and he stopped on the

threshold to stare up at dozens of glittering paper butter-flies, suspended on strings from the ceiling. "What's this?"

She leaned away from him to take a look. "Oh, the butter-flies. At night when I can't sleep, I count them." She paused. "Lately, I've counted them *a lot*."

He looked down at her face and met her gaze as she shifted back to him. "I know this wasn't what you wanted. I know you despise me. I would undo this if it were possible. You deserve someone nobler than me."

She put a hand on his cheek. "I can't complete the *breh-hedden* with you, Marcus, please understand that."

He nodded. "Understood."

Her gaze fell to his lips and the breath she drew seemed to skip into her chest. "But I want you, here and now . . . so badly."

He nodded. "Yeah." The word ground out of his throat like he'd dusted it with red pepper. He didn't comprehend all the mysteries of ascended life or what force had brought them together or even why they had to be together and joined in this way, connected in this way, but the hell if he could be close to her, guard her, and not be inside her body right now.

"And I need new memories in my head," she said. "This room frightens me."

"We'll fix that."

He glanced down at the bed. He released her, setting her feet on the floor long enough to jerk the comforter and top sheet back so that an expanse of black silk met his gaze. Her red hair would look beautiful on black silk. He turned back to her, nuzzled her neck, then licked in long slow glides over her vein until her body grew lax and she arched her head, giving him more territory to cover.

He put a hand on her shirt and folded it off along with her bra. Her breasts were so *perfect*. He fondled her.

"Oh," she cried. He kissed her and her fingers found his biceps. She started stroking his muscles through his shirt, clawing. He folded his clothes off. Skin met skin and the inferno erupted once more.

He didn't wait, but finished getting her naked. He pushed her back on the bed, half on, half off, and took her breasts in his mouth, taking deliberate turns, working her body into a matching inferno. Honeysuckle flooded the air.

Truth? His mind no longer functioned.

Havily threw her arms back against the sheets and trembled from head to foot as Marcus suckled her breasts, his hands cupping them. He tasted one, then the other, then back. He was thorough and she loved it. His erotic fennel scent drifted in clouds over his body.

She hadn't been with a man since Eric . . . a dry spell of fifteen long years. She hadn't exactly taken a vow not to be with another man, but she hadn't planned on it since the war . . . well, the war made everything dangerous and full of too much death.

However, Marcus had come to her in a strange and mysterious way, and with so much momentum and desire that she was allowing the connection . . . or perhaps more like *succumbing*.

But oh, his big warrior body was a heavy delicious weight on top of her, pressing her into the soft cushion of the mattress. Her lower half was bent over the edge of the bed, her feet flat on the floor, her legs spread, his heavy pelvis and powerful thighs pressed into various parts of her and . . . she loved it. Oh, how she had missed this, the weight of a man.

He dove his arm under her waist and held her tight, but his fingers reached upward behind her and found the lowest of her wing-locks. He teased the pad of his fingers back and forth.

She cried out. The combination of his suckling mouth on her breast and his drifting hand working a wing-lock quickly sent her into an outrageous state of need and desire. "Marcus. Please. Please. Please," rippled in a hoarse whisper out of her dry, open, pleading mouth.

She felt his mind reach for her and she released her

powerful shields to hear his words, *Please what, Havily Morgan?*

You're torturing me, she sent.

Good. The least you deserve for haunting my dreams.

She moaned as he bit at her nipple at just the right pressure. "Do more. Please."

He released her breast and shifted, moving his hips between her legs, and with his powerful thighs pushed her legs farther apart. She groaned at the touch, the feel, the strength of his legs holding her wide. She felt utterly exposed but very, very sexual.

His hand skated down her ribs, making her want to both giggle and moan at the same time. He grasped her behind her waist, lifting her upper body with one powerful arm and propelling her higher up on the bed so that she sprawled on the sheets beneath him. He then climbed toward her, one hand, one knee, opposing hand, opposing knee, his big warrior body prowling over hers. She felt weak and lethargic, like she could disappear into the mattress.

In her strange dream-fantasies, she was always on top, but this, being overcome by the sheer size of him, was . . . *better.*

His lips were parted as he looked her over from her eyebrows and eyes to her cheeks, lips, chin, drifting lower to her breasts. A faint growl sounded in his throat, a low rumble that caused her back to arch and her internal muscles to clench. She wanted him so much.

He had a faint dusting of black hair between his pecs that descended his abdomen to a line that led her eye to . . . his cock. She licked her lips and couldn't breathe.

She had felt him inside her while caught in her dream-like state, but this was different, so real, so *awake.*

It had been a long time. She had known two men before Marcus, and both men she'd loved. Now she would have Marcus, whom she did not love but whose body she craved as though even his skin meant life to her and his body every blessing possible in ascended life.

He pushed back on his arms and straddled her. He cupped himself, holding his erect cock in her direction. She looked up at his face, uncertain of his intention. His lips were still parted. His expression was serious, his eyes at half-mast, his chest rising and falling with deep heavy breaths.

Her gaze dipped low again, taking in the swollen head. A bead of his essence appeared at the tip. He still waited.

She leaned up on her left elbow and with her right hand she stroked him the entire thick length, from tip to the heavy thatch of black hair at the base. She brought her fingers up the back of his hand since he still held himself. More of his fennel scent teased her, sending shivers up her thighs.

He hissed. "Havily." Her name emerged from his lips on a growl.

She lay back down and looked up at him. "Let's do this, Warrior. I don't know the why of it, but I'm yours."

He groaned. He bent low and guided himself to her opening. "God, you're so wet."

"What else would I be?" How strange that tears rose to her eyes then slipped down the sides of her face into her hair. His gaze was fixed on her lower body as he watched his cock enter her in a series of slow firm pushes.

Her breaths came slowly and with difficulty. Marcus was big and each push was a little uncomfortable and yet like heaven at the same time as her body stretched to accommodate him. With each push tears rolled inexplicably, as though every moment of her life, even from the time she had stood at Eric's graveside, had been leading to this time with Marcus.

She had never thought to take a Warrior of the Blood to her bed. Yet here she was, with her inadequate powers, her dislike of his two-hundred-year absence from service, and her flaming, oh-so-irritating *breh-hedden* desire.

Once inside, he leaned over her, holding himself up by his arms. With a solid push, he rocked into her.

"We're joined," he said, again looking down at where they were connected.

"Yes."

He met her gaze, his longish hair falling forward on either side of his face. The ends curled under slightly. His hair moved in waves as he flexed his buttocks and pushed into her again and again.

She was grateful he didn't rush. This time with him seemed oddly precious, probably in part because there was no commitment on either side to take this farther than a few days.

He shifted his weight to the left and supported himself on one arm. With his right hand now free, he drifted a finger over her face, down her cheek, her chin, her throat. He pushed her hair away from her neck.

"I want what was stolen from me," he said, his voice a hard rasp. "But I don't want to upset you."

She felt his tension, his holding back on her behalf, because of what she'd just gone through.

She touched his face, and his gaze skated to hers. "You smell like licorice," she whispered. He groaned. His eyes had a wild look. He craved just as she craved. He needed what she had to give. She could no more have denied him in this moment than she could have left this bed.

She reached up and stroked his cheek with her hand. "I want you to take my blood," she said. She arched her neck away from him. "Make new memories for me."

Only a vampire would understand the presentation of the throat. She heard his sharp intake of breath. Using his forefinger, he stroked her neck in a long slow line just over her vein. Her heart rate increased since she knew what was coming, what he craved and what she craved for him to do. She wanted his mouth on her so that she might forget what had been done to her without permission.

He dipped down and kissed her neck then moaned and rocked into her, giving her a sharp thrust from his hips that made her cry out. *You fill me,* she sent.

He growled and thrust harder.

Her moans rose to the ceiling. The butterflies overhead moved as Marcus's hips disturbed the air beneath them.

The sensation over her tender flesh at the apex of her labia tingled anew and she ground against the thrust of his hips. He hissed between his teeth. He kissed her neck over and over.

"I want to taste you. May I drink from you, Havily? Do I have your permission?" His voice was low and resonant, thick with need and desire.

She clenched and on a heavy release of breath said, "Yes. Please. Yes. Now. Do it." She had lost the ability to form sentences.

He leaned toward her slowly, all the while his hips pushing and pushing, her body contracting around his cock, pulling him deeper inside.

Her hands crept around his waist, drifting up his back, and with spread fingers she positioned her hands between row after row of wing-locks. He groaned at the touch.

His tongue hit her neck and rasped a long glide over her vein. He repeated until her breath came in pants. She hadn't felt the sting of fangs, while in the midst of love-making, for fifteen years. She wanted the sting. She knew exactly where the corresponding sensation would strike, and her internal muscles clenched over and over in sweet anticipation.

"You're so ready for me," he whispered. She felt the tips of his fangs poised now, the barest pressure. "But I worry. Will this bring back memories?"

"Not the same thing at all. Marcus, you are the only vampire in this room right now. I want you to trust me in this. So please don't wait. Do it!"

He made a quick strike, to exactly the right depth. She cried out as her tender flesh responded in a sliding streak of pleasure so profound that as he began to draw at her vein and blood left her body, the first orgasm rode over her like galloping horses. Pleasure moved up and up through her core until she clenched around him repeatedly and screamed at the ceiling.

Honeysuckle, he sent, his voice inside her head enhancing the rolling tugging sensations. *You're coming.*

All that fennel. Oh, God. I'm coming. Oh, God, oh, God, oh, God.

A sharp grunt returned. She could feel Marcus tense. Was he ready to join her? So soon? She protested the thought. She wanted more of this, more of him, more of his body. Oh, just *more.*

Marcus lost part of his consciousness as Havily's honeysuckle blood hit his stomach and propelled into his bloodstream. Over the course of his four millennia, he had taken the veins of mortals and ascenders alike, but it had never, never, *never* been like this.

Havily Morgan had power in her blood, a stream of liquid fire that scorched his veins as the miracle of absorption took place deep within his belly.

He knew he was pumping into her as he sucked at her neck. He could feel her writhing body beneath him, but for the most part he felt the fire in his body as her blood began to seep into his muscles. Strength began to build, grow, *enlarge* every part of him.

Marcus, what's happening, pierced the dullness of his mind.

Not sure.

You feel . . . bigger . . . everywhere. She arched her back, which caused her hips to pull back and pull away from his cock . . . which was bigger. Holy shit.

He opened his eyes and though he didn't want to, he drew back from her vein. She was worried, surprised. "What's happening?" she asked again.

A new wave of power hit him. He threw back his head, arched, and gasped for air. He didn't know how much more he could take.

His body was in a frenzy as his hips moved in hard

rapid thrusts. The orgasm caught him by surprise as though coming from his body with a life of its own.

Havily's ecstasy arrived again at the same time because he could feel her hands stroking his pecs and shoulders and he could hear her screams but all he could feel was the pleasure that kept riding his shaft, coming and coming and coming, jets of liquid fire and pleasure and so much sensation he couldn't stop.

He just hoped to hell he wasn't hurting her.

Havily writhed under the muscular warrior body. Ecstasy had her trapped all over again, her body flailing beneath his, her feminine well clutching at the hard swollen member. She could feel his masculine orgasmic pulses and they just kept coming as though he couldn't stop and she didn't want him to because the pleasure she felt was indescribable. She felt as though she was drinking his essence into her body, absorbing, and with each pump of his hips, she took more in.

She knew she was moaning, screaming, crying out, but she couldn't quiet her voice.

Then, as if in a dream, she flew into that nether place, that in-between place that darkened all around the edges and . . . Marcus was with her.

"What the fuck?" His movements slowed but he panted over her neck. "What is this place? Oh, God." He grunted and groaned, his hips still rolling over hers. "It's never been like this before and now we're here, in that place again. Oh, God, Havily." He fell on her, weakened it would seem by the string of climaxes that had taken him.

She held him, her body shuddering beneath his.

She was breathing hard, her arms around his neck. She dragged her fingers over his back. He smelled so good, but what the hell had happened and where were they . . . again?

"It's like the dreams," she said, looking around wondering when her body would quiet. She still felt him inside her, swollen, erect. "Only this time it looks like my bed, not yours." She released another heavy sigh, still trying to catch her breath. "A line of darkness creates a border just as it did in your bed. Do you see it?"

He nodded and then he moved, one slow rhythm, a push in and pull partway out. The sensation, still mingling with her last orgasm, made her eyes roll in her head. The next moment his lips were on hers, a soft gentle kiss. His words eased over her mind: *I have never felt like this before, Havily. I need you to know that.*

Havily was overwhelmed. *Nor I,* she sent.

He deepened the kiss, his tongue filling her mouth, his hips still pushing and retreating, his cock still thick. His back where she touched him was slick with sweat. All the sensations reminded her of the past, the very best of her marriage so many decades ago, then later of her engagement to Eric. Now . . . Marcus.

Tender feelings rolled through her. She breathed in a long breath, her heart swelling. She wasn't supposed to feel this way, but she did. "Marcus," she murmured softly.

He nuzzled her neck, kissing her, suckling her skin. "Honeysuckle," he whispered. "I can't get enough." Again he pushed into her, and desire flowed in a beautiful wave until she was gasping and he was moving into her harder now.

"Your blood has done something to me," he whispered. "I'm not hurting you, am I?" His deep rich voice passed through her chest.

"No, of course not. You feel so good . . . so wonderful." She began to cry out again, her body heating up.

He moved faster now. He was hard and felt so good.

"Shit," he cried, "I'm going to come again. What the hell?"

The orgasm caught her, an intense surprise that had her crying out. He pumped fast now, lightning moves that carried her orgasm to a new height. He arched back and cried out, his thick pecs trembling as he spent himself yet again inside her.

He collapsed on her, once more panting over her chest.

Once more her arms encircled him. She slid a hand over his hair. His fennel scent surrounded her.

She remained like that, awed by what had happened between them and by where she was.

After a long moment, he eased out of her and rolled slightly onto his side He leaned on one elbow and looked around. "I think I know what this is, where we are? I just figured it out."

Havily once more glanced at the darkness that bordered the edge of the space, that seemed to drift on for miles. "Where?" she asked, confused.

"Of course. Havily, this is the darkening. You've brought us into the darkening, which is what you've been doing in your dreams."

"But . . . this is where Endelle hunts the Commander, isn't it? She chases him through the darkening?"

"I don't know about *chasing* him. More like she hunts him down. I don't think *he's* actually in the darkening, if I've understood Endelle's process." He then shifted slightly and looked down at her. He chuckled softly. "Well, for an ascender who has repeatedly disappointed Madame Endelle, you've got a goddamn righteous Third ability."

"No," she said and laughed at him, but he lifted a brow. "That's not possible."

"Yes. You do." He then kissed her forehead.

Her cheeks grew warm as his lips drifted to an eyebrow, where he placed another kiss. First a compliment, then a tender display of physical affection. She could get used to this. "So how do we get back?" she asked.

He shrugged. "I think this is your show, not mine. I told you yesterday that you bring me into this place, not the other way around."

Her thoughts took a hard turn. "Oh, God. If you're right, then that's why Crace came to me. This is why I had a guardian at my ascension, because I can do this, because I have darkening abilities."

"Yes, that would follow."

She overlaid his hand with her own and before she spoke the words, she knew exactly what would happen. "We'll return now."

Leaving the darkening felt as though she were being swept thousands of miles on a swift wind, then suddenly she was back in her real bed, Marcus beside her.

"That was . . . amazing," he said.

"I had only to think the thought and we were back."

He leaned down and kissed her again. "Look at me for a second."

She was staring into his eyes. "I am looking at you."

"I mean all of me."

Her gaze ran down his chest over his arms, down to his partially thickened cock and lower. "Marcus, you look different."

"I *feel* different."

Her gaze flew back to his. "How? Why? Is it the *breh-hedden*?"

He shook his head. "No. It's your blood. Your blood did this to me."

Havily's mouth fell agape. She touched his pecs and his biceps. Her brows rose. "You look like you've worked out nonstop for about a month."

*Because only rare anecdotal evidence suggests
that the occasional mortal has mounted wings
before ascending, a conclusion can be drawn that
first-flight falls into the category of myth.*

—From *Treatise on Ascension,* by Philippe Reynard

CHAPTER 8

Medichi sat on a bar stool at the Cave, the laid-back rec room used only by the Warriors of the Blood. He sipped a glass of Cabernet Sauvignon, the only Warrior of the Blood to prefer wine over hard liquor. The heavy tannin teased his tongue and he smiled . . . a little. He loved an excellent red wine.

He'd meant to head to his villa on the east side of the White Tank Mountains and crawl into bed. But after he'd been with Havily, after he'd comforted her, smelled the freshness of her shampooed hair, felt her breasts pressed against his chest, he'd been nerved up. Sleep couldn't have found him.

So he thought maybe a glass of wine in a room that smelled more of war than a woman's soft sweetness would ease him.

He was grateful Marcus had shown up. Of course he was. But for just a moment, holding Havily in his arms, he'd once again been reminded of what he'd missed all these centuries, and something in him had collapsed, fallen flat. His props had failed. All the reasons he used to justify his solitary state had exploded and here he sat, a burned-out shell, his loneliness exposed like an open wound.

Of course, life was changing for the Warriors of the Blood. And all because of the newest Guardian of Ascension, Alison Wells.

A shudder went through him at what her horrific ascension had put the warriors through: the increased battling with death vamps, the painful experience of watching a mortal woman forced to battle a powerful vampire on her own, the haunting image of Kerrick's near-death, then his incredible resurrection because of his *breh*'s immense abilities. Jesus.

But maybe worse than these traumas was the sight of Kerrick every night since, over the past four months, looking rested and content even though he battled harder than ever. The completion of the *breh-hedden* had done this for him. The bastard was happy, *happy,* even though nothing had changed for him in any other sense than that he took the same woman to bed every dawn, and, yeah, he had a child growing in her belly.

He knew what that was like. He could *remember* what that was like.

Shit.

He threw back the rest of the wine, something he never did. He always swirled and savored. Right now, for the first time in centuries, he wished for something harder. Scotch maybe.

A faint vibration of air near the new pool table had him off the stool and on his feet, his free arm extended ready to fold his sword into his hand. Who would be coming to the Cave midday? His heart rate shot into the stratosphere.

Thorne materialized.

Thank God.

They spoke at the same time and said the same thing: "What the fuck are you doing here?"

Medichi slumped back onto his stool and took a few deep breaths. His hands shook from the quick flooding of adrenaline through his veins. They were all on edge these days.

"So what the fuck are you doing here?" Thorne asked again.

Medichi turned into the bar and because of his trembling fingers, he had to work to refill the goblet without spilling. Eventually he succeeded. He took a solid mouthful then swallowed. He took a deep breath. "Got news, boss." He turned back to look at the leader of the Warriors of the Blood. Thorne's eyes were the usual—bloodshot and red-rimmed. Talk about never sleeping.

Medichi held the glass with both hands and worked at taking a few more deep breaths. He glanced at Thorne. They each wore jeans and tees, some indication they were both trying to dial it down. Wasn't working.

"News, huh?" Thorne had a split between his brows and he planted his hands on his hips. "Just tell me first why the hell you aren't home and in bed asleep."

"Why aren't you?"

"Asked you first, asshole."

Medichi would only lose this battle if he kept going, so he answered the question. "I went back to see Havily at her town house. Wanted to make sure she was okay."

Thorne walked in his direction, his gaze shifting over the back of the bar where the bottles were lined up as though waiting for target practice. The hunting stopped, no doubt on the bottle of Ketel One, his favorite drink. "How's she doin'?"

"Rattled. Her home was crawling with Militia Warriors."

"How many?"

"A couple of dozen, at least."

"Good." He reached for the bottle, unscrewed the lid, and poured three fingers, neat. He took a deep breath, tilted his head, and slid the contents down his throat.

Thorne was one wrecked warrior. He even had crow's-feet beside each eye, something that was supposed to be impossible on Second, but maybe not if you made war all night, battled with Endelle every off-minute, drank like a fish, and never slept. The only relief the man seemed to find was visiting his sister each dawn at the Creator's Convent. Thorne was a very devoted brother.

When the tumbler hit the bar, Thorne looked at him and said, "So what's your news? Or was that it—Havily's okay and Militia Warriors are guarding her town house?"

"Nope. While I was there, Marcus showed up."

He heard the quick intake of breath as Thorne grabbed his arm and squeezed. "Don't shit me now."

"He's back. The deserter is back."

Thorne's head rocked like he couldn't quite control his neck, and he released a ragged sigh. He righted himself. "To stay? Tell me Marcus is here to stay."

"He was pissed that I had my hands on Havily's arms."

Thorne searched his eyes. He nodded. He even smiled. "You think the *breh-hedden*'s got him?"

"Looks like it. His greeting to me was something like, *Get your hands off her, asshole.*"

Thorne's smile eased into a full-blown grin, which of course deepened the crow's-feet. But for just a moment he lost that we're-perpetually-fucked look. He released another long breath and once more reached for the Ketel. "Well. Thank the Creator for small favors."

When Marcus stepped out of the shower and started toweling off, he wondered what the hell he and Havily were supposed to do now. The problem was, he was ready for another round. He looked down at his subversive cock, thick and doing a righteous imitation of a heat-seeking missile. He wagged his head. "Don't even think about it."

Between the powerful effect of Havily's blood and the call of the *breh-hedden,* he shook with need. He tucked the towel around his hips and leaned forward to plant his hands on the counter. He forced his torso and shoulders to relax. He took deep breaths, a lot of them.

He had to get a grip. Somehow. After all, he hardly knew

this woman, her likes and dislikes, the essentials of her temperament or her temper. He did know she had a bit of a short fuse and that she was defensive as hell. And why wouldn't she be? Apparently, her boss, the proverbial bitch-from-hell, had let Havily know she'd been a disappointment to Second Earth from the moment she'd completed her rite of ascension. A hundred years of you're-not-good-enough had to take a toll.

But *holy shit* . . . her blood.

He lifted his head and looked into the mirror. He drew away from the counter and let his gaze drift over his body. Jesus H. Christ, he really did look stronger, his muscles better defined, larger, and that orgasm. Like taking off into outer space . . . again and again. Of course, dwelling on the recent experience was not the best strategy since his proverbial missile started throbbing.

He worked at breathing a little more and focused on Havily, the woman. They were going to be together for a few days, at least long enough to secure her future safety.

For starters, therefore, he should try talking to her, getting to know her. If she wanted to make use of his body now and then—well, he would be happy to oblige her. How generous of him. He smiled. She'd obviously enjoyed the recent lovemaking as well.

His thoughts took a more how-about-now turn.

Maybe . . .

He let the towel drop.

He moved out of the bathroom and was greeted with a strange sound, which he couldn't place right away. Havily lay on her side facing away from him in the direction of the window. She had a pillow pulled up to her chest, her knees drawn up.

What was that sound?

He drew closer. It wasn't quite like singing or talking. Somewhere in between.

He was at the edge of the mattress and listened hard, then heard a faint giggle followed by a murmur, then a sigh. His shoulders relaxed just a little. His woman had fallen asleep and in her sleep she made a series of contented noises.

He put a hand to his chest and listened. His heart warmed. He was drawn to her soft mumblings and sighs.

He didn't want to wake her but right now he needed to be close to her. Maybe it was the recent attack, maybe it was the *breh-hedden,* or maybe the sex, but, yeah, he wanted to be near her.

He put a knee on the mattress then the other. He ducked his head to keep from hitting some of the lowest dangling butterflies. He crawled toward her and lifted the sheet. Slowly, he eased himself down beside her. He inched toward her, pulling the sheet up over both of them.

The mutterings stopped. "Marcus?" But it was a soft, slurred question.

"Yes," he whispered. "Just me."

"Good. I'm glad."

"Go back to sleep."

She reached behind her and took hold of his forearm. She pulled his arm around her and pressed his hand between her breasts as though she had done so a hundred times before. He couldn't help that his cock responded, but that only made her wiggle her hips and press close.

He knew it wasn't an invitation, so he forced more air in and out of his lungs. He thought about *anything else.* Digging a trench. Yeah, he pictured the rocky hillside outside her town house and digging a trench, working hard under the sun, getting good and exhausted.

That helped. He calmed down a little so that he could press closer, embrace her more fully, plant his chest against her back, let her know he was here.

She murmured her approval. She had been up most of the night. His woman needed her rest and needed his protection. He could be here for her in both ways right now. Her soft mumblings started again and he smiled. He had forgotten, truly forgotten, what it was like to be close to a woman in this way, the comfort of her soft body against his hard warrior muscles, the sweetness of being physically connected that had nothing to do with sex. He had not allowed this kind of involvement in too many centuries to count. His last marriage had ended in AD 800. Death vampires had murdered his wife of five centuries, his beloved Neeja. His three sons were gone as well, warriors all, lost to the war before the advent of Christ. The pain . . . Jesus, he'd forgotten what that pain felt like until this moment because the *breh-hedden* had made Havily precious in his eyes. He'd promised himself *no more.* Now he was here, holding a goddess in his arms, an ascender who smelled so erotically of honeysuckle.

She was a balm against his burning skin, an unexpected ease to his soul. If this was her way of seducing him, damn it might just work. He had lived a solitary life for over a millennium. He'd found lots of ways to make it work, one of which was never getting involved with a woman. Another was having lots of casual sex.

But the *breh-hedden* had orchestrated this moment, which in turn had brought memories forward of former times when he'd known this kind of closeness and joy with a woman.

And in this moment, his heart began to hurt.

"Is this all the footage you've got?" Crace asked. He sat at his desk in the office he'd commandeered four months ago from one of Greaves's generals. Rith had just loaded a DVD of the attack at the Superstitions, the one in which Rith had personally detonated the incendiary bomb that was supposed to have offed Warrior Luken. Everything looked in order—so why had the mission failed?

Rith stood next to him and grew very still, the man's only tell. "Yes," he responded succinctly. "This is all I have. Warrior Thorne showed up thirty seconds after Warrior Luken hit the earth."

"Fucking bad luck," Crace muttered. He grunted his displeasure at the screen. He thought the height of the flames could be taller but he liked the colors, some pinks and greens, almost glittery, real spectacle-grade shit. But why the fuck hadn't the warrior died? What was the point of beautiful explosions if someone didn't get killed?

"There is something, however, I think you might have missed," Rith said. He gestured with both hands toward the keyboard. "May I?"

"By all means." Crace scooted away in his rolling desk chair, his hands in the air. He had an instinct about this vampire who pretended to be submissive. He should kill him right now and would have except that Greaves favored the bastard.

A few clicks followed. "There," Rith said. "A hint of red hair. I was too far away at the time and preparing to leave so I didn't see the arrival of a third person. I snatched the camera and tripod then folded away. I only saw this later."

Crace peered close. "Fuck. You think this is ascender Morgan?" He could still taste her exquisite blood on his lips. His heart rate increased, double time.

"Yes. I do."

"What the hell was she doing there at the scene?" Crace asked.

"The real question is—how did Warrior Thorne know to come to Warrior Luken's aid?"

Crace frowned. "Are you saying he was warned?"

"I'm not sure. But ascender Morgan has a special relationship with Warrior Luken. I believe she knew he was in trouble."

"A link?"

"Not necessarily, but I do think it's possible she had a link with Warrior Medichi and that's why he arrived at the town house so swiftly last night."

No shit, Sherlock, he thought. Aloud, he said, "Go on."

"There is no way Warrior Thorne could have known of the bomb at the Superstitions or that one of his warriors was down. I made certain that the Awatukee Borderland, where he was fighting, had a surplus of death vamps to battle. Even so, Warrior Luken fell hard to earth, and you can see by the footage that he was unable to make a call."

"But you think ascender Morgan somehow knew that he'd been hurt, then intervened?"

"Yes. I do."

"If not a telepathic link, then how do you explain it?"

"Do you recall the dispatches of yesterday?"

"Yes."

"One of the Seers spoke of *emergence*. There have been at least six more reports from Seers Fortresses about ascender Morgan in the past twenty-four hours. One of them spoke of darkening capabilities."

At that, Crace frowned. He was just a little skeptical about Seers' prophecies. "Are you suggesting that she located Warrior Luken through the darkening?"

"I think it possible. It would explain a lot, especially her increased appearance in the future streams."

Crace shook his head. To his knowledge only Endelle had darkening capabilities, which meant it was a Third Earth power even Greaves didn't have. Yeah. Skeptical.

"And you're telling me this because—?"

"Because I know you have an interest in her beyond her emerging powers."

Crace didn't trust Rith any farther than he could piss on him. He sensed in the man duplicity and schemes, plans of his own, but it didn't matter. Right now, for whatever reason, it suited Rith to share information with Crace about Havily Morgan, and that was good enough. Maybe it was simply that Rith wanted her out of the picture the way Greaves did. Making Havily dead would be a feather in his cap where the Commander was concerned.

Crace did indeed have an entirely different interest in Havily Morgan. Truth be known, he didn't give a damn about her emerging powers. What he wanted was her blood. Permanently.

He had never felt better in his long fucking life.

He flexed his right arm and felt the increased bulk of his bicep. Goddamn if the dispatches weren't right. Her blood had done exactly what dying blood could do: It had increased his physical strength, lit up his libido, improved some of his normal human abilities. Bottom line? He may have just discovered the mother lode.

Rith stepped away from the computer and rounded the table to stand facing Crace. "There's just one more thing. We have a convergence in the future streams."

"Between?"

For the first time since Crace had known Rith, the vampire's cheeks wore color—very faint, but the flush was there, a pale pink. What the fuck? "Ascender Morgan and the mortal-with-wings, a woman. She finally showed up in the future streams."

Crace jerked forward in his chair and rose to his feet. "What the fuck?" He moved so fast, however, that his chair skidded backward and slammed into the stone wall. "We've heard nothing about the mortal-with-wings in the past four months and suddenly we have a convergence between these two women? Are you fucking sure?"

"Yes."

Crace knew the bastard was holding something back, something big. "What do you want, Rith? Tell me."

"I want her, the one purportedly with first-flight capability, the mortal-with-wings."

"Why?" He knew for certain the next words his enemy spoke would be important.

"Because she is to me what ascender Morgan is to you."

A blood donor? No, not that. Then what? Shit. Rith would never tell him, and he'd never been able to read his goddamn mind. Well, wasn't this a day of surprises?

Crace relaxed his shoulders. "So basically, if I should happen to find the women together, as the future streams have suggested, then you want me to deliver the mortal-with-wings to you personally."

Rith met his gaze with a blank stare, his mental shields practically glowing. "I would be obliged to you for the favor."

Crace could lie with the best of them. "Then I'll just

have to see what I can do." There was more than one way to destroy an enemy.

When Rith left, Crace headed to the war room. He scouted the notables present and ignored five of the generals to glare at the sixth, General Leto, former Warrior of the Blood. He disliked Leto immensely and distrusted him even more.

He moved to the surveillance grid and changed the coordinates to reflect the Metro Phoenix area, Mortal Earth. A mortal-with-wings by nature would have a power-signature strong enough to show up on the grid. Once he had her location, he'd go after her.

He glanced at Leto. How he despised the bastard who had fought Alison Wells in the Tolleson Two arena and failed to destroy her. He was tall, taller than Crace by at least an inch, and well muscled. He had intense blue eyes and long black warrior hair, which he kept drawn back in the traditional *cadroen,* a reminder to his peers that he'd once been a Warrior of the Blood. So fucking what!

Crace was happy to make use of him, though. Greaves had given Crace power over all the generals for any assignment that came down the pike.

He called Leto over and instructed him to keep an eye on the grid, told him what he was looking for, and asked the man to summon him the moment he found a strong enough signature to indicate a mortal-with-wings. He'd be in his forge until notified.

Leto, to his credit, merely flared his nostrils slightly, then responded, "Yes, Mr. High Administrator."

Master would have been a preferred choice of address, but Crace thought it more likely he would ice-skate in hell first.

As he folded to the underbelly of the entire complex, deep in the earth—his beautiful forge—a shiver of anticipation went through him. If there was to be a convergence between ascender Morgan and the mortal-with-wings, then

Crace thought it likely he'd be in the presence of his preferred blood donor very soon.

How much he loved synchronicity.

As the hour neared seven in the evening, Parisa Lovejoy stood in front of the mirror in her master bath. She wore black lace French-cut underwear but nothing else. Her breathing was shallow, her eyes burned, and her back was on fire.

She had waited ten days. She could never go beyond ten days or the release occurred spontaneously. So far, in the past year since *the event* had overtaken her body, she had been able to mount her wings in complete privacy and secrecy. But she feared more than anything else in the world that her unique condition would become public knowledge.

She closed her eyes. She drew a deep breath and released it slowly. At the same time, she relaxed all the hard fiery lumps that ranged in a V down her back. The weirdest vibration, accompanied by an almost unbearable itch, followed. Nausea overtook her and she shuddered.

She should have done this sooner, but even though she knew quite a bit about the ascended world of Second Earth, she was still worried that as a regular human being, a *mortal,* she was able to mount a pair of wings. It just wasn't *normal,* at least not in her dimension.

She arched back then folded forward.

That was when the indecent pleasure began, almost like sex, as ripples of sensation flowed over her breasts and down deep within her. Okay a lot like sex. Then the wings came forth, gliding as though well oiled, from her body, just as they did for the other ascenders who mounted their wings. She was grateful she knew about the world of ascension; otherwise when her first wing-mount had occurred, she might have gone crazy.

When they were fully released, she straightened up. Her gaze fell to her breasts, which always looked like this, full and peaked as though she had just climaxed.

The nausea still worked over her stomach and she felt weak, like she could fall over if she wasn't careful. But her gaze was drawn to the feathers her body had somehow produced, at the sheer height and beauty of the cream-colored wings, of the tall span that reached all the way to the nine-foot ceiling. She leaned forward and stared into the mirror. She might dislike the fact that she was a complete anomaly on earth, but her wings were magnificent.

As she stared, a slight gasp left her lips. Today there was a difference, a very beautiful difference. Near the tips of the outermost feathers there had always been two bands, one black and one a soft burnished gold. But now there was a new color, the same color as her eyes, a light purple, not quite lavender, placed between the bands. When she held each wing to its fullest height and breadth, and drew them together to touch above her head, the bands made a perfect arch, black forming the outermost arch, then amethyst, then gold.

"So beautiful," she whispered, her gaze tracking the arch from left to right. Her heart ached at the sight and familiar longings trapped her breath in her chest. She felt a profound call on her life and she knew exactly what it was: She was being called to ascension.

She knew about the dimensional world because of another preternatural ability she possessed: She had *visions* of Second Earth. Or at least that's what she called them. When she made herself still and focused, she could see into the ascended world, like opening a window.

Of course, the strangest part of all was that these visions centered on one particular man, a very tall, muscular warrior, who proved to be a vampire and a warrior. But not just any vampire warrior. He served in a place called Second Earth with six other warriors, all of whom she knew by name. As a group, they were known as the Warriors of the Blood, probably because they were vampires.

Vampires.

She could say the word now, quite easily, though that hadn't been the case early on. She had felt ill. She had always believed that vampires were a dark mythology that arose from the collective unconscious of the masses. So when the world of ascension presented itself in the form of her unique visions and immediately presented as also the world of the vampire, well, that had taken some getting used to. But then so had her wings.

She manipulated her back muscles and the wings responded instantly, as though an extension of her muscles. She could make them unfurl almost to a full span and would have if the bathroom had been larger. She could pull the wings in tight to her body as well, even arching them forward to create a cocoon around herself.

She had a powerful urge to waft them downward and fly, which of course would only force her body upward and no doubt punch her head into the ceiling. She would probably break her neck.

She extended her left wing and stroked the feathers with her right hand. They were extremely sensitive to touch. Tugging on one *hurt*. But she separated the feathers and found the gossamer superstructure, thin filaments that must have bound the wings together once they released from her back. How this happened, she didn't know, couldn't imagine.

Her head waggled back and forth. There was so much she didn't understand. Her wings had appeared a year ago, demanding release initially at month long intervals but accelerating to ten days now.

As for her visions, the latest one had been particularly disturbing. She had seen Warrior Medichi visit with Warrior Luken in what looked like a hospital room. She didn't know exactly what had happened to the warrior except that he had been badly burned; the two men were concerned that he might have lost the use of his wings permanently because of the accident.

Warrior Medichi was so very handsome with pronounced cheekbones and smooth olive skin. His hair was black and very long. Sometimes he wore it in a leather clasp, called the *cadroen,* and sometimes he wore it free.

She met her gaze in the mirror, her amethyst eyes staring back at her. So what was going on with her? Why was she so fixated on Warrior Medichi? What did all of this make her? Was it possible she was going insane, that all these experiences and sensations were mere hallucinations?

She shook her head back and forth. No. What she experienced was real. She knew in the depths of her being that her wings existed, and that her visions were real. Maybe she couldn't explain any of it right now, but she didn't doubt the truth of what her eyes saw and her body felt. She gave the woman in the mirror, with the layered dark brown hair and amethyst eyes, a serious nod of her head.

Then she smiled. For a long time now she had wanted to try something new. She had considered performing this daring feat more than once, but tonight, for some reason, she had decided to take action. She would give her wings a test flight, albeit a very small test flight—more like a test *float*.

Still wearing just her French-cuts, she drew her wings close to her body by arching the top of the span and folding the layered feathers back almost behind her, the way birds did when they hopped about. In this configuration she could walk through her house without doing injury to her wings.

She moved to the small vanity area of the master bath, which had a door that opened onto a walkway and railing overlooking a small courtyard below. The courtyard was completely private, located in the center of the house. Not one window could be seen from the street or by any of her surrounding neighbors.

Two stories wasn't that far, and she felt certain if she expanded her wings, she could float to the pavers below.

At least, she hoped so.

She moved onto the walkway and, making use of a stepladder she'd planted by the railing earlier, climbed up the few steps. Was she really going to do this?

Her heart started to race. She spread her wings for balance, and by creating a little lift with a gentle downward sweep of her wings, she was able to rise onto the railing. She planted her feet on the wrought iron. She had to work to maintain balance—her toes curled around the rail as she extended her hands and manipulated her wings to keep from flying either forward or back.

Finally, she achieved equilibrium. She unfurled her wings and her feet were steady. She drew a sharp breath into her lungs even as tears touched her eyes. Was she really going to do this?

She couldn't imagine the picture she made, with just her lace briefs on, her breasts fully exposed, and her wings spreading above the courtyard. But how happy she was.

She knew there was a danger if she didn't do this properly, but she wouldn't think of that now. Instead, with a sweep of her wings, she dropped into the space below. Her wings, just as she hoped, caught air and eased her onto the hard pavers.

Oh. My. God.

First flight.

Her first flight!

She smiled and glanced from one tip of her wings to the other. Her heart pounded, loud and hard. She took a breath and drew her wings close to her body once more. She turned and stared up at the railing, at least sixteen feet above her, more than a story.

She thought of flapping her wings and seeing if she could regain the railing, but that was too much of a risk to attempt tonight. What if she flapped too hard and ended up clearing the roofline? What if a draft caught her wings and carried her toward the hill behind her house? No, she wouldn't do that, but she was willing to bring her wings in close, go back inside, and return up the stairs to the railing. Yes, this she could do.

And she did, again . . . and again . . . and again.

Nurture the gifted and a land will prosper.

—*Collected Proverbs,* Beatrice of Fourth

CHAPTER 9

Havily awoke and stretched. She glanced toward the window. She could tell by the fading light that it had to be late—at least seven, maybe later. The clock on the nightstand proved her theory. Almost seven thirty. She had slept through most of the afternoon and well into the evening. Of course when she thought back to all that had transpired the night before, beginning with a death vampire attack and ending this morning with an astonishing bout of lovemaking with Warrior Marcus . . . well, she wasn't surprised sleep had claimed her. At long last.

She heard Marcus in the other room, in her kitchen. She heard pots banging around. She extended her hearing. "There's really nothing in here but Yoplait yogurt." He grunted his displeasure. Who was he talking to? "Okay. So it's called Give Me Greek. No, that's okay. I'll call and order. Thanks, Jeannie."

Huh. Marcus had called Central, the place that oversaw the nightly war against death vampires, for information on local restaurants? Sometimes men were helpless . . . but at least Marcus was resourceful. But still, *Central*.

Mmm. Food. Her stomach rumbled.

She stretched. She glanced at the bathroom. A shower sounded like heaven as well. She slipped from bed and padded to the bathroom. A minute later she stepped into the shower, dipping her head below the heavenly spray.

Now that Marcus was separated from her by several walls, and his fennel scent wasn't burrowing into her brain, her rational mind had a chance to surface. What on earth was she thinking? She had slept with the one man on the planet she had considered the *last* man on the planet, any dimension, that she would ever sleep with—Warrior Marcus, the deserter.

She needed to get a grip, to remember one salient fact: that Marcus, despite the fact that he made love to her like a god, had deserted his brothers-in-arms two hundred years ago. What did that say of his character, of his worth? More than once while caught in the pleasure of his body over hers, tender feelings had surfaced, but this was nothing more than the horrible *breh-hedden* trying to work its wiles on her, seduce her into caring for someone she did not feel deserved it.

So there.

With that settled, however, her thoughts drifted back to making love with the deserter. Oh. Dear. God.

Memories rose and fell on her, knocking her flat, drawing from her body remembered pleasure. And yes, his exotic fennel scent had swamped her, but exactly what were the two of them supposed to do now? Keep tumbling into bed, keep exploring each other's bodies, keep drowning in each other's scent, keep kissing those lips and putting her hands in his hair, and letting her fingers rake his muscled flesh and oh, God, she was aroused all over again.

"Dammit, Havily," he called to her all the way from the

kitchen. "Would you stop throwing honeysuckle at me? I swear I'll come over there and break the door down if you keep that up."

He could smell her all the way from the master bath to the kitchen?

She was so screwed.

Even if she hadn't been drawn to Marcus by the *breh-hedden*, the truth was, she loved this. Oh, hell, she shouldn't, but she did. Warrior Marcus was in full caveman mode and she loved that she could work him up just by thinking a lusty thought or two.

The trouble was, she hadn't had a man in her bed for way too long and now she was just as bad as Marcus. She was a young woman on her honeymoon and everything she needed was in the other room.

She turned the shower off, stepped onto the bath mat, grabbed a purple towel, and dried herself off. She took her time working her Clinique lotion into every square inch of her skin.

She may be a vampire and she may heal fast but she vowed she looked better because of Clinique.

She heard a tapping on the door then a soft scratching. "Havily?" From beneath the door and around the doorjambs, fennel invaded the steamy bathroom.

Uh-oh.

"Yes." The word kind of squeaked out.

"We need to talk." Another soft scratching sounded. More fennel. Oh. God.

She drew a couple of deep breaths. "I know." But she didn't speed up her process. She tapped the moisturizer with her little finger very gently beneath her right eye, then her left. This really wasn't necessary, but the ritual calmed her.

"How long are you going to be in there?"

"I don't know. I feel safe in here."

"I'm not a monster."

"I know."

"Just wanted you to know."

"I know." He was just a deserter. But he'd also saved her life four months ago during an attack at Endelle's palace. The vampire wasn't all bad.

"Okay. I've ordered Greek."

"I'll be out in a few. I promise."

"Okay."

She stared at the door. So what was she supposed to do with this man?

Marcus felt lost as he stared at the bathroom door. He wanted to bust the damn thing down and drag Havily back to bed. He wanted to keep her there for maybe a year—or a century. He wanted to taste her . . . everywhere. He wanted her blood again.

He could smell her honeysuckle scent and his balls tightened. Dammit.

He turned on his heel and made his way out of the bedroom. He paced through the small suite of rooms that made up her town house, up and down the short hallways, through the kitchen back into the living room. He was uneasy and tense so he made this loop over and over, trying to just calm down.

Still, she remained in the bathroom, probably tending to her perfect hair and her stylish makeup. Okay, so he really approved of how she cared for herself. His approval wasn't helping.

He'd finally made love to the woman he'd been craving for four months and the experience had been . . . *incredible*. Trouble was, as soon as he'd detected her lovely honeysuckle scent wafting from the bathroom, he'd grown as hard as flint, all over again. With Havily around, it didn't take much.

He'd been awake for hours. He'd phoned Ennis several times, walking him through various aspects of his empire, things he thought Ennis would need to know. But the bastard sounded so fucking patronizing, *yes, he knew about the contracts that needed to be signed, yes, the board meeting had gone off without a hitch, no, he didn't think the COO of the corporation handling the horticulture exports needed to be replaced.* Blah, blah, blah.

He kept pacing. This not having anything to do, even for a few hours, bugged the shit out of him. He was a man of forward motion and action. But all he could do right now was wait for Havily to get dressed and for the food to arrive. Then what? He felt ready to jump out of his skin. He never had this much downtime.

After a good half hour of pacing, he turned on his heel, left the dining room, and marched through the kitchen, down the hall, to a closed door he'd been ignoring. He turned the knob and pushed the door open.

What he saw stunned him. In the very center of what proved to be an office was a huge architectural rendering standing at least three feet by six feet or so and rising some four feet in the air. What the hell was this? Looked like some kind of incomplete office complex.

He noticed that the topmost level had several wide stretches of green, which he knew represented areas of lawn, which meant that all the levels of the building below were actually underground. He saw miniature steel girders sunk deep, indicating that the building would be many stories in height. Was this what Havily did in her spare time?

"What are you doing in here?"

He didn't turn around immediately because he couldn't believe what he was looking at. "I didn't mean to pry. I'm a little antsy, but what is this? I'm really impressed."

He heard her sigh. "Just a project I've been working on in conjunction with an architect for the past several years. It's a military-admin complex. For a long time I've thought Madame Endelle's operation could be seriously improved starting with a new facility. I had a mock-up completed and ready to present, but it got annihilated by a flame-thrower."

He glanced at her over his shoulder. "What do you mean?"

Another sigh. "I tried to present my ideas to Madame

Endelle, but she took an instant dislike to my audacity. She torched the whole thing although I will admit my timing was atrocious. Still . . ."

Marcus turned around fully. "Well, I didn't mean to invade your privacy. I was trying to distract myself . . ." He looked her up and down and his lips parted. What she wore wasn't sexy, but it was stylish. He'd known a lot of models over the decades and he recognized the fashion influence. She wore silk cream pants cuffed tight at the ankle and leopard-print heels. The blouse was long-sleeved, rolled up to the elbows, in blue plaid, also in silk, very chic. She wore pearls in long loops. Her hair was a floating layer of red. Her makeup was perfection, as always, and expert shading and mascara enhanced her light green eyes. The woman knew how to put herself together.

She was a feast for the eyes and he devoured. Her gaze slid down his change of clothes as well and her expression flared. He had on a short-sleeved blue silk shirt and tailored slacks. He noted her approval. "I folded some things from home," he explained, essentially his Tom Ford collection. Given his profession, he wore jeans only on Bainbridge, the place no one visited, his sanctuary. Here? No jeans. "I'm planning on staying with you until we get your security situation figured out."

She nodded. "And I need you to be here. I know I'm not safe. And . . . you look really nice. What am I smelling? I mean the fragrance you're wearing."

He smiled. He couldn't help it. "Grey Vetiver. Tom Ford."

She responded with a smile; then her nostrils flared. "Would you knock it off with the fennel? Oh." He heard the vibration as she reached into her pant pocket. "Excuse me. It's *her*." She straightened her shoulders. "Yes, Madame Endelle." Her gaze was fixed on Marcus, the color on her cheeks heightened. "Of course. At once."

Havily stared at the phone and grimaced. "You know, she could have at least given us a lift. Now I have to call Jeannie."

"What's going on?"

"You'd better cancel dinner."

He lifted a brow. He wanted an answer first. He crossed his arms over his chest. "And where are we going that we can't simply fold to the location?"

She gave him a look. "Fine. That was Endelle. She wants us to come to the palace, as in now, but I have no idea why and the last thing I was going to do was ask for an explanation."

Marcus smiled. "Smart move."

"Yeah, well I've learned a thing or two working in close proximity to her over the past few months. My new office is just down the hall from hers. Believe me, on the best day, it's no picnic."

"You work on the same floor?" He smiled. "You're a woman of courage."

"Are you mocking me?"

"Hell, no. You forget, I've known the woman for a few millennia. In all that time she hasn't changed much."

He drew his phone from his pocket and hit redial. He canceled their dinner order. He shoved his phone back into his pocket. "So how do we do this?"

She still held her iPhone. After touching the screen, she lifted it to her ear. "Hey, Jeannie, it's Havily. No, I'm fine, everything's fine. It's just that Marcus and I have been called to the palace and we need a lift." Jeannie said something that made Havily laugh. "Well, I intended to suggest it to her since there's no way I can bypass the security around the palace, but you know how *patient* she is. So, can you do this for us?" As she spoke, she extended her hand to Marcus. He took it, thinking this was a very natural thing to do with her, like they'd known each other forever, like he could read her mind, like he trusted her and she trusted him.

He mentally calculated exactly how much time they'd actually spent together and didn't come up with much, a handful of hours, really, and yet . . .

"We're ready."

The vibration lasted a couple of seconds, a whisper of time through nether-space.

The next moment he stood in an all-too-familiar rotunda, the same rotunda where he had last seen Havily right after the attack on the palace. The memory flooded his mind. So, shit.

"Oh, my God," she whispered. She released his hand then turned in a circle. She was remembering as well since a roll of honeysuckle hit him in his gut. Yep, she was re-membering.

She turned away from him and faced *the wall,* the one where he had pinned her, had her skirts up around her waist and was ready to take her, his mouth glued to hers, when Luken had intervened. Now that he thought about it, Medichi had been there as well, yanking him away from her, and Jean-Pierre had held Havily back.

Marcus had been crazed, completely out of his mind. He had been convinced she was in danger and he had to get to her, to save her, which was ridiculous. The only per-son she needed saving from was him.

He drew close though she faced away from him. He wanted to touch her but he held back. "I never apologized for my behavior that night. Havily, I'm so sorry for what I did. I was *not myself.*" A profound understatement.

She drew in a quick breath but she didn't move away from him. He took a risk and put his hands on her arms. She gasped then took a deep breath through her nose. He thought he heard a moan but he wasn't sure.

"I always worried that I'd frightened you," he said, leaning close, dragging her sweet scent into his nose. "I hated what I'd done, what I'd been about to do to you. I worried that I'd ruined you, made you fear men after that."

"No," she whispered. "Not at all." Her voice trembled. "I wasn't frightened. I was . . . overcome. I *wanted* you as well. Whatever you were feeling, I felt it, too."

"I was completely out of my mind, lost, so hungry." The last word slid into a growl. He moved her hair away from her neck then planted his lips on her scented skin and suckled. He felt her knees dip but he caught her around the waist, kept her from falling. A heavy groan fled her throat.

As though it had happened yesterday and not several months ago, he felt the call all over again, the wildness in his spirit. He turned her to face him and as he had that night, he pressed his thigh between her legs and started pushing her backward once more toward the wall. She slung her arms around his neck and let him push her. Her green eyes flared and glimmered. Desire for her so muddied his head that he forgot where he was, why he was even here. All he cared about was getting her flat against the wall and finishing what they had started that night.

"I wanted you." The words rushed from his throat.

"I would have let you take me." Every word breathless.

At last, the wall was behind her. He moved in, pressing his body against hers, letting the wall forge their connection. He arched his hips to make sure she knew how hard he was for her, how completely worked up he was.

"Marcus," she whispered. "Oh, God. I want you all over again, just like that night."

She couldn't have spoken sweeter words. He lifted her shirt and had just worked the clasp loose at the waistband of her pants when he felt a powerful force behind him.

The words, when spoken, carried a swipe of sarcasm. "Oh, goody," Endelle's voice intruded, "a show. At least I get rewarded for having my meditations disturbed. No, please. Don't release her now, Warrior. You'll leave her in pain."

He turned to face away from Endelle. He wondered exactly how long it would take for his arousal to settle down. Right now it felt like it would need, oh, about a century. However, he kept an arm protectively around Havily's waist. She put her hand on his arm. She was breathing hard.

"I do beg your pardon, Madame Endelle," Havily said quickly.

Marcus glanced over his shoulder at Her Supremeness. She wore a long purple linen gown, something she put on when she did her darkening work.

"Well, this whole thing must be a bitch for you, Morgan. But if I were you, I'd complete the goddamn *breh-hedden* and put my man out of his misery. Though why you deserve to take a Warrior of the Blood to your bed, the hell if I know."

Those cutting words, spoken to his woman, had a cooling effect on Marcus's aroused state. Slowly, he turned around, and at the same time he stepped in front of Havily. "If you're wise, you won't talk to her like that, not anymore. You have a bitch's mouth, Endelle. From a sheer executive point of view, demeaning those who work for you is a perfect way to undermine your entire organization. You can never get the best from your people when you treat them like dirt. Bottom line, I want an apology." He might have been okay with this speech if he hadn't uttered the last four words. Endelle didn't *serve* as Supreme High Administrator, she *ruled*. Her commands were to be obeyed and her power was so great that to challenge her in this way was an act of stupidity.

However, right now, he didn't care. Havily deserved better because she was loyal and long-suffering. But the deeper truth was much simpler—everyone deserved to be treated decently.

Endelle lifted a brow. She crossed her arms over her chest. She folded a tall-back, throne-like chair into the room and sat down. "So you want an apology," she said, her tone clipped. "Well, unfortunately, *Warrior* Marcus, if I can even call you that anymore, you'll be waiting a long time for it, but be my guest. Fucking wait."

Marcus drew in a breath. His protectiveness was in high gear, but the hell if he would let anyone talk to Havily that way. "Then I'll take her back to Mortal Earth with me right now until you get this situation figured out. She doesn't need to listen to this kind of shit from you or anyone. I've known you a long time, Endelle, and I admire the hell out of you, but this needs to stop. Belittling your subjects won't fly with me."

She huffed a sigh. "Jesus H. Christ, who put the clamshell up your butt." She narrowed her eyes. "It's the fucking *breh-hedden,* isn't it? I have to say this is some crazy-ass shit. Very well. No more talking to Morgan like she's a flea's knob."

At that, some of the stiffness left his shoulders and he dropped back to stand beside Havily. She was staring at him, and he turned to meet her gaze. Her green eyes glittered in the dim rotunda light. "Thank you," she murmured. "That was . . . gentlemanly."

He was taken aback. Had she just approved of something he'd done? For whatever reason, her approval did him in. He felt the growl forming in his throat as he turned toward her, but she caught his elbow and gave him a jerk in Madame Endelle's direction. "Hold that thought," she whispered. To Her Supremeness she said, "So, exactly why did you bring us here?"

Endelle rose from her throne and scowled. "Thorne came to see me just a few minutes ago. His sister delivered a Seer's prophecy from the Creator's Convent, you know that shithole in Prescott. Apparently, the prophecy indicates that there's a mortal-with-wings, a female, and that we have to find her, as in right now, because if Greaves gets ahold of her he'll be able to start Armageddon, and no I don't know how or why."

"A mortal-with-wings?" Havily murmured.

"Has there ever been such a thing?" Marcus asked.

"Only once to my recollection," Endelle said, her voice low, her gaze suddenly fixed on nothing as though she looked deep into the past. "Luchianne."

Marcus whistled. Luchianne was the first ascender, the first vampire, the one who led the way, eleven thousand years ago, to Second Earth.

"The first ascender had wings before she ascended?"

Havily asked. "I didn't know that, but it kind of makes sense." She shifted her gaze to Endelle. "So where do we look for her? I mean she could be anywhere on Mortal Earth, right?"

"Lucky for us, she's in the Metro Phoenix area." Endelle's expression grew a little distant. From where he stood, Marcus could feel the ripples of her powerful thoughts flowing through the empty space. She continued, though in a more subdued voice, "I just wonder what the hell is going on."

She turned and moved toward the side of the rotunda that was open to the air. The space faced south with a view of a long stretch of the McDowell Mountains as well as the Valley below. The palace was at least a thousand feet from the foothills. In the winter, with a storm out of the north, snow would occasionally cloak the palace.

He caught Havily's hand and drew her with him to follow in Endelle's wake.

Endelle continued speaking as though to herself. "Alison had the ability to fold even before she ascended, and now she's a Guardian of Ascension with the self-proclaimed vision that she will be the instrument by which the pathway to Third Earth is finally opened. Now we have a mortal-with-wings. Shit."

She was silent for a moment as he drew close, still in possession of his woman's hand. She added, "I want you both to work from Medichi's villa and don't ask me why. It's just my gut telling me that's the best place for all of this right now. Between Havily's situation—whatever the hell that is—and now a mortal-with-wings, looks like the war is about to heat up . . . again. Don't worry. I'll cast a shield of mist over the villa so that even Greaves can't find it."

Actually, Medichi's villa made sense. Even before Marcus had exiled himself to Mortal Earth, Medichi had built a vast estate on the east side of the White Tank Mountains. Under the century-old COPASS laws, because Medichi was a Guardian of Ascension, his property was protected from attack.

So Havily would be infinitely safer at the villa than in her town house. Once . . . or rather *if* . . . they found this mortal-with-wings, they could bring her to the villa as well and afford her the same level of protection, at least for an hour or so. Mortals couldn't survive in the second dimension, not for very long. If trapped on Second Earth, an unascended mortal would die within twenty-four hours. The two-hour mark was usually more than most mortals could bear. But an hour would give all of them enough time to figure out a strong course of action.

There would also be plenty of room for privacy, and as he gave Havily's hand a squeeze and glanced at her, he knew he would be needing some privacy with her . . . soon.

Okay, he didn't need to think about that right now. He looked back at Endelle. "Did Thorne say in what part of the Valley we would find this mortal?" With a population of three million, the Phoenix area on Mortal Earth was one helluva haystack to sort through, especially with a critical time frame.

No doubt Greaves's war room was already on the task.

Endelle looked over her shoulder at Havily. "No, but ask her? She's the go-to woman right now. She's always got some plan for solving problems, getting shit organized. See, I don't think she's completely useless."

Havily laughed. "Was that a compliment, Madame Supreme High Administrator?"

Endelle stepped toward her and met her gaze. "Was that sarcasm, my little organizer?"

Marcus once more put himself physically between the two women. He thought he might have a conversation later with Havily about not baiting scorpions in general. He addressed Endelle. "There's something else you need to know."

She shifted her lined, ancient gaze to his. "What?" she snapped. "I don't have all night."

Marcus glanced at Havily and frowned slightly. "We need to tell her," he said.

"You mean about . . . earlier?"

"Yeah."

Havily lifted her chin but released a heavy sigh. "Yes, I think so, too. Shall I?"

He smiled. Maybe she'd been set back on her heels all these decades by Endelle's sour opinion of Havily's powers, but his woman didn't lack for pluck. "Go ahead."

Havily met Endelle's gaze head-on. "Earlier today, when Marcus and I were . . . *engaged* . . . I took him into the darkening."

He liked that she said it flat-out. He also enjoyed just how wide Endelle's eyes grew.

Her Supremeness blinked. "You did what?"

"For the past four months, I thought I'd been engaged in enjoying very intense, dream-like fantasies about Warrior Marcus. Two nights ago, when I had a vision of Luken with his wings on fire, I also thought it was a vision I was having." She took a deep breath. This couldn't be an easy thing for her to say, since she was essentially speaking about sex to the most vulgar, inappropriate, indiscreet vampire on Second Earth. Still, she pressed on. "However, today, this afternoon, when Marcus and I were . . . making love . . . we ended up in the darkening. I think all this time, I've been taking Marcus into the darkening, and when Luken was attacked I somehow took myself into the darkening and traveled to his location. Once there, however, I couldn't reach him."

"No one in this dimension," Endelle cried, "can go into the darkening but me, not even Greaves. So forgive me if I don't believe you. Settle down Marcus, what I mean is, why don't you describe for me what it was like, what it looked like, what it felt like, and I don't mean your warrior's cock. This is important, Morgan. I must know exactly what happened."

Havily took her time and described the experience. Marcus nodded his agreement.

When she had finished, Endelle just stared at her. "Holy shit," she muttered. "Well, you've described it exactly and I'll be a goddamn motherfucker if you don't have darkening capabilities. It's a goddamn righteous Third ability, you know." Her brows knotted. "Were you in two places at once?"

Havily shook her head. "No, never that. In or out, never both, although I understand splitting-self is a critical aspect of the ability. I never did that. I suppose you can."

Endelle snorted. "Damn straight I can." She narrowed her eyes. "And you're sure you weren't in two places at once?"

"I'm sure."

Endelle almost smiled. "Well, well, well. So you have some power after all. I'll see you in the office tomorrow and we'll talk about what to do next. For one thing, I'll need to teach you how to split yourself. Then maybe you'll be of some real use to me."

"Yes, ma'am."

Her Supremeness turned to Marcus. "Protect Havily and find this mortal-with-wings ASAP. Update Thorne then keep on updating him. He'll contact me if I'm needed. Okay. We're done."

Endelle lifted her arm and vanished, no doubt to return to her meditation chamber.

He glanced at Havily. "Medichi's first, then we'll figure out what we need to do next. How does that sound?"

She nodded, frowning.

"What?"

"Well, you know how odd Endelle's clothes can be? But she actually looked almost normal tonight, didn't she, like she was wearing a sort of Grecian robe?"

"When she does her meditation work, her darkening work, she usually wears something comfortable. At least that's how I remember her."

"It was just so strange not to see her in a tiger skin or . . . rabbit pelts."

"Rabbit?"

Havily laughed. "You know what I mean."

"I do."

He slid an arm around her neck, pulling her close. He held her in that position, locked against him, just looking into her eyes until her lips parted and he smelled a delicious wave of honeysuckle. He planted his lips over hers. He palmed her cheek and deepened the kiss. He made liberal use of his tongue until she responded with a soft moan. He stroked her cheek as he drew back. "We'd better get you over to the villa or I'm going to have you against that wall again."

She searched his eyes. "Do you know how much I'm tempted to keep you right here?"

He growled deep in his throat. A woman shouldn't say such a thing to a vampire, especially not to a vampire caught in the grip of the *breh-hedden*.

"Fennel," she whispered. She pressed a hand to her chest and gulped as she drew away from him. She brought her iPhone out of her pant pocket, touched the screen a couple of times, then pressed it to her ear. "Hi, Jeannie," she said after a moment. He still had hold of her hand. "Can you send us to Medichi's villa?" A pause, then, "Yeah, I've got him. Do your worst."

And the vibration began.

The hunt is the true elixir of ascended vampire life.

—*Collected Proverbs*, Beatrice of Fourth

CHAPTER 10

Havily released Marcus's hand as soon as she felt the planked wood floor of Medichi's villa beneath her feet. She was aware that if he so much as said the word, or came at her with a familiar wild glint in his eye, she'd fall right back into his arms and let him push her up against any of these walls.

She drew some much-needed air into her lungs and questioned all over again what she was doing with this man. She had never felt more vulnerable.

Marcus looked around. "I see he's made a few changes."

"Yeah. I guess it's been two hundred years since you were here."

"Yep."

Havily glanced around as well. She had been to the estate a number of times. Though parties were rare, if the warriors had one, Medichi hosted, as well he should. The dark, almost black wood floors were covered in fine woven rugs. Antique furniture, some quite massive pieces, ran stem-to-stern.

His villa was a work of art in the Italianate style, and he had expanded the property over many decades. He was wealthy but then he'd spent centuries building his investments, particularly in the import business from Mortal Earth. He also had a love of computers, so as soon as there were whispers on earth of the PC, Medichi had bought stock.

She stood with Marcus near the front door in the large central foyer. Opposite was a bank of French doors that led to a beige stone terrace and rolling lawns, which sloped upward in the direction of the White Tanks Wildlife Refuge. The desert of the refuge was a powerful juxtaposition to the green grass and the dozen or so palo verde trees staggered on that part of the grounds.

To the right, at the north end of the villa, a guesthouse and Olympic-sized pool sat at the entrance to extensive formal gardens. Hundreds of Italian cypresses created various boundaries throughout the grounds, delineating vineyard and winery, from an olive grove and press as well as from the main house and gardens. Medichi sold his wine, olives, and olive oil, but only locally as a hobby.

He read, he studied, he played the piano, and he owned several public gardens throughout the world, including the new hanging gardens of Babylon, reconstructed from the accounts of ascenders over the years, those who had been alive during the height of the Babylonian Empire. His gardens were open to the public, and it was said the combined annual receipts could have funded a small nation for, oh, about a hundred years.

Havily had often wondered why she wasn't more attracted to Antony Medichi, whose education, extraordinary physicality, and careful manners made him the object of overwhelming attention from the female of the species wherever he went. She adored him, of course, as she adored all the warriors. But the spark just wasn't there.

Speaking of sparks . . .

She glanced at Marcus as his gaze traveled over the foyer and moved to look down the southern hall at a series of connected rooms. He whistled as he had earlier at the palace. "Holy shit. Medichi makes me look like a lightweight."

And there it was, Havily thought, the difference that seemed to reach out to her every time she drew near Marcus of Mortal Earth. He was down-to-earth, single-minded, intense, and probably had little interest in collecting art.

When his gaze landed on an impressionist painting on the left wall of the entrance, she said, "Yes, that's an original Monet."

"No shit," he murmured. He drew close and stared. "Huh. I have a few nice pieces myself but . . ."

Havily tried not to smile and at the same time tried to ignore the swell of her heart. "Let me guess. You get turned on by the car photos in magazines—you know, the dark, moody pictures in black and white with the light angled to gleam off sleek sculpted lines and magnesium rims."

He lifted his brows. "I suppose you'll despise me for that."

She shook her head. She even shrugged. "How can I when I subscribe to *Vanity Fair* and *Cosmo* and think that the Paris and New York designers should form a committee to rule Mortal Earth, Vera Wang to serve as their high queen, of course."

He smiled. He even chuckled. "So . . . do you have any idea how we're supposed to locate this mortal-with-wings?"

Havily processed the question and what lay behind it. She had to admit she was surprised: Apparently he didn't think she was a complete moron. What a novel experience.

She nodded. "I do recall an anomaly from Alison's rite of ascension. Thorne mentioned it more than once, and we were all shocked. Even before she ascended, she was so powerful that her signature showed up on the grid, on Mortal Earth." Mortals never showed up on the grid. Ascenders, yes. Mortals, no.

"That's right," Marcus said, nodding. "I remember Medichi talking about it. So you think it might be possible?"

"Why not?" she said. "She's a mortal female *with wings*. That has to indicate an incomprehensible level of power."

"Let's do it then."

Havily pulled out her phone again and touched the screen. "Hey, Jeannie. What would it take to utilize Central's grid for a couple of hours to hunt for a powerful mortal?"

"How powerful?"

"Like Alison."

Jeannie whistled then tapped on the keyboard. "Well, we just have to punch in new searching coordinates. There is a problem, however. We use the grid one hundred percent of the time to scan for death vampires active on Mortal Earth; that way we know where to send the warriors. So what's goin' on?"

Havily explained the mission.

"Wow, a mortal-with-wings. It should work, but I don't have the authority to switch coordinates."

"Can you talk it over with Thorne?" As the leader of the Warriors of the Blood and the one who handed out the assignments every night and generally kept the brothers' activities coordinated, he would be able to say yea or nay.

"You bet. Stay on the line."

"Of course."

Havily moved to the table in the very center of the foyer, a large, round, inlaid piece on a massive pedestal. An artistic arrangement sat in the center of the table composed of stems, dried seedpods, mosses, tall branches, and living magnolia blossoms. The entire edifice was nearly seven feet tall.

Marcus took a tour of the space from the bank of French doors, past the art on each wall, making a complete circuit as Havily kept her phone pressed to her ear and waited. He wore a slight frown.

"I want to do better at this," he said.

"At what?"

Marcus waved an arm around the entire room. "Whatever this is that he does. Collecting maybe. And what the hell is this?" His gaze traveled the height of the floral arrangement. "You know, it looks like a work of art. Are the flowers *alive*?"

"Yes, they are. The flowers are self-generating, which is a more recent Second Earth technological development."

"How?"

"I have no idea. Something to do with the artist herself and her particular ascended power. She goes by the name Tazianne. A real celebrity in the elite horticultural circles." She smiled. "There is one significant problem with the arrangement, however. If Medichi leaves any of the doors open for very long, bees find their way into his house."

Marcus remained near the table, but stayed a few feet away from Havily. She had her phone to her ear, her expression serious as she waited for Jeannie to get back to her with Thorne's response.

So she liked *Vanity Fair*. Well, he loved how she looked, like a page out of the magazine. Somehow the silk navy plaid suited her red hair, which still floated in layers around her shoulders. Her green eyes glittered in the low light of the foyer. Even though she was focused on the event at hand, her scent filled the large space. He took a breath and flared his nostrils, bringing it in.

Oh, God, that smell, like the purest honeysuckle. Of all the aspects of the *breh-hedden* that battered him, this one was the most mysterious, the scents shared only between lovers. He remembered the first time he'd caught her fragrance. He'd arrived on Second Earth, at Endelle's administrative offices, ready to fulfill the vow she'd called in. But when he first entered the place, he'd been struck by a rich honeysuckle, which later turned out to be Havily. He recalled that he kept looking around the administrative office trying to find the source.

He later discovered that Havily had preceded him. She'd been to see Endelle that same night and left her signature

scent behind, a rich bouquet that had worked him up before he even knew the source or the why of it.

The second time her scent had pounded him was at the
Cave. And that was the first time he'd actually seen her.
She'd been surrounded by warriors, then something had occurred to make all of them turn in his direction, and there
she was, a red-haired goddess in a Ralph Lauren suit, staring at him first as though he had sprouted horns and then
as though she'd been struck down by the sight of him.

He'd been hooked since.

So had she.

Right now, especially since they were alone in the house,
if he didn't keep his distance he'd attack her again like he
had at the palace.

His protective instincts were firing off rockets as well.
His senses were on full alert, the way he had felt thousands
of times over all the centuries he had battled as a warrior.
Something was in the wind. The prophecy alone, of the
importance of the mortal-with-wings, had set his warrior
nerves to screaming.

So he breathed and kept a few feet away from her. He also
tried not to look at her. He was so fucking screwed.

"Yes, Jeannie, but hold that thought." She drew her phone
away from her ear and hit the speaker setting. "Warrior
Marcus is listening in. Go ahead."

Jeannie's voice entered the space between them. "Thorne
says to give you top priority. Do you know where we should
start looking?"

"Endelle said anywhere in the Metro Phoenix area."

"It's too bad we can't narrow that down but I'll set the
coordinates right in the middle, near Central and Bethany
Home. How does that sound?"

"As good as anything."

"Stay close to your phone."

"Will do." She tapped the screen and returned the phone
to her pocket.

Now they had to wait. He slung his arms behind his

back and turned away from her; otherwise he didn't trust himself. He could think of a number of things he'd like to do to her while they waited. He'd start with sucking on her neck. Okay, better not think about that.

He glanced into the north hallway. In the distance, beyond what looked like a receiving room with a whole lot of silk chairs and sofas, he spied a massive table with dining chairs designed to accommodate warrior bodies.

He jerked his head in that direction. "Does Medichi keep anything to eat in this joint?"

Havily smiled, that pretty smile of hers. His gaze fell to her lips, then he looked away . . . fast.

She started moving in the direction of the receiving room. "He always keeps his cupboards stocked since he'll have the warriors over at a moment's notice. A month ago they started having the occasional poker game, at dawn of course."

"I could use a bite to eat." He'd prefer to bite her but he kept that to himself.

He let her lead the way, but after a few steps she glanced at him over her shoulder and said, "What's with the fennel?"

"You, Havily Morgan, you're *what's with the fennel*."

He glared at her until she chuckled and started moving again.

At nine thirty Parisa had no desire to get ready for bed. She had enjoyed a dinner of pasta and a fine Cabernet Sauvignon. Clothed in her nightgown, she had relaxed in the private courtyard once more despite the June heat. And yet instead of fatigue finding her, she felt ramped up, totally stimulated, as though forces were at work she couldn't possibly understand.

Her heart beat a little too loudly and her ears rang. She had tried reading, her favorite pastime, but couldn't seem to concentrate and reread each succeeding page of *Anthony Adverse* at least three times before pressing on to the next.

The longing she had felt earlier returned in a broad sweep of sensation, and the small apertures on her back wept anew. She reached behind her—yep, the lace nightgown she wore was now damp.

What a strange life she led.

She was still excited about having jumped earlier from the upper railing and she wanted to fly again, right now. The desire to release her wings came to her, sudden and profound. She slipped the straps of her nightgown off her shoulders one after the other then tugged the lace until it glided over her hips. She stepped out of the gown and draped it across the chaise-longue.

She now stood naked in her private courtyard. She felt a little naughty but she giggled.

She spread her arms wide and closed her eyes. She thought the thought. The muscles and tissues of her back thickened, and the next moment her wings emerged. She let the resulting fiery sensation flood her mind, her chest, her heart. She opened her eyes and smiled. What ease, what bliss, just like . . . well . . . just like an orgasm.

She wanted to fly beneath the warm glow of moonlight. She brought her wings in very close to her body and went inside. She climbed the stairs and once more gained the railing, her wings at their fullest span. She took a deep breath, gave a little squeal and once more leaped.

Ah . . . what bliss . . .

Marcus finally decided to keep his meal with Havily simple, especially since he really couldn't cook. Even after four thousand years he had never had enough interest in fire, skillets, and spatulas to get a decent grip on how to make a meal. He had preferred, until about two hundred years ago, keeping his dagger and sword sharp and hunting death vampires.

He opened the fridge and started pulling things out to make sandwiches.

Havily jumped in and found bread, a fresh loaf of sourdough that needed slicing. She took a serrated knife and started in. Funny how they worked in tandem so easily. He opened a jar of mayo and one of mustard and started slathering. He stacked the meat. She washed lettuce and tomato, did more slicing, and before long he sat next to her on a stool at the same island where they'd prepared the meal.

Two bottles of Dos Equis flanked blue-gray ironstone plates. He grabbed his sandwich with both hands and took a bite. The sandwich was very good and yes, he was hungry. There was, however, one small problem. No matter how strong the flavor of the salami, or how spicy the mustard on his tongue, or how fragrant the sourdough, dammit, all he could smell was honeysuckle. For that reason, with each bite he took, he avoided looking at Havily. Whatever his need for her might be, he was damn hungry right now, and he could use the distraction of chewing and putting food into his empty stomach.

"So, how do you like ascended life?" he asked between bites. "Are you happy here?" He sipped his beer and glanced at her.

She chewed and stared at her sandwich. She dabbed at her mouth with a cloth napkin. "There is so much to be said for this new world," she began. "I feel satisfied here." She put a hand to her chest then sighed. "But I miss my life on Mortal Earth, at least the one I shared with my family."

"Your family?" Oh, this couldn't be good.

She looked at him, her chin lifted slightly. "I was married on Mortal Earth."

He lifted a brow. "You left your husband behind?" Somehow that just didn't fit with his instincts about her character. Havily would never have abandoned her man, an assessment of her essential strength of spirit that drove a spike straight into his heart. *Once committed, Havily would never abandon her man.* Oh, God, this just kept getting worse.

She sighed. He watched her shoulders fall. She picked at a piece of lettuce that had fallen to her plate. "Scarlet fever went through Vancouver Island and took him."

"I'm sorry."

"Me, too. He was such a joy. A really good man."

And very different from me, he thought. "What was his name?"

"Duncan Morgan. We had a farm, the most beautiful farm with dry-stone walls to keep the sheep in their pastures, turnstiles like the old country."

"So Morgan is your married name."

"Yes."

"No children?"

She paused and set her sandwich on her plate. He had a feeling she wouldn't be picking it up again. "Three daughters. Three beautiful little girls, all of them with the sweetest red hair." The words were quiet and fell like stones. Shit.

He was silent as he chewed. His thoughts whirred in his head. He knew the answer to the question he was certain he shouldn't ask, yet not to ask seemed rude, even insensitive. "Did you lose them at the same time?" The room felt suddenly shrouded in fog, the kind that dampened all noise.

He heard the choppy breath she took. "Yes." The word disappeared into the fog.

Jesus. What did he say now? "They must have been young."

"Yes. Very. We buried them on the farm. I wanted them near me. Then Duncan took sick and three days later he was . . . gone, too."

He set his sandwich down as well and turned toward her. He saw the stiffness in her jaw and shoulders and he knew a sudden truth about her. "You haven't told anyone here, on Second Earth, have you?"

She met his gaze. She shook her head.

"Why not?"

Her lips parted. A frown wrinkled the small space between her brows. She released a sigh. "I don't know. I'm not even sure why I told you but now that I have, given how old you are, and how alone you are in the world, I suspect you've had your own losses."

Not to share also seemed insensitive. "Through the centuries, yes. I had three wives. One divorced me and I don't know what became of her. Death vampires took my first and third wives. As for the children, one ascended to Third. I think about him, wondering what his life is, hoping he's still alive." He smiled suddenly. "I hope he is and I hope he's happy."

"I'm sorry about your families."

"And of course you know about Helena."

"Kerrick's wife, your sister."

"Yes." He looked away from her. Shit, his heart hurt just thinking about her, and it had been two hundred years. Would that wound ever heal, ever really heal?

She put her hand on his arm. "Tell me about her."

He took a sip of Dos Equis. The bottle clinked on the granite when he set it down. "You would have loved her but then everyone did. God, she was like sunshine. No matter how bad everything got, she could walk into a room and light up the dullest day.

"Maybe losing her was so hard because she was the last of my family left here on Second Earth. I'd come to rely on her. We were always in each other's houses, which meant of course that Kerrick was around her a lot. So of course he fell in love with her. I suppose it was just a matter of time." He still held the bottle of beer in his grip. He thumbed the condensation up and down.

"I don't think the warriors believed me when I said I'd kill Kerrick, but I would have. I was that crazed when she died." He glanced at her, saw the stricken look in her eye, and shunted his glance away. But he kept talking. She ought to know the worst about him. "I would have killed him because his marriage to Helena had gotten her killed. I'd begged him over and over not to marry her. I begged them both.

"I know you think I'm a worthless deserter. Maybe I am, but if I hadn't left that day, I would have killed him. And I was sick of it, all of it, of the battling without end, that my sister and her children died in that horrible explosion, and of Greaves's endless moves and countermoves.

"I snapped and I knew it. I think Endelle knew it, too. I think she knew I had to leave. Of course she yelled at me, but we'd known each other a long time and she didn't try very hard to prevent me from going. She only asked one thing of me—that if she needed me to come back, I would. Which I did four months ago." He looked at her and held her gaze. "And now I'm here again."

Without thinking too much, he leaned toward her and captured her lips with his own. She didn't retreat; instead she kissed him back, a tender action that surprised him, almost as though she expressed gratitude rather than desire.

This journey with her had taken a sudden sharp turn. She had borne children and lost them, not to a war as Kerrick had, or as he had lost a beloved sister, niece, and nephew, but to the diseased imperfect nature of Mortal Earth existence. Nor had she shared this information with anyone else. They were both intensely private people, one more similarity that seemed to be binding his heart to hers. So . . . yeah . . . shit.

Her phone chimed. She picked it up but held it between them, the speaker function still on. "Hi, Jeannie," she said.

"We've got her. A house in north Peoria and she's in full-mount."

"Right now? She's in full-mount right now?"

"You know what that means. If Greaves doesn't have her yet, he will soon. You ready to go?"

She dipped her chin to Marcus. He nodded. She took his hand.

"We're ready."

*Is there a vampire on Second Earth who does
not lead a double life?*

—From *Treatise on Ascension,* by Philippe Reynard

CHAPTER 11

Parisa stood in the courtyard, just outside the open sliders.
Her wings were fully emerged and she reveled in the cool
breeze that wafted from the air-conditioned house over her
naked body and into the warm dry outdoor air.

She had gone up and down the stairs and launched off
the railing about a dozen times. She figured it was time to
end her romp since her legs were trembling from so many
jogs through the house, up the staircase, up the stepladder,
and onto the railing, followed by a frightening yet exhila-
rating launch.

She could not have been happier and she felt incredibly
free doing the whole thing without a stitch of clothes on.

She was about to begin the process of drawing her wings
back into her body when she felt the air change within the
courtyard, as though another kind of breeze had blown
through.

A moment later, much to her shock, a man and woman, very stylish in their manner of dress, appeared as though having been beamed down from the starship *Enterprise*. What's more, she knew who they were from her visions that weren't visions.

The woman was Havily Morgan, a Liaison Officer whom she had seen most recently being comforted by Warrior Medichi. The man, who stood gawking at her bare chest, was Warrior Marcus. She had not seen him for months but recognized him even though his dark hair had been much shorter then.

Despite all that, she still asked, "Who . . . who are you?"

The woman, Havily, took a step toward her. "I know you must be frightened, but—"

"You're Havily Morgan and the man is Warrior Marcus. I know you both." Her gaze shifted back and forth between them. They glanced at each other then back to her.

"You know us?" Havily asked.

"Yes, Warrior Marcus was here several months ago for a few days while Alison Wells went through her ascension ceremony. Havily, I know you to be a good friend to Warrior Medichi." She put a hand to her head. She felt dizzy. Was this happening? Had these two worlds suddenly collided?

Havily took another step toward her. Her eyes were narrowed. "I beg your pardon, but you speak as though you're ascended."

Parisa shook her head. "No. At least I don't think so. I live here on Mortal Earth, but I have wings like Second Earth."

"But how do you know about Second Earth?"

"Visions," she said, but her voice sounded hushed.

"Visions?"

Parisa nodded. "I see things, so clearly. For instance, I recently saw how Warrior Medichi comforted you because you had been attacked."

"You saw that? How?"

Parisa shrugged. "I see things, mostly connected with Warrior Medichi."

The woman, Havily, let her gaze drift over Parisa's wings.

"Marcus, look at the wings. Do you see what I'm seeing?"

"I noticed."

"I've seen pictures of the ancients of thousands of years ago. There are portraits of many early ascenders who had similar wings. It's astonishing. There's even a portrait of Luchianne with these wings. These are *royle* wings."

For a long moment, both of her visitors stared at her wings as though awestruck. "What does *royal* mean?" she asked.

"It's not *royal* as in *the royal family*," Havily explained. "It's an ancient word, *royle*." She spelled it for her. "The literal translation is 'benevolent wind,' and it has spiritual significance in ascended culture." She smiled suddenly. "This must sound like gibberish to you."

Parisa blinked.

When the woman's gaze drifted to Parisa's breasts, Parisa remembered that essentially she stood naked before two strangers. Yet it didn't seem to faze her. Was she in shock? The man also stared at her breasts.

She looked down as well, seeing but not seeing, aware but not aware. Yep, she was in shock. "I must be hallucinating," she murmured, but she looked at her wings, the right one first, then the left. Her wings were real and so were the people in front of her and she knew them.

She glanced at Havily but the woman now glared at Warrior Marcus. "Are you looking at her breasts?" she cried. "For God's sake, why do you have to be such a guy right now."

He grinned ruefully, but he turned around.

Parisa shook her head. "It's just so strange. I mean, I knew the visions I had were real but it's still so different to have you standing here."

Havily moved the final few steps toward her until she

stood just two feet away. She also shielded her from Warrior Marcus even though he remained with his back to them both. "You're not hallucinating," Havily said, "but you are in danger. I take it you know something of our world?"

"Yes."

"You know we're at war?"

"Yes." She then expounded on her visions, which had revealed the dimensional world of Second Earth over the past year. "Does this mean I've been called to ascension?"

The Liaison Officer lifted her brows. "I . . . I don't know. I guess that's something we'll have to discuss, although I find it hard to believe that you're not called if *you* are able to tell *me* all about Second Earth. The problem is, this isn't the traditional order of events."

Parisa nodded then shook her head. "I just hope I don't have to fight in an arena like Alison."

"Okay. Wow. You really have seen a lot of our world."

Parisa's pulse quickened, and her mouth grew dry. "Can you tell me something?"

"Anything."

"Well, is Warrior Medichi as tall as he looks?"

Havily laughed. "Yes. He's six-seven."

"Uh, ladies?" Warrior Marcus called out. "Just want to remind you we might have a time crunch here since the enemy is on the hunt for a mortal-with-wings."

"Right," Havily called back.

Parisa looked down again. "You know, I really am naked, aren't I?"

"Maybe you could fold some clothes on? You know what *fold* means, right?"

"To materialize, but I've actually never tried it before. I don't think I can."

"Well, that doesn't matter. Let's get you dressed and then we'll figure out what to do next. But first, go ahead and draw in your wings."

Parisa nodded. She tried to relax but found that her heart was pounding. She took a deep breath and focused on her wings . . . and nothing happened. "I don't think I can, at least not yet. I'm kind of freaked out here."

"Don't worry. I'm sure we've caused you emotional distress, and the mounting of wings or retracting is often affected by our emotions. Try to take a few deep breaths. In the meantime, tell me your name?"

"Parisa," she said, dragging air into her lungs. "Parisa Lovejoy."

"Well, it's very nice to meet you, Parisa Lovejoy. I'm Havily Morgan and this is Warrior Marcus Amargi, Second Earth, though lately of Mortal Earth."

Parisa might have offered a word of welcome, but at that moment a man materialized several feet away from Warrior Marcus. He was tall and fierce-looking with long black hair and startling blue eyes. He wore the familiar warrior battle gear of black leather kilt, heavy black sandals, and weapons harness. She recognized him from her visions of four months ago, from Alison's arena battle.

"Warrior Leto," she said, stunned.

"Oh, my god," Havily cried.

A second later, swords flashed into each hand and the sound of metal on metal rang through the small courtyard.

Crace stared down at the grid he'd just turned back on. He hated General Leto. He hated him in a way that made his eyes bulge and threaten to burst into flames.

Leto had sent a message to the forge, letting Crace know that he'd found the mortal-with-wings, but then he'd left the war room at exactly the same time, getting a head start on Crace. Several of the generals had confirmed Leto's moves. According to witnesses, Leto had sent the message then dematerialized.

Crace knew exactly where he'd gone—in pursuit of the mortal-with-wings. He wanted the glory for himself, the chance to win favor with Greaves. Worse, when Crace realized Leto had folded and where he'd headed, he'd tried to follow after him but found his trace blocked. *Blocked!* Jesus H. Christ, Crace's head was about to explode.

So Leto had gotten a head start then had deliberately switched the coordinates on the grid to throw him off the scent. Goddammit. Crace had made a tactical error trusting Leto, but he had a few tricks of his own. He tapped on the keyboard, and the grid returned to the former position. Yep, there was the location with four strong signatures. *Four.*

Only then, as Crace stared down at the glowing lights, did his temper calm down as his heart fired up. Adrenaline streaked through his chest and his pecs twitched. Three powerful ascenders were with the mortal woman, and the mortal woman was a dynamo of power, hence her signature. One of the signatures would of course belong to Leto, but what about the other two? Undoubtedly, Endelle had sent a Warrior of the Blood to protect the ascendiate, but was it possible the final signature belonged to a certain red-haired Liaison Officer?

Crace smiled. His biceps flexed and he swiveled his neck to give his spine a good crack. He closed his eyes and breathed in hard through his nose. Was she there, the woman he'd come to think of as his *personal blood donor*?

Goddamn, she sure as hell could be, since Endelle would have naturally sent a top Liaison Officer to tend to such a powerful ascendiate. Wouldn't that just make his century if ascender Morgan was there? Holy shit.

He narrowed his gaze and determined exactly what he would do if his conjecture proved correct. He didn't give a fuck about the mortal-with-wings or Greaves's plans for world domination. He would fold to the location on the grid and if Havily Morgan was present, as he believed she was, then Leto could keep on fighting whatever warrior was there and he'd take care of the women. Hell, if he could get to both of them, well, that would be a cherry on top of this sundae.

He imprinted the coordinates into his brain, thought the thought, and the vibration began.

Havily couldn't get Parisa calmed down enough to retract her wings. Her own heart rate had kicked up in response, which wasn't helping.

She had ushered the mortal into the hallway, away from the courtyard and the battle of the two warriors, who had been clanging swords for the past few minutes. But they could still see and hear what was going on through the glass doors and windows. The whole time, she had talked quietly to Parisa and rubbed her arms and tried to get her to focus on her need to draw in her wings, but the woman couldn't.

Not that Havily blamed her. First, two unknown beings had showed up in her patio, then a third arrived—General Leto—in full leather-kilt-and-harness battle gear and started fighting Marcus with a sword. Of course, the weird thing was that Parisa knew them all, even Leto. Nor did the mortal-with-wings seem at all surprised by the presence of swords and subsequent fighting.

Leto's appearance, however, had reminded Havily that she needed to get Parisa to Second Earth, to Warrior Medichi's protected villa, *right now.* The enemy knew their location and Leto had even shouted a warning that more would follow.

The rest she could deal with, as in why Parisa knew who she was and what potential significance there might be to the woman having *royle* wings. Wow, *royle* wings.

Okay . . . focus.

But until Parisa drew her wings in, she would be unable to have Jeannie fold them through the dimension. Wings were just too fragile to make the trip.

"Please try again," Havily said. She even took Parisa's hand this time and squeezed.

However, instead of making an effort, Parisa's eyes widened as her gaze shifted to the courtyard and she gasped.

Havily turned and couldn't hold back a shriek of her own. There, beyond the warring men, was Crace, the death vampire who had attacked her in her town house, the monster who had taken her blood and wrecked her throat. He wore only a black leather kilt and battle sandals. He looked eerily pale—as he should, given his nature—and his dark hair hung uncombed almost to his shoulders. He was more monster now than High Administrator.

"Is he the one who drank from you?" Parisa cried.

Havily just looked at her. "You know about that?"

"I saw Warrior Medichi talking to you and comforting you."

Havily nodded. "Yes, he is the one, and he is really dangerous. Parisa. We have to get out of here. Now."

"I don't know what to do!" Parisa cried. She shook now, head to foot. "I just can't seem to make the wings retreat."

"You have to stop looking and listening. Warrior Marcus will take care of General Leto and Crace." But Parisa was wild-eyed, which was completely understandable. "Calm yourself down. Think of other things."

Havily started shoving Parisa in the direction of the south-facing rooms, but Crace caught sight of them. His gaze, now lowered, was not in any way directed toward Parisa, but was fixed on Havily. She shuddered, for in that moment she understood his intent—and it had nothing to do with the woman in front of her.

Havily took a deep breath and turned toward Parisa. She took both her hands and looked into her eyes. "Okay," she murmured. "Let's try something else. Do you have a boyfriend, someone you can focus on?"

"Oh. Yes, I do. I . . . I have *someone*."

"Good. Then focus on *him*. Think of being with him, of speaking with him, of having his arms around you. Pretend they're around you right now."

Crace lifted an arm. Oh, shit, he was dematerializing, which meant he would be next to them both in three . . . two . . .

Creator help us!

Parisa seemed to fall into the image with her entire being, and before Havily blinked Parisa's wings flew back through her wing-locks. The moment they did, Havily thought the thought, with Crace only a few yards away and reaching for the mortal. She couldn't take her far, not in this situation, so she landed in Parisa's backyard, right next to the pool. She drew her phone from her pocket and made a swift call to Central.

"Pick up, pick up, pick up," she muttered, hopping from one foot to the next still holding Parisa's hand. The trouble was, Crace would be able to follow them since the act of folding left behind a pathway of light, a trace, which any powerful ascender could follow. And yes, Crace had enough power, which meant she had only a few seconds to get this done.

"Jeannie here."

"Jeannie," she cried. "I've got the mortal. Send us to the villa now!" She screamed the words because Crace had materialized ten feet away from them. He smiled as he ran, but the next moment she stood with Parisa in Medichi's foyer.

She shook all over but she punched her phone. "Jeannie, we made it, but is there any chance Crace can follow us?"

"No chance in hell. Her Supremeness misted the villa. The mist will block the trace."

Havily finally released Parisa's hand. "Thank you. Thank you so much." She put her hands over her face and let a few tears leak out of her eyes. She had so much adrenaline in her system that she couldn't stop the tears or the shaking.

"Are you okay?" Parisa asked.

Havily felt the mortal's hand on her shoulder.

At that, she pulled herself together, because it was absolutely the most absurd thing in the world for a mortal human, who had just been dematerialized . . . *twice* . . . and brought to an unknown house in a different dimension to be consoling Havily.

"I'm sorry," she said, giving her head a shake. "But Crace is a monster and he would have hurt us both. I'm sorry I lost it. I'll try to do better."

Parisa nodded. She was looking white-faced and she was still completely naked. "So, what just happened? How did we get here?" She turned in a circle. She murmured, "I know this place."

"I called our Central Command, which has the ability to do jumps between dimensions. We call it folding, otherwise known as dematerialization. You are now officially in the Second Dimension. How do you feel? Any dizziness? Nausea?" Sometimes mortals didn't have a good reaction to Second Earth and had to be sequestered on Mortal Earth until the rite of ascension drew to a close.

Parisa, however, just shrugged. "Actually, this feels really wonderful, almost like . . . home. And I'm smelling . . . sage. A lot of sage."

"Herbs from the kitchen, maybe." She was distracted as she thought of Crace—and of Marcus possibly battling both Crace and Leto alone. She wasn't sure what she needed to do next, but she still had her link to Medichi. She used it now.

How strange to feel the tendrils that reached out for the powerful warrior. When she felt the connection touch him, she sent, *Marcus needs help. Leto and Crace attacking at the following location.* She then streamed the image of the house through the link, which in terms of ascenders locating a place worked as well as coordinates laid out on Central's grid.

On my way, came back to her in a rush of sensation, of power, of determination. He was in full warrior mode, which was to be expected since at this hour, nearing ten o'clock, he had been battling death vampires for at least two hours.

"Thank God," she murmured. She could only trust that Medichi would arrive in time to support Marcus against the two powerful vampires.

She glanced at Parisa, still nude.

Well, this was one problem she could solve right away. She might not be able to retrieve Parisa's clothes, but she could bring some of her own to the villa.

She moved to the large central table and brought an assortment of pants and shirts, even underwear from her dresser and closet, folding the pieces one after the other onto the table. "I think you should be able to wear some of these. We look to be about the same size."

The woman stared down at the pile. "How clever," she said. There was something of the intrigued scientist in her voice.

"You know, for someone who has just been introduced to a new dimension, you're taking all of this really well."

Parisa grabbed a black silk thong and stepped into it. "I don't know about that. I think I must be in shock. Yes, probably shock." She made use of one of Havily's bras, but her breasts overflowed the top. The woman had to be at least a double D. She quickly dove into a pair of jeans and a purple sequined tank top meant more for clubbing than fleeing from the Commander's henchmen, but the combination looked good on her.

Parisa blinked at her from a pair of beautiful amethyst eyes, the same color that she had witnessed on her wings. A faint smile drifted over her lips. "On the other hand, from the visions I've had, I've already seen a great deal of this world already and I know the men. I know Warrior Marcus from before, as I said, and Warrior Medichi, of course." She blushed as she said his name. "I know that something happened to Warrior Luken and that both he and Warrior Medichi are worried about his back, about his wings, I think."

Havily nodded, then told her about the attack on Luken at the Superstitions.

"Oh, God." Parisa started, a whole-body jerk, and her fingers flew to her lips. "I once tried to pluck a feather. I couldn't believe the streaks of pain that followed. I can't imagine what it must have felt like to be burned. But he looked perfectly well when I saw him in my . . . vision . . . in the hospital. How did he survive?"

"The ascended world is a world of near-immortality. Only the most brutal of events can take the life of an ascender. In all other situations, we heal miraculously."

"Oh." Her gaze shifted and then she sort of crumpled, dropping to sit down on the planked floor as though her legs simply wouldn't hold her up any longer.

Well, finally. A normal reaction.

Marcus smiled. He battled with his sword like the warrior he had been all those centuries ago. He and Medichi had Leto backed up into a ficus tree.

Leto had been a good friend to Marcus, a drinking buddy, in times gone by. Now he was a goddamn traitor— something he still found hard to believe.

The women had long since dematerialized, hopefully to Medichi's villa. Crace was gone as well. So now there was just the traitor to take care of.

Again Marcus smiled. And Medichi smiled. Because it was only a matter of time before they finished Leto off, but shit, the warrior was still an amazing swordsman.

Marcus pressed from the left. Medichi from the right. Swords clanged. Marcus felt a punch to his right side but ignored the sensation and attacked. Suddenly Marcus's sword hit what felt like a wall, his arm jarred from the vibration of the strike, but he wasn't anywhere near something that solid.

Fuck. Leto had cast one helluva shield. Who the hell could do that? He sure as hell couldn't. He struck again and was rewarded with another painful stinging vibration shooting straight up his arm. "What the fuck!" he shouted.

Medichi did the same and came away cursing with pain and holding his sword elbow with his other palm. "What the hell is that, traitor? A fucking shield? You afraid to fight, you goddamn motherfucker?"

Marcus stared hard at Leto. The bastard was sweating and breathing hard but then they all were. He looked from one to the other. "Nice to see you again, assholes, but I need you to get a message to Endelle. Tell her that there's a party planned for the Ambassadors Festival. Watch the skies."

"What *party,* you fucking traitor?"

But that was all Leto would say. He gave Marcus a wide smile, all teeth, flipped him off, then vanished.

Marcus turned to Medichi, who was still holding his elbow.

"What the fuck was that all about?" Medichi let go of his sword-arm and gave it a shake. He was breathing hard. He glanced at Marcus, at his abdomen. "Hey. You're bleeding."

Marcus felt the warm trickle and looked at his side. Leto had sliced him, deep and all the way through. As though acknowledging the blood had opened a floodgate, suddenly he felt the pain. "Aw, fuck."

Medichi bent over at the waist, catching his breath. "It doesn't look too bad. I've got to get back to New River. You know New River, that place where I'm doing that job you refuse to do?"

Marcus found breathing difficult. He wanted to flip him off but couldn't. He now braced his abdomen with his arm. As Medichi lifted up from the waist, Marcus asked, "How the hell did you know to come over here? Did Thorne send you?"

"Nope."

"Then how did you know?" Shit, his side had really started to hurt, and now he was bent over.

Medichi grinned. "Well, asshole, you're just going to have to find that out for yourself. But I guarantee you one thing, when you do find out, you ain't gonna like it." He tapped his forehead, laughed, then lifted his arm and vanished.

Marcus shouted obscenities after him or at least tried

to. What the hell did Medichi mean by that? Or was he just fucking with his head?

He clutched his side. Blood poured down his abdomen. His pants were getting soaked. Shit.

Whatever.

He folded his sword back to Bainbridge.

He needed his wound tended to and he also needed to get back to Havily and the mortal-with-wings. He'd seen them fold out of the house just before Crace got to either of them. Damn, his woman was good.

Oh, man, he couldn't breathe. He'd also need a boost through the dimension and oh, shit, it was going to hurt even more because of the sword slice. *Shit.*

He called Jeannie at Central. First things first. "Did Havily call you? Are the women okay?"

"Yep. She has the mortal at the villa."

"Good." He was panting now.

"What's wrong, *duhuro*?"

He didn't have the energy to argue with her over her form of address. "I got cut and I need a lift to the villa. Can you get me there?"

"Damn straight, but I gotta warn you, the pain will be worse."

"I know," Marcus whispered. "Just do it."

"Feel better. I'll send Horace."

"Thanks."

The vibration struck and as he moved through nether-space he knew he was screaming. When he landed in the entrance near Havily and a now-clothed mortal, he was still shouting like a sonofabitch. Words poured out of his mouth, inappropriate words, but the hell if he could hold them back.

He landed on his feet but fell to the floor and writhed. He forgot how bad it hurt to fold with a wound like this. Sonofabitch. He breathed hard. Sweat poured off his body. He lay on his back and hit the planked floor with one hand over and over. With the other, he held the wound at his side.

He felt a hand on his arm. When had Havily dropped down next to him?

"You're wounded."

"Yep. Horace on the way." He took one more deep breath then passed out.

Havily knelt beside Marcus as blood pooled from his waist. The cornflower-blue silk shirt he wore was torn and bloodied.

Horace didn't come.

He didn't come.

Where the hell was he?

Marcus moaned. Havily put her hand on his shoulder very gently. His eyes opened, but they looked wild with pain.

"Horace isn't here yet," she said, "and I know my blood can help. Will you take it?"

He nodded.

She put her wrist to her mouth and with her right fang made a nice suicide cut across all the veins. The sting of it hurt but based on what had happened when Marcus drank from her, she knew her blood would help heal him. She put her wrist against his lips and let him taste.

His eyes popped wide and, as though she'd offered an elixir of Olympian quality, he moaned and started taking deep pulls.

She heard Parisa gasp.

Havily turned in her direction and shrugged. "I might have forgotten to mention that Second Earth is also the world of the vampire."

Parisa nodded. "I knew that." She was still sitting on the floor. She stared at the joined wrist and mouth and put her hand on her neck. Her lips parted and the color on her cheeks turned pink, but not in embarrassment.

Havily looked away. Yes, the suckling motion, and the

exchange of blood to mouth, all spoke of a more intimate connection. She wasn't surprised that Parisa rose to her feet and without a word left the room.

So this really is the world of the vampire.

Parisa left the foyer, but once she entered the expansive formal living room, out of sight of Havily and Marcus, she turned swiftly to lean against the wall. She closed her eyes and took deep breaths. She put two fingers to her neck right above the vein. She hadn't been disgusted or even distressed by the blood-taking. It had seemed . . . natural . . . but very erotic.

In her visions of Warrior Medichi, Parisa had once seen him take a woman's blood. He'd been in some kind of club with red velvet booths and loud music and he'd taken a woman into one of the booths. He'd sucked blood from her neck while he'd made love to her and the whole time Parisa had wished she had been beneath his big warrior body. She was embarrassed by the memory, not because of what he'd done but because instead of retreating, she'd kept her special vision open and had watched the whole thing from start to finish.

She was such a voyeur.

Now she was here, in his home.

She hadn't told Havily, but she recognized this house. She had seen Warrior Medichi here many times before.

Many times.

She pushed away from the wall because she could still hear the suckling sounds. She moved into the room full of heavy antique sofas and chairs covered in cream silk. Large woven rugs anchored the furniture and olive-green silk panels flanked the windows at both the east and west sides of the room.

She needed separation from the oh-so-intimate contact going on in the next room. She sighed. How could she explain what it was she felt right now? From the moment she had entered Warrior Medichi's villa she had been overcome, not by fear, but by lust, pure, heavy, saturated lust that kept her sex in an uproar. She caught the scent of sweet sage everywhere and had to conclude that since this was Medichi's home, the sage smell must belong to him. Perhaps he used the spice a lot when he cooked. Whatever it was, her body loved it.

"Better?" she heard Havily say.

"Much," Marcus responded.

The sounds of their voices, so tender, forced Parisa to move on, deeper into the house, one step in front of the other. She knew exactly where she was going.

She crossed the room and found herself in a second but much smaller foyer. A rectangular oak table sat in the center of the space.

Branching off from this smaller connecting room was a wing that faced west; a window down the hall gave a view of a rolling lawn and mountains beyond. She had never seen Warrior Medichi go into these rooms during one of her visions. She supposed these might be guest rooms.

The villa hallway stretched to the south, and she knew that the warrior's private suite of rooms formed the entire southern wing of the house. Yes, she had been inside this suite of rooms in her visions as well. She felt a profound desire to explore them but squeezed her eyes shut and forced herself to set aside such invasive thoughts. She had no right to enter his rooms.

So she headed to the one room that made sense. To the east, opposite the supposed suite of guest rooms, was one very large room—the library. She had seen Medichi in this room numerous times as well. She was, after all, a librarian by trade.

She crossed to the arched doorway, and the smell of leather and sage drew her in. She couldn't imagine a more erotic combination than what greeted her. A love of books was in her blood, deep, passionate, ages old, so that she would have loved this room no matter whom it belonged to. But smelling that rich sage scent embedded in all this leather nearly sent her crumpling to the floor all over again.

She let the overwhelming sensation move through her. She breathed . . . a lot . . . then swept her gaze over what was a magnificent chamber. Leather-bound books rose all the way to the ceiling along wall after wall after wall. She moved in a circle and blinked. The room was lit in a soft glow, the lamps throughout the house already on—or perhaps had come on once they arrived, she couldn't remember.

But she wanted to see better so she searched for and found the light switch. She turned the dimmer mechanism. The room gradually flooded with light, directed downward from the ceiling, and a choir of angels began to sing . . . at least in her head.

She searched the shelves on the left and found an edition of *Pride and Prejudice,* no doubt an early edition. If the potential of immortality was part of life on Second Earth, just how old was Warrior Medichi? Was it possible he had purchased all of these books when each had first been published?

She took the treasured volume and moved slowly to a group of massive leather chairs, the size suited for big warrior bodies. The rich sage smell of the house rose up from one chair in particular. She drank in the scent. In her visions, she had seen Warrior Medichi sit here more than once.

She settled into the deep cushion of the chair and was immediately engulfed with what she now believed to be the warrior's scent. Her heart beat a furious cadence, one coupled with profound desire of a sexual nature, yes, but something more. No, this desire crossed the boundaries of the body into the deep places of the soul. She found herself, as she had so many times before during the past year, in a state of profound longing that caused tears to pour down her face as she pressed a hand to her breast.

She had come home.

Those were the thoughts that moved through her, beat

at her, caused the tears to flow so fast she had to set the book aside. The purple sequins could not in any way absorb the tears so she used her fingers, her palm, the back of her hand until a single thought brought her up short and the tears ceased.

She was a woman who had learned to live her solitary life, and she'd gotten so good at it that she never needed anyone. Long before she had released her wings for the first time, she had become comfortable with her isolated world.

When she was a child, she had moved a lot. Her parents used to joke about their itchy feet; changing cities, homes, and schools was the order of the day. Because of it, Parisa had learned early on that making friends with other children meant leaving them all too soon because of yet another move to another city.

The losses had soon taught her to keep to herself, a state she had never really minded. She had simply accepted the reality of her life. Books had become her refuge.

Later, when her wings had emerged, when she had begun having her special visions of Warrior Medichi, she had understood the value of all those early solitary lessons. She had even been grateful for them, since she could never have explained wings to another mortal.

What she hadn't planned, however, was that one day she would actually step into this new world. Now what was she supposed to do?

She took a deep breath and with a will she had developed from childhood, she pushed all the longings away. She moved from her heart into her head and started analyzing her current situation.

She had come to a new world, the world of the vampire, and yes she felt, *she knew,* she belonged here. She had even had the most erotic fantasies of letting Warrior Medichi take her at her neck.

However, this was also a world at war, and clearly *Warrior* Medichi played a constant part in that war. His death, therefore, was no doubt an eventuality. Ascenders died in this extraordinary world even though they were in most respects immortal, although that was an oxymoron if she'd ever heard one. How could anyone be immortal *in most respects.*

Whatever.

She might have a sense of having come home, but did she really want to ascend to a world so full of battle, of death vampires, and an enemy that threatened even the women of this world?

She rose from his chair and went in search of a bathroom. She found one en suite in a bedroom opposite the library. She grabbed a tissue from the counter, blew her nose, then wiped her face. Afterward, she crossed to the bed and sat down on the edge. She took deep breaths until she began to grow calm. She would need a clear head from this point forward to be able to chart her course. She didn't understand her life right now or what was expected of her.

She was here, in a new dimension, a place called Second Earth, a world of the vampire, of immortality, of war.

Her thoughts flew to images of Warrior Medichi in all the ways she had known him through her strange visions. Because of what he was in this world, she couldn't allow herself to become attached to him.

He was after all, a Warrior of the Blood, and his service to his world had only one likely end: He would fall by the sword as he had lived by the sword.

The last thing Parisa needed was to become involved with someone destined, no doubt, to die.

How proud she was of her analytical mind.

The myth of the breh-hedden *lives in the hearts of all vampires.*

—*Collected Proverbs,* Beatrice of Fourth

CHAPTER 12

Marcus released Havily's wrist unwillingly. The power of her blood worked in him now and thank God the mortal had left because his desire to engage Havily in some hard-core sex was like a jackhammer at the base of his brain. He was rock-hard and in need.

That his wound felt better was not a surprise given the powerful nature of Havily's blood, but he still required Horace's healing hands, the sooner the better.

Still, he licked his lips, savoring the honeysuckle flavor of Havily's blood. He was breathing in gasps and not from pain.

He palmed the back of her neck. "Come here," he whispered.

"Marcus . . . no. We have a guest in the house."

"She went down the hall. We're good." He didn't care whether they were good or not. Bad sounded really good. He tugged, pulling her toward him.

"You're injured," she said, but her tone had a lovely whimpering quality.

He tugged again. "Kiss me anyway." And she followed, her mouth on his in sweet surrender.

He breathed in her scent through his nose and at the same time tasted more of her honeysuckle flavor from her lips. He strengthened the hold on her neck and pressed so he could thrust his tongue and let her feel what he wanted to do to her.

She responded with a moan.

"I love your blood," he whispered. "I love you here like this and thank you for taking care of me."

"You feel better?"

"A thousand percent."

"Good."

However, a shimmering next to him put him in full warrior mode. He completely forgot about his wound and his aroused state.

He pushed Havily away as he sat up and at the same time folded his sword back from Bainbridge Island into his hand.

But holy mother of God. He grabbed his abdomen with his free hand and arm then rolled onto his side groaning. He had so many problems right now and so much pain he could barely function. His stupid arousal was bent and hurting like a bitch, he didn't have the strength or ability to face the enemy and protect his woman, and if anyone touched his identified sword they were toast, including Havily.

Fortunately, the intruder was only Horace, the gifted healer who worked the Borderlands all night, taking care of the Warriors of the Blood.

"Don't touch me," he cried. It wasn't pain that made him cry out but the dangers of his sword. If anyone touched the hilt, they'd die.

He leaned on his side and panted, his sword shaking in his hand. Shit, he was useless, so thank fuck it was only

Horace or his woman would be dead. At least his arousal had dimmed. Jesus, he was a mess.

Though Horace knelt beside him, he held his hands in the air in the universal sign of surrender. "Deal with your sword, Warrior Marcus." Even the healer's voice had a strange soothing quality.

All his fears eased, and the tension left his muscles. He folded his sword back to his Bainbridge house.

Relieved of the burden, he flopped onto his back and closed his eyes. He could hardly breathe. The pain in his side sent bolts of lightning through his body. Shit.

Then he felt Horace's healing touch and, with his hands held directly above the wound, the pain began to ebb immediately. Thank. God.

Horace never touched the wound directly but merely stationed his hands above Marcus's side and let his energy flow from his hands into the deep cut. Every second that passed eased more of the pain as his flesh began knitting together.

"Horace?"

"Yes, *duhuro*."

Marcus smiled at the ancient form of address, even if he didn't deserve it. He'd deserted his brothers-in-arms. He didn't deserve anything from the healer. "I can't remember when I first met you. Seems like you've been serving the warriors from the time I ascended. Has it been that long? When did you ascend? Was it before me?"

"Yes. Now, please, sir, let me concentrate."

"Right. Of course." So Horace was over four thousand years old. Now, why didn't that surprise him?

Havily rose and moved into the south wing, probably to check on Parisa who had headed that direction a few minutes ago. A few minutes later, Havily crossed behind him as she passed beneath the arched opening that led to the opposite room, then into the dining room. His gaze followed her, hungry, grateful, obsessed. In the distance he watched her leave the dining room, which meant she had probably gone into the kitchen. The doors were offset, so there wasn't a direct view from the foyer into the kitchen, a very nice arrangement.

A few minutes later she came back with a damp rag and a couple of dry ones. He wondered what for but without saying a word, she dropped to her knees, this time to the right of him, and started cleaning the floor. The white rags turned red.

"This isn't going to work," she murmured. She rose to her feet and headed back to the kitchen. She came back with a bucket of water, a sponge, and more clean rags.

As Horace worked, she stayed with her chore. She probably could have called Jeannie for cleanup, but instinctively he knew what Havily would say, that she didn't want to do anything to interfere with the warriors on duty. And she was right.

When Horace tipped him on his side to work on the hole in his back, he could hear the drop and squeeze of the sponge in the bucket and the soft slide against the floor. She worked quietly, steadily. There was something soothing about these small ministrations.

Oddly, his thoughts turned to Leto. During the past decades, the former warrior had developed some serious skills. He knew Alison was capable of throwing physical shields like that but he hadn't known Leto could, which made him wonder. Leto had fought Alison in an arena battle four months ago, a terrible engagement that Greaves had orchestrated and COPASS had supported. Alison had won that contest against Leto by casting a similar shield around herself. So why hadn't Leto done the same? Why had he put himself in Alison's power? Leto hadn't held back during the actual battle with swords, and more than once Marcus had been sure Alison would get skewered before she even ascended to Second Earth. Leto couldn't have faked his intent to make her dead.

But he had held back at least some of his powers. That

much was clear, which led Marcus back to the shield Leto had constructed around himself while in Parisa's court-yard. And what had Leto meant by issuing a warning about the Ambassadors Festival? After all these decades, was Leto having second thoughts about having aligned himself with Greaves?

Well, at least Medichi was in charge of delivering the message to Endelle, who in turn would know exactly what to do with the information. Not his problem. His problem was next to him cleaning blood off a wood floor.

When all the pain in his abdomen, front and back, dis-appeared, and when Horace sat back on his heels, Marcus put a hand to his side. He pushed gingerly, astonished as always at what the man could do. He sat up then rose to his feet, but damn—all he felt was the slightest twinge.

Horace hopped up as well and planted a hand on his shoulder. "A good night's sleep will put you right." He then drew his pager from his pant pocket. He arched a brow. "Looks like I'm headed to Awatukee. Santiago got a burn on his arm."

Marcus looked at Havily, who passed behind him carry-ing the bucket and all the rags back in the direction of the kitchen. He thought about Parisa still in the house, still under his protection. His warrior instincts were strong and he didn't like the idea of Santiago in the desert by himself, a new wave of death vampires probably on the way. He almost offered his help, but he had two women with him and no way of really knowing that Greaves wouldn't put together a new plan to come after them.

He therefore repressed the urge to draw his sword once more into his hand and tell Horace to lead the way. Even so, the words left his mouth in a rush: "Anything I can do?"

At that, Horace met his gaze, his warm brown eyes smiling. "Still a warrior, I see, but no. Your job is here."

Marcus nodded several times. "Right."

"Be well, Warrior," Horace said. He lifted his arm and vanished.

Havily returned to the foyer, bucket and rags gone. She nodded in the direction of the southern half of the villa. "I folded some of your things here for you to use, you know, from my town house. Let me show you to your bedroom."

He stopped her, taking hold of her arm harder than he meant to. "*Our* bedroom. You're sleeping with me."

Havily stared at a determined slash of dark eyebrows over very intense light brown eyes. These warriors, she thought, always ready to fight, even about sleeping arrangements.

"Yes," she said, agreeing with him so maybe he could relax a little. "Fine. *Our* bedroom. But just FYI, I intended to share your bed tonight anyway, because in case you haven't noticed, you're not the only one caught up in this ridiculous, obsessive, frustrating, oh-my-God-you-smell-like-fennel myth."

The fingers on her arm gentled and a smile softened some of his intensity. "Good. That's good." He nodded.

She didn't know whether to kiss him or hit him, which frustrated her all over again. "You'll want a shower and I'll need to get Parisa settled. I'm putting her close, across the hall from us."

"Wait a minute. Shit, I totally forgot. How long has she been here? Has it been an hour? Two? We need to get her back to Mortal Earth but where is she going to be safe? Shit, shit, shit."

"Uh . . . that may not be an issue."

"Why? You know ascendiates can only tolerate Second Earth for a limited time. You know that. I heard even Alison felt dizzy after two hours, and her powers approached Endelle's levels."

"Well, what can I say. Parisa has wings and she's not the usual mortal. But you should probably see her for yourself." She led him to the second smaller central hall and to the arched doorway of the library. But the dark brown hair of the ascendiate was all that was visible, her head tilted slightly. Asleep, maybe or perhaps unconscious because of being on Second Earth? Had she erred? "Parisa?"

The head bobbed. Parisa jumped to her feet, holding a small leather volume in her hand. "*Pride and Prejudice*," she announced. "Isn't this amazing? It's a really early edition. I think the first edition was in three volumes but still—"

Marcus tugged on her arm. "Okay. Exactly how long has she been here?"

Parisa glanced around the library, her gaze landing off to her left. She turned back to them. "I've been here two hours and fifteen minutes."

"How do you feel?" he asked.

"Really good but it's the weirdest feeling. I have to say, I'm a little giddy."

"Dizzy?" Havily asked, concerned all over again.

"No, not at all, just really happy."

Havily turned to him. "See what I mean? I noticed it earlier. Not even a hint of lethargy or anything."

"Is there a problem?" Parisa asked.

"Not exactly. It's just that you shouldn't be able to handle being here, in this dimension, since you're still unascended. Usually by now a mortal would feel exhausted, dizzy, sometimes nauseous."

She shook her head. "I don't feel any of those things. Is there something wrong with me?"

Havily smiled. "You're an anomaly, that's all."

At that, Parisa grinned then rolled her eyes. "Oh, that's all."

Havily felt Marcus sway into her, just a slight lean, then he righted himself. She glanced at him, noting that his complexion was still a little pale. She turned once more to address Parisa. "I'm putting our savior here to bed then I'll be back and we can talk. Okay?"

"Yes. That would be great."

"If you feel like it, Warrior Medichi has some excellent red wine in the kitchen, in a tall rack at the end of one of the counters. I know he would want you to feel at home, so if you're inclined . . ."

"Shall I pour two glasses?" Parisa asked.

"Perfect. I would like to sit with you for a while anyway just to make sure your overall incomprehensible comfort with Second Earth remains."

"I'd like that," Parisa responded.

When Marcus didn't protest, didn't *demand,* that she join him in bed, she knew she'd been right in her assessment of him. She took him in the direction of the guest rooms directly across from the library. She opened the door on the left. She thought he would appreciate the heavy masculine feel of this particular room, with the massive four-poster bed, a tapestry of a deer hunt hanging over a black-leather-encased headboard, and burgundy velvet falling to the floor from an enormous gold-leaf cornice high above the tapestry.

The rest of the furniture matched the bed—an antique armoire where she'd hung their clothes, a large chest of drawers opposite the bed in which she'd put miscellaneous articles, and three-foot-square end tables.

The window on the east wall overlooked a large stretch of sun-loving lawn, now shrouded in moonlight, and beyond that, rising in the distance, the White Tanks Mountains. Five miles away on the other side of the mountains, White Lake and at least a hundred hotels formed one of Second Earth's premier spectacle sites.

Marcus headed for the en suite bathroom but paused at the doorway, planting a hand on the frame for support. He looked back at her, his brows slashed in concern once more. "You'll let me know if we need to take Parisa back to Mortal Earth. We could stay at my place on Bainbridge. I'm sure Endelle would lend us her mist for the duration if needed."

She smiled, "All right, *Hercules.* I'll let you know."

Marcus smiled, just a little crookedly off the side of his mouth. "That poser?" But he laughed and went into the bathroom.

Havily smiled. Marcus was Sumerian in origin. Of course

he would disparage Greek or Roman mythological charac-
ters. Havily had seen the advent of electricity during her
youth a few decades ago, but Sumer was credited with having developed the wheel. Her mind boggled.

Shaking her head, she left the bedroom then returned to
Parisa. She once more asked the mortal how she felt.

"Just a little tired, but you have to remember, I worked
all day at the library, then I released my wings . . . twice,
which always fatigues me. After that, I kept running up the
stairs and launching from the railing. I must have made
two dozen flights if I count both times together."

She smiled as she continued, "Oh, and then I met ascenders from another dimension, then I was almost attacked
by a really crazed-looking, uh, *vampire.* And now I'm here.
So, yes, I'm tired." But she swirled her dark red wine in
her goblet and her smile broadened. Medichi preferred
Cabernet. She lifted the goblet. "This wine is excellent, by
the way. I don't think I've ever seen the label but I like the
wings, nice touch."

"That's Antony's label." Havily shook her head, stunned
by Parisa's apparent immunity to the effects of Second
Earth. "I have to say, you don't seem to be experiencing any
ill effects from being on Second, almost as though . . . well,
it doesn't matter." She took the other goblet, a third full of
the dark red wine. She sighed. "How wonderful this looks."

She sat with Parisa, drinking wine, for what seemed
like a long time, long enough for the front-yard automatic
sprinklers to come on.

But when Parisa yawned, Havily said, "I hate to ask you
this again, but I need to know if you're sure you're all right.
Really, Parisa. Twenty-four hours on Second Earth is lethal for mortals. And Marcus said he would take us to his
home on Mortal Earth if that's what we need."

Parisa took a deep breath. She frowned again. "I truly
feel fine. I'm just tired, like I said. Otherwise I have these
tendrils of euphoria floating around in my chest. I can't
explain it but . . . I love being here."

Havily thought of Marcus. That was exactly how she felt when she was near him, as though tendrils of euphoria floated around in her chest. "Well, how about we get you to bed. I've put you in the room opposite Marcus and myself." She couldn't repress the blush that touched her cheeks. The thought that they were acting like a couple made her really uncomfortable. After all, what did she really know about Marcus or the other way around? "If you start feeling ill at all, you can knock on our door and we can get you back to Mortal Earth right away."

Parisa nodded then rose to her feet. She held her goblet up. "I should wash these out."

"No, you shouldn't. I'll take care of them as soon as I have you settled in your room."

She led her to the guest room opposite then showed her where she'd put the clothes she'd lent her and the sleep gear plus the extra girl-stuff she would need. Parisa thanked her profusely then gave a little cry when she saw the black silk nightgown draped across the bed. "I have this exact same one."

"La Perla?"

Parisa nodded.

Havily laughed. "I knew you had excellent taste." As she met Parisa's laughing amethyst eyes, she had the strangest feeling she'd just made a friend, a good friend.

She returned to the library, picked up the goblets, then headed to the kitchen. She thought of Marcus sleeping in the bed they would be sharing and a shiver of anticipation ran through her. Ascenders healed fast, but how fast could he recover from a searing blade wound?

Well, she supposed she would find out.

For now, though, she had wine to put away and goblets to wash.

Marcus awoke to a dip in the bed and a sigh. He felt Havily adjust the covers very slowly as though trying not to wake him, but he was awake. He wasn't sure he'd even been asleep partly because he was still a little sore but also because he needed her in bed with him. He couldn't relax if she was anywhere else in the house. He needed to know she was safe. "She okay?" he asked, worried about Parisa as well.

A pause then a short sigh. "She's right across the way. I've instructed her to wake me if she feels in any way distressed by being here."

"Good. Now come closer and please don't tell me you put a nightgown on."

"How can you be wounded and still barking orders?"

He smiled.

He faced the window. Lace drapes showed dim landscaping lights in the distance, and through a couple of swirls he could actually see stars in the night sky, one or two since the skyline of the White Tanks was a dark distant presence.

Havily shifted in a couple of quick bounces over to his side of the bed and planted her warm and very naked flesh right up against his. He breathed in the scent of her—woman and honeysuckle—and released a sigh. He was aroused but too tired to do anything about it. At the same time, something deep inside started to relax. She was here. She was safe. She was in his bed.

When she draped her arm across his hip, he pulled that hand around to his chest and pressed it close, returning the favor since she'd done the same thing with him not so long ago. He closed his eyes and that was that.

Havily listened to Marcus breathe. Had he been waiting for her to come to bed before he could finally fall asleep? And why did that squeeze her heart so hard? He held her hand in a tight grip, perhaps fearing she would leave if he let go. Her nose was smashed up between his shoulder blades, which made it impossible to do anything but catch his wicked masculine fennel scent until her body was shedding fluids everywhere.

She was worked up but couldn't wake him.

Worse, she was so content, deeply content, and she didn't want to be, not like this, not with this man, not with this deserter, not with Warrior Marcus.

But she was caught in the teeth of the *breh-hedden* and right now she couldn't help being with him, being in bed with him, with her breasts tingling against his back and her thighs pressed against his buttocks and the back of his legs.

A couple of tears slid from her eyes.

She had felt like this before, many, many years ago with her husband, a man she had adored, loved, desired. She had forgotten how sweet it could be to share the same bed, to smell the rich scent of a man, to feel the heat from a man's body flooding an otherwise cool space and warming things up.

This was the same except multiply all those sensations to the tenth. That's what it was like with Marcus. She even had to throw the sheet off her back because he was a heat lamp right now against her front.

His warmth made her drowsy, very drowsy. She released a sigh and that was that.

The next thing she knew, she could hear the chatter of sparrows outside her room. *Their room.* Light from the early June morning had crept into the space. She was no longer smack up against him but rather lay on her stomach completely uncovered, arms spread wide, her left hand off the bed. She patted the sheet on the other side and though she felt the warmth of the fabric, Marcus was clearly not in bed. His fennel scent filled the room, though.

She drew her arms under her chest then lifted up a little to turn her head in the direction of the bathroom. Marcus stood in the doorway, leaning against the door frame and grinning. He looked warrior-gorgeous, completely nude, and muscled like a Greek god, but she was so tired.

He smiled. "My God you've got a beautiful ass."

"Pilates," she murmured, then let her head fall back on

the mattress. She felt like she could sleep for a year, but when a fresh roll of fennel struck her nose, her adrenaline shot into the stratosphere. Her body responded as though enthralled.

"Honeysuckle," he growled.

Havily felt strangely panicky. There was a part of her that didn't want this. She knew that the farther down this road she traveled with Marcus, the harder it would be to break with him when the time came. She knew that women bonded to men through their pleasure, through orgasm, and each time he came at her and brought her release, those "tendrils of euphoria" would wrap themselves tighter and tighter around her heart. Was she being wise?

Uh . . . no.

He moved to round the bottom of the bed then sat down on her left and rubbed her back. "What happened? You gave me this delicious wave of your scent then an ice wall."

His scent hadn't changed, he was one licorice twizzler and she wanted her tongue all over him.

She rolled on her right side so that she could look up at him, which of course exposed her breasts to him—and he didn't hesitate to take in the view. His lips parted and he leaned toward her but she put her hand on his shoulder, stopping him. "Marcus, what's going to happen to us? Because I swear every minute I'm with you, I'm getting sucked in deeper and deeper. I . . . I don't want to love you."

He shrugged. "Just fuck me then."

She laughed but couldn't help but notice that his smile didn't quite reach his eyes. So he was worried as well.

She lifted a brow. "I'm scared. You're . . . you're an awe-inspiring man, a warrior of excellence—"

"A deserter—"

"Yes. That disturbs me most of all. What if I fall for you, I mean really fall for you, and then you disappear because life gets a little too hard?"

He shifted so that he sat more evenly on the bed, closer to her. She could see that the small apertures of his wing-locks were moist with desire. She ran her hand over them without thinking. His back arched and he murmured something unintelligible. She couldn't mistake the response. "I love your body," she whispered.

"You know, if you're trying to push me away, you're doing a piss-poor job of it." There was an edge to his voice.

"You're angry."

"I'm frustrated. We're in the same boat, you and me. Life got to us, robbed something from each of us. I understand your question, the real question, as in, how can you love me, how can I love you when there is war and death and grief? And my leaving Second Earth when I did you see as the worst betrayal a man could make."

"Yes," she whispered, but her hand slid over his back again. She drank in the wave of fennel that once more wafted from his body, beckoning to her, speaking to her, drawing her in. Her hand fell low and she dragged the backs of her fingernails over his buttocks. "I'm just saying, don't expect anything from me."

He turned to look at her. His light brown eyes were drawn in pain. "I have nothing to give. It was all too much, Havily. Maybe that's the real plight of living a long life. One day you wake up and you just can't take it anymore. I don't know. So I guess the question is, do you want me to leave you alone?" He snorted. "Or at least try to leave you alone because so far it's been damn impossible."

"What if I said yes?"

He growled softly. As she drifted her hand over his wing-locks again, the moisture increased. By the time she reached his neck, her hand was wet. Eric's wing-locks hadn't shed moisture like this when aroused. But hers did. She and Marcus were alike in that respect. She slid her hand into his hair, grabbed on, then drew him toward her. He turned and planted his right hand next to her shoulder. He kissed her.

"I'm a hypocrite," she said.

"No. It's the *breh-hedden*. You could ask me to stay

away, but I couldn't, not right now. Maybe in time this stupid thing will fade, dim, release me, us, both of us."

"Then while we can, while we can bear it, we should be joined." Her gaze fell to his neck. "Marcus. I want your vein this morning."

He groaned. "You've got it." His voice was dark and husky.

Marcus crawled across the bed, over her body, until he was on the other side of her, his hands dragging across her peaked breasts. He stretched out on his back, one knee up. He tilted his head to expose his throat. She rolled toward him, her torso sliding over his. She caught his stiff cock in her hand until she rubbed just the tip with her thumb. God, it felt good. His woman knew how to touch him. She was familiar with a man's body. She didn't grab and pull, she stroked lightly and teased.

Her tongue fell against his neck and rasped over his vein on the left side so that he could feel her breasts rubbing against his rib cage and chest. He drifted his hands over her. He loved the body of a woman, he loved the smoothness of her skin, the silky quality, the way her ribs narrowed to her waist, the way he could put his hands almost all the way around her waist, the way she moaned when he squeezed, the way her hips flared, the smallness of her compared with the bulk of his muscles. He wrapped her up in his arms so that even though he had the strength to squeeze the life out of her all he did was cradle her gently.

He surrounded her as she licked his neck and brought his vein throbbing to the surface.

She tilted her head to get the right angle.

The taking of blood was pure sex, nothing less. She would be in a frenzy soon and he'd eventually find his way inside her, but there was always more than one means of giving her the pleasure she would need right now.

"Take me, Havily," he whispered. "Damn, I want you taking my blood."

He felt moisture drip onto his neck . . . then her fangs struck, swift and sure, practiced. She moaned as she began to drink from him in strong deep draws. He groaned and every muscle in his body contracted and released in one snake-like wave of desire. His shoulders lifted, then relaxed, his arms hugged, then retreated, his chest pushed against her breasts, then drew back to allow her more access. His hips rolled and his legs rocked against her and around her.

She kept suckling but her body responded in kind until she moved against him with each draw. She rubbed the juncture between her legs against the top of his heavy muscled thigh. Oh, yeah. He responded by flexing that muscle and pushing against her each time her hips rolled over him.

Her moans increased in strength and frequency and then her mind touched his.

Oh, God, Marcus. You taste like heaven. Fennel down my throat. My stomach is on fire and I want you, want you, want you . . .

His eyes rolled in his head. Her thumb still teased the head of his cock. "Havily," he murmured, his voice rough and deep.

You're weeping, she sent as her thumb stroked back and forth.

Yes. Yes. Oh, God, Havily, mount me. Let me take us both where we need to go.

Yes.

He held a strong arm against her shoulders to keep her mouth connected to his vein, then he carefully maneuvered his body under hers. It took a certain amount of skilled hip swiveling and positioning but finally his cock reached her opening and with a slow thrust he penetrated her.

She cried out even as she pushed her tongue against his vein and held him in place. Then she suckled harder.

She was so wet. Her moans sent lightning through his cock until his balls ached. Her hips bucked and she nearly let go of his neck but he sent, *Let me do the work. Just stay put and take what you need from me.*

Oh, Marcus. Why do you have to be so wonderful?

He smiled as he thrust, carefully at first; then he steadily increased the pace until she was barking her pleasure between sucks and murmuring inside his head, *Oh, God,* over and over.

It had been a long time since a woman had taken his vein, over two hundred years. Yes, he'd taken some veins in between, but all those women had been mortal and couldn't return the favor. He had forgotten the sex of it, the pleasure of it, the feelings of oneness, of communion, to be the one allowing the invasion, giving the most essential life fluid. He caressed her buttocks and groaned. He was so close now and she had grown tight, a sure sign she was ready to take flight herself. And he knew exactly what she was doing when her right hand crept around his waist and slid beneath his back.

His balls tightened a little more. He wanted her to do it. *Yes,* he sent.

Oh, shit. Her fingers found a ridge, just one wing-lock, and she began to rub.

Havily. Shit. Are you ready? Because what you're doing is going to take me the distance.

A moan was her only response, her mouth working wildly at his neck now. He took that as a yes and increased the pace, his hips bucking, his cock thrusting in and out. She dragged a nail over the ridge. He cried out and before he could warn her he began to come but she was ready. She finally released his neck and arched over him, rising up, staring into his eyes, then capturing his mouth with hers. She moaned at the same time, and he could feel the grip of her core pulling at him as he spent his seed.

He surrounded her with his arms and held her tight as he thrust his tongue into her mouth. She dueled with him. Her body continued to buck and pull at him and his orgasm spun out like a wild ride at Six Flags. So, shit.

After her body quieted, she pulled back—but only far enough to then fall against him, her arms spread out on either side of him. He chuckled. He held her close and his pecs flexed against her chest. She cooed her pleasure. He kissed her neck, her cheek, her beautiful red hair.

Your blood is like heaven, my dear man.

God, I love you in my head.

Ditto. That was . . . just . . . amazing. You're amazing. You're so damn strong. When you were powering into me. Oh. My. God.

These words couldn't have pleased him more. He pushed her back then rolled her carefully so that they were still connected. For just a few minutes, he wanted to be on top and to look at her.

Her gaze fell to his neck and touched the spot over his vein where she'd taken him. Withdrawing the fangs left behind a healing potion that sealed the wound. With the quick healing of Second Earth, what would have been a bruise would be little more than a pair of small red marks in an hour and nothing within the space of another thirty minutes. He moved over her and pressed into her mons. She responded by tightening her muscles, holding his cock tight. He chuckled. "It's like we've been married for years."

She smiled and huffed a sigh. "I loved being married. I was looking forward to being married again."

He nodded and ran his finger down her cheek and over her lips. "To Eric."

"Yes."

"Did you love him, Havily, really love him?"

She smiled but her eyes tightened. "I did. I fell hard for him. I hadn't expected love to find me again."

"Did he take your blood as I have?"

She looked at him, her hands now stroking his shoulders, her thumbs lower as she rubbed his pecs back and forth. "You're not going to get jealous, are you?"

He shook his head. "Just wondering."

She huffed a sigh. "Well, I was nervous at first, either

direction, but yes, we exchanged blood. He was my first, my only, until now. It was . . . extraordinary. What about you?"

"Yes, I mean no. I mean, I've taken blood in the last couple of centuries but I've not had a woman at my neck since I left Second Earth." He stroked her hair and kissed her cheek, her chin, then lower to press his lips against her throat. "I loved it. I truly had forgotten how wonderful it could be."

He felt dizzy suddenly, as though he stood on top of a tall building, peering over the edge. He let himself drift forward and he fell. Yes, he was falling, that was the sensation he felt, falling and falling but there was no ground to hit, just an infinite abyss full of pleasure, ease, comfort.

What did it mean that being connected to Havily made him feel like this?

CHAPTER 13

Fabulous, hot, steaming water broke over Havily's shoulders, and she let out a soft moan. Bathing on Vancouver Island in 1910 meant building a fire and heating water on top of a coal-burning stove. The good old days had nothing on water heaters and indoor plumbing. Hallelujah for a hot shower.

She breathed and breathed, the moisture of the shower a relief from the dry desert air. As she lathered, her head wagged back and forth.

With every molecule of space Marcus took up in her life, with every millisecond she was with him, the bond was growing. She could feel all those tendrils weaving through her body and tightening his hold on her, and he wasn't even doing it on purpose.

Earlier, she had tried to tell him that she didn't want to be near him and then she had stroked his wing-locks. What

an idiot. But it was clear that even though her mind might
be able to make sense of things and shoot off warnings
every now and then, her body was completely in control.

Memories jostled her as she rinsed off.

She had taken his blood. *She had taken his blood.* Her
knees buckled in the shower and she only just caught herself from falling.

His blood, oh-my-God, his blood had been incredible.
She could feel it now singing through her veins. The power,
the sheer power of taking blood felt as though light and heat
vibrated within each muscle of her body, warming her,
opening her heart, even her mind.

And the sex? Once more her knees weakened, threaten-
ing to send her down to the tile. Even if she could make a
rational decision to stay away from him, just how was she
supposed to do that when right now, if he busted through
the door, she'd just open her arms wide and take him inside?

Parisa had awakened to the sounds of sex, beautiful throaty
sex in the room opposite. She was both embarrassed and
aroused. The shower had been running off and on for some
time, so she supposed the latest round was over.

She sighed heavily as she sat up and slipped her legs
over the side of the bed. She adjusted the black silk since it
had gotten caught between her legs. Her body was heated,
her mind distressed.

What was this place she had come to?

Second Earth. A new dimension. A place where wings
were normal, which meant she was normal.

Lace curtains covered the window. A thick lawn spread
out to a considerable distance. If she understood where the
villa was located, she was looking at the eastern slopes of
the White Tank Mountains. Same earth. Different dimensions. Even the place-names were kept the same to avoid
confusion.

Her brows rose as she crossed to the window. She pushed
back the curtain and found a deer on the lawn, long neck

extended, munching happily. On earth—Mortal Earth—she knew that deer lived in the White Tanks. Therefore, that would also be true here on Second Earth.

But how out of place the animal looked on a manicured lawn. And what a lawn! Very few homes in Phoenix had lawns like this anymore, water being the scarce commodity it was, despite the underground rivers. Maybe resources were apportioned differently on Second Earth.

The doe lifted her head, her ears swiveling. Something had disturbed her and she bounded away, in the direction of the mountains.

Parisa felt like that, ready to run. She was torn about her experience so far. In one sense, she knew she belonged here, despite evidence of a serious war. But another part of her, so used to earth, longed to go home, to live in the comfort and safety of her known life. She wondered how soon she could go back to her house, when it would be safe for her.

She sighed. What was she even doing here?

In strong contrast with her deliberations and confusion, her stomach rumbled. She put her hand to it and smiled. "Well, at least you always know what you want."

After the night's fighting and a brief conversation with Thorne at the Cave, Medichi folded directly to his personal suite of rooms at the southernmost end of his villa. Thorne had informed him that he had guests—Marcus, Havily, and the mortal-with-wings, a woman by the name of Parisa Lovejoy. He thought he'd get cleaned up in case the women were around. They really didn't need to see him covered in a night's worth of blood spatter.

He had delivered Leto's message to an incredulous Thorne. Trouble at the Ambassadors Festival in three days. Actually, two now. So, shit.

What he didn't understand was what Leto meant by giving them a warning. Could he be trusted? Who the hell knew? He would leave it to Endelle and Thorne to figure this one out.

The only thing he really did understand about Leto's warning was that he had to keep a lid on it, as in a deep mental shield so that anytime a powerful entity—like that prick-of-all-pricks, Greaves—decided to do a mind-dive without Medichi's knowledge, he wouldn't find out the truth, at least not from him. If for some reason Leto was having second thoughts about his defection, or if his conscience had returned, Endelle's administration could use all the help it could get.

As he folded his battle gear straight to Murphy's Laundry on Union Hills and Cave Creek, Second Earth, the fine establishment that kept his uniforms in top shape, he moved into the shower. Ten years ago, when he'd seen the bathroom overhaul in Kerrick's basement, he'd hired the same contractor to outfit his shower with a similar fine array of eight heads. Damn, he liked a good shower.

He turned all of them on full blast.

Heaven.

Fucking heaven.

He turned in a slow circle, letting the water beat on him from every possible angle, which brought a heavy sigh rumbling out of his chest. The resulting intake of air, straight through flared nostrils, however, popped his eyes open.

What the hell was that scent? He'd been through citrus groves that smelled similar, especially if you took an orange, punctured and peeled the skin, then sucked at a juicy wedge.

Only it wasn't the scent of an orange exactly. He breathed in again. Nope, not oranges. More like tangerines.

He laughed. Why the hell would his house smell like tangerines?

He had a cleaning service on call, the Merry Ascenders, but they wouldn't have installed Air Wicks without letting him know. Although the smell pleased him so much he might just make a phone call and see if the company made a tangerine scent. He laughed again.

He laughed until, as he continued to breathe the fragrance in, over and over, he started getting *aroused*. What the fuck?

Whatever.

He shrugged, palmed his cock, and stroked a couple of times. He really liked the sensation, especially coupled with the tangerine fragrance. Talk about erotic. Then he remembered that he had guests in his house and somehow jacking off in the shower then greeting everyone bugged the shit out of him. Even then, he wasn't sure why.

Pressure formed in his chest and a deep profound longing ensued, the way he'd started feeling when Havily was around.

Goddamn, he needed a woman. What he wanted was someone he could bang on a regular basis without any emotional commitment, date on a casual basis, someone he could get to know but not care too much about. This showing up at the Blood and Bite in the evenings and chasing a piece of mortal tail around hoping to take some of the edge off had gotten about as thrilling as plucking nose hairs.

He shampooed his long warrior hair and used a crème rinse, which made him less than a man in his opinion, but if he didn't, his ritual long hair was a bitch to keep in the equally ritual *cadroen*. He had thick hair, and yeah, he had to work to keep it in shape.

Every once in a while, though, the scent of tangerines struck his nostrils and yeah, each time, his cock responded as though hit with punch of Viagra.

Sonofabitch, what was that?

He needed to find the source and get rid of it. Otherwise he'd be walking around with a hard-on and scaring his guests.

He released a heavy breath and turned in a circle, letting all that beautiful water pound on his skin. Finally, he hit the lever. He stretched his hearing to see if anyone was up and about. In the distance, two women talked and laughed together.

"Do you smell that?" the unknown female said, the mortal, no doubt. Parisa. She had a confident way of speaking, and something about the tone of her voice eased the pressure in his chest. "It's stronger now. I mean really strong."

"That sage scent you were smelling last night?"

"Yes. The one all throughout the house. The chair I sat in was drenched with it."

"Is that why you sat there? Oh, now you're blushing."

The women laughed together.

"And now your cheeks are bright red."

"Stop, Havily."

"So you're smelling sage?"

"Yes. Isn't that strange?"

"Maybe. I don't know."

Havily still served every once in a while as a Liaison Officer, though less often because of her increasing duties as an executive in Endelle's administration. Medichi smiled. The pitch of a woman's voice was higher and lighter than a man's. Yeah, he had forgotten how much the sound pleased him.

Marcus awoke to the sound of feminine laughter and not close by, but in some distant part of this big-ass house . . . villa . . . whatever.

What do you know? He'd dropped off to sleep after making love to Havily. The last thing he remembered, she was in the shower.

Ah. Making love to Havily. He folded his arms behind his head and smiled up at the ceiling, carved beams in a coffered pattern of the same heavy wood as the bed. He liked this room. Of course it helped that he still had Havily's scent in his nose, thick this time, rich with sex. He licked his lips and tasted his blood on his mouth because she'd kissed him right after she'd taken his vein. Oh . . . yeah.

He slid a hand from in back of his head and touched his

neck. Not even a bump. He would have preferred to wear the red burn as a badge this morning, to see it in the mirror, to see Havily's gaze drop to the results of her penetration, to watch her eyes flare as she remembered.

Those thoughts brought a sudden new arousal and, if they'd been alone in the house, he'd have called Havily back to bed. Yeah, that's exactly what he would have done.

He touched his side where Leto had stuck him with the blade. Not even a fucking twinge. He ought to send Horace flowers or something. What a gift the man had.

But the healed wound sent his thoughts flowing in the direction of the death vampire known as Crace. Havily had been right, he was big like Luken. The thought that he had been at Havily's neck balled his hands into fists. He wanted the vampire dead and he wanted him dead now.

So who was he exactly? Endelle had said he was a High Administrator aligned with the Commander but apparently he was operating in Phoenix now and had a new passion in the form of securing blood donors. The next question was simple: Had he come to Parisa's home for her or for Havily? Could he have even known Havily was there?

Thank God Crace had been unable to trace to the villa. The women wouldn't be alive otherwise. Shit, this whole situation was setting his teeth on edge. He knew how Havily's blood made him feel, which meant that Crace had experienced the same damn sensations. A long line of obscenities possessed his mind, swirling around until his head pounded. If he were in Crace's shoes, he'd want more of Havily's blood because, based on all the reports he'd ever heard about dying blood, Havily's blood was a fucking match.

Jesus H. Christ.

He rolled out of bed. Though Medichi's home had the best possible covering of mist, in addition to COPASS's protection under the law of Second Society, he felt a profound need to be near Havily right now, to keep his guard up, to watch the skies.

He went into the bathroom and found his shaving gear lined up against the mirror. Havily's doing. He smiled but shook his head as he picked up a can of shaving cream and squirted foam into his hand. She was a woman of detail. He liked that. He was a detail man himself. But those thoughts led him down a different path, and though his fingers were now covered with shaving cream all he could do was stare at the white cloud.

Havily had been right. What the hell were they doing getting so involved when neither of them had the heart for it? He sure as hell didn't. He loved being with her for obvious reasons but right now, his chest felt weighed down when he thought of the next day and the next. He couldn't give something to this woman that he didn't have to give. Four thousand years of living, of losing those closest to him, had ripped his heart from his chest.

For a minute, he could hardly breathe.

Shit.

The women's laughter struck his extended hearing. He drew it in then cast his hearing in a southerly direction. Medichi should be home by now. What he heard there surprised him, since he detected a faint, guttural moaning followed by a very precise, "What the fuck is that?"

Yeah, Medichi was home and apparently agitated about something. Maybe all the laughter was keeping him awake when he was trying to fall asleep for the day.

Havily hadn't enjoyed herself this much in a long time. Parisa had a sharp wit and strong intelligence. She stood at one end of the dark soapstone island in the kitchen and Parisa at the other. They were talking like college roommates, sipping coffee and comparing the warriors.

"Santiago has the most interesting nose," Parisa said. "It's curved and very sexy."

"You should see Luken with his hair down," Havily said.

"I have, remember? His hair was over his bare chest in the hospital."

"That's right. You saw us there in one of your visions."

"Yes, I did." Parisa shook her head. "You know, there's almost too much raw muscle among these men. I swear I'm ovulating even as we speak." Then she laughed.

Havily, having been trapped by the sensual delights of the *breh-hedden* for the last several days, giggled along with her.

Parisa wore a pair of Havily's jeans again but instead of the purple sequin tank she had donned a red silk blouse, which was, of course, a little too snug across the chest, but that couldn't be helped. If Parisa stuck around on Second, Havily would definitely need to take her shopping unless they could find some way to sneak back into Parisa's home without getting attacked by death vampires.

Hmmm. Shopping or death vampires. Now, there was a tough choice.

Parisa was something of a mystery in many respects: her *royle* wings, her visions, which seemed oddly focused on Medichi, and her ability to handle being on Second Earth. All these things indicated strong preternatural powers. Yet she couldn't fold, nor did she seem to have telepathic abilities. So she had phenomenal powers in some respects, yet in others she was totally lacking. Which made Havily like her very much.

"You're sure you're all right?" Havily asked.

Parisa shrugged. "You've asked me three times this morning and I'm fine." She tilted her nose off to the side and sniffed. "You know, that sage smell is getting even stronger. In fact, it seems to be coming from the direction of the foyer."

Havily turned and took a deep breath. "Actually, I do smell something but it's more along the lines of licorice."

"Licorice?"

Havily felt a blush creep up her cheeks. She then spent the next few minutes explaining about the *breh-hedden* and the warriors, about specific scents that indicated the ritual had been triggered between a warrior and his *breh,* and how the same experience had struck down Warrior Kerrick and Alison four months ago.

Parisa frowned. "What are you saying? Do you think I'm Warrior Medichi's *bray* or whatever it is you said? Do you think this sage I'm smelling belongs to him?"

"Of course not . . . that is . . . oh, my God." The owner of the villa suddenly appeared in the doorway, his long, thick black hair, still damp from a shower, draped over his heavy pecs and down his back. The man wore nothing but a towel, a black terry-cloth towel wrapped around his waist that was tented ominously. "Medichi? What's . . . going on?" Havily was shocked. Of all the warriors, Medichi was the most . . . gentlemanly.

But, damn, he was one gorgeous man. He was also in a profound state of arousal, and it was as though he didn't even see her. His gaze was fixed on Parisa, his chin dipped low, his dark eyes glittering. His pecs flexed, relaxed, flexed, relaxed. A low growl reverberated through the room. She realized she had never seen him without a shirt on, but wow was he built . . . and aroused . . . and acting like a beast.

Which reminded her of Marcus on more than one occasion . . . and that's when all the puzzle pieces fell into place: that Parisa could smell sage, that her visions had focused on him, that he was now behaving in a completely uncharacteristic manner.

Oh, dear God.

Trouble was, she didn't exactly know what to do.

But as bad as it was that Medichi stood in the doorway, obviously aroused and looking like something from the Roman pantheon of gods, the warrior then did the unthinkable. He unhooked his black towel and let it fall to the floor almost as though he wanted Parisa to see . . . oh-my-ever-loving-God.

Havily whirled around, turning her back on Medichi.

She had no right to see what he'd come to show... Parisa.

But how was the woman taking the situation? She was probably embarrassed, maybe ready to faint.

From her peripheral vision, she could see that Parisa hadn't moved. Instead, her gaze was fixed low on Medichi, her lips parted, and she was stroking her neck with her fingers. Her cheeks were pink. Her breathing shallow.

Well... she certainly wasn't *embarrassed*.

Holy shit! The *breh-hedden* had struck again!

Havily couldn't bear looking at her because she knew exactly what Parisa was feeling, the depth of the sexual desire and attraction, the flood of scent that was right now passing only between the two of them, specific scents meant only for each other.

"Warrior Medichi," Parisa whispered, her voice a soft erotic caress.

She started moving down the length of the dark soapstone island, clearly intent on going to him. Havily didn't know what to do, a confusion that intensified when Parisa's eyes went wide with horror and she cried out in a loud voice, "Warrior Marcus! No! Don't hurt him!"

At that, Havily whirled back around. All she saw was Medichi flat on his back and the towel he'd dropped bunched over his hips and covering his arousal. Marcus stood next to him, his fists bunched.

Thank God! Marcus had arrived and immediately assessed the exact nature of the situation and intervened.

She glanced at Parisa and said, "How about we go for a walk?"

Parisa turned to her and murmured, "He's... so big."

Havily thought of Marcus and a little shiver traveled down her spine and teased her wing-locks, every damn one of them. "I think it's a warrior thing."

She didn't say anything more, but Havily knew Medichi. He defined the word *gentleman,* and this whole situation would mortify him once he came to his senses. She hooked Parisa's arm and guided her in a northerly direction toward the pool and the formal gardens.

Medichi stared up at the ceiling. He wasn't sure what had just happened but his jaw *hurt*. He pressed it with his hand and moved the hinge around. At least nothing was broken. He blinked.

"I see stars." Someone was bending over him. Oh. Marcus. "What the fuck did you just do to me?"

Marcus sat back on his heels but he was grinning, the bastard. "Saved you from a rape charge. Or don't you remember dropping the towel in front of the ascendiate for her viewing pleasure?"

Oh, dear Creator, what had he done? He crossed his hands over his stomach, but he didn't want to look. He whispered, "Are Havily and the ascendiate still standing on the other side of the island?"

"No. Havily took her outside. Dragged her, actually." Then he smiled. "Well, dumbfuck, how do you like the *breh-hedden* now? Isn't it just the bomb?"

Medichi flipped him off. "So, shit. *She's* here."

"Looks like it."

"What the hell is going on? First Kerrick, then you, now me? Don't you think this is a little bizarre?"

"At the very least. So, did I break your jaw or what?"

He rubbed it again and once more worked the hinge. "No, but I could use some ice. I'd call Horace but this is just too goddamn embarrassing. Shit." When Marcus rose up then headed toward the fridge, he called out, "So did the ascendiate just arrive or what?"

"She's been here all night."

At that, Medichi leaped to his feet and shot in the direction of the pool, the towel once more forgotten. "It's not safe," he cried. "She'll die!"

Marcus watched Medichi blur past him and move swiftly into the hall that led to the patio. He was about to call out for the warrior to stop, but his gaze fell on Medichi's back.

Holy shit. Scars crisscrossed the broad muscled expanse in a multitude of flat silver lines. All the decades of wondering why the hell Medichi never mounted his wings suddenly came home to him loud and clear. But the vampire was moving fast, intent all over again, apparently, on getting to Parisa. He didn't really have time to wonder what had created the scars.

Marcus knew Medichi wasn't thinking. He'd been there, done that. He knew the powerful instincts boiling in his chest.

He swiped the towel off the floor . . . again . . . then folded straight to the doors leading to the pool area and met a blazing-eyed warrior who had drawn his sword. Marcus lifted his brows, cocked his head, and wagged the black terry cloth in front of him.

Medichi stared at the towel but merely scowled hard, dipped his chin, and for a moment looked like a bull before a red flag. Clearly, he had one goal and that was to bust past Marcus no matter what.

"Medichi!" he shouted. "Where the hell do you think you're going?"

"Outside!" the warrior bellowed in return.

"You want to put on some clothes first?" He held the towel even higher.

Then Medichi blinked and blinked again. Finally, a long string of obscenities flowed from his mouth, a sure sign his rational brain had started to kick in. Marcus could only grin at him. "I feel you, brother. I really do."

"Fuck," Medichi spit. He folded his sword away, took the towel, then wrapped it once more around his waist. "This is hell. My brain isn't functioning."

"Preaching to the choir. So what went through your head right now? Why did you suddenly decide you had to go after her?"

Medichi shook his head. "You said she'd been here

overnight. She can't stay here. Marcus, you've got to get her back to Mortal Earth. Now. She only has twenty-fours and then she's dead. How long has she been here anyway? Goddammit, Marcus, what have you been doing? Manscaping your pubes? Why haven't you fucking secured her safety?"

"Easy, Antony. I'm not the enemy, and I promise you there are answers to your questions if you think you can hear me."

Medichi took a deep breath, but his brows were pinned low on his forehead. He was one breath away from losing it again, and Marcus knew exactly how and why he felt the way he did. Maybe talking would help. "Parisa is still here because Endelle's mist is the best possible protection. But beyond that, Parisa is *unusual*. She's not feeling the effects of Second Earth like most ascendiates. She's fine. Believe me, we keep checking."

Medichi's shoulders dropped, and his brow grew pinched like he was in pain. "Okay. I guess I can deal with that. But shit, I feel this ache to get to her, right here." He punched his chest, between his pecs. "Just tell me, are you absolutely sure she's safe? Even Alison felt dizzy at the two-hour mark when she was on Second Earth and not yet ascended and you know how fucking powerful she is."

"Havily keeps asking Parisa but the ascendiate's comments range from how at home she feels to sensations of euphoria. She's fine." He turned slightly in the direction of the door that led to the patio. "Of course, I'm not crazy that the women are out there without one of us guarding them." He turned back to Medichi. "How about you go to bed, or do whatever you do after a night of fighting, and let me see to them?"

"You stay away from Parisa," he barked.

Marcus could only laugh, which made Medichi glare and bunch his shoulders.

Marcus just lifted a brow.

Finally, the warrior huffed a heavy sigh, then turned on

his heel and headed back the other direction. This of course allowed Marcus a second look at the warrior's scars even with all that thick black hair hanging to the middle of his back. There wasn't an inch of his skin unmarred. There was a possibility he couldn't even mount wings.

Marcus wasn't surprised when Medichi came to a halt and looked back at him, a stricken light in his eye. "Shit. No one knows. Please don't say anything."

"I give you my word," Marcus said quietly, a fist to his chest. "And I'll deep-shield the memory as well."

"Thank you." He didn't say anything more but continued in the direction of his rooms in the southern wing.

Endelle scratched just below the halter's hem. Damn. This kangaroo hide made her itch, but then she'd been warned, since she insisted on keeping the fur attached instead of having the hide tanned. Her snug suede pants had been dyed to imitate leopard print. They rocked.

Maybe she'd do some embroidered leather next. The idea appealed to her.

She knew everyone thought she was nuts, but she liked the way the various skins, furs, pelts, and feathers felt beneath her fingers. And . . . she really liked watching everyone go through the gyrations of initial disgust to forming expressions of proper blankness. It always made her day. That and the stuttered compliments.

Idiots.

She was in her office with three women opposite her: Morgan, Alison, and the mortal, the woman called Parisa. She had thought to deal with Morgan's darkening ability today but apparently that would have to wait. Right now, she had a mystery to solve involving the mortal.

The women were each dressed differently. Alison wore the usual soft stretchy pants, her body already swelling. She had on a blue silk top that looked like water flowing in diagonals. Havily had on more formal office wear, pressed slacks in brown, three-inch heels, a solid cream blouse with some kind of ruffle in the front, and a beige silk jacket heavily embroidered at the hem. The one thing Endelle would say about her, she always looked like a million bucks and Marcus would like that, so good for her.

As for Parisa, she wore jeans and a red top that pulled way too tight across the breasts. Havily's clothes, probably. Endelle nixed a plan to go back to the Peoria house. She didn't want any of their lives risked just for a fucking change of clothes.

She leaned her ass on the front edge of her marble desk and stared at the latest ascendiate, whose current rite of ascension, if it could even be called that, was already a complete anomaly. For one thing Parisa Lovejoy hadn't yet *answered* her call to ascension in any discernible manner. She hadn't made her way to one of the Borderlands, nor had she demonstrated preternatural power, since mounting a pair of wings didn't fall into that category.

Of course it didn't help that Greaves had sent his minions, both Leto and that bastard, Eldon Crace, to attack the mortal in her home. If she had been in the middle of her call to ascension, how the hell would anyone know?

Thank fuck for Marcus, though. He'd made it possible for both women to get out safely even though Leto had all but gutted him. While she had the women in her care, Marcus had excused himself to do cleanup on his sword in his Bainbridge house. He'd be back in a while. In the meantime, there was no safer place on Second Earth for either Havily or Parisa than right here in her office.

She scanned the ascendiate now but for the life of her she couldn't figure out what she was seeing. She addressed Havily. "So what the fuck is this, Morgan, some kind of joke?"

Havily actually looked shocked. "I don't know what you mean."

"Well," she drawled, "first we get word about some kind of mortal-with-wings, and how critical she will be to the war, then you bring me this." She waved an arm at the tall beauty with dark brown hair and amethyst eyes. "So I figure it must be some kind of joke."

Havily narrowed her eyes and shook her head. "There is no joke here, Madame Endelle. I'd like you to meet ascendiate Parisa Lovejoy, lately of Peoria, Arizona, Mortal Earth. She's a librari—"

"She's a goddamn fucking *ascender,* you nitwit, but then why the hell should I have expected anything more from you than this kind of screwup?" She gestured with a flip of her hand to Parisa. "This woman is ascended."

Havily shook her head. "I'm sorry to disagree with *Your Supremeness,* but no. She's not." Ooooh. Sarcasm. Havily dipped her chin as well, and her light green eyes flared. Now, that was one thing she liked about Havily, the woman could take it on the chin, repeatedly. If you were going to swim in the big pond, you'd better be prepared to get your ass-fins thrashed by bigger fish.

Alison stepped forward. "Take another look, Madame Endelle." That empathic part of Alison swept over Endelle in a powerful wave of peace, which at first irritated the hell out of her then calmed her down. She had a real love–hate relationship with her new executive assistant. For one thing Alison wasn't afraid of her *at all* and for another, she was right most of the goddamn time.

Endelle huffed a sigh, jammed her hands together behind her back, and struck the would-be ascendiate with a nice punch of power straight from her mind, which flung Parisa against the wall. Hard. Though Parisa cried out, Endelle wasn't done. She slammed her thoughts into Parisa's mind, intending to dive deep and bring about a confession, but the would-be ascendiate lifted her palm and sent a blast that flung Endelle up and over her desk and into the plate-glass window of the northern wall.

Shiiiiiit.

It all happened so fast. She'd almost flown through the glass, but at the last nanosecond Endelle released a burst of energy that kept the window from shattering on impact. She still landed on her ass, on the floor, behind her desk.

"What the fuck?" she cried.

She stood up, rounded her desk and, at a run, moved to stand in front of the fake-mortal. "So you have hand-blast capability? Who are you? Where have you come from? Why do you have shields I'm finding it damn hard to penetrate? Do you belong to the Commander? I'll have answers or by God I'll raise my hand and strike you dead right now." She lifted her hand high, ready to follow through on her threat.

The woman with the violet eyes did the only sensible thing she could do. She dropped into a faint.

"Oh, for fuck's sake. What did she go and do that for?"

Alison moved to stand next to Endelle then crossed her arms over her chest. "Oh, I don't know," she said. Alison, too, had learned some sarcasm. "Maybe because she is exactly who she claims to be and you're a goddamn ill-tempered bitch who needs to be put in stocks for about a century?"

Havily, kneeling beside Parisa and stroking her cheek with her forefinger, called out, "I'll volunteer to throw the rotten cabbages . . . or rotten tomatoes, cow pies, sheep intestine, really hard dirt clods would do. Hmmm, what else? Let me think."

Endelle lifted her arms, preparing to hit both women with a hand-blast, but Alison just met her gaze. Then she smiled.

Oh, the depth of understanding in those lovely blue eyes rimmed with gold. Alison reminded Endelle of Thorne. Both had the kind of loyalty that shook her soul. In the same way she trusted Thorne with every atom of her being, she trusted Alison. Besides, that smile was as amused as it was instructive.

Endelle sighed. She was having one shitfest of a bad week. The Ambassadors Reception was about a breath away and she hated the idea of greeting all those fucking foreign dignitaries, Luken had gotten himself burned to a crisp out at the Superstitions and almost died, Havily had been attacked in her home by High Administrator Crace, who'd obviously gone to the darkest of the dark side, then Leto had issued a warning about the Ambassadors Festival. Leto, who might or might not be on her side, but whom Alison said was at least on the side of some Sixth ascender by the name of *James*.

So . . . shit!

Now she had to deal with this fake-mortal.

The thing was, Thorne had come to her the night before with word from his sister. He'd been adamant that one of the sisters with powerful Seer ability had had some kind of vision of Parisa while taking a little jaunt in the future streams. No details. Of course not. That would be way too easy. But the message had been that this fake-mortal, still lying unconscious on the floor with Havily petting her cheek and speaking in low tones to her, would make a difference in the war.

Endelle huffed a sigh. "Tend to her, Lissy, will you? I'll behave." She moved toward the windows that overlooked the eastern desert and waited. She turned, crossed her arms over her chest, and watched the tender scene from afar.

Alison dropped beside Parisa and put her hand on the woman's forehead. A moment later the fake-mortal awoke and stared first at Alison, then shifted her gaze to Endelle. She struggled to her feet with both women supporting her. Endelle meant to apologize, but Parisa looked back at Alison and asked, "What did I just do to Madame Endelle? How did I send her flying into the windows?"

Alison smiled at her. "You threw a hand-blast, from the palm of your hand."

Parisa looked at her hand. "I've seen this done, in my visions I mean, but I didn't know I could do it as well. My hand and arm feel a little numb."

Alison patted her shoulder. "The sensation will pass."

"What do you mean, *your visions*?" Endelle called from across the room.

"I don't know how to explain them exactly. Sometimes I just see things."

"Huh," Endelle murmured. She wasn't sure what to make of this. Maybe the woman had darkening capability, which would again confirm her opinion that she was looking at an ascender and not a mere mortal.

Parisa added, "When I see you in my visions, you're always in a rage."

"There, you see," Alison cried. "We really do need to work on your anger management skills."

Endelle rolled her eyes then addressed Parisa. "I will try very hard not to yell at you again."

"And . . . ," Alison said.

Endelle drew a noisy breath through flared nostrils. "And I apologize if I frightened you."

Parisa blinked. "What do you want from me?"

"I want to know the truth. I want to know why you're pretending to be a mere mortal when clearly you're already ascended."

Havily put an arm around Parisa's shoulder. "Show Madame Endelle your fangs. Your vampire fangs."

Parisa just looked at her then shook her head. "How do I show her something I don't have?"

"Like this," Havily said. She smiled very big, pulling back her lips just a little, so that her incisors showed. She lengthened them.

Haltingly, Parisa drew her lips back.

Endelle left her controlled position by the window and moved back to the three women still clustered near the door. She got up close and stared into the woman's mouth, but there were no fangs. *There were no fangs.* "Jesus," she whispered.

"What?" Parisa asked.

"It's not possible to be ascended and not have fangs.

Vampire fangs always come with ascension." Endelle still didn't know what she was looking at. "You make no sense to me but I still can't believe you're not ascended. Let's see your wings."

Parisa looked down at her shirt and shook her head. "I can't. Not . . . not like this."

"Well, take your fucking clothes off."

The fake-mortal blushed.

Endelle groaned. "Creator, save me from modesty. Parisa, I know this is trying but it would help me a great deal if you would mount your wings."

Parisa removed her red tank and then her too-tight bra, oh-so-slowly.

"For fuck's sake, we're all girls here. Who gives a rat's ass except, well now, don't you have the prettiest breasts. I actually think they might be bigger than mine. Huh."

"You're not helping," Alison cried.

Endelle again rolled her eyes.

"Try to ignore Madame Endelle's lack of manners," Havily said, glaring at Endelle. "She lost her filters a few millennia ago. Now take your time, and as soon as you're able, mount your wings."

Parisa, still wearing her jeans, closed her eyes. After a few minutes, her wings flew through the wing-locks, interfacing at the same time with the mesh superstructure.

Endelle took a step back. She gasped. "Holy shit." Parisa's wings were huge, especially for someone who was apparently un-ascended. "You've got goddamn *royle* wings. I've not seen these wings on anyone in five, maybe six millennia. Well, have you flown yet, un-ascended ascender?"

"I've only jumped from a sixteen-foot railing, but I have longed to fly. I have had such yearnings to take to the skies. But I was afraid to because—"

Endelle nodded, "You were afraid you'd get caught. Well, if you really are what you say you are, that was a smart move. A lot of idiots on Mortal Earth. You would've been taken to Area Fifty-one and dissected." She let her gaze drift over the wings, which were among the most beautiful pairs she had ever seen and that was saying a lot. She glanced at Havily. "And she's been here how long?"

"Almost eighteen hours now."

"Wow. Okay. Parisa, this might feel uncomfortable but I need to get inside your head. I need to see exactly what's going on with you. When I came at you with my mind earlier, you were a wall of shields, which reminded me of Morgan here. But if I'm to know how to act on your behalf, I must see exactly who and what you are, do you understand?"

"No," Parisa barked, but then her lips curved.

Even Endelle smiled. "Keep doing that. You're going to need a sense of humor on Second Earth, especially with this level of power. Ready?"

Parisa nodded.

Endelle placed herself within a foot of the mortal and put her hands on either side of her head. "Now you're going to release your shields so that I can see your life. I want you to relax and just let everything go."

Endelle closed her eyes and as if by magic the woman's shields melted away. She eased her mind within Parisa's; when she felt no resistance or panic, she dove and began a long run through the woman's head. This would tell her everything she needed to know.

By the end, she pulled out of Parisa's mind and stared at her. "Well, you are definitely mortal and un-ascended but are you kidding me? Sage? Warrior Medichi smells like sage?"

Steps on the path grow clumsy,
When the shoes outgrow the feet.

—*Collected Proverbs,* Beatrice of Fourth

CHAPTER 14

Crace walked in a slow circle all around the patio in the center of the Commander's peach orchard. He had been in this place many times before. Greaves liked to entertain here.

The hour wasn't yet noon. He knew Greaves tended to work around the clock so he figured meeting his master here, at this hour, would be as acceptable to the Commander as any other. He still wore his leather kilt and battle sandals but nothing else. He'd thought about changing to something more suitable but he just didn't give a fuck. He had work to do after this meeting that wouldn't involve a shirt and tie.

The setting was also symbolic since below the orchard, running for miles under the earth, was Greaves's compound and Command Center, many stories deep, and the place where he barracked the death vampires he imported nightly from all over the world. Crace was fairly certain Endelle had no real idea of the vast nature of his growing empire or that the compound itself was in a continual state of expansion deep within the earth.

The peach orchard was a calculated work of horticultural advancement and preternatural power. An environmental shield, constructed by Greaves, allowed for a dozen microclimates. Each microclimate created a month of the year and therefore peaches were being grown at every possible stage of the trees' annual cycles, which meant that fruits were being ripened on the stem every goddamn month of the year. Not only had Greaves won awards, but the sheer power of sustaining these microclimates kept High Administrators around the world in a state of awe. There were so many ways to win a war.

Crace approved of the strategy. Let the sheep be seduced however they may.

On the other hand, with Crace's evolution of physical and preternatural power, he'd begun to view the Commander in a different and perhaps less exalted light. Some of the glimmer on Greaves's shining armor had dulled in his opinion.

From the first he'd had a lot to offer and now he had even more, which meant it was high time Greaves allowed Crace some real autonomy and some say in the progress of the war. At the very least, he ought to be able to direct things in Metro Phoenix Two without hindrance from that bastard Rith.

As far as he knew, Rith's primary function involved surveillance. He was a goddamn spy. Not even a lowly administrator, never mind a High Administrator. So what the hell did the man bring to the table? Squat.

Beyond that, Rith had his own ideas about how the pursuit of the two women should be conducted. He had commandeered critical personnel to perform surveillance at Endelle's headquarters. Crace knew, he *knew,* Endelle would protect them. No way in hell would Her Supremeness let Rith or his cronies get within a hundred yards of either the mortal-with-wings or ascender Morgan.

Trying to apprehend them at headquarters was about as

useful a strategy as tickling a flea's balls. He'd argued with Rith, but the vampire had been adamant and refused to be moved from his position. He also had Greaves's sanction. Rith, in his opinion, was a fucking idiot.

Crace knew exactly where the women were. By an instinct he couldn't explain, he could sense they were holed up at Warrior Medichi's villa. Not only did the location make sense because it belonged to a Guardian of Ascension, but the property couldn't be goddamn located, which meant mist. But not just any mist. Endelle's fucking mist.

They were there. All he needed was every resource placed in the surrounding vicinity and as soon as either of the women made an appearance, dammit, he'd have them.

But Rith didn't put stock in Crace's *intuition* and he had his forces scattered from Sedona, by Thorne's house, down to Tucson, where Warrior Santiago had his main residence. So . . . fuck.

What he needed, therefore, only Greaves could give— permission to redirect personnel.

The air shimmered next to him. A moment later, the Commander appeared, his expression inscrutable, his bald head gleaming, the claw on his left hand snapping once. He looked like a picture out of *GQ*. He wore, as always, fine-pressed wool, the best of Hugo Boss. His shirt was lavender silk. He smelled, also as always, of lemons and maybe turpentine, a really odd juxtaposition to his suave, immaculate appearance.

Whatever.

Crace was about to speak, but the second snapping of the claw gave him pause. Greaves didn't always sport the unnatural appendage, just when he wanted to remind his subjects of his inherent preternatural power.

"To what do I owe the honor of *this summons*," the Commander said, his voice low and way too soft.

Crace felt the first inkling of his error by the way sweat popped out all over his forehead. The second inkling came from a wave of nausea. Jesus.

He wasn't daunted, though. He had a mission—to acquire his blood donor no matter the cost. "Warrior Medichi's villa should be our only priority. The women are there. I know it in my gut, but your servant, Rith, has staff as well as several squadrons of death vamps stationed at every property throughout the Sonoran Desert, even Tucson. I demand—" His voice broke off as Greaves's large round eyes narrowed.

Crace hissed since within the space of a millisecond he found himself facedown on the rough patio pavers. He also felt a blade at his neck. His head was turned onto his right cheek so he could see his master's fine Italian footwear moving from one end of the patio to the next, which meant that Greaves held him down and kept the knife at his neck by the sheer breadth of his personal power.

After what seemed like a century, the Commander seated himself opposite on a cement bench. He crossed his legs at the knee, the gentleman that he was.

Crace couldn't turn his neck far enough to see anything more than the lowest button of the Commander's coat. If he dared to move even one centimeter more, the blade, which had already broken skin, would slice deep, too deep. As it was he could feel the blood weep down both sides of his neck. His heart beat like a jackhammer.

Fuck. He had so many beautiful plans. Was he really going to die now?

He heard the heavy sigh. *"What am I to do with you, my dear Crace?"* Greaves's long-suffering voice had split-resonance and at the same time rattled through Crace's mind. He closed his eyes and moaned. Voice and mindspeak combined, especially weighted with resonance, caused so much searing pain, like knives whirling through his head and slicing the whole time.

"I fear you've gotten a little ahead of yourself here, especially with me. Since when do you decide, ever, that I must come to you?"

He wanted to bleat his apologies, to retract his words,

his request for an audience, but he couldn't make his lips move.

"So impatient. I thought you had grown a little at the end of our last adventure with ascender Wells, but I do believe you've actually regressed. I am so very disappointed, although this I believe is my fault. I should never have given you *dying blood*. And yet how could I have known you would take to it with such fervor?"

The blade disappeared, and Crace took his first normal breath. He remained, however, in the prone position.

"You may rise."

As Crace pushed up from the patio, his arms shook. Christ, his powerful, muscled arms actually shook.

Even so, he wanted to argue, but as he rose to his height and looked down at his still-seated master, he felt very small and insignificant, a cockroach that the sleek Italian shoes could squish with just a thought.

"You will do as you are told, Crace. My servant, Mr. Rith, has done as I have asked him to and you will respect his position in relation to me. *Are we in agreement?*" The last phrase was spoken both aloud with resonance and telepathically, which meant the knives started whirling through his head again. Crace fell forward straight onto the pavers once more, his cheek yet again pressed into the rough cement-formed, terra-cotta surface.

He lay prostrate until, after several minutes, he realized he was also alone and he wasn't held fast to his position.

He drew back to his knees. He took several deep breaths until his heart settled down, his head didn't hurt quite so much, and his hands stopped shaking.

He tried to take Greaves's rebuke to heart, he really did, but all he felt was enraged and the object of his rage had a wide forehead, a broad nose, black hair and came from somewhere east of the Caucasus. Bastard.

He gained his feet. He shifted his attention to the north. After all, from this position Medichi's villa was only a few miles away. Greaves and Rith could go fuck themselves for all he cared. He knew Havily Morgan was there, waiting for him. Even if Endelle's mist did protect the property from detection, GPS could at least put him at the boundaries, where he would wait.

Yes, goddammit, he'd wait, with three squadrons of death vampires. Then he'd take what he had already claimed for himself.

The only thing that ever really wearied Greaves was the moment a servant rebeled. Only then did he feel a sense of failure that very infrequently accompanied his efforts to subdue Second Earth. He did not mind a verbal battle with Endelle or even the effort to travel to various Territories through the night in order to secure new squads of death vampires to send to Phoenix Two. Nor did he mind the serious diplomatic twists and turns required to get a High Administrator to abandon Endelle's administration and join his forces. He even tended to enjoy the farcical COPASS hearings.

But when one of those allied with him made these ridiculous power plays, like *summoning him* from other parts of the world, only then did he feel the desire to maim and kill.

He'd come close to taking Crace's life, but for decades now he'd had a serious policy in place of always letting others do his dirty work. He needed his record clean, so clean it would be. Besides, he strongly suspected that Eldon Crace, despite his growth in surprising preternatural power as well as physical strength, would be his own undoing. If the vampire could get himself killed by stealing from the nest of a Warrior of the Blood, so much the better.

He folded back to Rio de Janeiro Two and begged the Brazilian High Administrator's apologies for his lapse in manners at having to leave the negotiations so abruptly. He spoke Portuguese, of course. Fluently.

He had already maneuvered the woman from behind her desk, that seat of authority behind which he could not allow her to continue addressing her concerns. Some things were very simple when it came to managing a Coming Order.

She now sat in a chair and he stood in front of her. "As I was saying," he said, noting again the large ruby she wore on the ring finger of her left hand, "I have a top-functioning mine in Burma near Mogok, which I would be only too happy to offer as a token of good faith. I want all my High Administrators to understand their importance to me personally as well as to my Geneva Round Table." She was actually quite lovely and he sensed her . . . *arousal*. Very good.

He also saw the flash of light in her eye as he spoke of the ruby mine he owned. He shared that flash of light, of greed, of hunger, and he knew negotiations over the next few weeks, perhaps even days, would fare extremely well.

"You are most greatly generous," she responded, her English less than perfect, but he appreciated the effort. His gaze drifted down the silk blouse she wore, unbuttoned at the third button. The signal was not lost to him, but he never mixed business with pleasure—unless of course he could put the High Administrator in thrall and slice her memories later, something he might just do. He was still irritated by the interview with Crace. A little relief would be welcome. She would find herself bruised afterward, inexplicably, but some things couldn't be helped.

He tested her shields and was both stunned and pleased that, though she had many powers, shielding capacity was almost nonexistent. Well, it seemed he had just found a soothing balm for his recent encounter.

"May I sit down?" he asked.

She inclined her head. "Nothing would please me more."

He smiled.

As Havily opened the door to the office, Marcus moved up the hall in her direction. He was a welcome sight after the usual harrowing encounter with Endelle.

She held the door for Alison and Parisa, the former

talking in low tones to the ascendiate, her arm around her shoulders.

"How did it go?" Marcus asked, his hand touching her elbow.

"Oh, the usual," Havily whispered. "But you should have seen Parisa. When Endelle punched at her from across the room with her powers, Parisa returned the favor and Endelle landed on her ass. I was shocked . . ."

The door opened. Oh. Shit. Preternatural hearing. She should have at least waited until she was back at the villa before she started gossiping about Endelle.

"Havily, tell me something," Her Supremeness began.

She turned to face her employer. "Yes, Madame Endelle?" Could her voice get any higher?

"I've been thinking about this recent battle in Parisa's courtyard, playing it over in my head. How the hell did Medichi know to show up exactly when he was needed? Thorne said he didn't send him there. Do you know anything about that?"

Havily released a sigh of relief. She'd expected to get reamed because of what she'd been saying to Marcus. Instead, it was just about the courtyard incident. "That's easy. I called him." She tapped her forehead. "I have a link with Warrior Medichi. We set it up after I had the vision of Luken getting wounded. They were both concerned for my safety, and as it turned out they were right. That's how Medichi . . . arrived . . . at the town house . . ." It struck Havily that Endelle would already have known all about this. And why was Endelle grinning?

When Endelle just lifted a brow then shut the door in her face, it took Havily a few seconds to realize exactly what Her Supremeness had meant by the whole thing and just how seriously Havily had erred.

She felt a rumbling beside her that quickly turned into a growl at her neck. Marcus's hand found her nape and held her firmly. "Break that link now," he cried.

She withheld a heavy sigh. If Endelle weren't so damn

powerful she'd plot how to get back at her, but the woman would probably know her plans before she could even form them.

Fine.

Now, what to do about the jealous beast beside her.

Down the hall, Alison and Parisa stood close together conversing. Alison gestured with flutters of her hands and Parisa smiled. In a few minutes, Havily had another meeting with the various committee heads to finalize both the Ambassadors Reception and the Festival.

"Break it now," Marcus growled, adding resonance, which forced her to turn and face him.

"It's no big deal," she tried to reassure him. "And if memory serves, that link saved your ass."

Those were so the wrong words to say to a Warrior of the Blood, on so many levels. That she would suggest Marcus wasn't fully capable of defending himself or her or Parisa was unforgivable. So was challenging him about the right of another man to have possession of her mind, even in this small, superficial way. She might as well have trumpeted a call to arms.

The release of a torpedo of fennel caused her to gasp. She took a step back and weaved on her feet. She saw stars, she really did. Holy shit.

She glanced at Parisa and Alison. She met Alison's gaze and sent, *Would you see to Parisa? I seem to have a situation.*

Alison glanced her direction, lifted her brow when her gaze shifted to Marcus, then guided Parisa into the executive dining room. She closed the door with a quick snap.

Before Marcus gave vent to the rage so evident in the way his light brown eyes were almost glowing, Havily jerked her head in the direction of her office. She moved with preternatural speed, pulled the door open and went inside. She knew he'd followed with the same blast of speed because his thighs were up against her, shoving at her, each step of the way.

Oh, boy was she in for it now.

Before she could open her mouth to either protest or explain, he had her pinned against the wall. Though the front part of her office had glass windows, the south wall was solid and separated her from the entire administrative pool. Only if someone happened to walk by could they be seen. The plate-glass window on the east wall was open to nothing but miles of desert.

His body was pressed the full length of hers, and the release of all this aggression had tainted his fennel scent with such a heavy dose of pheromones that her knees no longer existed. "Break it," he whispered deep into her ear.

His breath, his fennel, the erotic feeling of being pinned by this warrior, caused Havily to breathe in light little gasps. Dammit, she was panting. How quickly the man could sex her up. Not only that, she couldn't form a single rational thought. Instead, she wondered if she ought to just fold off her slacks and her thong and let him take care of business. That he was a hard length grinding between her legs wasn't a surprise.

What was it she had meant to say to him?

"No one takes your blood," he said, measuring each word, his breath still driving into her ear, "and no one gets inside your head." He drew his hips back slightly, and his hand went low as he caught her between her thighs. He cupped her . . . hard . . . and it felt so good. "And no one gets in here." *All of this*, he sent, *your mind, your body, your blood . . . these belong to me. Do . . . you . . . understand?*

Havily opened her mouth to speak, knowing she should argue, maybe set some boundaries, but his lips were on hers and his tongue took possession of her mouth in hard thrusts. After a moment, his cock once more formed a powerful ridge against her. He drew back but just enough to meet her gaze. "Break the connection." He ground his teeth. "Now. I need this."

"I can't," she responded breathless. "I would, but I don't know how. I think Medichi has to do it. Besides, I'm still not certain if it's a good idea."

He growled and pressed his hips against hers. "Not an option," he said. "Let's go back to the villa. I'll wake him up and we'll get this thing taken care of."

"Marcus," she whispered, turning her head. "I have a meeting. It's important, especially after the warning Leto gave you about the Ambassadors Festival. Besides, Medichi should sleep. You of all people know how important that is."

He was breathing against her neck and licked her throat.

She groaned, her eyes rolling back in her head. She would love to just throw away all her responsibilities, even her sense of what was right in this situation, but there was a little more at stake than the *breh-hedden*'s absurd call on them both.

She wedged her hands against his chest and pushed. Reluctantly, he gave way and stepped back, if not very far.

"Come to the meeting with me," she said. "And as soon as I can I'll sever the link, but I must conduct this meeting now."

He closed his eyes and she watched the struggle. The hands clenched on her arms gripped too hard. His jaw ground back and forth and he forced several deep breaths.

"Fine," he muttered, at long last, but his face had a ruddy color. "But I'm not happy about this."

"No shit," she whispered. That made his expression soften a little, since she rarely used profanity.

The meeting, however, did not flow quite as smoothly as she had hoped, but that was to be expected with one pissed-off-looking warrior vampire leaning against the door as though he barred all the other vampires from leaving.

Despite his brooding presence and the way his gaze followed her no matter which direction she moved, Havily listened to reports from each of her heads and had a good sense that both the reception, to be held on the following night, and the Festival in two days' time were well in hand. She would have expected nothing less. She had chosen her people with great care.

Finally, she broached the matter of security. Endelle wanted Leto's warning known, without revealing the source.

She kept the message succinct, then added, "Given the attack on Warrior Luken, there is strong reason to suspect we're talking about an incendiary threat, probably in the air."

The head of security, the Militia colonel by the name of Seriffe—and one powerful warrior—sat forward in his chair. He had short black hair, dark eyes, and a deep olive complexion. He was almost as big as Marcus. "So what are we talking about?" he asked. "Are we talking about during the barge parade or the following spectacle? Maybe the fireworks? The route is fifteen miles long and even though we'll have ten thousand Militia Warriors on the ground and another five hundred in the skies patrolling, how the hell are we to watch every movement, especially along the fireworks battery lines? Did this source indicate if there were concerns about the reception?"

Havily glanced at Marcus. She lifted a brow. Marcus had heard Leto. He would know that answer.

Marcus leaned away from the door and stood upright. He took a deep breath and some of his broody demeanor fell away. He shook off the effects of the *breh-hedden* and assumed his most professional manner, very in control, very much the man who had met her in the lobby of his building and escorted her upstairs to his office. Had that only been a couple of days ago? "The source referred specifically to the fireworks display. Nothing was said of the reception."

"Well, that's something then," the colonel stated. "So we'll focus our efforts on the fireworks batteries in the White Tanks. Beyond that, we'll have to rely on the vigilance of our Militia Warriors to report any undue activity."

Havily glanced at Marcus, at the slash of brows over light brown eyes, and a strong sensation of admiration rose in her chest. She hadn't wanted to feel this way about him, that on top of the *breh-hedden*'s call for communion, she could actually admire the man, but so she did. He had tremendous presence, the kind a man emitted when he'd been used to governing, in this case, a large number of corporations. His gaze shifted to hers abruptly. His eyes narrowed; then a faint smile and a nod of his chin gave evidence that her sudden emotion had communicated in no doubt a release of what he kept calling *honeysuckle.*

Naturally, *naturally,* he sent his own little fennel message, which brought on the familiar shortness-of-breath-and-watery-knees syndrome. She looked away from him and forced her attention back to Seriffe. She encouraged the colonel to lead the discussion, which drew Marcus well into the mix because his empire made extensive use of security. Corporate spies were busy everywhere. With Marcus thus engaged, she could breathe . . . a little.

By four o'clock, the meeting drew to a close. "I want to thank all of you for doing such an amazing job. With your outstanding teams in place, I'm sure this will be one of the finest events the administration has hosted." Smiles followed, and quirks of lips, since *the administration* hadn't hosted an event in decades.

She stood by the door as everyone left. She clasped hands, spoke more words of gratitude, and even exchanged a joke or two.

As best she could, however, she tried to ignore the vampire at her elbow, who sent a whisper through her mind, *Break the link, Havily, as soon as we get back to the villa.*

Once the last chairperson left the conference room, Marcus would have folded Havily straight back to the villa to take care of business, but Havily reminded him that they had a mortal-with-wings to tend to. He made short work of rounding up Parisa and getting both women back to the house.

But his attention was all for Havily. Damn, he hated being such a bastard about this, but he needed the link gone . . . now.

Parisa, fortunately, said she needed some alone time and intended to prepare a cup of tea and enjoy a piece of solitude. She pointed behind her. "I'll be in that small room at the top of the stairs, you know, just beyond the kitchen."

"The turret bedroom," Havily said. It was the only second-story room in the villa.

"If it's all right with you both," Parisa said, glancing from him to Havily, "I . . . I really would like to be alone for a while."

"Of course," Havily said.

Marcus had never been more grateful in his life, because right now he needed to get Havily alone and have a little *talk* with her.

When their winged ascendiate took off in the direction of the kitchen, his previous drive and instincts, with all the subtlety of a sledgehammer, pounded him again. He crossed to her and took her hand. "You," he said quietly. "Come with me. We're going to wake Medichi up then we're going to have . . . a discussion."

Havily opened her mouth to protest then clamped her lips shut. "Very well."

He started to pull her hard in the direction of Medichi's suite.

"Hey," she cried, jerking her hand out of his grasp. "Could you slow down a little? I'm wearing heels."

He turned back to her. "I apologize." He slid his arm around her waist and stared at her. He stared until a resulting wave of honeysuckle flowed over him. "Good," he said with a firm nod.

He remained glued to her side, walking at a pace she could easily maintain, until he got her to Medichi's bedroom door. He knocked several times. He had to repeat this again and again, getting louder each time, until the door opened and Medichi, with one eye still closed, asked in a deep voice, "What is it?" He didn't open the door farther than the width of his palm.

"Break the link."

Medichi's brows rose and his closed eye flipped open. He glanced from Havily to him and back. He closed both eyes this time for the space of about six seconds. Marcus glanced at Havily and watched as her head jerked and her brows rose.

"Done, asshole." He shut the door with a snap.

Marcus turned to Havily. "We good?"

She drew in a deep breath. "He broke the link."

Marcus growled then guided her back up the long hall to the intersection of the guest rooms. He made a hard left, then another, herding her into their bedroom. He shoved the door shut with his foot.

He picked her up, moved to the bed, and dumped her on her back. She gave a cry of surprise, but he had a point to make and he needed her to understand exactly what that point was.

She scrambled backward, but he leaned forward, put his hand on her stomach, glared at her, then folded her clothes off, even her thong.

She gasped then laughed. "What is with you?"

"I already told you but I don't think you've taken me seriously on this subject."

"Marcus . . ." Her tone was chiding, her head tilted.

He unbuttoned his shirt slowly as his gaze roved her exquisite breasts, her flat stomach, the rise of her pelvic bones, the soft thatch of red hair between her thighs. He unbuttoned his slacks, unzipped, and peeled them down his thighs. He didn't have patience with the shoes and socks. These he got rid of the old-fashioned way as he thought the thought.

When he stripped off his briefs, he had the satisfaction of watching her gaze track down his chest, lower and lower, then latch onto his stiff cock. She licked her lips. He growled. He moved onto the bed, hands and knees, until he was over her. "Just so we're clear," he said, "you're on bottom until I say otherwise, *if* I ever say otherwise."

She nodded. He could tell by her scent, which flooded the space between them, and by the way her breaths were short and light, that he could have told her to stand on her head and she would have agreed to it. Good. He took her right arm and drew it straight out from her body. He took her left arm and did the same. Then he focused on each wrist and set small shields at the base of each of her hands. He might not be able to do big shields like Leto, but these he could do. It wouldn't take much to break the preternatural bindings, and she could if she needed to, but right now he wanted her to feel restrained and bound.

She gasped. "What did you just do? I can't move my wrists." A wave of honeysuckle once more flooded his sinuses. For a moment, he couldn't breathe and his cock throbbed.

"Shields." His voice deepened. "You're not allowed to object." But he watched her carefully. He would relent if he saw the smallest sign of distress. However, a moan left her throat, she drew a ragged breath, then licked her lips, and honeysuckle once more assaulted him. Good. This was very good.

"Now, present your left vein."

She tilted her head to the right, stretching it as far as she could. He shifted over her, his heart pounding. He was worked up, but he needed her to understand. "Mine," he whispered. "Do you understand, Havily? This is *mine*." He positioned his fangs over her vein then struck. She gave a little cry as he started to drink.

"I want my hands on you," she cried, as she struggled against the invisible bindings.

Hush, he sent. But it pleased him.

He didn't drink much before he withdrew from her vein, the tips of his fangs releasing a chemical that sealed the membrane. "Now your other vein."

Havily rolled her head, this time to the left, and felt tears burn her eyes. He was too far away from her and she needed her hands on him, her arms around him, yet the restraints aroused her. Oh, his fangs sank into the other side of her neck and he was drinking again. She ached deep in her abdomen, within the well of her body. She felt her fluids seep from her. Even her wing-locks were wet beneath her back.

She moved her hips, trying to reach him, but he shifted away from her, all his actions designed to torment. So what did he need from her?

After less than a minute, he drew back from her neck. Then he lowered himself and cupped her left breast in his hand. She watched his fangs emerge again and he struck, not hard, and not for long. "Potions," she murmured. "Oh, God. It's been so long."

Yes, he sent straight into her head as he withdrew his fangs.

Her back arched as he started to lave the already puckered tip. The potion worked fast, a wonderful burn that seeped into her nipple, her areola, then kept spreading until the breast he kneaded with his hand was an organ of intense pleasure.

She cried out and tears fell in earnest down her face.

He shifted slightly, his fangs poised over her other breast.

"Oh, Marcus," she cried out. She didn't know how much more she could take.

He struck again. The sting of his fangs penetrated her skin and caused her to clench, hard. Once more the potion was an erotic burn so that now both her breasts were on fire in the best possible way. She writhed beneath him.

Marcus kneaded the breast as he licked and suckled. Havily moaned, her hips swayed and rocked. Her legs caught him about the waist and worked hard to pull him into her, but he stayed just out of reach. She had physical strength; all vampires did. But he was male and he was stronger and he wouldn't allow her release until she'd learned her lesson. She was in agony and he was pleased because when her release came it would be hot.

By now both breasts would be on fire. He pulled back and watched her, satisfied with her suffering as she writhed under him. "You should have told me you had a link with Medichi. You were very bad not to have broken it the same day I arrived and took you to bed. I need you to know that."

But she was arching off the bed, her breasts puckered and reaching for him. If her wrists hadn't been pinned, she would have wrapped her arms around him hard. The sight of her worked up just barely kept him from grabbing her about the waist and thrusting into her. However, he was just getting started with this instructive session.

Her legs scissored around him, trying to gain control of his hips. But he pushed back and broke the connection.

"I need you," she cried. "Please."

He put his hands on her legs and with his pecs and biceps flexing with effort, he pulled her legs from around him and spread them wide. He closed his eyes and the same clamp-like shields took hold of her ankles, pinning her spread-eagle on the bed.

All that could move now were here hips and her head. Both thrashed as she called out, "My breasts."

"You want me to suckle your breasts?" he asked.

"At the very least," she cried. "Marcus, what have you done to me? I want my hands on you."

He suckled and played with her breasts until she was weeping all over again.

"Marcus," she whimpered.

"No more telepathic links."

"No. Never again."

"Promise?"

"Oh, God yes. Anything."

Anything. Now there was a temptation, but he restrained himself. Instead, he responded, "Good. Now that we have that settled, what is it you'd like me to do for you?"

"Take me," she wailed.

He took hold of his cock in his right hand and rose up so that she could see him. "You mean with this?" He was fully aroused, weeping.

"Yes, yes, yes," she hissed. "Oh, God, yes."

He shook his head, smiled, and stroked himself in long pulls. "You're not ready for me. I can tell." A complete lie.

He was sure if he put his finger in her she'd be wet, hot, and swollen.

She squeezed her eyes shut and groaned. "The potion is going deep now, traveling down my abdomen." Her hips arched. "Marcus, please." Her light green eyes were wild, her lips puffy, her chest rising and falling.

He laughed again. Her rich honeysuckle scent flooded the room. He loved having her at his mercy.

He knelt low between her legs and kissed her thatch of red curls. He separated her labia with his fingers. He bent down and in one long stroke licked her from her opening to the top of her clit. He had never heard a woman make a sound like that, a cross between a moan and a cry, a wild animal in torment. He moved in with his lips and sucked. Her groans turned deep and guttural and within a few seconds she was screaming her orgasm.

He wanted to stop what he was doing, leap on her and bury himself deep. But another part of him wanted to take this all the way, keep her pinned like this until he'd done what he'd started out to do.

He released her then moved up to her groin. There were veins he could tap but they were deep.

"Marcus," she whispered, her breaths still little more than a lusty pant. "What are you thinking?"

He licked the space at the juncture of thigh and pelvis. "I think you know."

She moaned at the ceiling and he swore the sound reverberated around the room.

But he wouldn't do this without at the same time giving her another release. He slid a finger into her core, withdrew, then gave her two. Very slowly he stroked her, in and out, her body gripping him, her hips moving in a corresponding rock.

"Be still," he commanded. "You need to be still when I do this." She stopped and her breaths were now quick and shallow.

He positioned himself carefully and with a practiced

strike, hit the vein on the right side of her groin. As she cried out in pleasure all over again, he sucked hard and worked her with his fingers, moving faster and faster.

Havily was on fire, her body incinerating under the multiple sensations. Her breasts still throbbed and the chemicals he'd released into them had traveled down her abdomen, below her belly button now, and sought the center of her body. At each point where he had taken her vein, she throbbed. That she was pinned to the bed and couldn't move was incredibly erotic. She wasn't afraid. She knew Marcus. She trusted him.

But the implied threat worked her like nothing else.

Your blood is intoxicating, he sent.

She lay trembling, her hips rocking into his hand, his mouth pressed close to her sex as he drank from her. That she was giving to him as he gave to her also wound her up. But the friction of his fingers was heaven, dragging out, pushing in, going faster and faster until the pleasure reached the knife-edge. She trembled as ecstasy streaked over the most tender part of her, drove up her core and punched at her in a blaze of orgasm so powerful she cried out then screamed, his arm a piston as he worked his fingers in and out, over and over, his lips sucking her essence from her vein.

Oh, God.

Only as her hips settled did he stop the motion of his hand and arm, then finally withdraw from the vein. He kissed her skin above the two red points where his fangs had sunk deep. He kissed her over and over and with the back of one finger stroked her gently between her legs.

After a minute or two, he once more sat on his heels and looked at her. His eyes were hazy and he had her blood on his lips. He looked so pumped, even wired. She wanted to reach up and touch him because he looked dazed. "You okay?" she asked, her breaths still in little gasps.

He nodded. He closed his eyes and took deep gulps of

air. His muscles looked larger, just as they had the last time. He flexed his pecs, opened his eyes, then looked down at his erection.

He was massive. She clenched unexpectedly as she saw that he wept from the tip. She wanted him so much. For all the incredible pleasure he had just given her, she wanted him inside her, joined to her, connected, *one*.

"Marcus," she said quietly, meeting his gaze. "Out of respect for you, so long as you are with me on Second, I will not form another link. I hereby make this solemn promise."

His smile was slow, and he looked satisfied, like a man who had gone on a hunt and brought down his prey. He nodded. "Good."

She felt the shields release one after the other, soft little pops of power. She flexed her arms and drew her legs up, bending at the knee. But she kept her legs spread wide . . . for him.

He settled between her thighs, his cock at her opening, pressing just a little. He leaned over her, planting his hands on either side of her shoulders. She put her hands on his chest and in slow strokes covered the breadth of his pecs. She flicked his nipples. His head arched and he moaned. She drifted her hands down his sculpted abdomen, lower and lower until she had her palms against his groin. "I want to take you there." She pressed her fingers against his vein and stroked upward. "I want my fangs in you and sucking your blood just as you took mine."

His hips bucked. "Havily, this is madness."

"Yes," she murmured. "A very sweet kind of madness." She reached her right hand low and surrounded his cock. "Inside. Now, Warrior. All the way."

His eyes flared as he met her gaze. He moved fast, jabbed, and in a single smooth stroke penetrated her. She cried out at the invasion and the pleasure, both of which made her so happy. But he was big and it took a minute to adjust to his size. In this, he took his time, moving in short strokes and grinding against her in a circle as her body stretched and accommodated him. She slid her arms around his neck and held on.

This wouldn't take long. He was worked up and she was ready again, her body trembling, the fire of the potion gripping the core of her. She clenched around him, stroking him, savoring the feel of him deep inside.

As he started pumping into her, she closed her eyes and eased back on the bed, letting her arms slide over his shoulders. She focused on the beautiful sensation of being taken by him. There were many sexual pleasures, but this one, of having what was most essentially male driving into her, affected her the most, not just physically but emotionally. Her chest filled with an ache she couldn't explain but which grew more profound the longer he pumped into her.

Havily, he sent. *I want in. Now.*

She could feel his mind press against her mental shields. Her body was on fire again, but this was different, this would change things. Adrenaline joined the mix and though she felt like she should tell him no, she couldn't resist. She wanted Marcus in her head, taking her in deep mind-engagement, one more step along the path to full communion.

Yes, she whispered, and the last of her reserves fled as he entered her mind.

Marcus was so powerful that when his mind moved inside hers, she was at first overwhelmed by his presence. He groaned and his hips jerked against her. He dove through her thoughts and her memories. Her body responded, the pleasure she had felt turning from a solid blaze into an enormous bonfire. His presence in her mind, the fire in her breasts, and the deep pleasure between her legs converged. She was all arms and legs, stroking, holding, hugging, wrapping, and undulating under him until his hips moved faster.

With her legs, she locked him against her, arched her back, and screamed as he pushed her once more over the edge. He joined her, also arching back, pulling away and shouting his release.

Oh. God. Pleasure barreled through her up and up until even her chest was filled with ecstasy. She screamed again and then his mouth was on hers as he pumped the last few bits of his seed into her, his harsh breaths battling her own deep pants.

"Oh, my God," she whispered against his lips. Her body was locked around his, her legs entwined and holding him seated against her, both her arms snaked around him, one surrounding his back, the other his neck, her fingers trapped in his hair.

He lay on her, breathing hard, his mouth on her neck.

"Havily. Havily," he said against her skin. He kissed her and she smiled, her head falling from one side to the next and back. His kisses followed. She was so happy, glowing, content, and he was still inside her head. She could feel him, a warm comforting presence.

For the first time in fifteen years, since Eric died, she didn't feel alone. She smiled at the ceiling and sucked in more much-needed air. Her shoulders relaxed and her legs finally released him but she hoped he would remain inside her, both his mind and his cock. She didn't want this moment to end, not now, not yet, maybe not ever.

Oh. God.

Marcus was in trouble.

He knew that now. He hadn't gotten it before, but reality was starting to sink in.

He'd been inside Havily's mind and though it was impossible to see everything about a person in a single mind-penetration, he had seen her, really seen her, the depth of her, even though she pretended not to have depth, the kindness of her, though she could take what was dealt her, the breadth of her ability to love, though she kept her emotions tight, controlled, remote.

Yeah, her ability to love swamped him, not that she was

loving him right now but that she had such profound capacity, and he yearned for that as though he'd never had a yearning before. He wanted her love, now and forever.

He dipped his arms beneath her back and held her to him, wanting that heart of hers to press against his chest and slide inside. Then he drew back, his arms as well. He put his lips to hers and kissed her. He kissed her, full-bodied kisses, his tongue dipping and tasting, reaching her, the depth of her.

He kept kissing her until her body once more moved and undulated. He hadn't meant to suggest that he make love to her again, but he was still connected and when her hips moved and created more friction he was ready with just a few strokes. This time he kept his connection to her mouth until she was moaning once more. He was still inside her mind. *I want you, Havily, all of you,* he sent.

You have me returned.

He didn't have her, though, at least not yet. But somehow making love to her made him want her as he hadn't wanted a woman in over a millennia. He felt anxious in the midst of the pleasuring and connection. With so much flowing between them, with the taking of her mind, just how easy was it going to be, once he'd made her safe on Second, to step away from her and let her live her life without him?

His heart seized and he forced the difficult thoughts away. She was here, she was his *now.* He never broke the connection of his mouth to her mouth or his mind to her mind. He just kept working his hips, moving against her in strong pulses, pushing then drawing back.

You're mine.

I'm yours.

He sped up, and he took her again. He took her until she was screaming at the ceiling, pinning her legs around his hips, again and again and again.

CHAPTER 15

Parisa was a very wicked woman.

She sat barefoot on the bottom step of the stairs that led corkscrew fashion up to the turret room. She had been in the second-story room for half an hour then decided to come downstairs to fix something to eat.

She'd gotten as far as the bottom step when she'd heard the throaty cries from all the way down the hall. If she hadn't known *who* was in the house, or if she hadn't already slept in the room opposite Havily and Marcus, she might have wondered if a crime was being committed.

The trouble was, she had finally come to understand the nature of the power she possessed, a power that allowed her to *see* what others were doing.

When she had told Havily about her visions, that they most often if not always involved Warrior Medichi, she had believed they were connected to him.

Not so. In the past few minutes of having focused on the activity in the southern part of the house, she had opened a sort of window to the events in Marcus and Havily's room, and she had watched the lovemaking like a voyeur, like one who prowls outside windows at night and looks in to see what's going on. Only it wasn't nighttime and she wasn't outside a window.

And yet she could see into the couple's room as surely as she could see the planked floor beneath her feet. Even now, she watched Marcus and Havily and she just couldn't seem to look away.

She leaned over and planted her elbows on her knees, her fists cradling her cheeks.

She had never seen anything so beautiful as the way Marcus kissed Havily while he made love to her. Their bodies glowed with tendrils of light, some pale green, others a golden brown, but all sparkling like diamonds. Yes, so beautiful. Marcus had to be *in love* with Havily but did he know it? Did she?

Her fingers were wet.

She glanced down then swiped her cheeks. She'd been weeping.

And why wouldn't she be when she was so moved? Her heart ached at the sight of them together, connected at their hips, joined fully, for she had even seen him enter her.

But she really was a wicked woman to be watching.

Her conscience finally smote her and she drew out of the room, closing the mental window.

So all this time, that's what had been happening to her. That's why she'd been able to see all these warriors, especially Antony Medichi. For some strange, impossible reason, she had the ability to *see* these people, to *see* Warrior Medichi, to watch them all in the midst of their lives, while they ate, made war, made love.

She sat back and stared at the small sunroom across from the stairs. The view opened onto the front lawn. To the left was a pathway arched with vines and a lovely purple flower.

She didn't know what to think of this world. If Havily was to be believed, then Parisa was Warrior Medichi's *breh*. But that seemed so absurd. She was a librarian on Mortal Earth, and she really didn't see how she could possibly fit into Medichi's warrior lifestyle.

Beyond that, she didn't want to be here, not really. She didn't ask to have these powers, to be able to knock the Supreme High Administrator backward with what Alison told her was a hand-blast. She didn't ask to have wings, or to have this freakish ability to spy on others without their knowing. It was so wrong.

She sighed heavily. She wanted to go home, pour herself a goblet of Cabernet Sauvignon, prepare a bubble bath in her soaking tub, put on Holst's *The Planets,* sink to her neck, and get lost in the music for the next century.

She wasn't built for this world or for a warrior who was as tall as an NBA player.

She covered her face with her hands because one particular image of Medichi zoomed through her mind—that moment when he had appeared in the doorway of the kitchen and dropped his towel to expose himself to her.

The tears ran faster now.

How could she explain how much she loved, *loved,* that he had done that for her—as though, on a very elemental level, he trusted her. But in the same way, she trusted him because she already *knew him.* After all, she'd been *spying* on him for over a year, and she knew that in the depths of his being he longed for the same things she did—to be touched, caressed, kissed, made love to.

But it wasn't going to happen.

She wanted to go home, and as soon as Madame Endelle figured out how to make her safe on Mortal Earth, she was going back.

Havily lay on her back, still in bed, listening to the shower run.

She was sated, beyond sated, so well used she wondered if she would even be able to stand, never mind walk.

She looked at her wrists, wondering again how he had bound her but hoping it wouldn't be the last time. She ran a finger over the place he'd taken her at her groin. A lump remained and she touched it gently. She closed her eyes, remembering.

What a session that had been.

Wow. Shivers ran over her shoulders.

She still couldn't believe that Marcus had taken her the way he'd taken her—and so thoroughly. Then he'd kissed her and kissed her and with his mouth pinned to hers he'd given her round two, or was it three, or was it seven?

She chuckled. Then she sighed. What bliss.

But as she recalled what it had been like to have Marcus in her mind, her amusement dimmed. Something troubled her about that, something she couldn't quite define. Except, what if he now had different expectations of her? What if he wanted more from her?

She tried to think back over the past day or two. Had she made it clear that she wasn't interested in a long-term relationship with him—and not just because he would always be a deserter in her mind?

They hadn't exactly had time to talk. Either they'd been engaged dealing with her work or protecting Parisa or they'd been in bed . . . busy.

Her thoughts traveled back to Eric's funeral and how blasted she had felt, so deeply hurt that she vowed she would never go through that again. Grief was a powerful antidote to falling in love. Enough grief and why would anyone go through such terrible loss again?

It didn't take long for other thoughts to arrive, ones from a hundred years ago when she had buried her family in four graves all within one single horrible week. The month had been April, and even now she could smell the hyacinths in bloom, that light powdery fragrance, the flowers that came up by bulb just outside her kitchen window.

She sat up, the pain of remembered loss pressing on her.

She lifted her gaze to the bathroom. She heard Marcus humming and her heart hurt a little more.

She slid her legs over the side of the bed. She grabbed a robe and a change of clothes. There were several bathrooms in the villa, and without examining the why of it, she left the bedroom and went down the southern hall to yet another hub in the center of another group of rooms. In one of those, she found a bathroom and closed herself inside.

She turned the shower on, wrapped her hair in a towel, and when the water was warm, she stepped inside. She washed her arms, her shoulders, her breasts. Her hands traveled lower. She felt the faint bump on her groin again, then her hand went between her legs and she felt his seed. Marcus had left a lot of himself on her and inside her.

For some reason, the tears came, hot on her cheeks as she bent forward out of the spray. She didn't even know why she was crying except that Marcus's seed had reminded her of being married once, of having loved being married and content in the safety of her world until disease stripped her naked within a handful of days.

She had been hysterical that first night. During the painful days that followed, grief had stolen her heart utterly and completely

She marveled only at one thing, that eighty-five years later she had actually allowed Eric into her life. How and why was the mystery, except that somewhere in her mind she had thought maybe ascended life would be different and she had given herself permission to risk loving again. Then Eric had died and her heart had closed up once more.

Reminded of the depth of that loss, and the terrible losses before Eric, she knew one thing—she could never go through it again.

A few more minutes in the shower, as her tears lessened and finally ceased, she felt calmer, more at ease, more like her old self. Her heart felt safer, more secure.

She dressed in jeans, two tank tops, one white, the other

black and off the shoulder. She folded her makeup from the other bathroom and made use of under-eye concealer. She tended to her makeup as she always did, blending the foundation carefully, applying the proper layers of eye shadow and liner. She got very close to the mirror and tweezed her brows. The routine of it further eased her heart.

When her hair was brushed, teased, combed, and shaped, when she had donned several rings, two sets of pierced earrings, and a simple silver chain necklace, when she was satisfied with her appearance, only then did she leave the unfamiliar room and head in the direction of the kitchen.

By the time she entered the foyer, two aromas reached her. One belonged to onions and garlic simmering in olive oil, and the other was a rich fennel scent. Her stomach rumbled at the first, but her heart seized at the second.

Whatever.

Somehow, she was going to have to get used to the call of the *breh-hedden* and not take it so damn seriously.

She straightened her shoulders. As she neared the kitchen, she called out, "What smells like heaven?"

Marcus sat on a bar stool on the nearer side of the dark soapstone island. He wore a fresh, white silk, short-sleeved shirt; slacks; shoes; and socks. This was casual Phoenix, but she had the impression that what he wore right now was about as casual as he would ever allow himself to get. But jeans would be a great look for him, jeans and maybe nothing else. Commando would add the finishing touch. Okay, she needed to stop these thoughts right now because they weren't helping her to stay focused.

He turned toward her, a forkful of pasta near his mouth. The fork paused midair as he looked her up and down, his light brown eyes flaring. He licked his lips. "Parisa cooked."

When another rush of fennel struck her, she ignored the way her heart rate climbed. She looked past him to Parisa, who stood on the opposite side of the kitchen island. "So I see. It smells wonderful."

Parisa dished up a plate for Havily and dressed it with

fresh basil and a squeeze of lemon. "I found the ingredients in the fridge. I made a lot because I know I was starved and I figured you both would be as well. I wasn't sure about Warrior Medichi."

Havily took up a stool next to Marcus and before she could warn him away, his hand was on her thigh. She looked down at it, uncertain what to do.

"Hey," he murmured. And before she could stop him, he leaned close and kissed her, full on the lips. Ohhhhh . . . damn.

Havily drew back and looked at him, fear striking her heart like a well-swung mallet.

"What's wrong?" he asked. But just as quickly as the concern entered his eyes, understanding followed, and the hand on her thigh slipped away.

She wanted it back.

No, she didn't

Yes, she did.

She took a deep breath and concentrated on her pasta.

Parisa sat down beside her. "I've been meaning to ask, what is that mesh-like structure in the air above the villa?"

"You can see that?" Marcus asked, then whistled low.

"It's called mist," Havily said. "A powerful ascender can create it. Marcus can. Medichi. All the warriors, I think. I haven't developed the ability yet but then essentially I'm very young in ascended terms. That you can see it is rather amazing; it indicates your level of power. It is the rare ascender who can actually see mist. Although I must say I'm not surprised by this ability since you're not only a mortal with wings but you can also throw a hand-blast. Amazing."

Parisa shook her head back and forth. "I can't believe I actually slammed the ruler of Second Earth against a plate-glass window because of power I released from my arm and hand."

Havily laughed. "It was the highlight of my day, let me tell you."

Parisa smiled, but her gaze shifted in the direction of

the exotic dome over Warrior Medichi's property. "Well, I think her mist is beautiful. It reminds me of a very fine white lace." She was silent for a long moment, chewing on the tender pasta, then asked how old everyone was.

Her eyes widened when Havily gave both Endelle's and Marcus's ages. "Medichi of course is younger. He ascended around AD 700."

Parisa laughed and shook her head. "You know what's funny? Of all the things you've told me, for some reason speaking of having lived in terms of centuries has made me dizzy." She lifted her hand, palm facing both of them, and added quickly, "I'm fine. I swear it."

Havily laughed, Marcus as well. "Parisa, the pasta kills," he said. "Thanks for cooking. I would have offered but when it comes to culinary ability, I'm basically cooking-challenged."

Havily glanced at him. Now, why did he have to be such a nice guy? Why couldn't he have said something offensive, or not been grateful that Parisa cooked, or worse, *bragged* about what a great cook *he* was? Why couldn't he just man up and give her a reason to dislike him?

"You're welcome," Parisa said. She then drew in a deep breath. The fork that twirled her pasta slowed and stopped.

Havily noted the serious frown between her brows. "What is it?"

Parisa met her gaze. "I know that there are bad guys out there looking for me, but do you think there's someplace we could go so that I could try out my wings? I mean, I don't want to make anything difficult for either of you, but if you only knew how much I long to fly—"

"Absolutely," Havily cried. "I haven't flown for a week and I know exactly what you mean. I get a little antsy, even irritable, if I don't take to the skies on a regular basis. But you haven't really flown at all yet, have you?"

She shook her head. "Just that little jump off the railing, which was really more of a floating experiencing than anything else."

Havily felt relieved. Supporting Parisa through her first few flying experiences was just what she needed to get some distance from the warrior beside her. "I'll bring over a couple of my flight suits. They're made with halters. I'm sure one of them will fit, although it might be a little snug through the chest."

Parisa grinned. "Thank you. I can't tell you how much this means to me."

After the dishes were cleaned up, and Medichi's dinner put in the warming oven, Havily returned with Parisa to their rooms. She folded the suits from her town house, gave Parisa one, then changed into her own.

When she left the bedroom she shared with Marcus, he was standing at the end of the hall, near the rectangular table, as though he'd been waiting for her. He opened his mouth to speak but Parisa exited her room at the same time and called out, "Yes, it's tight, but I think I can manage."

Havily's gaze fell to the beautiful long line of cleavage that overflowed the haltered top then dropped to examine the waist, which was loose. "I can adjust this for you," she said. "The clasp is in the back."

Parisa put her hands on her hips and turned around. Havily adjusted the waistband, making it snug. "There's an entire industry geared to women's flight apparel."

"I can just imagine."

"There. I think we're both ready. Let's fly."

As Havily turned toward Marcus, she saw that his gaze was settled on Parisa's cleavage—and why wouldn't it be, since the snug fit pushed her breasts up and out? Still, she rolled her eyes.

Directing Parisa toward the front door, she let her get in front of them a few paces. When there was sufficient distance, she elbowed Marcus. "Do you have to be such a guy?"

He looked at her, startled, then glanced up at the ceiling. "Sorry, sweetheart. Old habit."

"Yeah, well, get some new ones. And what's with the *sweetheart*?"

"Darling?" he suggested.

"Aack," she cried, and walked faster, moving ahead of him.

"You know," he called after her, "for a second there you looked just like Endelle."

She ignored him and focused instead on teaching Parisa the basics of flight.

Havily wore an emerald-green flying halter, boned to support her breasts and tight around the waist to keep the whole thing from sliding around while she maneuvered through the air. The black pants, snug at the ankle, were a stretch knit that gave ease of movement.

Her back itched and tingled, the wings ready to come.

She stood opposite Parisa, whose breaths were high in her chest in anticipation, her amethyst eyes glittering. The un-ascended non-ascendiate hopped from one foot to the next. Her flight suit included the same black pants, but the halter was a sexy boned creation made of supersoft black leather. She really couldn't blame Marcus for staring. The woman's cleavage was spectacular.

Both sets of feet were bare since they'd be practicing on the front lawn beneath the shelter and protection of the enormous dome of mist.

Havily smiled then closed her eyes. She hadn't mounted her wings in over a week and she tried to fly often. Her preferred place to take to the air was off the Mogollon Rim, near Thorne's house in Sedona. Though it had taken a good decade to gain real confidence, she loved launching from the two-thousand-foot cliff and flying through the canyons, catching the currents, floating, feeling the eddies tease her wings as unexpected drifts of air appeared from hidden canyons.

Yeah, she loved it.

Parisa, already filled with the longing for flight, would be crazy about the Rim. Maybe one day they could fly it together.

Havily took a deep breath and spread her arms wide.

This was the moment she treasured, in her opinion the most important gift of ascended life, the blessing of flight.

Her wing-locks hummed, vibrated, and wept with fluids to ease the emergence of the feathers and attendant mesh superstructure from the locks. As the wings began to glide in a swiftly flowing sweep out of her back, she arched slightly then gasped. The sensation, so much like ecstasy, caught her behind her knees. She honestly would have fallen but the wings themselves kept her aloft. Once extended, she opened her eyes to find herself staring at Parisa, who had pressed her hands to her cheeks, tears shimmering in her eyes.

"Your wings are so beautiful," Parisa cried.

Havily preened. "I know." Her wings were light brown and speckled with dark brown spots in increasing numbers toward her back. A light green about two inches in diameter formed a band a few inches from the tips of the outermost feathers. She turned this way and that. The movement of course sent her rising off the ground a few feet as the curve of hundreds of feathers caught air. She gave a flip of both wings and twirled in a spiral. She drew her wings in and landed on her feet.

Parisa clapped her hands. "Oh," she cried. She closed her eyes, and a moment later she mounted her wings.

Havily sucked in her breath. "Whatever mine are, yours are *majestic*."

Parisa threw her arms wide. "I need to fly," rushed from her lips. She lifted her wings then flapped.

"Wait!" Havily cried. She had made the same rookie mistake, flying straight up into the air without either instruction or practice.

Havily launched after her and, as the resulting forward spin threw Parisa in what could be a deadly maneuver for the mortal, Havily caught her bare feet and gave a downward tug. The movement forced Parisa to lift her arms, which brought the wings up and out. The resulting parachute effect permitted the untried ascendiate to drop gently back to earth.

As soon as Parisa touched down on the grass, she brought her wings in close and dropped to her knees. "Well, that was foolish," she cried. She took deep breaths.

Havily floated down beside her and also brought her wings to close-mount, chuckling. "I tried to warn you but you took off so fast. Sorry, I should have said something ahead of time. As much as you think you'll know what to do, there is still quite a bit of skill involved."

Parisa looked up at her, a hand pressed to her chest. "I was so sure I could do it." She blinked several times. Her cheeks were flushed and Havily could almost hear the loud hammering of her heart. "I hate to think what would have happened if I'd fallen to the ground."

"You have no idea. I spent a week in the hospital in my early days. Broken feathers, or feathers ripped from mesh, hurt like a bitch."

Parisa started to laugh then covered her face. A few more breaths and she rose to her feet once more. "Okay. Teach me what I need to know."

Marcus folded a lawn chair from the pool area to the front patio. The moment of sheer panic he'd experienced when Parisa's first flight resulted in an out-of-control forward roll had dissipated as he watched how Havily, with a piece of clear thinking and expertise, pulled on Parisa's feet and brought her safely to ground. Genius.

He locked his hands behind his head and smiled. His woman had chops.

These were two beautiful women, lean and fit, and both pairs of wings were exquisite.

Parisa's *royle* pair still stunned him. He wondered what her wings could possibly mean for Second Earth. There were several myths surrounding *royle* wings, primarily indicating that a vampire who presented *royle* wings had the capacity to bring peace to a land, a quality that the first ascender, Luchianne, had.

Marcus snorted. He was very old and he knew one significant truth about Luchianne: She brought peace to the land by battling death vampires from the time the first vampire used his fangs to take dying blood. So, yeah, Luchianne had brought peace, through her ability to wield a sword.

Whatever.

Well, Parisa's wings weren't exactly his concern and certainly not what kept his gaze fixed on the women. Yeah, he was a man. He enjoyed watching the women move, backs arched in short climbs or dives, breasts thrust forward.

But more often than not, his gaze was fixed to Havily, whether she was in flight showing Parisa the basic movements of the wings or steadying the ascendiate with one hand while Parisa practiced a downward flap. It was like watching someone beginning to swim, learning which movements kept you afloat instead of sending you to the depths, which kept you from rolling or pitching left or right.

For the most part Havily kept the mortal just a few feet off the ground.

Yeah, she was a good teacher, patient, encouraging. How many times had she clapped her hands at something Parisa did? Fuck. His admiration for Havily was growing. That's all he needed, to admire the hell out of her. Great.

Parisa was an interesting woman to watch as well, despite that occasionally his gaze drifted to her . . . yeah, well, he was trying not to be such a guy. When he was able to keep his attention *elsewhere,* the woman's concentration was so fierce she barely blinked, as though she wanted to learn everything about working the air in the next three minutes.

He'd ascended such a goddamn long time ago that he'd forgotten the wonder of it all, the pleasure of flight, of wings, of soaring through the air high above the earth. The sight of Parisa's sheer joy at the process warmed his heart, his ascended heart, that part of him that belonged here on Second Earth.

His gaze drifted up to the shield of mist over the property. He frowned. He thought he saw something. Yep. There it was. He sat forward as shadows passed straight overhead. He sharpened and lengthened his vision. Shit. Squads of death vampires, already in the air, hunting no doubt for the mortal-with-wings. Which of course meant that Greaves had a legion of his warriors out searching for her.

He eased back and forced himself to relax. Both Parisa and Havily were completely safe beneath Endelle's monumental creation of mist.

He thought back to the attack on Parisa's home. If Marcus understood the workings of that bureaucratic mess called, appropriately, COPASS, Endelle had to file a complaint with the committee about the attack. Leto and Crace showing up, armed, had to be a major violation. But like any good bureaucracy, filing complaints, then having those complaints acted upon took *time,* usually lots of it and rarely with an acceptable outcome.

There was only one crime on Second Earth that COPASS acted upon with speed—assassination. Justice was always served within hours. Unfortunately, *assassination* was narrowly defined as the taking of a life whose designation involved an official, government capacity. The mere slaying of an ascender by a death vampire was considered a homicide, which in turn would take months going through the process of Second Earth's criminal justice system, not too different from Mortal Earth.

Marcus had always preferred warrior justice—a sword straight through the neck, the head separated from the body samurai-style.

Oh . . . yeah.

Shadows once more moved beyond the mist.

"Havily," he called out as she took Parisa higher into the air.

Havily took Parisa's hand and steadied her, both women flapping their wings in a slow movement and hanging suspended in the air. She called down to Marcus. "What is it? Everything okay?"

"Don't go beyond the mist."

"We won't."

When he saw Parisa nod, he relaxed and released a deep breath.

Okay. The women were safe.

That was good.

Good.

Medichi held a hot plate of pasta in his hand and from the vantage of the steps leading to the front lawns from the pool side of the estate, he watched the women flying. He was grateful for the distance. He needed the distance.

Parisa's wings had stopped him dead in his tracks. In all his thirteen hundred years, he'd only seen wings like them once. They were very, very familiar and he didn't know what to make of it, or if there even was any significance to the similarity.

Whatever.

Damn, but this was good pasta. He'd have to thank who-ever had cooked it—probably Havily, who was comfortable in his kitchen.

He lifted a goblet of Cabernet from off the stone hand-railing then sipped. The bottle had been left on the dark soapstone counter to breathe. Good wine, good pasta, and one helluva fine view.

He sharpened his vision, preternatural-style, and had a good clear look at . . . his *breh*. Jesus H. Christ, even say-ing the word in his head gave him the shakes. He returned the glass to the stone rail and picked up his fork again.

Parisa was beautiful, tall, with dark brown hair. And her eyes, violet and so intense.

And her body . . . the fork stopped just short of his

parted lips. She had a narrow waist he wanted his hands around and full breasts that made his jeans shrink.

He put the fork in his mouth and dropped his gaze to the plate.

Even at that distance, her exotic tangerine scent reached him, small wafts of scent meant just for him, which plucked at the sensitive nerves all along the insides of his thighs.

The call on his body was ridiculously strong and resulted at the very least in the incessant pounding of his heart. Parisa Lovejoy—even her name got to him—was a pull on his soul that felt like strong fingers working in his chest, kneading and tugging. He wanted more than anything in the world to be right next to her.

Suddenly she cried out.

His gaze shifted. He watched her tumble high in the sky a few feet from the dome of mist. He dropped his plate to the cement step at his feet, and the jerk of his arm knocked the goblet off the railing.

He was ready to sprint forward, his wing-locks humming, but Havily caught her hand and give her a quick, skilled jerk and the tumbling ceased. As practiced, Parisa made scoops of her wings and floated back to earth. She drew her wings in close-mount and, as she had done earlier, she leaned over, no doubt calming her heart and catching her breath.

He bent over the railing, also catching his breath. He retrieved the goblet, which had fallen on a spread of natal plum and wasn't even chipped. He rose up and looked at the shattered dark blue stoneware. There were clumps of pasta here and there that would leave oil stains. The resident ants in his garden would be all over it within the next few hours.

He picked up the fork and the broken bits of his plate, fully aware that his hands shook. He scooped the leftover pasta onto the largest pieces. He headed back to the kitchen. He didn't think he wanted to keep watching the flight training, for several reasons, least of which was that he never mounted his wings in front of other people and the only way he'd be able to be of use to Parisa was if he did. So . . . shit.

The sun was setting and he'd be assigned to one of the Borderlands in just a little while to do the usual. Right now, no doubt the rest of his brothers were at the Blood and Bite, enjoying a final drink and taking a romp in the red velvet booths, all except Kerrick of course. He'd be at his mansion, with his *breh,* doing exactly what Medichi wanted to be doing with Parisa.

Whatever.

When he'd disposed of the pieces of stoneware, he put the fork in the dishwasher and washed and rinsed the goblet. Afterward, he moved in the direction of his rooms at the south end of the villa.

As he walked down the central corridor and glanced through the windows that faced the front lawn, he caught glimpses of the fliers. Parisa, despite the recent near-miss, was back in the skies. He liked that a lot. The woman was tenacious. She'd already moved past at least two minor traumas and gotten back on the horse. Good for her.

But when he heard her laughter, dammit his heart hurt.

He turned away from the sound and moved with preternatural speed the rest of the distance to his bedroom. He shut the door a little too hard. The frame rattled in protest.

Shit.

He folded off his jeans and T-shirt. He walked into the expansive master bath, all glossy black marble. He stared at himself in the mirror, not looking into his eyes. He knew what he'd see there, the great loss of his life, too enormous to permit another love to pierce his past failures.

Now *she* was here, the woman meant for him in the second dimension, the one he had never believed existed, not even after Kerrick had been hit with the *breh-hedden,* not even after he'd dragged a crazed Marcus off Havily four months ago. But *she* was here and his soul cried out for her.

But the reality of his life, of his history, was much more powerful than any bizarre warrior myth. The last thing he could ever do was allow Parisa into his life.

He turned slightly so that he could see the scars that crisscrossed his back, the hundred slices of leather whipped over his skin, cutting him while he heard not his screams but those of his wife, raped at his feet, her belly full of a child that died within her womb as she died. No, the *breh-hedden* was nothing to these truths.

But despite this reality, he felt the cramping of his wing-locks. He hadn't released his wings in almost two weeks, so the need had grown profound. For whatever reason, wings needed to be mounted on a regular basis.

He had hoped the scar tissue would in time disappear in his ascended life, but it hadn't. His wing-locks, however, had made all the necessary adjustments, and a year after his ascension he'd mounted his wings for the first time. He allowed his wings to release now. They were enormous, a match for his considerable height, almost as expansive as Endelle's, the apex reaching to the fifteen-foot ceiling above.

They were cream in color, the same as Parisa's wings.

They had three bands at the tips, just like Parisa's.

And just like the ascendiate's, the bands were gold, violet, and black.

So, yeah, he had *royle* wings, just like Parisa.

So, shit.

The bands meant that both he and Parisa, however much they were separated by centuries, had some connection with ancient ascenders, in particular with the first ascender, Luchianne. He knew of the myths surrounding *royle* wings, but in his opinion that's all they were, myths, children's stories of how *royle* wings could bring peace to a land, to all of Second Earth. Was it significant that he and Parisa shared identical wings? He didn't know except that it was extremely rare in the vampire world. Right now he chose to think of it as a coincidence, nothing more.

He remained still for a few minutes to give his wings a

chance to breathe and to relax. He flew regularly, usually on his estate beneath a cloak of mist. He kept in practice in the same way he worked out with weights and on treadmills. He may never have mounted his wings in front of his warrior brothers, or anyone else, but he had always thought, somewhere in the back of his mind, that he should be capable of flight no matter what.

After a few minutes, he drew his wings back into his wing-locks then dressed in his form of traditional battle gear: black cargo pants, a heavy-duty black T-shirt, steel-toed boots, and black silver-studded wrist guards. He also wore the same weapons harness as the other warriors so he could have a dagger on his chest ready for battle.

He had just made it to the front patio, where Marcus reclined watching the show and the landscaping lights had just come on, when Havily cried out. "Parisa, stop! Not past the mist!"

But her warning was too late and Parisa, clearly exhilarated by the experience, shot through the boundary.

Medichi's heart fired up. He knew what no doubt waited somewhere beyond the edges of his property. Thorne had already texted him with the warning of death vampires near all the warriors' properties and hangouts.

He knew what would follow.

He folded his sword into his hand as Marcus leaped out of his chair, folded off his shirt, and mounted his wings. Marcus was in the air, sword in hand before Medichi had taken three steps forward.

Damn, the vampire was fast, even after two hundred years on Mortal Earth.

CHAPTER 16

Marcus hadn't waited. The moment Parisa left the protection of the dome of mist, he knew exactly what would happen. He plowed through the air and was beside Parisa within the space of three seconds. Not fucking bad.

Despite his efforts, however, once he was guiding a startled Parisa back toward the mist, with Havily on the other side of her, the worst had already happened. She'd been spotted by the enemy.

Dammit. The breach in the mist would no longer offer the necessary protection, not until Endelle could do the repair, which meant someone had to contact her. Right now there was no time even for that.

Three squads of death vampires, and that bastard, Crace, headed straight for them. So, yeah, the warriors' estates had been under surveillance for signs of the ascendiate, which of course meant that Greaves wanted Parisa bad.

As he flew back through the mist, he shouted at Medichi, "Thirteen incoming."

"Bring the women to me," Medichi returned, his voice booming across the airspace. Marcus still had hold of Parisa's hand and, as soon as he drew near the patio, he took both of her hands, popped his wings into parachute mode, and brought her squarely to earth. "Draw your wings in as fast as you can," he cried. He didn't want to think how hard that was going to be since her eyes were the size of saucers.

Havily, bless her, already had her wings within her body. She went to Parisa, but the mortal cried out, "I can't do it. I can't do it."

As Marcus also drew his wings into his wing-locks, Medichi crossed to Parisa and put his large hands on her shoulder and neck. He looked deeply into her eyes. "You can do this," he said quietly. He even smiled a little.

The mortal heaved a sigh and closed her eyes. The next moment, her wings retracted. Thank God. Havily took her hand and hauled her into the villa.

With the women on foot, Marcus had already made the decision to battle next to Medichi, and protect the entrance to the house. He knew Medichi's style of warfare, having battled beside him for centuries and more recently four months ago. He held his sword in both hands, knees bent. Another second and the pretty-boys poured through the opening in the mist, Crace pulling up the rear.

He heard Medichi on the phone. "Thorne. We need backup at the villa. Have Jeannie do the fold. We had a mist-breach and we've got thirteen landing on the property now." Pause. "Yeah, three squads and that big motherfucker, Crace, pulling up the tail, fucking coward. You know, he's almost as big as Luken now." Pause. "See you in a few."

From his peripheral he watched Medichi replace his phone into the pocket of his cargoes.

Marcus stayed close to Medichi, back-to-back, swords drawn. The attack came. Six remained in flight and six landed. Crace kept his distance, his glossy black wings

plowing the air. Coward wasn't the half of it. He traversed
the air in front of the southern villa, peering through the
windows, hunting his prey. So, yeah, he was after the women.

Marcus put at least six feet between himself and Medichi.
He flexed his sword in both hands. From the ground, the
first pretty-boy offered him a smile and a hard stare. He
laughed. Did the bastard actually think he could enthrall
him?

"*Enthrall this,* asshole." He moved with preternatural
speed, whirled and plunged his right arm. The sword struck
deep. The smile faded. The body fell sideways.

One approached from the air. Marcus swung in a wide
arc, levitating at the same time. The second flying bastard
screamed as Marcus severed an arm and part of a wing.

He engaged a third and fourth. He worked hard to protect Medichi's back and to keep any of the bastards from
getting past the door. He saw a blur to his right and a bad
feeling came over him. Where the fuck had Crace gone?
But he already knew.

He fought harder, using preternatural speed again, and
took down a third. He engaged the fourth, his heart pounding in his ears. He had to get to Havily. Crace wanted
Havily's blood. He had to get to her.

Shit.

Across the lawn, reinforcements arrived—Thorne, Jean-
Pierre, Santiago, and Zach. Thank you, God. They'd probably been relaxing at the Blood and Bite.

Havily took Parisa in the direction of the turret and pushed
her up the narrow winding staircase. Parisa was shaking
but then Havily wasn't exactly a smooth ride of nerves
herself.

"We're under attack," Parisa cried.

"You're doing fine." *Oh, dear Creator, help us.*

The turret was a small bedroom with a canopied bed
tucked into the corner, a small barred window near the
bed, and below it an oak chest of drawers.

Havily shut the door and turned the key.

"Hav . . . ily . . ." The singsong voice sent a spear of dread through her. "Open the door, babe. It's me. Eldon Crace. Come on, sweetheart. Don't be shy." Laughter followed, deep, low, menacing.

Parisa drew close and slipped her arm around Havily's.

Havily waited for the latch to lift. Instead the air shimmered and the monster without was suddenly within. Together, the women backed up until Havily felt the bed at the back of her knees. She turned to grab Parisa, but Crace was before her. He held Parisa against him with one arm. With the other, he formed a brace at the back of her head. Oh, God. One quick twist.

Havily didn't think. She just moved, not in Crace's direction but straight into the darkening. At the exact same moment, her thoughts pulled Parisa in with her in a quick swish of momentum. They stood facing each other, the space similar to the turret bedroom but fading to black all around the edges. Her heart slammed against her ribs. She reached out and grabbed Parisa's arm just to make sure she was real. The moment she made contact, Parisa's face crumpled. She covered her face with her hands and started to weep.

She pulled Parisa against her and held her fast. "You're safe. You're safe," she whispered. "I should have done this the moment you retracted your wings. I wasn't thinking. But you're safe now. Truly."

The librarian of Mortal Earth couldn't be consoled as she cried over and over, "It was my fault. My fault. I passed the mist without thinking. My fault. I don't belong here. I shouldn't be here. My fault!"

Crace twisted his arms but hit only air. "What the fuck?" The woman was gone. The mortal whose neck he'd intended to snap with a quick jerk of his arms was gone. Vanished.

But where the hell had she gone? And where was Havily?

Damn, they must have folded away. He had to act fast if he had any chance of getting to them before they disappeared beneath another cloak of mist somewhere else in the Valley.

He turned in a circle searching for the streams of light that would allow him to trace after Havily. He didn't give a tick's ass about the mortal-with-wings, but Havily was *necessary*. He'd hammered out a special pair of manacles just for her, engraved with butterflies the entire distance around, a real fucking work of art. "Havily," he called softly, "where are you?"

He made a circle and searched for the trace, but found nothing. He turned in a second complete circle then a third.

Shit. Where the fuck was the trace?

When he heard the heavy thump of feet up the stairs, he knew he'd just run out of time and somehow his blood donor had gotten away. He prepared to fold, but he thought he'd have a little fun first.

From the stairwell, he heard Warrior Medichi's deep voice. "She's in here. I can smell tangerines." The doorknob turned but the key was in the lock. The next moment, damn if Medichi didn't shove his boot at the door, making a sound like a gunshot. The door flew open, hard, and snapped off the top hinge.

The warrior appeared on the threshold in avenging glory, with sword in hand and dark eyes blazing.

Crace met his gaze, laughed, then flipped him off as he lifted his arm and vanished. He hoped Medichi would follow him, because he was folding into the bowels of Greaves's compound and he'd have the bastard.

Crace arrived next to his forge.

"Yeah, follow me, asshole," he cried.

But no one came.

Adrenaline pumped like fire through his body. He paced and shouted at the enormous ceiling, a vaulted space of heavy carved rock. His voice bounced back. He shouted again. He'd failed on both counts. No Havily and no dead Parisa. *Fuck.*

But if Havily hadn't dematerialized, then where the hell had she gone? Where the hell had the mortal gone? And who had taken her away? What kind of power had been in that room that could have made the women disappear without leaving behind the signature of even one trace?

He cursed and stomped around for a good loud minute until he saw what would calm his nerves. The latest mortal he'd apprehended stood shivering in white gauze against the walls, her arms manacled overhead. She was still fresh, not even drooping yet. Good. She'd probably put up a fight.

He approached her, ripped the gauze, pushed her head to one side, and buried his fangs.

The screams and fists only made it better.

God, he loved being a vampire.

Marcus stood beside Medichi in the small turreted room. No Havily. No Parisa. Where the hell were they?

Medichi ducked beneath the canopy and smoothed a hand over the black-and-red quilt covering the bed. "Parisa was here. Her scent is near the bed. Do you think somehow Crace got her?"

His dark eyes were wild as he met Marcus's gaze.

"I don't know. I'm trying to figure out what happened." Havily had definitely been here as well. He could smell honeysuckle thick in the space. He took a deep breath and calmed his racing heart. He folded his sword to Bainbridge since the space was so confined. Medichi followed suit, his sword disappearing as well. Identified swords were dangerous.

He searched for folding traces but found, thank God, only one faint telltale stream of light, which meant Crace had dematerialized alone.

"I'm only seeing one trace," Marcus said. "Not even two, never mind three."

He saw the small door off to the side. He opened it and found one helluva small bathroom, a shower in the corner, toilet, a sink the size of a tortoiseshell. But no one was in there.

He turned back into the bedroom and met Medichi's tortured gaze.

"Where are the women?" Medichi asked. Sweat from the recent battle flooded his face and dripped down his neck.

In that instant, Marcus knew exactly what had happened to them. "Havily," he said in a strong voice. "You can come out now."

Medichi frowned, turned toward the bed, and dropped to his knees. He peered under. "They're not here."

"If it's where I think they are, they're safe. Really safe."

"Well, where the hell do you think they are?"

"The darkening."

Medichi rose up and stared at him. "You're shitting me."

Marcus shook his head. "Nope." He even smiled.

Medichi glanced around the room once more. "I won't believe it until they're standing right next to me."

And then there they were, both women, standing right next to him. Havily had her arms around Parisa, who in turn was weeping against Havily's neck.

The sight broke his heart. His smile dimmed.

"My fault. My fault," Parisa sobbed.

"Hey," Marcus called softly. He met Havily's gaze, but she shook her head.

"I'm not sure what to do," she said softly. "She blames herself."

Marcus glanced at Medichi, whose gaze was fixed to Parisa. Medichi paled as he stared at her. He blinked a couple of times then started backing out of the room. The next moment he disappeared through the doorway. Medichi's heavy boots could be heard thumping down the spiral staircase.

Marcus turned his attention back to the ascendiate. "This was not your fault, Parisa," he said. "You are never to be blamed if an attack comes."

Suddenly he was angry. He hated that this innocent woman had been attacked, he hated the war, he hated death vampires, he hated that Endelle's administration was so ineffectual, she'd lost ground in the past decade. "goddammit, Parisa, it's not your fault!"

"Marcus," Havily said, her eyes wide. "I don't think you're helping." But Parisa turned in her arms, her eyes wet and puffy, and looked at him.

Marcus couldn't contain his rage and he cried once more, "It's not your fucking fault!"

Parisa hiccuped and a new wave of tears slid down her face.

He was out of control and he knew it. He wanted to hit something. He swiped the back of his hand over his forehead. Sweat flowed.

Havily was right, he wasn't helping. So he turned on his heel and hurried down the narrow staircase, just as Medichi had and maybe for the same reason. One shoulder or the other jostled the plastered walls as he moved. He cursed the entire distance.

When he reached the hallway, he punched the air several times then saw a flash of light outside where the battle had taken place. Central had just done cleanup on Medichi's front yard. He drew a deep breath. For some reason that settled him down. Twelve pretty-boys out of the picture permanently. Go fucking team.

He made his way through the kitchen, dining room, and receiving room to the foyer. The massive front door was wide open; hot June air assaulted the cooler interior.

He followed the sound of male voices.

When he reached the threshold, he paused.

There they were. The Warriors of the Blood, all of them, with the exception of Kerrick. Even Luken had arrived in the interim, bearing his sword and wearing flight gear. Flight gear. Holy shit. Was he really ready to start battling again? Even flying?

Something gentled within Marcus at the sight of him. Luken was healed up and ready to make war again. To a man, the warriors had gathered around him.

Luken held his arms akimbo and flexed his biceps and pecs, all the while smiling as he struck a bodybuilder pose. The next moment his wings flew with preternatural speed through his wing-locks and a fully restored pair emerged, popping high into full-mount. He had elegant, powerful wings in a light blue. How the hell had he healed so fast? Well, wasn't that ascension for you?

Slowly, Marcus made his way across the lawn. His heart swelled at the sight of the men who had come so fast to take care of business.

Zach shoved Luken's shoulder. "Who the hell could keep you down for long?"

Luken grinned. The warrior was happy to be back. Yep, ready for battle.

Jean-Pierre lifted his hand. Luken gripped it hard, then dragged the Frenchman against him for a hug, his wings shimmying with the movement.

Thorne stood apart and smiled at his men.

Medichi was next as he cupped the back of the warrior's neck. He put his forehead on Luken's. "Welcome back, big guy."

"I get Luken tonight," Santiago cried out. He had a cloth in hand, wiping down the blade of his sword. "Okay with you, *jefe*?"

"I'll leave that up to Luken."

Luken met Marcus's gaze. "I'll take Marcus if you're battling tonight."

Marcus shook his head. "Would if I could. I'm on guardian duty."

"You staying long?" Luken asked.

Well, wasn't that the million-dollar question. Marcus shrugged. "I'm taking it one day at a time."

Luken's smile broadened to a grin. "Sounds like a yes

to me." His gaze moved past Marcus and he added, "Of course there is one reason I'd like to see you go." His smile dimmed as affection filled his eyes.

"Luken," Havily cried from across the lawn. "Your wings!"

Marcus turned and watched her start to run. She still wore flight gear, which hugged her body like a wet suit. He had a powerful impulse to step in front of her and block her as she drew close, but somehow he mastered the overwhelming instinct.

"You've got wings. Your wings are back!"

She ran into Luken's arms and Luken swallowed her up in a hug. He twirled her in a series of big circles so that Havily's legs were almost parallel to the ground. His wings moved and lifted them both into the air. Havily squealed and laughed.

Marcus started breathing hard. His woman, his *breh,* was in the arms of another man. *She was in the air and in the arms of another man.* He felt Thorne come up on his left and grip his left arm. Medichi whirled back, took one look at him, and caught his right arm going the other direction.

"It's just friendly," Medichi whispered. "Luken would never hurt her, and if he hasn't won her in a hundred years, he won't today."

Marcus heard the growl in his throat, his vampire nature in ascendance.

Luken grinned at Marcus from about twenty feet in the air. His wings flapped and he moved slowly downward until his feet touched earth. With Havily's naked back on display and her arms still wrapped around Luken's neck, the bastard flipped him off.

If Thorne and Medichi hadn't held him back, he would have leaped at Luken and knocked him flat, or at least tried to. Luken was one big motherfucker.

"Uh, Havily," Thorne called out.

She slid her arms from around Luken, took one look at Marcus, and blanched. "Oh, God." She patted Luken's weapons harness. "Glad you're back." She turned around and headed in the direction of the house. She didn't stop to say anything to Marcus nor did she look at him, which was probably wise.

"That went well," Thorne muttered.

Luken drew his wings in. He approached Marcus and said, "She's yours, asshole. We all know it. Just please stick around and take care of her. At least in that way you can put me out of my misery."

The sad expression in Luken's eye dimmed the rage that boiled in Marcus's veins. Luken had had a crush on Havily apparently since he'd served as her guardian during her rite of ascension. So . . . shit. How much simpler all of this would have been if Havily had been Luken's *breh,* instead of his.

Sometimes he thought destiny had one sick sense of humor.

Marcus turned as if to follow after Havily but Thorne held him back. "I'll have to give Endelle a report. Tell me what happened with Crace."

When Havily returned to Parisa, she found the mortal had begun weeping again, not hysterically but in that exhausted way of someone who had been through way too much in too short a time. First the thrill of flying, then being chased by a maniac who tried to kill her, then finding herself in the darkening. Not to mention that she'd had one swift dunk into the world of the vampire.

She led the ascendiate back into the house, her arm around her shoulders. She was grateful to have a distraction. The look on Marcus's face had frightened her. She'd never quite seen him that enraged, and it hadn't escaped her that both Thorne and Medichi were physically restraining him.

She took a deep breath, guiding Parisa in the direction of the kitchen. Maybe a glass of wine would help . . . both of them.

She drew a bottle of Cabernet from the wine rack and two glasses from the cupboard. Then she had another thought that might be of even more use than the wine—but she'd need her phone. Before she set about opening the bottle, she closed her eyes. She actually had to search her memory to figure out where she had left her iPhone. She found it on the dresser in her bedroom, *their* bedroom, then folded it into her hands.

She guided the screen. A moment later Alison, her voice a little breathless, said, "Havily. What's going on?"

In the background, she heard Kerrick say, "Come back to bed. I still have twenty minutes before I report to Thorne." A growl followed.

Havily felt a blush on her cheeks. She almost said she would call back later, but Alison said, "Just ignore that. What's going on? How can I help?" A pause, and Alison's voice was muffled as she said, "Stop that. Havily needs me." She came back on the line. "Well, that's settled . . . for the moment. Talk to me. I can feel your distress."

Havily felt an instant calm descend over her. Thank God for Alison. She relayed the events that had just occurred, then her request that Alison come to the villa and spend some time with Parisa.

"Of course I will." Another pause, then, "Will ten minutes be all right? I'll come now, if—"

"Make it fifteen," Havily said, rushing her words.

"Good that's good. See you in fifteen." Then a sound like the phone had hit something solid, like a wall. "Kerrick," Alison cried, her voice distant. "We can't keep buying new phones. Oh, stop that." A lot of giggling ensued followed by a series of moans. When things got serious, only then did Havily break from the really improper listening in and end the call.

She stared at her phone for a long moment. She knew what they were doing and for some reason it made her want to cry. They were so in love, so completely bonded. They were married now, if not by ceremony then by their bond, their commitment, their unity, by the completion of the *breh-hedden*.

For the past four months, their happiness had been a thorn in Havily's side. She had once been that happy with Duncan. She knew what that kind of happiness felt like.

"What is it?" Parisa asked. "You look so sad right now."

"Do I?" Havily asked. She then gave her head a shake. "Alison will be over in a few minutes. She'll help get us through this."

Medichi paced the length of the dining room table.

He didn't dare get any closer to the kitchen.

He heard the distress in Parisa's voice. He could *feel* her distress as though she stood next to him and stared into his eyes.

He wanted to go to her, to put his arms around her, to comfort her. He ached to be with her, to calm her. But he couldn't. Of course he couldn't.

Where the hell was Alison? Havily had said she would be here in fifteen minutes. Fifteen minutes had come and gone. Now it was seventeen minutes. Where the hell was the empathic wonder who could keep Endelle calm and make anyone around her feel like life would be okay just because she was close by? Yeah, where the hell was she?

He ground his teeth. He paced from the window to just in front of the opening that led to the dining room. He didn't want to see Parisa or be seen.

He headed back to the window. Where the fuck was Alison?

He felt a movement of air from the foyer. He stalked in there and glared. "Finally," he all but shouted.

Alison's brows rose. "Medichi, what is it? Has something else happened? The ascendiate, is she all right?"

"No, she's not all right. She's really upset." He flung a hand in the direction of the kitchen. "She's in there!"

Alison held his gaze as she moved past him in the direction of the archway that led to the kitchen.

He continued to glare, letting her feel just how much he disapproved that she hadn't arrived exactly when she said she would. She should have been here three minutes ago. Okay, two. No, three now. Three lousy minutes.

But Alison stopped in her tracks and turned to face him.

"Go," he cried, his arm still pointing the way.

She shook her head. "Not until you tell me what's going on and why you're about an inch away from striking me with a bolt of lightning."

His nostrils flared. "Because she needed you here sooner." He glanced in the direction of the kitchen, still standing out of range.

"Havily? Havily needed me here?" Her eyes had narrowed, those blue eyes that always searched to understand. He felt her empathy surrounding him, reading him, wanting to be of use to him.

"Would you stop that? *I* don't have need of your services. And no, I'm not concerned about Havily . . . it's her, the ascendiate . . . *Parisa*." The last word came out, much to his horror, like a caress.

Alison's mouth opened then closed. Her eyes glittered. "Oh, Antony, are you kidding? Are there to be more of us?"

Medichi took a step back. He sucked in a tight breath. "Fuck," he muttered. "Just take care of her."

He lifted his arm and dematerialized the hell out of there.

Crace sat in the low chair in his deity's office. Even with his increase in sheer muscle bulk, the chair barely put him at neck level with the edge of Greaves's enormous black desk. He understood the purpose of the relationship of the low chair to the big desk, a symbol of power and submission that he used to admire as very clever. Now he was just plain pissed off.

Was it only a few months ago that he had sat in this exact chair, in this spot, leaking sweat like lemon juice squeezed through a strainer? He had a hard time remembering the why of all that sweat.

Of course part of the reason had to do with his current state of mind. He wasn't exactly *present* in this room. He was back in Medichi's villa with his blood donor. Dammit, he'd been so close to achieving his goal. Right now all he could smell was Havily Morgan's blood in his nose and feel his desire to have her blood down his throat. But where had she gone?

He watched the Commander's mouth move. Half of what he said, he spoke in the direction of Rith, who stood a few feet back and off to the left side of Crace. The vampire brown-noser was dressed in a suit and looked like a cheaper version of Greaves.

Crace was pissed off. He'd been within a pig's snout of snatching his prize and somehow she'd gotten away from him, but how? If she hadn't folded somewhere, then where the hell had she gone?

His attention was drawn quite suddenly away from his concerns by a paper flying off the desk and floating toward him. Crace plucked it from the air. He stared at it frowning. Shit, he needed to get his act together and afford this meeting at least some attention. He scanned the document. "I don't understand," he murmured. "Why do I need to know the details about the warrior Thorne's movements?"

"My dear Crace, you weary me with your inattention. I have been speaking of this for the past ten minutes. Do I need to take your forge from you?"

Crace felt his temper spike but clamped his lips shut. He'd always hated being talked to as though he were a child.

Greaves narrowed his eyes at him, something he'd been doing a lot lately. Crace lowered his gaze and took deep breaths. "My apologies, Commander. I have a lot on my mind. The mortal-with-wings . . ." A fucking lie, but *whatever.*

He felt a sudden pressure on his mind, but his shields had gained strength. Though he couldn't prevent Greaves from entering his head, he could still bury certain memories very deep and overlay them with impenetrable mini shields.

The pressure increased. He began to perspire, and his head felt as though Greaves had just stuffed a watermelon between his ears. Now he remembered the cause of all that former sweat. Jesus. H. Christ.

"What are you hiding from me, I wonder?"

Crace didn't relent. He wouldn't release the mini shields even when stars danced in front of his eyes.

The pressure stopped and only with a profound act of will did he keep from vomiting. Sweet motherfucker, that hurt.

"The whole point, my dear Crace, is that you aren't yourself these days and I am . . . disturbed. However, if you will look the document over, these are the essential details you'll need for the assassination of Thorne and no, I do not expect you to do it yourself. But I want you to arrange it. Can you do that for me? The assassin will of course be executed immediately by COPASS, which cannot be helped, but I feel a very powerful need for a demonstration at the Reception to be held in honor of the ambassadors. The Reception, Crace. Not the Festival. Are you hearing me?"

Crace shifted to stare at Greaves. "Yes," he stated. But he was now in shock. Greaves meant to take out the leader of the Warriors of the Blood? This was one helluva bold step. He approved. He even sat up a little straighter, or as much as he could in this fucking chair that angled back like he'd be getting his teeth cleaned next. "I'll see to it. You can rely on me."

Greaves smiled. "There is one more thing, which ought to please you. I want you to know that I very much approve of the incendiary bomb you used at the Superstitions. I regret that Warrior Luken did not die, but the attempt was quite lovely. Rith provided a DVD of the event. Very well done."

"Thank you." He was startled by the praise.

"Yes, the bomb was quite effective, and I understand

you have a little demonstration planned for the spectacle over White Lake."

Crace couldn't withhold his smile. "Yes, master, I do."

"More firebombs?"

"Combined with fireworks."

Both of Greaves's manicured brows lifted in approval. "I look forward to the event with great interest. In the meantime, tell me what happened at the villa."

Crace drew in a deep breath. He spoke of the breach in the mist by the mortal-with-wings, which seemed to interest Greaves very much. He detailed the loss of the three squads to the Warriors of the Blood and ended with the inexplicable disappearance of the women.

"They vanished *without a trace*?" Greaves asked.

Crace stared at his master. Had he just made a joke? "Yes, master, without a trace, without a single trail of light to follow, and you know I have power in that area."

Greaves leaned forward slightly and his eyes flared. "You know what I think this means?"

Crace shook his head, but his heart rate had started to climb and a shiver slid down his neck and arms. He was about to receive a revelation.

"One or both of these ladies have darkening capabilities."

The moment the word was spoken, Crace knew it to be true. Shit. The darkening. Of course. Rith had even told him of the Seers' prophecies. "Yes," he said. "That fits the situation exactly. I should have thought of it."

"Well, what do you know. No wonder the future streams have been all lit up about these women. Very, very interesting." He nodded then said, "I expect you to continue your vigilant efforts to find the mortal-with-wings, but I think I want her alive in case she is the one with darkening abilities. Are we in agreement?"

Before Crace could reply, Greaves once more dove within his head, a torpedo of sensation that hurt like a bitch. The sweating started all over again. "Yes, master," he cried. "I will see to everything."

As quickly as it had begun the pressure released. He was left with a fucking migraine.

The Commander rose from his chair. "Excellent. Then I'll leave you to it. Rith, you will come with me." He lifted an arm and both men vanished, Rith folding away while in the middle of his most obsequious bow.

Darkening capabilities.

Coordinate Thorne's assassination.

Shit.

Crace leaned over the side of the chair he hated so much and threw up.

The teacher sometimes needs the lesson.

—*Collected Proverbs,* Beatrice of Fourth

CHAPTER 17

Havily always felt like she was facing a firing squad whenever she approached Endelle's office. After Thorne had reported to Endelle on the attack at the villa, Her Supremeness had summoned her to the administrative offices even though the hour was now past nine o'clock.

Marcus had insisted on accompanying her while Alison remained with Parisa, to continue to counsel her. Havily knew Marcus didn't like leaving the women alone, but Endelle had repaired the breach in the mist so they were once more under a cloak of safety. Also, because of Alison's bond with Kerrick, the warrior would know instantly if the women were in trouble and could fold directly to his *breh,* without the assistance of Central or anyone else. In that way, both Parisa's and Alison's safety were ensured.

Havily knocked on the door, her heart an annoying thump in her chest. Endelle's answering bark, "Come," didn't help.

She straightened her shoulders and gave the door a shove. She walked in with Marcus right at her back as he had been since the attack. She could even feel his breath on her neck, his left hand a light touch against her waist.

The attack had nerved up his warrior instincts, and he'd become a second skin. Damn her for liking it as much as she did. And seeing him in battle gear? *Whoa*. She was a sucker for a man in a kilt, always had been. Besides, the wing-serving weapons harness displayed his muscles *to perfection*.

She was still distressed by the whole thing, by having watched Parisa lose herself in the thrill of flight only to fly straight through the mist barrier and initiate a crisis. Dammit.

Now she was here, facing her personal firing squad, yet again.

She'd exchanged her flight suit for jeans and a light blue silk tank top. She wore lime-green heels as well for the simple reason that if she didn't add the inches to her height, Endelle would tower over her. The last thing she needed with any interview in this office was an extreme disparity in height. It was really hard to stand up to someone who was a foot taller by means of *her* stilettos and *your* flats. So, yes, she wore heels.

She folded her arms over her chest and met Endelle's gaze squarely. The woman wore the same outfit as earlier and scratched at the fur halter. She couldn't figure out what kind of fur it was, only that it seemed to irritate Her Supremeness. Her suede pants were spotted like leopard.

She had no idea what fault Endelle intended to find with her tonight, but the bitch could kiss her ass on this one.

However, the wooded appearance of the Supreme High Administrator's eyes somehow knocked sideways what little confidence she possessed. Havily couldn't imagine having lived on Second Earth for nine thousand years. What had Endelle seen during that time? What had she been forced to endure as Supreme High Administrator of Second Earth?

Endelle said, "I wanted to let you both know that tomorrow I have a meeting with COPASS so we can figure out what to do with Parisa. I will insist on a ruling before I'll ever allow her to return to Mortal Earth or whatever the hell she's supposed to do next. I know those assholes won't have the sense to discipline Greaves as he should be disciplined, like put his ass in a sling and keep it there. However, I intend to make public that some of Greaves's high command have been after Parisa without cause."

"Well," Marcus said, nodding, "it's at least a place to start."

Havily frowned as she looked up at Marcus. He was being reasonable . . . again. She wished everything was different. This situation had started wearing on her, the powerful sexual nature of their current entanglement as well as all the ways this kind of intimacy reminded her of how much she'd loved being married and how much she'd lost.

And now here she was with Endelle and waiting for the other shoe to drop. She repressed a sigh.

Her Supremeness folded her arms over her chest and pursed her lips. She held Havily's gaze and didn't hold back her sigh. "Alison tells me you pulled Parisa into the darkening and saved her life."

"Yes," she responded, but she felt uneasy. "Crace was ready to . . . break her neck." She described the event in detail. The whole time Endelle kept her eyes narrowed and nodded several times.

Endelle surprised her, however, because an odd expression overtook her face and she smiled. She smiled and nodded. "Well, ascender. This is a big fucking deal, you know. Darkening abilities are considered Third abilities. Even Alison can't go into the darkening. Aren't you just a little impressed with yourself? I know I am."

Havily couldn't have heard right. Endelle was impressed

with her? Impossible. But even if she was, Havily didn't exactly feel grateful. Instead, she lifted her chin and let a fair dose of sarcasm flavor her words. "Well, how nice that you actually think I might be worth something."

But Endelle only laughed. "What the hell do you care what I think anyway? The warriors know the truth. The war stripped me of my humanity at least two millennia ago. You need thicker skin, Morgan. Now let's get down to business. Take me into the darkening."

Havily lifted a brow. "I have no idea how to do that."

"How did you take Parisa?"

Havily shrugged. "I really don't know."

"Well, then," Endelle murmured, her eyes narrowing. "Looks like I need to teach you, and we're going to start right now."

Havily did not like the look in the woman's eye . . . at all. So that's why she was here, to receive a darkening tutorial from the worst teacher in the world. *Great.*

The next moment, she stood in a space that resembled Endelle's office in essentials. She could detect the presence of her massive marble-topped desk, the north and east walls constructed of plate-glass windows, the west wall bearing a rarely used fireplace, the south wall solid except for the door, but the edges of the space melted away to a thick darkness.

Havily planted her hands on her hips. She frowned. "I know now that this is the darkening, but where exactly are we?"

"Nether-space, like the Trough. This might even be a space between dimensions. Nobody really knows." She huffed a breath. "All right, ascender, I brought us here. Now you take us back out."

But all Havily could do was stare at her and once more shrug. She looked Endelle up and down and realized they were both standing with hands planted on hips.

"Well, that's just fantastic," Endelle drawled.

The next moment they were back, but Marcus stood in a

different place, near Endelle now, and said, as though in mid-sentence, ". . . like tangerines. I think it's the weirdest part of the whole process."

Havily didn't exactly understand but Endelle turned and winked at her. Then she understood. "You were in both places?" Havily cried. She took a step back, a big one. Because of Endelle's regular use of obscenities and because she seemed so *normal* in ascended terms, she often forgot the level of her power.

Marcus glanced from Havily to Endelle. "You took Havily into the darkening and continued talking to me? You were in two places at one time? What the fuck?"

Endelle smiled at Marcus. "Did I seem very different to you? My speech patterns were pretty good, weren't they? I can't hold the position very long. Usually, to split-selves I have to recline, as I do in my meditation chamber, and the primary self remains quiet and relaxed."

"Shit, Endelle," he cried. "How long have you been capable of talking while in two different places?"

"About a century." She turned her attention to Havily. "But I was able to do a split-self almost immediately after learning I had darkening abilities, and for whatever reason, Morgan, I need you to learn that and be quick about it. My ill-formed clairvoyant abilities are ringing right now. Apparently for you it's a real matter of life and death that you learn to split-self, so let's get on it."

"Now? But it's so late."

"So the fuck what? Oh, that's right. You need your goddamn beauty sleep. Well, princess, *them days is ovuh.* Get used to it." Endelle then descended on her, both hands outstretched as though she meant to cup her face.

Havily batted them away. "What are you doing?" she cried. She also had a bit of prescience going on and she could suddenly see her future, bound ankle-and-wrist to Her Supremeness. The last thing she wanted was to get caught in that trap.

"Morgan," Endelle growled. "Get your ass over here.

All I'm going to do is download a couple of my experiences straight into your head. You have a disconnect between your gift and your rational mind." Endelle lifted her hands, ready to place them on Havily's head.

But Havily blocked her again, striking at her forearms and once more backing up. "Hell, no," she cried. "You'll fry my circuits."

At that, Endelle laughed. "I'm not an idiot. I'll go slow. Oh, and just so you know, you don't have a fucking choice. I don't run a goddamn fucking democracy, remember?"

Havily released a punchy sigh. She knew better than to argue with Endelle. The woman had a bee in her bonnet and the truth was Havily could also sense her need to learn this skill as quickly as possible.

"Fine," she said. She huffed another sigh and closed her eyes. She really didn't want to be looking into the ancient eyes of her Supreme High Administrator while the woman shunted memories into her head. God help her.

Endelle's hands were warm on her face, and the warmth increased. *Release your shields* drifted through her mind. How strangely gentle the tenor of the words were, not the usual thing for Endelle.

Havily sighed again and let the mental shields back away, like a big piece of machinery in reverse.

Nice, Endelle murmured, again, inside her head. *The memories will come at you fast. Just keep your mind loose. Don't fight and don't try to make sense of it. Got it?*

Yes, she sent. She sort of understood. Maybe.

Basically, she stopped thinking, and before she knew it Endelle withdrew from her head.

She stared into the bark-lined eyes once more. She stared and weaved a little on her feet. She felt the strange whooshing sensation and she was in the darkening alone. She had taken herself there because she had Endelle's memory of how to do it. She thought the thought and allowed the whooshing sensation to return. She faced Endelle once more.

Endelle nodded. "Good. Now put your shields in place and do it again."

Havily searched her mind. "They are in place," she said.

"No shit. Well, that's excellent then. Do it again."

Havily repeated the exercise several times until it felt really natural. "This is awesome," she cried on about the fifth try.

"Now see if you can do a split-self. This is the really critical part about darkening work. When you can split yourself, you can travel all over the globe. Taking yourself or someone else into the darkening is a one-place-only kind of deal. You can't move around. So I want to help you figure this out right now. You ready?"

No. God, no. "Yes," but it came out on a whisper.

Endelle rolled her eyes. "Way to commit."

The next few hours *hurt*. There was never anything easy about Endelle anyway, but being under her tutelage was like picking up big armloads of cactus and carrying them around just for fun.

By midnight Havily could barely stand, and though she could easily take herself or Endelle into the darkening, she'd never once been able to do a split-self. Which meant, of course, that Endelle's temper had just gotten better and better.

Marcus smiled. He sat on a couch by the east window, his arms stretched out across the back cushions, just enjoying the show. Only a good dark beer and maybe some popcorn would make this better.

The two women had long since forgotten he was in the same room, and after this many hours it was like watching two whirlwinds face off against each other.

He'd never seen this side of Havily before and he was pretty damn sure she didn't know who she was . . . yet.

He knew one part of her from being inside her head while making love to her, but this part of her had surprised him and, fuck, aroused the hell out of him for reasons he couldn't exactly explain.

From the time he'd met Havily, she moved around people, even him, with a high degree of uncertainty, as though not quite belonging or maybe not wanting to get too close, he wasn't sure. This uncertainty had translated into weakness, but there was nothing *weak* about the woman standing opposite Endelle, her shoulders hunched, her hands fisted, as she glared at Her Supremeness. If anything, he saw a profound resemblance to the woman she battled and because he'd always admired the hell out of Endelle, despite her scorpion temper, he was damn pleased with what he now saw in Havily.

He wasn't sure if she was transforming into a different person or if this was who she'd always been. He suspected the latter.

"Well, you gonna stand there, ascender, and just pick your nose? Or are you going to show me something? You were always such a sniveling twat."

Havily's eyes flared. "Oh, shut the fuck up, Endelle!"

Marcus's brows rose, but Endelle wasn't mad, she looked hopeful.

"Try it again, dipshit!"

"Fuck you!" But Havily closed her eyes and focused, her brows drawn together.

When nothing happened, Endelle lifted her hands as though to send a hand-blast.

Marcus thought the time had come to intervene.

"Ladies," he called out in a sharp voice.

Both women, at the exact same moment, turned to him, eyes flaring, as they shouted in unison, "What?" The plate-glass window behind him rattled.

He grinned. "I think we're done. It's that or I can see blood all over these walls next. Whadya think?"

Endelle frowned slightly then looked at her hands lifted in aggression. "Shit," she murmured.

The color rose on Havily's cheek. She put her fingers

against her mouth, her eyes wide as she turned back to Endelle. "I am so sorry. I didn't mean to speak to you that way."

"Shut the hell up, Morgan. Goddammit, it's after midnight. Oh, shit. All right, I have to get to the darkening and get some *real* work done." She glared at Havily. "I hope you'll take the time to do some practicing. Maybe let Marcus get you on your back and worked up. Given your history with him, I'll bet you can do a split-self then. He seems to be one of your triggers. Of course, if sex does it then your warrior's just going to have to keep his dick handy. Hah."

Marcus shook his head but he laughed. "Endelle. Enough. You're making me blush."

Endelle rolled her eyes, lifted her arm, then vanished.

As soon as she was gone, Havily stumbled sideways. He moved with preternatural speed and caught her before she toppled over and twisted an ankle on her heels.

"That woman makes me crazy," she cried.

"Yeah. She has that effect on all of us."

"I'm so tired. I can barely stand."

"I've got you." He put his arms around her. She sighed and rested her head on his shoulder. But her head jerked upright as she asked, "Did I actually tell her to fuck off?"

"Yes. Beautifully."

"Oh, God."

"Forget about it. I'm sure she already has. She probably even respects you a little more because of it."

"She's a monster."

"Yep. But she's on the side of right so it's okay."

"Take me home," she whispered. He liked how she had both arms around his neck.

He kissed her forehead then folded them both back to Medichi's villa.

When Marcus materialized in the foyer with Havily in his arms, Alison waited near the Monet. She looked a little bleary-eyed but none the worse for wear.

"How's Parisa?" Havily asked. She kept her arms locked

around his neck and her head still rested on his shoulder. He loved it.

Alison lifted a brow as she met Havily's gaze. "She's fine. She went to bed around ten. I see Endelle worked you over."

"Understatement. She tried to teach me a darkening skill but I just couldn't get the hang of it."

"I'm putting her to bed," Marcus murmured. "She's done in."

Alison smiled. "I'm not surprised. It's the usual result of spending that many hours together with Her Supremeness."

Marcus chuckled then asked, "You okay?"

Her hand went to her bump. "I'm fine but I'm ready for bed so I'll say good night."

Marcus nodded. "Good night."

Havily contributed a soft "Night."

Alison lifted an arm then disappeared. He stared at the empty space and marveled that the woman had been able to do that before her ascension while still a mortal. He tried to recall when he'd developed the ability to dematerialize. Was it a decade after he ascended or a couple of centuries? Well, that was one problem with living a long time—the memories really got muddled.

With his arm holding Havily around her waist and her head still leaning into the well of his shoulder, and with his complete unwillingness to move her even a millimeter away from him, he walked her slowly in the direction of their bedroom.

He had a small problem. Watching his woman for hours had given him a profound need for her—but she was exhausted. So what the hell was he supposed to do?

He knew the answer and sighed. Only a cold shower would do, but the idea irritated the hell out of him.

After a trip down the hall that took much longer than usual, he guided her to the right then to the door of their room.

"Is something wrong?" she asked, as he shoved the door

open. He turned sideways to get them both inside without losing contact. "You seem really tense."

"No, nothing," he murmured. "I'm tired, worried, whatever."

He felt her sigh against him. "Me, too. I should shower."

"Just get in bed. You can shower tomorrow."

She pushed away from him. "No. Must shower. Now." Her eyes were at half-mast as she kicked off her heels then stumbled into the bathroom.

"Fuck," he murmured. He could hear her stripping her clothes off.

He grabbed a robe. He hunted in the south rooms for another bathroom. Finding one in a second suite of guest rooms, he folded off his clothes, turned the shower lever, and stepped into an icy spray of water. He shivered as he stared down at his ready-for-anything hard-on. Even the cold water wasn't helping, which was in itself some kind of cruel joke.

Whatever. He wanted Havily. He wanted her now. He shut the water off then smoothed over all his goose bumps with a towel. Jesus, he was still hard.

Maybe, if he took it slow, worked Havily up a little . . .

He took deep breaths. Yeah, maybe that would work.

He slid his robe on. He even took a minute to brush his teeth.

But when he returned to the bedroom, she was facedown on the bed, her red hair fanned over her back, her skin still damp in places from her shower. A full moon lit her naked body in a glow. Worse, she was lying on his side of the bed. So . . . shit.

"Hey," she whispered.

Hope burgeoned. "I thought you were asleep."

"No. I have your fennel scent in my nose and I need you."

He sat down on the edge of the bed next to her. She slid her hand on his thigh and he hissed. It would take so little . . . but . . . "Your eyes aren't even open," he said.

"Don't need 'em open." Her words were slurred since

her mouth was pressed against the pillow. Then she opened her eyes and a wave of honeysuckle wafted over him, not strong, but his cock didn't seem to care. Dammit.

"You sure about this? You sure you don't just need to go to sleep?"

"Take me, Warrior. I can always wake up for you."

She rolled oh-so-slowly onto her back, and since she was naked he couldn't help himself. He crawled over one leg and planted himself between her knees. He leaned over her and kissed her forehead, her cheeks, her mouth.

"Mmm. Minty." She giggled, but her eyes were once again closed. He had the worst feeling this was not going to end well . . . for him.

He dipped lower and kissed her breasts. Her body undulated at the light touch. A warble sounded in her throat. He figured he was headed in the right direction.

He kissed down her abdomen and swirled his tongue around her belly button.

"You are the smartest man ever," she whispered, her voice still a little slurred.

He moved lower and was thankful Medichi had had the foresight to put oversized beds in this room. He could maneuver.

When he had his arms slung under her knees, he settled in and got to work. Yeah, his woman was tired, so he'd get her where she needed to be.

Havily was in that delicious place of fatigue and pleasure that kept her body so loose that she swore she could feel every practiced flick of Marcus's tongue without any distraction. The man had a tongue that knew a woman's body, and though she might have felt jealous that he'd had a lot of practice, she couldn't really repine not when . . . oh. She groaned as his tongue went low and took her in a long swipe then penetrated her. Ohhhhhh.

Her head lolled first to one side then the other. With his hands, he pinned her hips down so he could keep thrusting into her in deep hard jabs until she was crying out. She knew he was aroused as well, since her nostrils were flooded with his scent, which in turn built tension all down her tender nether-lips as he plunged his tongue into her.

She closed her mouth and dragged more of his scent into her nostrils. She dragged and dragged, which enhanced the sensations building and building. He groaned now, lost in the magic of sex, of giving. She got lost in the repeated waves of fennel.

She cried out into the dark of the bedroom they shared, her body undulating and writhing.

He worked her hard, his chin banging against her low and increasing the dazzling sensations that . . . oh . . . my . . . God now streaked liked lightning along her sensitive flesh and drove inside her until she was crying out. The orgasm caught her hard, tickling her feet, drawing her stomach into a blissful knot, and making her heart ache. Her core pulsed and pulled and the whole time he tongued her.

When her body started to settle, his movements slowed. Only her harsh breaths punctuated the air of the room as her lungs caught up with how much oxygen she needed.

"Amazing," she murmured. She thought she pulled him on top of her, but her mind had turned to mush and instead, in a strange moment of awareness that disappeared as swiftly as it came, she realized she'd pulled her knees up to her chest and turned on her side. She called his name, but she thought maybe that was just a wishful dream.

She was so tired.

Damn Endelle anyway.

Marcus rose up, still on his knees. His woman had drawn into the fetal position and dragged a pillow against her stomach and was . . . God help him . . . already asleep.

The sigh that came out of him was part groan. Goddamn *breh-hedden*. If this had been any other woman in any other situation, he would have gone straight to the shower and taken care of himself. But he knew, *he knew,* that Havily was what he needed right now, her honeysuckle scent in his nose and her body taking him deep inside until he released his seed. Dammit.

With great care, he eased himself down beside her, not too close. His cock was at a perfect right angle to his body and, built the way he was, any closer and he'd be touching her. He'd never had this particular experience before. He knew that for whatever reason, the ritual called the *breh-hedden* had hooked him hard and was taking him for one painful ride.

He trembled now and his balls ached. Eventually, he was sure he would calm down, but with her honeysuckle mixed with the rich heady smell of sex, he was rigid as hell.

He kept breathing, but that smell was *intoxicating.* Honeysuckle whirled in his brain and for some reason his chest started to hurt. He wanted to touch her, to put his hand in her hair, on her shoulder, over her arm. He needed the connection.

She was a treasure, his treasure, made for him, meant for him.

The trembling worsened and the bed shook. He tried to calm down but couldn't.

Shit. He thought about leaving the bed, but he couldn't make his body move. He was where he wanted to be, needed to be.

Havily was in that strange ethereal space between waking and dreaming. She didn't understand why the bed was jiggling—or was that a dream? Dreams could be really strange.

Yet something nagged at her, really bugged her, made her uncomfortable. She had left something important undone, but what? What?

She rose into her consciousness another step. She'd been working with Endelle to improve her darkening skills. Endelle had been horrible but Marcus had been there.

Oh . . . Marcus. Her body relaxed and she dropped down a layer of consciousness. He had been with her and so kind . . . the nagging sensation returned and the jiggling on the bed got worse.

"I'm sorry." The voice came from so far away, that wonderful deep, masculine voice. Marcus had made love to her. "Go to sleep," the same magical voice repeated.

She wanted to sleep, but something was troubling her. But what?

Her eyes popped open. She stared at the lace curtains of the window, the outdoor lights of the garden. Where was Marcus? Why was the bed shaking?

She gasped and awoke completely. She turned over and stared at him.

"You're awake?" He looked panicked.

She put a hand on his shoulder. "You're shaking."

"Yeah."

"I must have fallen right asleep after you . . ." She couldn't say the words, *licked me, tongued me, brought me to a shattering orgasm*. She smoothed her hand down his arm. *He* was what was wrong with the bed.

She pushed back the sheet, saw that he was stiff, erect, and probably in pain, then her body relaxed. Of course. This was the important thing left undone. She dropped her hand low and in a long sweep she stroked him.

A groan gushed out of him.

"Oh, you idiot man. Come. Take me. Now. I'm still wet as hell." She rolled onto her back and pulled him over her.

She lifted her knees and he plunged into her, forcing her entire body up toward the headboard. It was about the best sensation in the world and she cried out. The pleasure of his presence in her body was incredibly intense, probably because she'd already orgasmed. He was too far gone to be gentle and that was so awesome. His movements were just right, very quick, and he was hard as granite. Her body responded by shedding a new wave of fluids.

He grunted, groaned, and moved over her like a beast.

She loved it.

Her body adored it.

"Honeysuckle," he cried out.

One last long intake of breath right behind his ear so that fennel rushed into her brain and her body splintered into a thousand particles of pleasure. She could hear herself screaming at a distance but her mind was all for the exquisite lightning streaks of pleasure that gripped the core of her body.

Marcus groaned as he released his seed, his body writhing as his ejaculation continued on and on, his groans harsher, his throat releasing a series of anguished cries until finally he was spent.

When he collapsed on her, she was only partially prepared. Her breath got squished from her lungs but she didn't care.

He immediately apologized and rose up, but she held on to him, her arms crowding his neck and holding him fast. He fell back on top of her. So . . . gooood.

"I've never felt like this," he murmured into her hair.

"I know." She breathed hard. Her chest filled up with such need and longing, painful yearning, the real hallmark of ascended life. "And you were being such a gentleman." She kissed him on the lips.

"I knew you needed to sleep."

She released her stranglehold on his neck and fell back against the pillow. "You know, you could have gone into the bathroom, and you know—" She didn't like to talk about self-pleasure but she wanted him to know that she understood. "I wouldn't have minded. I understand that men have needs." She felt the need to share, "Women, too."

His expression surprised her, the smile on his lips, the warmth in his eyes. Then he kissed her hard on the mouth. He looked at her again, his light brown eyes glittering in the dim light. "Normally I would have," he whispered. "You needed to sleep, but I . . . couldn't. I . . . Havily . . . you were what I needed, to be inside you. I can't explain it."

She felt as though he had shoved his hand up her rib cage, grabbed her heart, and squeezed. She gasped at the sensation. "Marcus, what's happening to us? I mean, I never wanted this again, not just with you, but with any man. I didn't want to love again. I *can't* love again."

He kissed her again and oh, damn, his eyes were wet. "I know," he murmured. "I've been inside your head, remember? I get it. We're the same in that way."

He was still connected to her, still inside her. Tears slipped from her eyes as well. "What are we going to do? This *thing,* this horrible *breh-hedden,* has me tied up in a knot. I can't be with you but I can't keep away from you and the longer I'm with you and the more times you give me such pleasure, the more I want you, crave you. Marcus, this has to stop."

The only thing that stopped were her words because he kissed her again and pushed at her with his tongue until he was inside her mouth and plunging his tongue into her tender recesses.

She kissed him back, all her earlier fatigue replaced with a combination of her frustration and despair that for some absurd, ridiculous, and completely useless reason communicated all her need to the sensual nerves of her body.

Before she even understood, before she could react in a rational negating sense, Marcus once more moved his cock within her body and her body once more wept for him, surrounded him, *loved* him. Once more he was hard as a rock. Tears streamed down her face this time as he again took her to the pinnacle but the whole time he kept his mouth connected to hers.

When she came, when he was arching over her and filling her once more, making a complete mess of the sheets, she cried out, part frustration, part ecstasy.

Then, as she settled down once more, as he left the well of her body, as he climbed from bed, as he went into the bathroom then returned with a washcloth, as she jammed the terry between her legs, as he climbed back in bed but cursed the wet mess he'd made, as he drew close to her from behind and spooned her, as he surrounded her with his arms holding her fast, only then did she release a quavering sigh, falling asleep with the certain knowledge that she was 100 percent screwed . . . in every possible way.

Marcus didn't fall sleep right away, though he knew Havily had.

He needed to think.

She had protested the *breh-hedden* at the precise moment that he'd had the worst epiphany of his life—he'd fallen in love with Havily Morgan, not a small kind of love, but the kind of love that made its way into sonnets and ballads, into pop songs and wedding rituals. He was in love with her. He loved her. *Breh-hedden* or no *breh-hedden,* he loved her.

Maybe he felt this way because he'd been inside her head and knew her basic generous nature, or maybe it was seeing her face off with Endelle, meeting her temper head-on by using the F-bomb, or maybe it was having her wake up and take care of him sexually that had pushed him over the edge of the cliff. Whatever it was, he was flying right now, so completely aware of this woman that for the longest moment, he didn't ever want to be separated from her. He wanted to be attached to her side by a tether, keeping her close to his body, his mind, his protective sword.

As sleep began to dull his mind, however, an old memory grabbed hold, the time he had last seen his sister, Helena, two hundred years ago. She'd been dressed in a lavender cotton gown gathering flowers from her extensive garden, the one she had designed specifically for making arrangements for the house, a true cutting garden.

He had argued with her again about her safety. He wanted her to stop driving the carriage into town with the children to buy supplies. He wanted her to send the servants instead. Dammit, he wanted her safe.

She had caught his arm, looked into his eyes, and pinched

his cheek. "Dearest brother, we all die even in this ascended world. Let me live as I choose. When my time comes, I am ready. Do you not ever feel that you and I have lived far too long as it is, perhaps on borrowed time?"

"No."

He had argued with her. He needed her and the children. They had been his saving grace, that which had made his warrior job tolerable each and every night.

"Marcus, you sometimes forget that I'm almost as old as you are and worse, I have lost children in this war, grown children. I have lost two husbands. Wedding Kerrick for me was the only thing I have wanted in the past thousand years. The only mistake I believe I made was not marrying again right after my last husband died. Life is for the living, and until I am committed to the earth I will live. I hope you will do the same."

She had perished in an explosion two weeks later, a gift from that bastard Greaves.

She had been the last of his family, she and her children.

When they died rage had flooded him and all that anger had become focused on Kerrick, as irrational as it was. He'd had a choice to make—stay and kill his fellow Warrior of the Blood, his own brother-in-law, or seek refuge and exile on Mortal Earth. He'd chosen the latter.

Now he was back.

He reached toward Havily and touched the bed just short of her body. She moved slightly in her sleep. Maybe his thoughts were too loud.

Havily was the first woman he'd wanted, *that he'd loved,* in longer than a thousand years. But already his heart ached with the impossibility of it all.

He thought of her darkening abilities and something clicked in his brain, the meaning of it, maybe even the purpose and why those abilities had first surfaced in her desire to be with him. In an elemental sense, the *brehhedden* was a demand for openness, commitment, belonging. Havily lacked all of these things just as he did.

In that intuitive aspect of ascended life, perhaps connected to basic clairvoyance—of a sense of knowing the future will be impacted by the issue at the moment—he knew that if Havily was to be safe, given the enemy's drive toward her, he must help her, somehow, to engage her darkening abilities, which meant he needed to open himself to her, to truly loving her.

Endelle was right. From this point forward, Havily's life depended on her ability to move in and out of the darkening at will—and even more important, to split into two realities, one self that could function in the darkening, while her other self rested in the real world.

When he had come back to Second Earth, returning to guard her, he had believed his job was to stay close and defend her with his sword. How strange to think that securing her safety meant he needed to love her better.

Only after he made this leap did he finally fall asleep.

The dawn illuminates change.

—*Collected Proverbs*, Beatrice of Fourth

CHAPTER 18

The next morning, Havily awoke on her side. Her gaze was fixed on the lace curtain of the window, the morning light having lit the eastern side of the White Tank Mountains in a glow. The sky above was a deep blue that would appear to fade during the day because of all the intense June sunlight. But for now, she saw one of the beauties of the desert world: the clear cloudless sky, the light, a sense of the expanse of the world.

Thoughts of what her day would be, of all her concerns for the success of the Ambassadors Reception, threatened to take over her mind. So for just this moment, before her day could steamroll her deepest thoughts, she blocked her responsibilities. She wanted time to think.

Marcus wasn't in bed, the shower wasn't running, and the room was quiet. Where he'd gone, she didn't know, but her thoughts turned to him. She rubbed her lower lip with her forefinger and smiled. Shivers traveled over her bare shoulders. Marcus.

She drew in a deep breath, released a deep sigh.

Marcus.

She smiled and a soft chuckle broke from her throat as she remembered awakening after a post-orgasmic doze to the bed shaking and her vampire lover so aroused, yet so restrained, that all his repressed need had set his limbs to trembling. Yeah, it made her laugh but it also made her heart constrict as she considered his character. Dammit, the man was thoughtful. He had fully intended to let her sleep even though his need for her bordered on torture. How could a self-proclaimed hedonist and narcissistic empire-builder of Mortal Earth also be thoughtful?

This wasn't helping her situation *at all*. She needed Marcus to be a prick so she could walk the hell away from him. Didn't he get that? She needed him to live up to her opinion of him as a disloyal bastard so she could let the *breh-hedden* run out of steam. Then she'd tell him to go back to his *small* life on Mortal Earth and she'd be able to get on with her own dedication to Second Society.

The trouble was, every minute she was with him kept proving that his essential character was very different from what he projected. He wasn't selfish; he was generous. He wasn't self-involved; he was thoughtful. He wasn't disinterested; he cared.

When Parisa had accidentally flown through the mist and Marcus had appeared in the air within seconds, in full-mount, ready to protect them both, her first thought had been, *Thank God*. Her second had been, *Who is this man?*

She released a heavy sigh. From the time she'd met him four months ago, during Alison's ascension, she'd known she was in trouble. Her crazy attraction to him was simply overwhelming. Add to that a subsequent four months of having sex with him in the darkening, acknowledged or not, and connections had been forged between them that should never have been built in the first place.

And oh, God, could the man make love. She didn't know if it was the *breh-hedden* or if it was just four thousand years of excellent practice or what, but damn he knew how to work her body. Desire rippled over her and resulted in a full-body shiver. She squeezed her eyes shut and for one ridiculous moment thought about calling Marcus back to bed. She moaned.

Okay, this was so not helping her time of reflection.

The trouble was . . . *the trouble was* . . . the longer she was with him, the more she enjoyed him, being with him, talking to him, sharing this difficult journey by his side, his sword drawn half the time, his body pinned to her the other half. She loved it so much, the connection, the physical oneness, the shared bed.

Yeah, she loved it all.

There was only one problem, the same issue she'd had from the beginning—she didn't want to be in a relationship. She didn't want her heart to swell with love and risk being punctured, deflated, obliterated by yet another death.

With the loss of her entire family so many years ago and later Eric's death, she had learned to live a serene, unruffled, unemotional existence because she had determined in her heart that she would never be in love again, never be married again, never risk losing someone she loved. The pain had been too much, and her ensuing commitment to a solitary life had been profound and purposeful.

A tear slid over the bridge of her nose. When had she started to cry? Only then did she understand that though she could intellectualize her situation, her heart knew she was in serious trouble.

She drew a deep breath and sat up.

Reflection time was over. She had to face the day. She had work to do, and it would include figuring out how to do a split-self so that she could engage in darkening work. In fact, with her ability to be in the darkening she might just be of some real use in the war effort. How happy that would make her, to have one more tool by which she could honor Eric's death.

A light knock sounded on the door. She dragged the sheet up around her bare breasts and covered her hips. "Who is it?"

"Just me," Marcus said.

She smiled, surprised that he would knock. "Come in."

He opened the door and stepped inside. He wore what she'd come to think of as his casual uniform, a short-sleeved silk shirt, this time in navy, and cotton slacks with a perfect break in the cuff. He also wore a variety of casual but expensive loafers, this time in dark brown leather. His hair was damp and combed behind his ears. He looked fantastic and, oh, damn, her heart swelled at the sight of him. His gaze slid over her face, her hair, her shoulders and her arm pressed beneath her breasts to keep the sheet in place. His eyes flared. She glanced down. Oh. She wasn't exactly covered.

When a wave of fennel washed over her, like licorice and grasses and summery scents, she closed her eyes and swayed even though she was sitting on the bed.

She expected him to slam the door shut and throw himself on her. Instead, he stayed put. Did he know she wouldn't have turned him away?

She opened her eyes and glanced at him. She lifted her brows, a silent question.

"Bad news," he said. "Endelle wants to work with you this morning."

Havily's first reaction was simple. "I can't. I have final meetings with my team leaders today and then the Reception this evening. I don't have time."

"Endelle rescheduled for you. She says this is more important."

Havily swallowed hard. Great. Then she noticed that Marcus's eyebrows were low on his forehead and he still hadn't advanced into the room. "There's more, isn't there?" she asked.

"Shall I tell you straight-out?"

Oh, God, what? "Yes."

"Only this—I feel it as well, this pressing need for you

to figure out how to do the whole weird splitting-self skill. I'm afraid I'm with Endelle today. Your safety is at stake."

"You're really serious."

He nodded.

What a great way to start the day.

As though he'd read her mind, he smiled. "I do have some good news. Parisa is making frittatas for breakfast."

She wanted to smile in return but she couldn't. She looked away from him, her gaze drifting to the lace curtains and the blue sky beyond. Well, she had wanted to be of real use to the war effort, but she wasn't exactly happy about having to endure Endelle's bucking-bronc style of tutoring again. Her head ached just thinking about it.

She glanced back at him. "I'll take a quick shower then join you in the kitchen."

When another wave of fennel pushed over her, when he growled but left the room, she knew she wasn't the only one making sacrifices this morning.

She showered then donned a gray silk dress and water-marked gray silk scarf. She wore heels. In gray. She felt gray as she ate her frittata then headed with Marcus and Parisa over to the admin building.

But when she saw Endelle, she felt even worse. The woman wore a black leather bustier, of all things, as well as a black-and-white-striped skirt made of some kind of animal fur. Havily so didn't want to know where the fur came from.

Whatever.

By the end of the second hour of enduring Endelle's strident method of teaching, Havily's brain had turned to mush. Her Supremeness had tried every possible means of forcing her to do a split-self. She had given her new memories, she had showed her by example, she had yelled at her, she had even folded a chaise-longue into her office so that Havily could practice while reclining. But nothing seemed to work. For whatever reason, she just couldn't make sense of the process.

By the end of the third hour, tears streamed down her face and her head was killing her.

Endelle paced and shouted, "You should be able to do this. I don't get it. What the hell is wrong with you?"

Havily would have responded but words wouldn't leave her lips. She wondered if she might have permanent brain damage from all the ways Endelle had invaded her mind trying to get her to understand the skill.

But it was Marcus who stepped in front of Her Supremeness and said, "Maybe it's the goddamn teacher."

Endelle lifted a hand, surely to strike him dead.

Havily even rose to a sitting position, her mind spinning wildly, her hands outstretched as though ready to stop the slaying, but Marcus smiled and dipped his chin.

Endelle, much to Havily's surprise, started to laugh.

"How about we try again after lunch," Marcus suggested.

"Fine," Endelle barked.

Havily didn't want lunch. She wanted to crawl under a rock. And never return. Her head ached as though someone had moved a boulder inside her head, then sat on it, was still sitting on it, was jumping up and down on it.

A soft knock on the door, then Alison entered. "Lunch is ready. Anyone hungry?" Her timing was perfect, which Havily suspected wasn't mere happenstance.

Her gaze fell on Havily and her eyes widened. As though she always did so, she crossed the room and put a hand on Havily's forehead. Havily gasped because it felt as though sheets of warm water spilled through her brain and eased her, *eased her*. The boulder disappeared along with the six-foot-five creature that had done all the jumping, thank you very much.

More tears fell, but this time with relief. She felt an arm under her elbow, Alison's arm. "Come on. I ordered spaghetti with Italian sausage, your favorite."

"My first meeting is at two," Havily said as she reached the conference room. She paused on the threshold. She had intended to argue with Endelle about continuing the lessons after lunch, but she was too stunned by the state of the long executive table. There were fresh pink and white roses in a large silver vase in the center. White ceramic bowls, filled with spaghetti and the promised sausage, sat on maroon silk place mats. The smell of the sauce caused Havily's stomach to set up a dedicated rumbling.

She took a seat next to Parisa in a chair opposite the door. Goblets containing Medichi's Cabernet label sat above a fork and a large spoon. There were even linen napkins.

Endelle plopped down in a chair next to Marcus. She frowned at the food. "COPASS has set up Parisa's hearing for tomorrow at one. Can you believe that shit? The same day as the Festival."

Parisa, who had just taken a sip of wine, choked. "I have a hearing?" she cried.

Endelle rolled her eyes. "It doesn't concern you. I mean, you have to be there, blah, blah, blah, but basically Greaves and I will square off and we'll see who wins." She pointed to herself. "That will be . . . hello . . . *me*."

Havily glanced at Parisa and tried to catch her eye, to somehow encourage her not to take Endelle too much at her word. Instead the ascendiate set her goblet down and put her hands in her lap.

Havily glanced at Endelle. She wanted to kick some sense into the administrator. The woman had no idea how her flippant, scornful, way-too-casual remarks could be interpreted. On the other hand, assuming Parisa chose to align herself with Endelle, the mortal-with-wings probably needed to get used to Her Supremeness.

Havily used her fork and swirled the spaghetti against her spoon.

"So Greaves will be there?" Marcus asked. "Somehow I thought he played an invisible role here in the Valley."

Endelle, sitting to the left of Marcus, shoved the empty chair next to her away, leaned back, and angled her legs up onto the table, crossing them at the ankles. The heels of her stilettos looked like a pair of daggers. Havily shook her head. The black-and-white-striped fur had a faint musky odor and slid up her thighs. That and her black leather bustier just didn't add up to "Supreme High Administrator."

She shrugged at Marcus's question then folded a bottle of Dos Equis into her hand, apparently uninterested in the wine. She flicked the lid off with the tip of her finger, which created a spark, then drank deep. Afterward, she belched. What a fine example of womanhood. "Oh, the bastard shows up when it suits him and COPASS suits him." She turned to Alison, who sat on the other side of Marcus. "I'll want you to do some empathic surveillance work, take the temperature of the room, see how many more of these freaks he's turned."

Parisa once more picked up her wine. She still hadn't touched her spaghetti. She'd grown very quiet.

Endelle glanced at her then said, "Just so ya know, I have the worst manners on the planet. I have no subtlety and I hope you can get used to it. Thorne said he's sure I've had a couple of strokes given how old I am, which has inhibited normal social screening. I told him to go fuck himself."

Parisa stared at her for a long moment. "We had a part-time librarian with your attitude. I fired her sorry ass the second day after I got promoted."

Endelle lifted her brows, her lips parted. She chuckled. "Well, then let's hope you don't get promoted over me." She took a long swallow of beer then released a sigh and another belch, only this time she politely covered her mouth with her hand. "You'll need to be tough in this world, ascendiate. Just remember that. Ascension ain't for sissies."

"No shit," Alison murmured.

Havily's gaze shot to her then she laughed. Alison so rarely made use of profanity that when she did, it was always funny because it always unexpected. Marcus smiled as well.

Endelle pursed her lips. "I know this hasn't been a barrel of laughs for you, Parisa, but I want you to know that I've decided to assign Medichi as your Guardian of Ascension until we can make you safe here. In the meantime, I want you to stay at his villa. We'll let him sleep the rest of the day; then he's to stick close to you until you've completed your rite of ascension. You do know about all this shit, right?"

"Yes," Parisa said, her gaze fixed to the untouched pasta. "Havily explained everything to me."

"Good. And don't worry, we'll get all this sorted out at the committee meeting tomorrow."

Parisa released a heavy sigh.

After lunch, Marcus leaned an elbow on the mantel of the fireplace on the west wall of Endelle's office. He looked his woman up and down. She wore a mid-calf gray silk dress and a dappled scarf, tall gray leather heels. Dynamite. And so at odds with the skunk-lady.

What a contrast between the women, at least from a fashion viewpoint. One thing about Havily, she set an excellent tone for the administrative offices.

But in the past hour, as Endelle barked her way through the coaching session, Havily had made little progress. Though she reclined on the chaise-longue intended to encourage her darkening abilities, Marcus felt certain, given what he understood of Havily's temperament, that her concentration was fogged by the fact that she had a meeting in less than an hour with her committee heads.

"But I can't even feel," she said, "anywhere in my body or in my mind or over my nerve endings, a sensation that remotely resembles splitting myself into two parts. It makes no sense."

"It's not supposed to make sense," Endelle cried. "What are you, a fucking moron? How many times have I said this is an ability, a power, just like dematerializing. You can't *think* yourself into a self-split, you just have to feel it."

"But I can't *feel* it," Havily shouted. She swung her legs over the side of the chaise-longue. "I can't do this. I know I need to, but there's nothing there, no sensation, nothing. Every time I think of the darkening, swoosh, I'm there."

"Then stop thinking!"

Marcus tried not to smile but there was something perverted in the male psyche that liked to see two women, two *beautiful* women fight, maybe with the hope that they'd get physical and start wrestling. The thought of Havily on the ground wrestling with another woman did him in.

Havily turned toward him very slowly, her mouth agape. "Why am I smelling fennel?" she cried, her temper now raging in his direction as she rose to her feet.

He could only shift and rest his back against the mantel. He crossed his arms over his chest. He shrugged and said, "I was just hoping this was going to turn into a catfight. One of my favorite things."

Havily hunched her shoulders, narrowed her eyes, and growled. "You'd better be careful, oh-grinning-bastard, or you'll be dead meat in about two seconds."

Okay, he was enjoying this way too much and completely at her expense. He turned away and tried to compose his face but he couldn't keep from smiling and chuckling. When from his peripheral vision he could see that she had now planted her hands on her hips, he said, "I'm sorry."

"You are no help at all," she cried. "Maybe you should leave the room. Or help us out here. Do you have any suggestions?"

This time Endelle chuckled. "You know, Morgan, for a minute there, with all that sarcasm and the wag of your head when you said that, you sounded just like me."

Havily gasped again and whirled. "And you," she cried, her light green eyes blazing as she shot a finger sword-like in Endelle's direction, "You're the worst!"

Endelle, instead of throwing the woman to the floor and planting her stiletto on Havily's neck, threw her head back and laughed, not a simple trill, but the full-throated, deep-chested laughter of a woman who had seen and done everything.

The room calmed down and Havily once more sat on the chaise-longue, her knees together but her feet splayed to the side. She looked like she was about ten except that her gaze moved back and forth over the zebra skin in front of the desk. Her lips worked and her brow crinkled. The funny thing was, she didn't seem all that upset. She was like Endelle in that once she gave vent, the moment passed.

Marcus watched her and put his mind to the difficulty. He wanted to help but he'd never done anything split-self. He couldn't imagine the difficulty involved. Finally, he said, "I know I don't have a basis of experience from which to offer advice, but Havily maybe this is more about you than about the skill itself."

"What do you mean?" Her brow was still wrinkled.

"I'm going to get into so much trouble saying this, but I think it might go to the issue here."

"Just say it," Endelle snapped. "Havily's not as delicate as she looks."

Endelle was both right and wrong on this one. Havily was a helluva lot stronger than she looked, than she presented herself. But she could be wounded . . . easily. Still, he knew he was on the right track when he said, "You don't trust yourself, you don't trust life, and I don't blame you. So how can you even think about splitting yourself into two pieces when you've spent the last century holding yourself together?"

The room got very quiet.

Havily rose once more from the chaise-longue. She looked like he'd slapped her, hard, right across the face. She rubbed her forehead and shook her head. "If that's the case then we're done here."

She moved around the bottom of the chaise and headed to the door.

"Where the hell do you think you're going?" Endelle cried. "We're not finished! We've just gotten started."

Havily kept moving. "I have a meeting I need to prepare for. We can practice tomorrow if you want."

"Get the fuck back here."

"Endelle," Marcus cried. "Let her go. This is enough for one day and she has the Reception tonight."

Endelle turned on him just the same. "But you've felt it,

too. I've seen it inside your head. She has to figure this out . . . now. Her life depends on it."

"I know," he said. "Damn, I wish we were both wrong about this but I'm going to the meeting. I want to talk to the head of security."

"Ten heads of security won't matter if Greaves gets involved tonight or tomorrow, you know that."

"Then I'm just going to have to stick damn close so that if he messes with Havily, I can be the physical shield she needs."

At six in the evening, long after Marcus and Havily, as well as Parisa, had returned from the administrative offices, Medichi approached the library, his tread slow and measured. Marcus and Havily were dressing for the Ambassadors Reception while he had orders to stay with Parisa at his villa, serving as her goddamn guardian.

He'd accepted his new orders from Endelle but only after he'd shouted at her for about ten minutes, paced her office a dozen times, then cursed her for laughing at him. He'd almost lost it when she'd spoken the word *breh-hedden*.

He had never hated her quite so much as in that moment.

But if all that hadn't been enough, he'd actually suggested she assign guardian duty to Santiago. But the moment the words had left his mouth he'd started listing all the parameters he would require for his brother warrior to be around Parisa, to wit, a female Liaison Officer would have to be brought on board to stay twenty-four/seven by Parisa's side, she must sleep in Parisa's room, she should be someone Santiago could neither seduce nor manipulate, and Santiago should be required, *required,* to sleep in a tent on the villa grounds and not inside the house.

Endelle had laughed so hard she'd started to cry. And so his rant had continued in its completely irrational way until Her Supremeness, eyes streaming, had actually fallen on her ass in front of the fireplace, exclaiming that she'd just peed her skunk skirt and would he please get the hell out of her office.

So here he was, rattled as fucking hell. The worst possible thing had befallen him in having been assigned to guard Parisa Lovejoy until she completed her rite of ascension, which, if he understood, still hadn't started, which meant that he couldn't even say he had to do this for only three more days.

So . . . shit.

He stood at the threshold of the library and there she was, so beautiful sitting in her cloud of tangerine, curled up in a chair near the south wall. His heart fucking hurt just looking at her. She wore a silk tank top, turquoise this time, and jeans, clothes she had borrowed from Havily. He wondered if he should make an attempt to get into her house just to bring her something to wear. Well, there was plenty of time to sort that out. Better she was safe first.

He called to her softly, not wanting to startle her. "Parisa?"

She had a book open on her lap and looked up at him. She smiled and said, "Did you know that Luchianne ascended all by herself, that somehow she passed through the Trough on her own power, and that she never felt the smallest effects of the second dimension? She's really amazing."

"And you share that quality with her since you're not feeling the effects of this dimension, either." Just looking at her, he felt as he did when his wings needed to release: on edge, hungry, his body humming with energy.

She nodded. "Yes, that much is true," she said. There was something reflective in her expression, as though she was weighing his words and her thoughts. "I know that part of my experience is similar to hers, but I don't think I could have handled what she went through, always being the first to do these incredible feats. I'm just getting to the part where she discovered the existence of and fought the first death vampire. I feel so . . . inadequate next to her. I could never wield a sword."

He glanced at the book. It was the one he'd recommended to her, a large tome filled mostly with anecdotes of the history of Second Society. Kerrick had once hunted through the same book looking for references to the *breh-hedden* in his hopes of finding a way to deflect all his possessive, jealous, and protective urges toward Alison.

Now here he was, Antony Medichi, ascended out of Italy some thirteen centuries ago, and caught so hard by the *breh-hedden* that visions poured through his head of crossing the room, picking Parisa up in his arms, carrying her to his bedroom, and taking her in every possible way.

That he'd been assigned as her guardian sure as hell didn't help since it now increased the time he would have to be with her.

She glanced up at him quickly. Her nostrils flared. Great. She could smell his desire for her.

She buried her nose back in the book, her hand on her cheek. He detected an answering wave of tangerine, but her body language told him to back off. Fine. Good. Great. Wonderful. Shit.

"I came to tell you that I've been assigned as your Guardian of Ascension."

She nodded, looking up at him again. "I know. Endelle told us at lunch today."

"I would change this if I could."

"It's for the best," she said.

"And how is that?" Okay, so there was an edge of hostility to his voice. He moved to his chair, wondering if he should sit down. He remained standing.

She leaned back and looked up at him, closing the book over her left hand, holding her place among the pages. "Obviously, we have to learn to be around each other despite this . . . this *thing* between us. Like you, I have no interest in it. I think a warrior's life is . . . unmanageable." She huffed a sigh, then dipped her head once more to the book and let the pages flop back open.

Well, how do you like that? She was dismissing him

and she'd called his life unmanageable. Which it was, but that wasn't the point. He was a goddamn Warrior of the Blood. He'd had women chase him all hours of the day and night *for centuries*. He could have any woman he wanted. He was revered in their society and she wasn't even ascended, dammit.

Unable to contain his absurd reaction, he turned on his heel and left what had always been his sanctuary.

Antony, came softly, so softly inside his head, he wasn't certain he'd heard her, but it was Parisa's voice. Did the ascendiate have telepathic abilities as well? Great.

He listened, but nothing followed. He thought about responding but what for?

Instead he went into the kitchen and opened a bottle of Cabernet. He poured two glasses. He knew she liked his label. He felt damn sad as he returned to the library carrying both goblets.

He set one at her elbow. "I'm sorry to invade your space like this," he stated in as formal a voice as he could muster, "but because of the recent attack, I have to stick close. I'll try not to disturb you."

He turned his back to her and took up his favorite chair opposite the window that overlooked the front lawn. He stretched out his long legs. He brooded.

Antony entered his mind once more. He glanced at her. Was she trying to communicate telepathically? Could she even do that? But she didn't lift her gaze. He frowned. She sighed. Yeah, he was probably imagining it because his name on her lips, aloud or in his mind, was exactly what he craved.

He pulled a book from his stack of must-reads. He opened *The Good Earth.* He lost himself in a completely different world, or at least he tried to.

Honoring the traditions of a culture
Casts a brilliant light over the world.

—*Collected Proverbs,* Beatrice of Fourth

CHAPTER 19

Marcus stood in the southern hall, waiting for Havily to emerge from their bedroom. He had showered and shaved in one of the other guest rooms, leaving her alone to dress in private. He'd donned his favorite tux, a kick-ass piece of workmanship by Tom Ford. He had his hands in his pockets and felt like a teenager. All he lacked was a set of keys to jangle.

He was wound up for several reasons, not least of which was because his *breh* was dressing in a nearby room, which meant for part of that time she had to be naked. How he kept from busting the door down, he didn't know.

So, there was that.

His mind kept going to the future and whether or not they would have a future *together*. If not, exactly what would the future look like living apart from her? Would he always feel this way about her? Would the insane attrac-

tion to her, the need to be right by her side at all times, ever
dim? If it didn't, how the hell would he be able to stay
away from her? Or worse, how the hell would he ever bear
the sight of her with another man?

Jesus.

So, there was that.

But probably what kept his nerves feeling like they'd
been stuck with cactus spines had to do with the Ambassadors Reception. He didn't like the idea of being in a large
exposed room, with hundreds of people milling around.
Anything could happen. A vampire with sufficient power
could wreck the place.

So, yeah, he was in a state.

He glanced in the direction of Medichi's private quarters then turned and let his gaze ramble all the way to the
northern reaches, at least as far as his eye could travel. The
entrance from the massive dining room to the kitchen was
offset and not visible from where he stood.

But what an elegant stretch of rooms, not quite a palace,
so yeah, *villa* was exactly the right word. He hadn't had
time to explore the outlying property yet, which apparently
went on for miles north, south, and east. The west boundary
stretched only as far as the White Tanks Wildlife Refuge.
The estate supported an olive grove and press as well as a
good-sized vineyard and winery. Whatever Antony's life
had been on Mortal Earth so many centuries ago, he'd made
a real place for himself on Second Earth, something that
resonated with Medichi's history in old Italy.

Marcus shook his head. So what exactly was an ascender
out of Sumer in 2000 BC supposed to create on Second
Earth that would make sense of four thousand years of living? Dammit, he hated this feeling that nothing in his life
was settled. Even the texts he received from Ennis let him
know he should be on Mortal Earth taking care of business.

"Hey." The word floated toward him from the direction
of his shared bedroom. A wave of honeysuckle followed

and his skin tingled from the assault. He flared his nostrils and drank the fragrance in as he turned toward his woman.

But it was the sight of Havily that took all those tingles and turned them into a goddamn roaring fire over his entire body. "Holy shit," he murmured.

What she wore looked like couture because the strapless black silk was sculpted to her body and flared toward the floor in gentle waves. She must have had on very tall heels because she could almost meet him eye-to-eye, which for him was a couple of major turn-ons; first because he loved women in heels and second, with her height, holding her in his arms would be incredible.

Her makeup, flawless. Her hair, a work of art that traveled in careful waves down the back of her head. But the best part of the whole look was the snug fit of her gown and the long keyhole that exposed her beautiful cleavage. Damn, he wanted his tongue right there, right now. She was so his kind of woman in every goddamn respect.

Pure desire rampaged through him. He was hard as rock all over again, as he so often was when she was near.

He watched her stagger a little on her feet and she put her hands out as though balancing herself. He moved swiftly to her side and steadied her.

"Fennel," she murmured. A heavy bout of honeysuckle slammed over him in response.

He didn't wait but turned into her and took her in his arms. He slanted his lips over hers and kissed her, a full wet kiss. He lifted her off her feet, pushed her back quickly, and pressed her against the wall next to the door of their bedroom. She panted over his mouth.

This is ridiculous, she sent. *You could take me right now and I wouldn't even protest, even though it took me an hour to do my hair. Oh . . . Marcus . . . shiiiiiit.*

The last word, so unlike Havily's usual choice of word or phrase, made him laugh. Damn, he was weak in his gut and at his knees. This did not bode well for exactly how the evening would progress. He'd be aching in his lower extremities before the clock struck midnight and this was just the sort of affair destined to last way, way, way too long.

He panted against her neck and hoped to hell he hadn't wrecked the fall of red waves down her back. "Let's get you to White Lake," he muttered.

Of all the reasons Havily had to be grateful for the success of the Ambassadors Reception, she had not expected one of those reasons to involve keeping her from feeling so darn much where Marcus was concerned.

They'd barely been able to leave the villa without doing a quick wall workout. What was it with them and walls. Honestly!

However, her teams worked together like magic so that Endelle, to whom the ambassadors paid homage, was able to meet and greet each of her Territory representatives.

The costumes alone were a pleasure to view. In the ascended world, all traditions were welcomed and honored, especially as reflected by the costumes of meaningful rituals, religions, and societal customs throughout the ages.

Cries of appreciation and rounds of applause accompanied the most intricate traditional garb as one by one the ambassadors, supported by their individual security details, administrative support, and significant others, approached Endelle's seat of rule.

The Bredstone Hotel had the most elegant rooms, this one with expensive Italian white marble on the floor. The unique gleam of gold leaf shone everywhere.

The tall domed ceilings were painted with historic and mythological scenes from every country around the globe. Looking up, she could see a Japanese shogun in what looked like full battle regalia. The Bredstone had definitely been the right place for the Reception.

To her right, on a raised platform in the very center of the room, a small orchestra played Mozart, the classical structure designed to keep the rational brain at the fore and the Reception on an even keel.

She stood off to the side, opposite the ambassadors' line, in order to monitor the flow of the room. The team leaders had been instructed not to approach her except in an emergency so that essentially no one knew she was in charge. She preferred it that way. Endelle and the ambassadors were what mattered. Period.

She had chosen a position in the room about ten yards from Endelle. Her protocol team worked the line, speaking with interpreters, answering questions, offering guidance.

Her gaze drifted to Endelle who sat in regal splendor on what amounted to a throne, her expression impassive, respectful, a unique state for the prickly administrator. Havily smiled. She even wore silk instead of hide, also a unique state.

Her gown of deep purple flowed in the ancient Greco-Roman style with gold bands encasing her narrow waist. Her long black hair was a masterpiece of loops and at least six more gold bands. For once she actually looked like the ruler of Second Earth.

Havily was proud of her. Unlike almost everyone present, she knew what it cost Endelle to sit still, to nod formally, and above all to keep her temper.

Thorne stood behind Endelle and to her right. He wore formal Warrior of the Blood ceremonial dress: a black leather tunic, streamlined leather battle sandals and shin guards, a brass breastplate, and a purple cape flung over one shoulder. His sandy-colored hair was slicked back and held tight in the *cadroen*, which accentuated his high cheekbones. His gaze traveled over the crowd in a slow continuous motion. He may have been at Endelle's back for official reasons, but the leader of the warriors was working tonight. More than once Colonel Seriffe, head of security for the evening, approached him for a quiet consult.

Warm hands moved around her waist from behind her. Marcus. She drew in a deep breath and smiled. Ordinarily she would have discouraged this possessive display of affection, but she stood in the shadows of a massive grouping of palms.

She covered his arms with her hands.

"Everything is in perfect order," he whispered. "You've done beautifully here."

"*My teams* have done beautifully."

"And exactly how many hours did it take you to assemble your teams?"

"About a gazillion."

He chuckled then kissed her neck. "I want to take you home."

At that she turned to look at him over her shoulder. "Hang tough, Warrior. It's only ten. This won't be over for at least another three hours."

"I want you naked and in *our* bed."

"I'm getting that, O fennel-master. Calm the hell down."

"How can I when you look like a goddess this evening?"

Havily wanted nothing more than to fold out of the hotel straight to the villa and oblige him. She opened her mouth to say something, when a terrible prickling sensation moved across her neck.

Marcus stepped away from her because no doubt he felt it as well. But she whirled on him and held up a hand. "No swords. Not here."

He lowered his chin. "Not yet," he growled.

"Fine." She turned back to the crowd, her gaze shifting back and forth. He drew close once more, a hand on her waist.

She remained in the shadows. "I can sense something, but nothing *looks* different. What do you think is going on?"

"We'll soon know."

She scanned the assembly. And there it was, a shimmering in the center of the room, not far from the multicolored robes, gowns, and costumes of the receiving line.

"Oh, shit," Marcus cried. He stepped away from her again. She didn't try to stop him this time as he drew his sword into his hand.

Greaves had arrived along with several of his generals, including Warrior Leto.

Marcus resumed his place next to Havily, but she held him back with a lifted hand. "This part is for show. I'm sure of it. What do you think?"

"Looks like it."

She watched her security team move into place surrounding the intruders, more than two dozen well-trained Militia Warriors, a sword in each hand.

A ripple of tension moved through the line of ambassadors as feet shifted, as costumes got plucked with nervous fingers, as anxious glances landed on Greaves and his entourage. Colonel Seriffe motioned to the orchestra conductor, and the music stopped.

Havily glanced at Endelle. The woman met her gaze and jerked her head in the direction of the ambassadors' line, which meant Endelle had her own instincts firing off.

She leaned close to Marcus. "Did you see Endelle?"

"Yes."

Endelle rose up from her throne, her gaze now fixed in the direction of Greaves. Thorne drew up next to her. The ambassador from the Argentina-Chile Territory, who had been kneeling at the base of the steps, rose to his feet and moved aside to give her room.

Endelle was an imposing figure, at least six-ten in her stilettos, and so beautiful, something Havily often forgot given the prickly nature of the woman's temperament. She looked like a princess from the Middle East.

She closed in on her enemy, moving within five yards of Greaves. Power shimmered in waves around her. She had set up an iridescent shield around herself. Havily thought it a thing of beauty.

"Why are you here?" Endelle asked in a carrying voice, her gaze fixed on Greaves.

"To congratulate you on a very fine event," the Commander responded, his voice cool, even.

"You were not invited."

He lifted a graceful hand and clucked his tongue. "Then my invitation did not merely get lost in the mail?" A couple of his generals snickered.

Havily experienced a profound sense of dread, her stomach sinking hard. Greaves defined charisma. Certainly he had a warrior's physique. He was tall and powerfully built, the size of his chest and arms evident even beneath a well-crafted tux. His bald head gleamed beneath the massive chandelier high overhead.

She wished the light fixture would fall on him.

At the very moment that her thought turned to the absurd, he shifted in her direction and his gaze found hers, as if by design.

He was in her head?

She could not have been more shocked. She began systematically building up her shields, like slamming steel doors one after the other. The Commander's lips parted and his eyes narrowed. She kept slamming until . . . there . . . she knew she had just shoved him out.

The bastard inclined his head. She would have felt a sense of triumph had she not been so distressed by the fact that, without her knowing, he'd been in her mind searching her memories.

Marcus leaned close. "What's wrong?" he whispered. "What did he just do?"

She turned to him, met his gaze. "He was in my head."

"Who? Greaves? Fuck."

"He's gone," she said, overlaying his arm with her hand. She felt his muscles twitch beneath her touch. He still held his sword, gripping it hard.

Endelle told Greaves to take himself and his party home. An argument ensued but Havily didn't listen. Her instincts clanged in a different direction as the hairs on the back of her neck rose once more. Again she turned her gaze to the line of ambassadors.

"Do you feel that?" she whispered.

Marcus murmured, "Yes. I think this whole thing has been staged as a diversion."

Parisa had fallen asleep curled up in her chair but she jerked awake because something had given her a mental tap, some danger.

She awoke and glanced around the room. Was she under attack again? She had the worst feeling and her neck felt like all the little hairs were standing up perfectly straight. Medichi stood by the window.

"Antony," she said softly.

He shot his gaze her direction. "What's wrong?"

She shook her head. "I don't know. Something." Her thoughts turned toward Havily and once more she felt uneasy.

He drew near and looked down at her from his formidable height. But she didn't meet his gaze. Instead she turned inward, thought of Havily, and opened up her voyeur's window. Havily came into view, with Marcus beside her. Both of them looked very intent, as though something was wrong. She panned back and the huge ballroom came into view as well as a long line of notables in a variety of cultural costumes and ceremonial dress.

She could see Endelle, looking magnificent in purple. She stood across from a number of men in black-and-maroon uniforms headed by Commander Greaves. Some argument was in progress.

But that didn't hold her attention. She was all for Havily and Warrior Marcus. They stood off to the side opposite the line of what must be the Territory ambassadors.

To Medichi, she said, "Commander Greaves is at the Ambassadors Reception. I remember him from the arena battle. He's brought some of his generals with him, including Warrior Leto. Havily and Marcus seem distressed but I don't think it's focused on Commander Greaves or his entourage."

"You can see all this?" His voice was sharp, worried.

She didn't look at him. She felt the need to keep searching, a profound impulse that caused her to pan left and to move her window backward several steps so that she could view more of the room. There. A death vampire cloaked in mist. She would know one anywhere, the porcelain bluish complexion, the extraordinary beauty. He moved steadily, hidden by the line of ambassadors. He drew closer to Madame Endelle and Warrior Thorne.

"Antony," she said. "Can you fold me directly to Havily? I have to warn her. I can see a death vampire not far from Madame Endelle. I can see him near the line of ambassadors hidden by mist."

She put her hand on his arm and relayed the vision to him as well as Havily's location.

He did not hesitate because the next moment she stood beside Havily. Medichi had his hand on her arm, supporting her.

Havily jumped at the sudden presence of Parisa and Medichi next to her. She gasped and put her hand to her chest. "What are you doing here?"

Parisa didn't say a word. She just planted both her hands on the sides of Havily's face and, with the same ability that Endelle possessed, imparted what she knew.

Havily gasped and watched the replay of some sort of vision, one of Parisa's visions. She saw the death vampire, disguised by mist, moving up along the far side of the ambassadors' reception line. He was almost opposite Endelle and Thorne.

The death vampire slipped through a break in the line. He was focused on Thorne. He lifted his arm and metal flashed.

Havily didn't hesitate. Even from the distance of several yards, she concentrated on Thorne. Just as the death vamp drew his arm up and back, she took Thorne straight into the darkening.

Thorne weaved on his feet, looked around, and drew his sword into his hand all at the same time. His gaze landed on Havily. "What the fuck?" he cried. "What have you done? Where the hell are we? Shit. Is this the darkening?"

"Yes."

"Why?"

"Death vampire and a very sharp dagger aimed straight at you. Do you trust me?"

Thorne shook his head, clearly stunned, but he cried, "Hell, yeah."

Marcus watched the pretty-boy's dagger fly from his hand, through empty airspace, to embed in one of the palm trees not far from where Marcus stood. Holy shit. That blade had been aimed at Thorne, but Thorne had vanished a split second earlier.

He looked around. Havily was gone as well, and a tremor went through him. If he understood what had happened, Havily had just swept Thorne into the darkening, which meant she had just saved Thorne's life. Holy shit!

Marcus focused his attention on the death vampire cloaked in mist and invisible from most of the eyes present. He folded directly behind the pretty-boy. "You looking for someone?" Marcus asked quietly.

The pretty-boy whipped around and met his gaze. His eyes flared as Marcus lifted his sword. With preternatural speed, before the death vamp could move, Marcus sliced in a strong swift arc at the bastard's neck. He made quick work of it, which unfortunately sent a fine spray of blood in every direction. At least the vampire was no longer breathing when he fell headless to the white marble floor and his constructed mist disappeared. His head rolled, thankfully, away from the line of ambassadors.

A cry went up at the same time and the reception line fell back, forming a half circle around the bloody sight.

Endelle joined Marcus then glanced at Medichi, who

drew up on Marcus's other side. "What the hell happened here?" Endelle cried. She looked down at the death vampire. She peered around, hunting. "Where the fuck is Thorne?"

Marcus explained. Medichi added information that concerned Parisa and a sudden vision.

Endelle listened, her striated eyes widening, her cheeks turning a dark red, her lips thinning. She seemed to grow an entire foot, and electricity began to spray from her head, her arms, her shoulders in brilliant green and blue flashes. She turned in Greaves's direction. The crowd parted.

She moved to stand once more in front of the Commander, the flashes turning red. "It would seem one of your own has made an attempt on the life of one of my Warriors of the Blood. So unless you wish to face me now, a challenge I would gladly accept, you had best get the hell out of here. Do you understand me, *Commander*?" The last word, spoken aloud and with unfathomable resonance, brought half the ambassadors to their knees along with most of Greaves's war party.

Greaves, however, didn't move; nor did he meet Endelle's gaze. His attention was elsewhere. He even frowned as he glanced around. Marcus watched him closely.

When the Commander's gaze landed on Medichi and Parisa his frown deepened. Medichi, however, stepped in front of Parisa, his sword drawn. He looked goddamn righteous in battle gear, his weapons harness strapped to his chest, over his black tee. His height was unmatched in the building by any other man present, the strength of his features enough to give even the most powerful death vampire pause.

And still Greaves didn't seem to care. He kept searching the room.

Then it dawned on Marcus what he was looking for: Thorne and Havily. But the hell if he was allowing Havily to be called back while Greaves was in the goddamn building.

Time to end this.

Marcus crossed the room and drew close to Endelle. He cried out in his loudest, most commanding voice, also splitting resonance: *"You've got your marching orders, asshole. Get lost! Now!"*

More groans erupted from several quarters, but Greaves leveled his gaze on Marcus. He felt the punch inside his brain but Marcus pushed back with a powerful, effective shove. Greaves wasn't getting anything out of this little show, not command of his mind, not clues to Havily's whereabouts, and not the death of a Warrior of the Blood.

Hell. No.

Greaves backed down. He bowed to Endelle. "I shall see you tomorrow at the committee hearing."

And that was that since Greaves lifted an arm, then he and his contingent, as one, disappeared.

Damn, that vampire had power. Bastard.

Endelle turned to Marcus then glanced at the body of the death vamp. She made a careful assessment. "So he was after Thorne." Whatever her temper might be, her mind was quick.

"Yep."

"And Havily has him."

Marcus nodded.

"Well, if he wanted to make a statement, taking out my second-in-command would have done it. Thank fuck he failed."

"You noticed Greaves looking around?"

Endelle nodded. "I saw."

"Do you think he meant anything more by it than wondering where Thorne and Havily were?"

She sighed and shook her head. "Greaves is no fool. We both know Havily's powers are emerging. He must have information about her from the future streams." A soft stream of obscenities left her mouth. "And now he sure as hell knows about her darkening abilities. Goddammit."

"I think I should get her back to the villa."

Endelle nodded but frowned. "What about all this?"

She waved a hand toward the line of ambassadors. Everyone was staring at Endelle, waiting, distressed.

Marcus had already thought this through. "Havily trained her teams well, and you need to continue honoring those ambassadors who have had the courage to show up for this reception and for the Festival tomorrow night."

He glanced around. "As for this mess, Jeannie can do cleanup. If she does it in small increments, the flashes won't do any damage."

"Get it done, Warrior," Endelle said.

Marcus drew his phone from his pant pocket then touched the screen.

"Good evening, Warrior Marcus. How can I help?"

"Hey, Jeannie. We need cleanup at the Bredstone at my location. Small doses. Just give me a minute to get this organized." He lowered his arm and called out, "Eyes closed." He repeated the command and waited until all necessary translations had been made. He brought his phone back up to his ear and gave Jeannie the command.

"You got it."

Marcus closed his eyes as well. A series of small flashes of light ensued. He opened his eyes and *poof,* death vampire and attending debris gone.

Endelle met his gaze. "Good job," she said quietly.

Marcus felt his future crowding him. His warrior instincts were firing off one after the other. He still held his bloodied sword in hand.

Something needed to be done about how this war was being managed, but what?

So far, by making use of his most powerful mist, Crace had been able to disguise his presence from the august gathering. He knew he didn't have much time to figure out what had happened. There were too many powerful entities present who would eventually see his mist for what it was: a projected image of a palm tree.

He'd been watching the show with great pleasure, right

up until the moment that Parisa had shown up with Warrior Medichi in full guardian mode. From that split second forward, his plans fell to shit.

Before the assassin could complete his assignment, both Havily and Thorne had disappeared simultaneously; then Warrior Marcus, having caught the death vampire in the act, had struck him down. He didn't give a toad's ass about the death vamp, only that his plan had fucking failed . . . again.

But where had Havily gone? Where was Thorne?

Once again, Crace hunted for Havily's trace as well as Thorne's but found nothing, which meant Greaves was right, the bitch had the ability to go into the darkening. She also had the capacity to take others with her. In this case, she'd just saved the life of the fucking leader of the Warriors of the Blood.

His first instinct was to report to Greaves, to tell the Commander what he believed had happened, but he belayed that impulse. The Commander wasn't high on his list of must-grovel-to right now. He was still pissed at having been humiliated in the peach orchard and he despised that Greaves actually favored Rith-the-weasel. So, the Commander could go fuck himself.

He was also intrigued that the mortal-with-wings had somehow learned of the impending attack and had informed Havily of it. So the women were working together? There was that *convergence* theory again.

Whatever.

He just couldn't work up a fly's armpit of interest in the mortal-with-wings. He wanted his blood donor and he wanted her now.

His pecs swelled and flexed in anticipation. Yep, Havily was what he needed, but shit, darkening capabilities.

In quick stages, he became aware that if he intended to hold his blood donor for any length of time he would have to deal with her ability to disappear into the darkening. He knew next to nothing about this power, since it was primarily a Third Earth ability, but if she could remain indefinitely in the darkening—or worse, leave from one location into nether-space then move to another—he would have to find some way to immobilize her.

The next step in the process led him to consider the use of drugs. The mind guided every power. If Havily's brain were melted down into a useless soup, she'd stay put. Besides, he didn't really need her thinking.

Already his mind whirred as a new plan began to form, one he could execute in tandem with his fireworks display at the Festival tomorrow night. He smiled. Damn, he loved it when a plan came together.

As for the botched assassination attempt, he knew Greaves would be disappointed but right now he didn't give a fuck. He thought about returning to his forge and getting started on what he'd need in order to contain Havily but he really wanted to see his suspicions confirmed. He wanted to see her bring Thorne back from the darkening.

He settled in for the wait until he felt a sliver of energy pierce him, a little zing that burned like hell. His whole carefully constructed shield of mist started to disintegrate, and now he stood exposed in his leather kilt and battle sandals for all to see.

He turned and sought the author of his shield's disintegration. Just in time, he caught Endelle's hostile glare and her upraised hand, palm aimed at him.

Aw fuck, the bitch was about to throw a hand-blast.

He lifted his arm and got the hell out of there. However, when he arrived back in his forge, a portion of his side was burned all to hell. Shit, she'd hit him.

He started to shake. That was a close one. If he hadn't escaped when he did, he would be a collection of charred carbon all over the wall of the Bredstone. Shit.

Expanding awareness,
Opens the universe.

—*Collected Proverbs*, Beatrice of Fourth

CHAPTER 20

Havily went with her instincts and waited to be recalled. Both Endelle and Marcus were present, and she knew that either ascender was powerful enough to communicate with her in the darkening. They'd certainly done so before.

"Havily," Endelle barked within nether-space. "Please return with Thorne."

Havily glanced at him and dipped her chin. "You ready?" she asked.

Thorne smiled. "You're fucking amazing, Hav." He nodded in return.

Havily couldn't help but give him an answering smile. She closed her eyes and thought the thought. The swishing began.

When she opened her eyes, she stood near Endelle with Thorne right next to her.

Marcus moved in close. He slipped his arm around her

waist, tighter than before. She leaned into him. His body was a rock wall of tension, which for some reason eased her. "You okay?" he asked.

She nodded.

Thorne took a moment to scan the entire room. When he was satisfied, he turned to Endelle. "So, what the fuck was that all about? What happened? I take it Havily just saved my ass."

Endelle jerked her head toward the side wall in the direction of the palm trees. "Colonel Seriffe is collecting the evidence right now. A death vamp would have had you if our girl, here, hadn't taken you into the darkening."

Thorne glanced at the Militia Warriors clustered around the dagger. One of them had a plastic Baggie, and another wore gloves. He whistled then turned to Havily and clapped her on the shoulder. "Thanks, Hav. Well done."

"My pleasure, boss."

He chuckled. "You'll do."

"There's more," Marcus said. "Crace was here."

"Crace?" Havily cried. A shiver went down her back, and she couldn't keep from also taking a quick look around.

"Shielded," Endelle explained. "But I felt him, felt his presence. He has a lot of power. When I located his mist, I sent a little gift package. He folded at the same moment but I might have winged him."

Havily shuddered. "Are you sure it was Crace?"

"I recognized him," Endelle said. "And Morgan . . . good job."

"Thank you." Her fingers trembled. Too much adrenaline. She glanced toward the center of the room. "I see the party left."

"Yep," Endelle said. "He didn't have the balls to stay and fight even though I offered. One day I'm going mano-a-mano with that bastard." She blew the air from her cheeks. "Well, I guess we'd better get on with the show, but as for you, Morgan, I want you back at the villa. That's an order."

"May I ask why?" She hated the thought that she might have let Endelle down in some way, but she honestly didn't know how she could have prevented an attempted assassination, not with Greaves and his generals able to get into the building despite all their security precautions. That Crace could get in as well was equally alarming.

Endelle shifted her gaze to Marcus then back to Havily. "I have reason to believe that Greaves was hunting you. Your powers are emerging, which means that you've probably been lighting up the future streams and God knows Greaves has turned enough High Administrators to have access to any number of Seers Fortresses around the globe, the prick. That's the why of it and for fuck's sake don't read anything else into this."

Well, that changed things. "Okay, but please call if you need me."

Endelle smiled. "Damn, Morgan, you just keep disappointing my *lousy* opinion of you." She laughed at her joke. "But believe it or not, we can see a goddamn reception through without your help. Now get going. I'm sure you'll figure out something to do with your time." She threw a knowing glance at Marcus then turned on her heel and headed back to her throne.

Thorne fell into step beside her as if nothing untoward had just happened. However, his right hand flexed as though he felt the need for his sword. He followed Endelle up the steps and flanked her as he had before, his arms crossed over his chest as he once more surveyed the crowd.

He was all man, all warrior. He carried the lion's share of the burden for the Warriors of the Blood.

"What are you looking at Thorne for?" Marcus asked, his arm tightening around her waist.

"I really admire him," she said, completely without thinking. But she understood her mistake when she heard a low growl right next to her ear.

"You admire him?"

Havily couldn't help but smile. Maybe she shouldn't

have, but she loved that he was jealous. "I admire him as a leader," she stated in as cool a voice as she could manage. "He's carried the load more than any other warrior here on Second Earth."

Marcus turned slightly to watch Thorne. He could have been killed tonight. Instead Havily had saved him so that he could keep on keeping on. Christ, he even shared a telepathic link with Her Supremeness. Havily was right: Thorne carried the load.

Guilt pounded Marcus. He'd been gone for two centuries while Thorne and the warriors took care of business. If he was coming back, he had a lot of making up to do, and he could begin right now by doing everything he could to keep Havily safe.

He took Havily's hand. "Ready?"

She nodded.

He thought the thought. He felt the blinking out then sudden hard awareness. When his feet touched the planked floor of Medichi's villa, he still had hold of her hand. She gave it a squeeze and smiled at him.

He was about to gather her up in his arms when Medichi walked into the foyer from the direction of the kitchen, his brow low. His nostrils flared as he said, "This guardian business is for shit." He then closed his eyes and sucked in a deep breath. He made an attempt to relax his shoulders but didn't quite succeed. He looked like Atlas struggling to hold up the world.

"What gives?" Marcus asked. He wanted to be understanding but he sure as hell hoped Medichi would make it quick. Havily was still wearing her high heels.

He jerked his thumb toward the south wing. "I have Parisa with me . . . in my bedroom . . . for the night." His molars made a grinding noise. "Hey. Don't look at me like that. My suite has a den. I'm sleeping in there."

"What's going on?" Havily asked.

He looked about ready to bite her head off. "What's

going on? This house is too fucking big, that's what's going on. How can I protect her if she sleeps across from your rooms?"

Marcus grinned. He couldn't help it. He knew all too well the pain of wanting something, with all the gentleness of a tornado, and being unable to have it, take it, be with it, plan a future with it. So, yeah, he grinned.

Medichi huffed a heavy sigh. "I'll say good night. Parisa's not happy, either, but she's showering and I'm closing the door. Once we're locked in, we're in for the night."

He didn't wait for a response but turned and marched, shoulders once more around his ears, in the direction of his suite. But he called back, "I've left the motion detectors off but don't open any doors or windows, got it?"

"Got it," Marcus called after him.

"Wow," Havily murmured. "I think he's got it bad."

"No shit."

He turned to Havily. She held her arms pinned around her chest, like she was barely holding herself together. "Are you sure you're okay?"

She glanced at him. "Yeah. Just a little rattled still."

He inclined his head toward her tightly folded arms then lifted a brow.

She laughed and uncrossed her arms. She showed him her shaking hands. "Adrenaline."

He nodded. He understood completely. "Breathe."

"Trying to."

"You were fantastic," he said. He took a step toward her and stroked the back of her arm.

She met his gaze, still looking a little wild-eyed. She tilted her head. "The thing is, Marcus, after tonight, I really think I can start making a difference in the war. I saved Thorne's life."

"Yes, you did and yes, you can. I think you already have. What you've done with Endelle's administrative offices alone is a wonder. And that was a top-notch reception you put together tonight."

"I was referring to the darkening."

He slung an arm around her waist and guided her in the direction of the north wing. She allowed him to ease her into the adjoining receiving room. She was keyed up as hell and he needed to talk her down. He also had a plan, a serious plan that involved his hands, and other things, all over her body.

"Because of Parisa, I saw the death vamp just in time. I didn't even think the thought, I just latched onto him with my mind and took him into the darkening. I still can't believe I did that."

"Amazing."

"Yeah. It really was."

He glanced at her and felt an inkling of unease. "You still need a lot of practice to figure this thing out, though."

"Yes, yes, I know. Oh, Lord, I must sound like I'm so full of myself right now but I didn't mean it that way. I just can't believe that I helped, I really helped."

He moved her through the dining room and into the kitchen. He led her past the island and farther down the hall.

Near the doors leading to the patio, he guided her to the left through an open archway.

"The music room," Havily murmured. "What do you have in mind, Warrior?" He loved that she called him that. Her gaze fell to the couch with a connected chaise-longue. A little swirl of honeysuckle made him smile as he moved past her. Yeah, there were a lot of things he could do on that couch.

"Just wait," he murmured.

He hunted through his CDs and found the one he wanted. Decades ago, he'd seen the artist perform live, one of the singular advantages of immortality. He'd seen a lot of artists through the ages perform live.

He enjoyed a cross section of music, and this choice was exactly what he wanted to play for Havily right now. The weight of it, he ignored. This was what he wanted no matter the consequences.

The sultry dark voice of the female artist and the driving rhythm moved through him.

Havily frowned then smiled. "Who is this?"

"Anita Baker. R and B."

Havily narrowed her gaze at him. "And the name of this song?"

" 'Sweet Love.' "

"Oh. It's really . . ." She closed her eyes and the beat caught her. She swayed. "Lovely."

Oh. Yeah.

He drew close and cupped the back of her neck. She melted against him and he held her close, loving the additional height her heels gave her. And, yeah . . . her heels. A shudder went through him and he slid both arms a little tighter all the way around her back. She rested her arms on his shoulders as he burrowed into her neck. Now he could mess up her hair. He wanted to mess it up a lot.

He swayed her to the erotic rhythm. He released her just enough to allow one of his hands to creep onto her bare back. Yeah, he had plans, and this one began right here. He drifted his fingers lightly over her wing-locks.

A soft moan followed and a sweet wave of honeysuckle. "This is our time," he said softly. "Yours and mine. Together. Now."

"Yes."

Havily felt herself falling. She was lost, caught up, entranced. His fennel scent washed over her in waves. Did he have her in thrall? The words of the music, all about *love,* should have sent her anxiety on a death spiral. Instead, Marcus was doing something to her, something that felt like seduction, sweet seduction.

He kissed the side of her neck and licked over her vein. "I want this tonight," he murmured.

Desire flowed and something more, a powerful sensation that kept moving through her. What was that? What was he doing to her?

He kissed down her neck and put a hand on her breast. "I want this."

"Yes." Her voice sounded hoarse.

He kissed her on the mouth, his lips forceful. She parted her lips and he drove inside, *very determined*. He was possessing her. His body was tense, his muscled thighs pressing against her legs, his thick, heavy arms engulfing her. She felt like a delicate flower surrounded by the power of him, the force of him, the determination.

She pulled back and looked into his eyes, a slash of brows over light brown eyes.

"Marcus," she said. "What's going on? You feel different tonight."

He whispered against her lips, "Be strong for me."

What did he mean?

He kissed her again then his mind pressed against hers. He sent, *Let me in, Havily, all the way.*

There was nothing in her, not one thing, that rose to resist, so she relaxed her shields, just let them disappear. He rolled through her mind, another possession, another taking, another invasion. *Mine,* drifted through her head, a seductive pull that dragged at her ankles.

The falling continued, that sensation that the earth was opening up and she was tumbling inside. She fell down, down, down.

Marcus, she sent. *What are you doing to me?*

His kiss deepened and she whimpered against his mouth. He pressed his thigh between her legs and she was back at the palace the very first time he'd kissed her, as he pressed her with the strength of his powerful body, back, back, back until she hit the wall and he was all over her, pulling her dress up around her waist and her panties down.

She was there again, unable to resist him and falling, falling.

When had he taken her down on the sofa? He put a hand on her side and her gown disappeared. He groaned. He must have thought a second thought, because he was suddenly naked against her, pushing her thighs wide, the crown of his cock already finding her and driving inside. How had the vampire moved without her knowing it?

The music had moved on as well, building, building, pulsing from wall to wall, heating everything up.

So perfect.

He pushed and pushed. He pulled out then pushed again. He set a driving rhythm and pushed.

Mine, once more rolled through her mind. *You're so beautiful. Your thoughts warm me.*

Havily no longer existed within her body. She was floating in some kind of delirious state in which his powerful body drove into her and his mind pressed and stroked her.

I'm yours.

She broke the kiss but only so that she could turn her head and present her throat to him. She needed another invasion of him, another way he could be inside her body. And oh, his fennel scent was another intoxication.

I need you now, she sent.

He didn't wait, thank God, but struck in a quick erotic jab. He was all sex and yet so much more as he drew on her vein, as though all the ways he took her body pulsed in rhythm with the beat of her music.

She felt the heavy thuds of her heart as he drew on her vein and took the wealth of her body into his mouth and down his throat.

He moaned. *Your blood feeds me.*

Yes, she responded.

You're mine.

Yes.

Each thrust into the well of her body sent shock waves up and up, through her abdomen, her stomach, the cage of her chest, up through her neck and into her mind.

Her eyes were closed now, the sensation of his presence in her mind, his mouth sucking at her vein, his thick cock pushing into her and connecting them as nothing else could, sent shards of pleasure to every nerve ending. Her toes and fingertips tingled, chills rained down her neck, her back, her sides. Her wing-locks, forced as they were against the nap of the sofa beneath her, were on fire.

She scrambled for air, to remember to breathe as he pushed, sucked, and rolled. He possessed her completely.

Her body held him now, gripping his cock. He groaned with each thrust. He was close. She could feel it in the increase of pace and in the way the muscles of his back flexed, the way he rose up off of her just a little even though she had a stranglehold on his back.

He released her vein and drew back.

She opened her eyes. He was watching her. She put her hand on his cheek. "What are you doing to me?"

"Everything," he whispered. "God I love being inside your mind." He still thrust, his endurance preternatural. Oh, yeah, ascended life. Vampire power. How could the *breh-hedden* be more than this?

Will you permit me to enthrall you?

You want to put me in thrall.

Yes. Will you allow it?

Her body answered the question by tightening and shivering. She wanted it. She'd never been enthralled before but she'd heard it was out of this world.

She took a deep breath as his gaze held hers. He would have complete power over her. Did she trust him? Yes. She nodded. *Yes. Do it.*

She felt the tendrils reach for her, a strange weaving of light and thought, of *purpose*.

What he did next didn't feel real. He held her mind, inside her mind. She felt *captured* and *bound*. She reveled in being at his mercy.

Mine once more flooded her brain. All the previous sensations sped through her, doubled then tripled in intensity as once more he took her at the neck, between her legs, and held her in a completely submissive state.

She felt something leaving her body. What was that? Then she knew.

Oh. My. God.

Marcus?

I feel it. Let it happen. Let go. You can do this.

Her second self, the split-self, was leaving, was entering the darkening!

Stunned, she was suddenly a second corporeal being inside the darkening, and alone. A profound sense of freedom came over her, that in this state she could go anywhere she wanted to. And she knew exactly where she would go.

She thought Endelle's name and swooshed through nether-space. She called out to her. She could see her now, sitting on her throne, still receiving at the Ambassadors Reception. The woman turned to look directly at her. She then whispered something to Thorne, who stood behind her and to her right.

Thorne nodded, moved down three steps, and said something to the ambassador now kneeling. While he held the attention of the ambassador, Endelle's split-self entered the darkening in an extraordinary cloud of golden light.

Havily lifted a hand to block the glow, and yet again she was reminded of the level of Endelle's power. She had been in the darkening but she had never looked like this. Must be something only a split-self could see.

Well, ascender, you made it. She looked Havily up and down. *No modesty this time but I like your heels.* She seemed to collect herself then asked, *How?*

Marcus holds me in thrall. We're . . . joined.

Endelle closed her eyes and after a moment smiled. *And he's fucking your brains out. No wonder you have a fiery red aura right now. Go back to him and for fuck's sake practice. See if you can figure it out . . . how to get back here. And Morgan, know this, your life depends on it. Now get the hell out of here.*

Havily didn't wait. She pictured Marcus in her mind and her split-self rushed through nether-space and re-turned to her initial point of departure, a couch that wasn't a couch. Another second and her two parts re-formed. She was once more within her body, on the couch, with Marcus, yes, pounding into her.

She was also on the cusp of ecstasy and she cried out, which in turn triggered his release. Oh, God, he was hard as a rock as he thrust into her. The now familiar lightning streaked over her, then pulsed upward into the well of her. A sensation flowed upward, like a river rushing through a narrow canyon gorge, grabbing her stomach, her chest, her heart, her mind until ecstasy tore her voice from her throat and she was screaming at the ceiling.

His orgasm went on and on, the pulses of his cock jabbing at her, which again ignited the powerful upward flow of sensation.

She arched her back up and off the couch.

The moment she did, all sensation joined yet again and formed a stream of pleasure as ecstasy once more took her into the heavens. She was beneath him panting and writhing, squeezing the last bit of pleasure from her body. He jerked at her movements, groaned and sighed.

At last, she eased back, relaxing onto the sofa.

You did it, he murmured within her mind. His warrior body, stretched out on top of hers, was another kind of ecstasy. She surrounded him with her arms. She loved his body. She loved his kisses, his mouth at her neck. She loved . . .

The word, so nearly spoken within her thoughts, had him drawing back and looking at her. His light brown eyes in the dim light of the room questioned what she meant to say, but she couldn't continue because she didn't know what the unspoken word meant.

She closed off the thoughts and he nodded as if he understood. He withdrew from her mind, which left a rubbery boomerang sensation within her head. Oh, she was alone again. Marcus eased out of her and his fluids rushed from her body. She caught them with a hastily folded wad of tissues. She looked down at her legs and noticed that she still had her heels and black thigh-high stockings on. She giggled then laughed. Well, he'd folded off *most* of her clothes.

She met Marcus's gaze and a smile lit his eyes. "What can I say?" he said. "I have a thing for a woman in heels. Come on." He picked her up. "Let's get you to bed. You've had one helluva night."

As he reached the door, with the music still playing, he turned and the music ended abruptly. He must have used his mind to shut the system down.

Havily leaned her head against his shoulder, the tissues still pressed between her legs. Everything about love-making was so wickedly personal, something that viewed from the outside must seem absurd, animalistic, without meaning, and yes, messy, but she loved it. She'd loved it with her husband, with Eric, and now with Marcus.

Yes, with Marcus.

The center of her chest lit with a warm glow, the heat spreading to envelop her heart.

This was love.

She didn't want to admit it, but, yes, this was love.

Sweet love.

Sweet Love.

Could she do this? Could she be with Marcus? Have a relationship with him? Have a life with him?

Yes, of course she could. She'd saved Thorne's life to-night. She could do anything.

But she sighed as anxiety rippled through her, a serpent in the garden. Who was she kidding? She had only to think about either Eric or Duncan and she lost heart. But that didn't mean she couldn't enjoy Marcus while their time together lasted.

"I'm going to fold us to our bedroom," he said, "be-cause the hell if I'm going to chance Medichi seeing you like this."

Havily kissed his cheek as together they dematerialized.

Marcus knew a bureaucratic farce when he saw one. He'd
dealt with committees on Mortal Earth like this, a growing majority of the members tied to special interests, deals
done behind closed doors, alliances formed, the original
purpose of the institution mired in rules and regulations,
bribes and more bribes.

The greater trouble with COPASS, however, stemmed
from something more insidious than just greed. According
to Endelle, at least a third of the members were addicted to
dying blood, having been seduced to the experience by
Greaves, who provided an antidote. But then, apparently,
the Commander also provided the dying blood to sustain the
addiction. How many deaths were required to feed these
heinous appetites?

And this committee was to decide Parisa's fate?

Over his dead fucking body.

He glanced at Medichi. He noted the tense line of his
jaw and the unblinking stare fixed on the back of Greaves's
head.

Over Medichi's dead body as well. The warrior stood
close to Parisa, almost touching her. Marcus knew exactly
what that instinct felt like.

He turned and looked at Havily who was, yeah, about
two inches away from him. Maybe one and a half. She wore
a conservative two-piece in navy silk, the jacket shaped
with attractive pleats and a slight flare at the hem. As always,
dynamite.

She smiled at him and he felt that tug, that need, the draw
she had on him, that made him think of the bed they shared
and getting her back there. He'd awakened this morning with
her on top of him and not in the darkening, just on top of
him in a really basic way.

And because it was morning, he'd been ready for her.

What he hadn't expected was how she'd gone for his neck. He still ached a little from how profoundly she'd drawn from his vein. Something about that made him wonder just how far down this road she'd progressed. He'd already gone the distance. He knew what he wanted: Nothing less would suffice than to complete the *breh-hedden* with her. He almost talked to her about it this morning, but Parisa had called to her, distressed about the upcoming hearing.

So here they all were confronting the enemy, this time in a judicial setting. Even his former warrior brothers were in attendance, all of them in battle-scarred flight gear because, as Jean-Pierre had said, these COPASS bastards needed to remember exactly what the Warriors of the Blood did each and every fucking night. Santiago stood next to him, his expression dark and brooding. He didn't carry his sword, but he had his jewel-encrusted dagger with him, which he flipped in his right hand over and over, also making his point.

Zacharius stood at a little distance talking quietly with . . . Kerrick.

Marcus watched his former brother-in-law for a long moment. Surprise. Ever since Havily had invaded Marcus's life, his hatred for Kerrick had diminished in stages, though he wasn't certain of the why of it. Four months ago, Medichi had told Marcus it was time to move on, to get over the rage that had forced him to leave Second Earth in the first place.

Kerrick caught his gaze, his expression somber. He knew what Kerrick wanted . . . forgiveness. But could Marcus do that, really go the distance? On the other hand, what kind of hypocrite did it make Marcus to be intent on keeping Havily in his life but being unwilling to forgive Kerrick for having married Helena.

Marcus looked away. The trouble was, they had something in common now. They both had *brehs,* women for whom they would each, without question, lay down their lives. Neither of them had asked for this to happen, but here they were, bonded to powerful women, their lives apparently changed forever. And now Medichi was headed down the same path.

The committee chamber was a long stone building, structured like an old English church, complete with fan vaulting and stained-glass windows, depicting the rule of law or a thriving society in the colored glass. Marcus thought it one big fucking sham, at least at this point in time. Maybe at the inception of the committee, things had been different, but you give one depraved man enough time, a man with all the gloss of a saint and even a bedrock of granite could be blown all to hell.

In the center of the chamber, side by side but at two separate podiums, Endelle and Greaves prepared to do verbal battle. Greaves looked his usual elegant self in fine-pressed wool. Endelle, on the other hand, wore green suede pants and some kind of white feathery halter made up of ostrich feathers, maybe. Her black hair was dressed in a tornado of curls. She looked like she'd been out clubbing all night . . . or turning tricks.

"Chairman Harding," Commander Greaves began, his resonant voice as always silky smooth. With him in the gallery to his right were, again, his generals, including Leto. "With all due respect to my esteemed rival, the Supreme High Administrator had no right under existing law to offer a shield of mist to the ascendiate. Madame Endelle has violated several rules of ascension and I hereby demand the redress of unrestricted and solitary access to the ascendiate for a similar period of time."

A general violent hiss erupted from the Warriors of the Blood, not unexpected. Parisa would be dead within minutes of being locked up in Greaves's world.

Endelle had no problem chiming in. "With all due respect to my most revered rival—" Here she turned toward Greaves slightly and flipped him off out of the view of the committee members. "—Commander Greaves had two of his most powerful warriors breaching the ascendiate's home on Mortal Earth before she had even answered her call to ascension."

"Not true," the Commander responded in his even tone.

The committee comprised ninety-eight members and one chairperson, the chair to serve as a tiebreaker. A simple majority was needed for any resolution to pass. The members sat facing one another, and the chairman sat at the head of the room on a throne-like chair. Harding wore white robes as though he were a god. Fucking hypocrite. Was there a soul in this exalted building who didn't know he belonged to Greaves?

Harding spoke now. "The matter before us is not simplistic in nature, but I think everyone can agree that the most basic purpose of the committee is to establish order between the opposing sides of our society. That order must be upheld. I think we can also agree that given Madame Endelle's breach of our established ascension rules, Commander Greaves has a right to exclusive time with the ascendiate."

The warriors booed him one and all.

"It's a death sentence," Santiago cried out. "And you know it."

Harding slammed an old-fashioned gavel down hard on a block of wood. "I will have order from the galleries or we will make this a closed hearing. Do we understand each other, Warrior Santiago?"

Endelle turned around and gave Santiago *the look,* as in he'd better shut it or she'd have him by the short hairs.

What Marcus didn't know was how the hell this was going to end well for Parisa.

Alison stepped up to the podium and whispered something in Endelle's ear. Endelle nodded. Alison withdrew.

"Mr. Chairman, I believe we've overlooked something."

"What would that be, Madame Endelle?" He had already motioned for Greaves's generals to apprehend the ascendiate.

Endelle took a deep breath. "Parisa Lovejoy never formally answered her call to ascension. She was never given the opportunity. The attack on her home took place before she had the chance to reach a Borderland, and as you know answering a call to ascension must always include a demonstration of power at a Borderland."

Pandemonium broke out as those who needed to support Greaves began shouting their objections while everyone still aligned with Endelle gave a rousing cheer.

Marcus smiled. Well, didn't that shift things in the right direction.

"I hereby suggest," Endelle called out in a loud voice, settling the committee members down, "that Greaves's claims on her are not valid and I have been acting as I would toward any guest on Second Earth—I have been assuring her safety since she was attacked not only at her home on Mortal Earth but at Warrior Medichi's villa as well. Unless of course Commander Greaves has evidence to the contrary."

Greaves wasn't happy. He glanced first at Endelle then at Alison behind her. Marcus thought there was fire in his eyes. The Commander's left hand, bent slightly at the wrist, trembled as he put it back on the podium. He tried to argue that Parisa had indeed answered her call to ascension when she first mounted her wings.

Harding consulted with two men behind him. One brought forward a large book, which he opened and pointed with his finger to a particular passage. When Harding turned around, his complexion had paled; even at this distance Marcus could see a distinct sheen on his forehead.

He addressed Greaves. "There are strict rules about this, Commander, as my esteemed colleague has reminded me by referring to the committee inception documents of 1901. Responding to a call to ascension must always occur at one of the Borderlands. This has been the tradition since ancient times and it is written into COPASS law. I fear . . . Madame Endelle in this particular has the law on her side."

Murmurs went round the room.

The warriors cheered.

Marcus could see the factions clearly, and those ascenders not yet belonging to Greaves sat with arms folded over chests and expressions resolute.

Harding mopped his brow with a hastily folded kerchief as he further addressed Greaves. "Because the mortal has not answered her call to ascension, there can be no rite of ascension. The laws do not apply." He swallowed visibly.

Someone's ass was going to hurt like hell later.

"I believe I must apologize," Greaves said, "for taking up the committee's time. I was gravely misinformed." He turned to Endelle and bowed to her. "I do apologize."

"Oh, eat shit and die, you fucking asshole."

Marcus grinned. It was moments like these that Endelle's rough-hewn exterior made him happiest. She was totally out of order, but since Greaves simply lifted his arm and vanished, taking his ass-lickers with him, well, no harm, no foul.

She turned back to the warriors and lifted her fist in victory. There was only one response: The warriors as one raised their arms and gave a powerful shout in return.

Even the most careful plan
Succumbs to the power of the unforeseen.

—*Collected Proverbs*, Beatrice of Fourth

CHAPTER 21

Later, at the villa, Marcus watched Havily once more work with Parisa on her flying skills. The air temp was in the hundreds and he was sweating, but he didn't care. The women had changed into their flight suits. Both were a pleasure to watch. Both were perspiring as well and also didn't seem to care. Havily looked *happy.*

This time, however, Medichi was the one to set up a lawn chair on the front patio. He reclined, albeit scowling, as the women went through their various maneuvers.

Marcus stood beside him for half an hour, his heart weighted. His gaze rarely left Havily's brown-spotted wings and flame of hair. She was as beautiful in flight as on the ground.

He physically ached to be with her.

He wanted to complete the *breh-hedden,* but Havily held back. He could feel it, see it in her eyes. He knew her thoughts, that she feared loving him or any man because of the losses she had endured. She was close, though. When he'd been making love to her, she'd almost told him she loved him, stopping just short of the words flowing through her head.

But what would it take for her to be ready to commit to him? Did she still see him as unreliable because he'd lived in exile on Mortal Earth? And was he truly ready to take this step?

"Why are you shaking your head?" Medichi asked.

"Because that's the only thing I can think to do." His voice sounded hoarse, low, lost. Shit.

Medichi grunted his understanding.

"There's something I need to do," Marcus said. "I'll be gone about half an hour. Can you guard Havily as well?"

"Sure. Heading back to Mortal Earth?"

Marcus glanced down at him. He heard Medichi's tone. "Now, why the hell would you say that?" Yeah, he was a little touchy on the subject.

Medichi folded his hands behind his head. "Thought you might be anxious to check up on your empire, get back to business."

"No," he responded. The funny thing was, he meant it. "Back in thirty minutes."

He went to his room and folded on battle gear, a black leather kilt, weapons harness, black leather shin guards, wrist guards, and heavy sandals. He also sported Ray-Ban Predators. Where he was headed, the sun would be setting and in his eyes.

He called Jeannie and got a fold to the spectacle landing platform, that place designated for all security and performance personnel. An event this size limited the places for dematerialization arrivals and departures. The rest of the land was crisscrossed with anti-dematerialization grids that prevented folding, real high-tech shit. It was just common sense with so many death vampires in the Metro Phoenix area.

When he arrived, four Militia Warriors, swords at the

ready, faced him. A few feet more, and a dozen waited as backup. He lifted his hands palms-up. If any of the pretty-boys showed up, they'd face an army.

"Warrior Marcus," the officer in charge called out. Marcus was still surprised he was so easily recognized, which of course meant that his reputation was alive and well in the ranks, even after two centuries of absence.

"I'm looking for Colonel Seriffe." The colonel was in charge of security as he had been at the Ambassadors Reception.

Marcus was sent in the direction of a massive white tent at the south end of the White Tanks, which he could only reach by way of another landing platform. The officer made a call and Marcus entered a second platform designed just for departure. The whole system was simple, sensible, easily controlled. Part of the tension he was feeling dissipated, at least a little, and he thought the thought.

A moment later he materialized on another platform. Seriffe was right there to greet him and shook his hand.

When he explained what he wanted to do, Seriffe nodded, spoke a few words to his second-in-command, then met his gaze in a hard stare. "The assassination attempt at the reception has us all troubled. We're doing everything we can to get the security locked down tight for the Festival."

"I didn't come to bust your chops," Marcus said. "Greaves was at the reception. He has enough power to bypass any security system."

"But he wouldn't have done that, not without repercussions. We think he had an accomplice, someone other than the death vamp who threw the blade."

Marcus felt all his tension return, focus, sharpen. He nodded. "I would have to agree. Did Madame Endelle or Thorne mention a death vampire by the name of Crace? Madame Endelle fired on him with a hand-blast."

He nodded. "She thinks he might have been powerful enough to bring a death vampire in without our security system picking it up. You know what this means?"

"Yeah. We'll have to be on our guard tonight."

Seriffe nodded. "Yes, we will."

"In the meantime, I want to have a look at your setup. Do you have someone who can give me a tour? I'd like to go all the way north."

"Mind if I go with?" he asked. The man was a bruising warrior and had seen some eight hundred years in the Militia ranks. He'd always been just short of Warrior of the Blood status but he didn't seem to mind. He had a wife and young children. He liked his position just fine.

He excused himself, moved to the landing platform, and dematerialized. A minute later he appeared on the arrival platform wearing a flight jumpsuit that teed at his shoulders and ran in a thick strip down his back to allow for full-mount. The fabric was black and military grade, just short of battle gear. He was fit as hell.

He met Marcus's gaze and sent, *You good with telepathy?* Marcus nodded.

Seriffe drew in a deep breath and mounted his wings, a powerful silver pair. Marcus followed suit.

Within seconds they were airborne.

Once in the air, at full-mount, Marcus had a unique view of the staging area for the spectacle. A good square mile below was nothing short of a fairground designed to house the spectacle performers. Enormous generators looked like a line of tanks on the southern border, providing much-needed air-conditioning for all the temporary housing. A hundred and five degrees made for dangerous conditions, even for ascended vampires. The necessary blue castles sat clustered in elegant circles throughout hundreds of tents.

How many performers? Marcus sent.

About four thousand. The squadrons of performance birds are in the range of ten times that.

One last glimpse and he turned north, flying beside Seriffe as they passed over the White Tank Mountains just to the east of the massive White Lake Resort Colony, the name given to the fifteen-mile stretch of hotels and public gardens on both sides of White Lake. In terms of spectacle sites, the place had no equal, not anywhere else on Second Earth.

But none of that mattered to Marcus. He just wanted to see and understand the entire security system so that once Havily was on the ground, anywhere, he'd have the best chance of keeping her safe.

Seriffe guided him in flight, directly over the fireworks battery sites. In quick succession, as he plowed his wings swiftly through the air, the enormous fireworks stations came into view. Seriffe sent, *The Hummers belong to security. I have two at each site. Every ascender working the batteries is checked and rechecked at twenty-minute intervals per the warnings from your undisclosed source.*

Leto's warning.

Good. Marcus flew in deep thrusts of his wings, his legs angled back in the natural flight position. He flew the entire distance to the very end of the mountain range then made a wide sweeping turn to the left to inspect the barge landings. *So, the ambassadors finish here?*

We have heavy security checkpoints and strong anti-dematerialization grids set up throughout. Do you want to have a look at the North End Command Center?

Yes.

Marcus landed with Seriffe at a separate location designated for anyone in flight. He drew in his wings, as did Seriffe, who led him into the command center.

The tent had guards surrounding it, every four feet, armed Militia Warriors, swords drawn. Nothing was being left to chance.

When he entered the tent, the tightness in his chest eased a little more and he had the thought that maybe everything would be okay, that maybe this creeping sense of anxiety was unwarranted.

The North End Command Center was an electronic dream. "How many of these do you have up and down the lake?"

"Thirty in all, one on each side, every mile. The grids overlap."

Marcus stared at an electronic display just smaller than a movie theater screen. It was huge.

"Good. This is good," he murmured.

Seriffe clapped him on the back. "Every hotel has secure landing platforms as well. All guests have had scheduled folding times. Anyone arriving early or late or not on the checklist undergoes interrogation. No one in or out without our people checking then double-checking."

Marcus met his gaze but he saw in the warrior's eyes the same thing he knew. Greaves could get through. Maybe one of his minions, so shit. Neither of them spoke the unnecessary words aloud.

Seriffe took a deep breath. "I have to get back. My second has been beeping for the past ten minutes. But I can bring someone here, one of my aides, to take you anywhere you want to go. Up to you."

"Thanks, Seriffe, but I've seen enough. I appreciate you taking the time."

Seriffe nodded and smiled, sort of. He looked sad. "We heard about the attack at the villa. Havily Morgan is one of ours, you know."

He did know. She was beloved among the Militia Warriors. He nodded.

Seriffe entered the dematerialization departure platform, lifted an arm, almost a salute, then vanished.

Marcus took the platform next. He gave Central a call and asked for a fold back to the villa. With Endelle's repaired mist still intact, he'd need assistance. He asked Jeannie to give Medichi a heads-up. Less than a minute later the vibration began.

Havily stood in the bedroom doorway as Marcus sank down on the side of the bed facing the window. He still wore full-on battle gear but seemed distracted.

She was frustrated that he'd just taken off without telling her what he intended to do. "Why didn't you ask me to go with you? I would have appreciated seeing the whole setup from the air as well."

But Marcus didn't look at her. Instead he flicked the hilt of his dagger several times with his thumb, his gaze fixed outside. She wasn't sure he'd even heard her. His hair was every which way from having been flying, and sweat trickled down his neck. He had the smell of the outdoors on his skin. Her nostrils flared as his fennel scent brought a shiver rippling down her neck.

Focus.

His posture struck her as odd, even deflated. "Okay. What's wrong? Were you dissatisfied with Seriffe's security measures? I thought the plan from the beginning was extremely thorough."

Marcus turned to look at her over his shoulder, one fist planted on his thigh. He scowled. "I'm sorry, what did you say?"

She tried again. "From what you observed, do you think Colonel Seriffe has done an adequate job? Do I have cause to be concerned?"

"Concern? No. Oh, hell, no. He's got fifteen miles of lake and desert locked down like a virgin wearing a chastity belt."

"Well, that's certainly an interesting image." The man had seen some history.

But he didn't smile. He just stared at her and grimaced then turned once more in the direction of the window.

Okay, something was wrong.

She moved from the doorway of the bedroom to stand opposite him, blocking his view. She crossed her arms over her chest. He looked hot as hell sitting there in a black leather kilt. The traditional warrior harness put his heavy muscled arms on display.

Again . . . *focus.* "Marcus, what's wrong?"

He huffed a sigh. "We need to complete the *breh-hedden*."

"The *breh-hedden*? You're thinking about that right

now? I thought you were worried about security for the spectacle."

He shook his head. "The entire time I was out there, all I could think was that if Greaves got his hands on you, or that bastard Crace, I wouldn't be able to find you. So yeah"—he lifted a mulish chin to stare at her, his lips in a grim line—"we need to complete the *breh-hedden* and we need to do it now."

Well, how romantic.

She shook her head. "Uh . . . *no.* I thought I made it clear that though this has been nice, and at times quite extraordinary, I can't, I won't become that involved with anyone again and especially not at the level of the *breh-hedden*."

He rose up, his fists bunched at his sides. "Dammit, Havily, we don't have a choice here. My instincts are firing off grenades right now where you're concerned. You're in danger. I can't explain it, but I know. And if we're bonded, wherever you are, I'll be able to get to you, to protect you. Right now that's all I care about."

Havily took a step back. She wasn't going to be pressured into completing the *breh-hedden,* not by him, not by anyone. "Well, tough shit, Warrior. The hell I'm going to bond with you when I have little doubt you'll be headed back to Mortal Earth as soon as your 'instincts' tell you it's okay to leave again. Or did you think I'd forgotten about that?"

His face paled and his slash of brows sank low. "So that's it? That's the sum total of your opinion of me? Even if I say I've returned, you'll always see me as a deserter, nothing more?"

She had really screwed up. Marcus had more than proven himself over the past few days, as well as the enormous thirty-eight hundred years before exiling himself to Mortal Earth. She wasn't even sure why she'd dragged all that out again, except that he'd gotten in her face, her heart had started hammering, and she'd met his aggression

head-on, the way she'd been meeting Endelle's aggression
for the past four months.

"I didn't mean it," she said.

A cold light entered his eye. "You didn't?" he asked in a
way-too-soft voice. "Then what did you mean?"

Thoughts flooded her head—that she was too frightened to complete the *breh-hedden,* that she was too attached to him already, that if anything happened to him, if
he died, she'd have to bury someone else she loved.

Someone else she *loved.*

Oh. God. She squeezed her eyes shut and put a hand to
her chest.

So there it was, the hideous truth she'd been avoiding
from the first. She'd fallen in love with Warrior Marcus,
head-over-heels, 100 percent, fallen in love.

She felt his hand on her shoulder. When she opened her
eyes, he shook his head back and forth. "Don't sweat it,
sweetheart. I think I understand what's going on in that
head of yours. You don't respect me. Fine. No *breh-hedden,*
no nothing. You've been a good lay and you're right, as
soon as I can manage it, I'm back to Seattle One, right
where I fucking belong."

He moved past her and left the bedroom.

Her head wagged as though she had no control over it.
What had just happened? How had they gone from conge-
nial to breaking up in the space of about a two-minute
conversation?

Great. Just great.

Two hours later, dressed in a mid-calf, silk sundress against
the June heat, Havily stood in the most centrally located of
the security command centers. Colonel Seriffe oversaw the
entire operation from this tent, which had been set up on
the Bredstone Hotel grounds. This command center was
the hub and drew in feeds from all the others. It was essentially the control room for the entire operation.

Seriffe sat in a chair and wore a headset.

The main concern involved the fireworks stations set up throughout the White Tanks. The video displays off to the right showed a continuous revolving feed of the various batteries.

Marcus stood near her, off to her left side and back a foot or so. She hadn't exchanged but a handful of polite words with him since the argument about completing the *breh-hedden*. Which was just as well. She needed to be focused on the spectacle. Although she didn't seem to have much cause for concern as her gaze shifted over the vast array of screens in front of her. The colonel had everything in hand.

Spectators had arrived from all over the world. They filled the several hundred grandstands up and down the lake, enjoyed private parties on hotel balconies, and those who couldn't afford the pricier tickets spread out blankets lakeside. Sporadic cheering erupted from the southern reaches as the spectacle, conducted on and over the lake, reached the various hotels and stands.

The decorated barges arrived first, ten in all. Each barge carried at least eight ambassadors. Thirty Militia Warriors, in full-mount, flew in protective formation around each barge. The vessels moved swiftly over the water and would reach the north end of the lake within an hour. With the sun still present in the western reaches of the sky, every barge was fully visible the length of White Lake.

Havily watched the monitors, her eyes flickering back and forth constantly. The hour seemed to drag from the time the last barge began its journey and ended at the North End Command Center. When Seriffe received the report that the last of the ambassadors had folded back to a secured landing platform, Havily released a sigh of relief. One event down. Two to go.

Cheers coming from the south indicated that the spectacle performers were nearing the Bredstone location.

She glanced at Marcus, forgetting for a moment that they were at odds, and smiled. He seemed to understand since he dipped his chin, a very approving gesture, and smiled in return. He then moved a little closer and whispered, "Sorry I pressed you earlier."

She turned into him. "I really am sorry for what I said. I spoke defensively and I apologize."

"Apology accepted." But he didn't touch her, not even a brush of his hand against hers. The disconnect *hurt*.

"This is fantastic," Seriffe cried. "Havily, you should go outside and watch the show. I've got things here. Look at those swans in formation. How the hell do they do that?"

The monitors provided ongoing footage from dozens of stationary cameras all along the route. Images were fed into the command center and managed by three ascenders working from computers.

"I'd love to," she murmured. Only then did Marcus take her hand.

"Come on," he said. "These events don't happen every day and I haven't been to a spectacle in decades. And no, Alison's arena battle does not count."

She glanced at him. "Okay. For a little while. Seriffe, I'll be just outside the tent if you need me."

He waved a hand but didn't take his eyes off the monitors.

Once outside, Havily set her gaze to the skies. With the last of the sun's rays setting a golden glow on the performances, she didn't have the heart to move from the spot. Spectacle performers had the courage of the warriors matched with tremendous artistry to do what they did while in full-mount. Their elegant tumbling maneuvers through the air as well as their ability to handle squadrons of DNA-enhanced swans, geese, and ducks was beyond comprehension.

In addition, each act that passed by included a light show executed mostly from the ground but occasionally with floating robotics. Accompanying music blasted from speakers all along the lake route.

After a few minutes, she started to relax as she applauded one performance after the next. A few minutes

more and Marcus had his arms around her waist from behind. She didn't hesitate, but leaned into him. Nothing was
settled, of course, nor was their situation in any way simple, but for this moment they were together and, oh, damn,
she *loved* him.

She also suspected that though Marcus had tried to
force the *breh-hedden,* his heart wasn't in it. He was just a
warrior trying to do the right thing. For that, she could
admire him and appreciate his most basic character, but
she wasn't persuaded to go any farther than this.

As she waited for the next act to appear, Marcus leaned
low and planted a kiss on her neck. An accompanying
swell of fennel sent shivers over her shoulders. She turned
into him and his lips met hers.

"We need to talk," he said. "I came off like a Neander-
thal earlier. I'm sorry, Havily."

She met his light brown eyes, glittering in the fading
sunlight. "What I said, Marcus, I don't believe of you, I
really don't. I fell back into an old pattern."

"I would never abandon you. What happened two hundred years ago—" He broke off, took a deep breath. "How
can I explain it? I'd served in the war for almost four millennia and when Helena died, my heart broke. I just
couldn't go on and I would have hurt Kerrick. I need you
to understand that. I completely blamed him for my sister's
death and the deaths of their children. I . . . I still haven't
truly forgiven him."

She searched his eyes. "I believe you. I'm not that old,
but what I've experienced of life in only a century has
made me wary. Four millennia? Maybe my actions wouldn't
have been so different from yours."

Applause and cheers erupting from the south indicated
another act nearing the Bredstone.

He squeezed her again. "When we're done here, we'll
go back to the villa and talk. How does that sound?"

"I'd like that."

He growled softly. "If I can keep my hands off you."

Since clouds of fennel now enveloped her, she said, "Well, maybe we can talk *after*."

He growled and hugged her harder.

She laughed then released another deep sigh.

At last the flight performances ended and the final act of the spectacle began—the fireworks.

But Havily felt compelled to rejoin Colonel Seriffe. As much as she would have loved to watch the skies light up, this was the section of the program that concerned them all the most. Bottom line, the fireworks display would provide the best cover possible for the use of incendiary bombs. If Greaves or his minions intended to disrupt the Festival, now would be the time.

However, watching the display from the enormous monitor, and all the monitors below, became an event in itself. Colorful dragons, whales, schools of fish formed above the mountains and dipped as though flying over the waters. This was one of Second Earth's finest advances. The fireworks were amazing. The cheering from the crowds had never been louder.

As minute succeeded minute, Havily had to remind herself to breathe. She didn't know what she expected to happen but her fingernails were pressed into her thighs through the thin silk of her dress.

Fifteen minutes passed.

Half an hour.

Forty-five minutes.

Only fifteen minutes left to go.

Ten. Nine. Eight . . .

She started to breathe. Was it possible all their worrying was for nothing?

The grand finale began to form on the screen. The fireworks opposite the Bredstone suddenly shot up great walls of color that took a new shape in the form of brilliant blue and green flames topped with pink and lavender. They almost glittered. "That's magnificent," she cried. And . . . *familiar.*

"Something's not right," Marcus said.

Havily suddenly recognized the flames from the night Luken had been burned in the air by an incendiary bomb!

Colonel Seriffe shouted, "Those aren't fireworks!"

The entire sky over the lake was on fire in a several-hundred-yard arc directly in front of the command center. The incendiary device had just arrived. What had started as an astonishing display became a nightmare of showering sparks and fire.

Explosions followed and Havily watched in horror as the monitors showed people scattering everywhere, whether escaping from the grandstands or racing away from the banks of the lake. Even the hotel balconies were deserted in no time flat as fiery particles rained down from the sky. The screams came from everywhere.

"What do we do?" she cried.

Colonel Seriffe was talking madly into his mouthpiece.

But before another question could rise to her lips, dozens of fireboats raced across the waters. Within seconds of the call to arms, massive amounts of water were propelled from the boats to douse the flames. Several of the major gardens were on fire.

"Thank God," she murmured, but tears rolled down her cheeks. "I can't believe this is happening."

"Believe it." The words were spoken so softly that Havily didn't know the source. She whirled around. Marcus's arm fell away from her shoulder.

"Did you hear that?" she asked.

"Hear what?"

"A voice, a man's voice, said, *Believe it*."

"Fuck."

"Greaves?" she asked as Marcus also turned in a circle.

"I want my sword but there are too many people around."

A loud explosion outside the tent on the south side sent Havily running with Marcus to the door flaps on the north side. Once again, people scattered, running madly every which way.

"We can't fold out of here," Marcus cried. "Security has

everything locked down. I'm calling Jeannie. She'll fold us back to the villa."

"I should stay here."

But he met her gaze. "The hell you should. Trust me, Seriffe will take care of business."

She nodded, but she hated the thought of leaving. The Festival had been her idea. Yes, the colonel was in charge, but she'd put him in charge, which made her responsible.

As Marcus released her to retrieve his phone, a different arm surrounded her neck from behind and choked her. "Hello, Havily," a heavily masculine voice said into her ear. "Miss me?"

She recognized Crace's voice, but she didn't understand what was happening or why Marcus didn't do anything to help her. Instead he stood in front of her, not two feet away, as though paralyzed, his phone in his hands. He stared up and to the right of her at some object she couldn't see.

She craned her neck, a hard thing to do because Crace had her trapped, but she now saw what Marcus was looking at. Crace had a bomb in his hand, which he held high overhead. It was a strange-looking cylinder with an old-fashioned lit fuse. The length had already burned down to within three inches. Two-and-a-half. Two. She couldn't breathe. She felt light-headed. Her vision sparkled.

"Bye-bye, Warrior." Crace laughed.

Everything happened so fast. Marcus took off at preternatural speed in the direction of the lake, which was away from crowds. Crace threw the bomb straight for him.

Havily saw the explosion, as flames in red and yellow rising to green and lavender spread over her vision. At the same moment, her world turned to black.

When a sword falters,
The brotherhood gathers.

—*Collected Proverbs*, Beatrice of Fourth

CHAPTER 22

Havily awoke to searing pain around her wrists, both wrists. Her neck hurt and her back. Her shoulders were killing her. In addition, sweat poured off her forehead into her eyes. The combination of the salty perspiration and her makeup made her eyes burn.

She was in a sitting position, sort of draped with some kind of see-through gauze-like fabric. Underneath, she was naked. Something supported her but it was very hard, like a low wooden bench.

She had trouble forming thoughts, and her eyes felt so heavy. She wanted to open them so that she could figure out why she hurt so much, but she couldn't.

And why was it so hot?

Her neck felt bruised and raw. She wanted to rub her neck, ease some of the pain away, but she couldn't move her arms. She must be restrained in some way.

She was so weak.

With great effort she opened her eyes, the barest squint. She couldn't make sense of what she was seeing. A kind of rope or plastic tube was attached to her left forearm, and where it was joined, it hurt. She lifted her head and saw that an IV dripped into the tubing.

Oh. She was being cared for. Had she been in an accident? Was that why she hurt so badly? Why couldn't she think, and why did her right forearm burn in exactly the same way as her left forearm?

With great difficulty, she turned her head in the other direction. More clear tubing, only it was red this time. A transfusion? She followed the line of the tube. It didn't go up, however, but down, and the bag holding the blood sat on the floor, a stone floor, a dirty stone floor. What kind of hospital was this and why was she sitting on a bench so near the floor?

She leaned forward but she couldn't get far. She was restrained around her waist.

She knew one thing. She needed to get the tube out of her right arm, the one carrying her blood away from her body. Someone had made a mistake. She tried to reach over but she couldn't move her arm very far.

She turned once more and saw a black chain. She lifted her hand. The chain was connected to her right wrist by a heavy black bracelet decorated with butterflies. It was pretty in a way but more goth than she liked.

"I don't intend to drain you, if that's what you fear."

The voice was male, sort of familiar, and sounded chipper.

Drain her? That made no sense. Why would someone in a hospital talk about *draining* her and of what? Her blood?

She looked at the man and worked hard to focus. His features started to take shape through the fog of her mind. She had seen him before.

A whisper of fear moved through her. She was looking at Crace, the death vampire who had attacked her in her town house. Why was he in her hospital room?

"Yeah, I had to give you a drug, otherwise you'd just fold out of here or worse, head into the darkening, and I can't have that. But don't worry. The bruises will heal. Don't you remember? You struggled when I put the manacles on. Again, don't worry. The manacles are high-tech. They have clip releases and hinges because every once in a while I'll need you out of chains." He laughed.

"It's hot," she whispered as more sweat dribbled into her eyes and burned all over again.

"You're in my forge, Havily Morgan, and you're going to be here for a long, long time. Welcome home."

Marcus lay shaking. He drifted from complete blackout, to awakening in so much pain he would do a dry heave then black out again.

He woke up this time, his sight bleary, and turned his head to empty his empty stomach once more. He remained awake despite the sensation that all his skin had been peeled from his body.

Jesus H. Christ.

He ignored the pain. "Havily. Where's Havily?" What had happened to his voice?

"Good. You can talk."

He shifted his gaze, turning his head slowly until a mountain of black hair came into focus. She'd looked the same way at the COPASS hearing, like a wild child. "Endelle? Did you find her? Is she dead?"

"We haven't found her yet."

"Crace has her." He struggled to sit up. "I have to get to her."

"Easy, Marcus." Endelle again. "We know. Let Horace and his team take care of you."

"I ran away from her. He had her and I ran away. I abandoned her. She'll never forgive me now."

"No, Marcus." He knew that voice, Kerrick's voice. It came from behind him but very close. "I saw what happened. Crace had a bomb in his hand, lit, ready to go off.

You ran away from the crowds, to direct the explosion toward you. You saved a lot of lives tonight."

He tried to sit up. "I have to get to her. I have to find her."

Kerrick, however, pinned him down with hands on his shoulders. "We've got to get you healed first."

He shifted to try to look at him. Pain streaked through him, all over his skin, into his muscles. "Kerrick. Go after her. Find her. Please."

"Marcus, ease down," Kerrick's voice sounded anguished. He put his hand on Marcus's chest and held it flat, a weight that . . . settled him. His chest had been bouncing. Oh, shit, he couldn't see because he was crying. Fuck.

Marcus shifted his head toward Endelle. "Can you find her with your voyeur's eye? I know that's one of your powers."

"I've tried," she said. "But I can't get a fix on her. She must be in one of Greaves's locked-down military facilities. Sorry, Warrior. When we've got you on your feet, I'll go into the darkening, but without a location it will be a goddamn crap shoot."

Kerrick leaned close. "We'll find her," he said straight into Marcus's ear. "Somehow. We'll find that bastard. We'll slay him, brother, if it's the last thing we do."

Marcus turned once more and met Kerrick's gaze. He'd missed the bastard. Goddammit, for two hundred years he'd missed Kerrick. Now Kerrick was making promises about finding Havily and avenging her kidnapping.

Oh, dear Creator, was Havily still alive? She had to be.

He nodded and his eyesight dimmed. He faded again. Dammit.

Endelle stared down at the mess that was Warrior Marcus. She had rare moments when she felt like this, not enraged because *enraged* was too small a word. Explosive. Yes, more like that. She wanted to stretch out her arms, draw in power from every corner of the universe, let it flow through her, then annihilate the entire planet.

If she understood what had happened, High Administrator

Crace was now a death vampire of tremendous power and he'd made it his priority to gain control of Morgan, which he had. The few people in the vicinity who had seen the abduction and were still alive told the same story: A huge, muscled man, shirtless and dressed in a black kilt and battle sandals, had put his arm around Havily's neck then disappeared with her.

That he'd been able to fold into and out of a locked-down site like this . . . Shit. She could do it. Greaves could, which meant there was another entity on Second with powers that could challenge hers . . . so, yeah, shit.

Though she rarely made use of her healing gifts, she employed them now. She put her hands over Marcus's face. His eyes, now closed, were blood red. His cheek and neck were burned into deep tissue. She worked over his eyes first as Horace worked his legs, where the greatest damage was done. Horace had summoned healers from all over the globe to help with the disaster. Several worked beside him now just on Marcus, his skin knitting together by magic beneath so many sets of warm, glowing hands.

As for the attack, it would be weeks before she had a report from Seriffe on exactly how the bombs had been cached in the fireworks batteries, whether they'd arrived as part of the original orders or if some other kind of stealth had been employed. If Crace had been behind the incendiary bombs then probably *stealth*. So, again . . . shit.

The death toll, however, hadn't risen very high so far, just eleven confirmed, and thank the Creator the number was so small. But in her opinion, one was too many.

Within an hour she was sweating, but Marcus opened his eyes again and this time he didn't hurl. He started to talk but she said, "We're about halfway, Marcus. Just try to relax. We're healing you as fast as we can. You feeling better yet?"

"Yes." But the word came out hissed.

"Good. Now relax."

"Fine." He closed his eyes, and though she could tell he was still conscious and anxious to be moving, he stopped struggling against his incapacitation.

She glanced at Kerrick, surprised that he was the one cradling Marcus's head on his lap. "You okay?" she asked.

"Too many fucking memories."

She chuckled. "No shit."

Kerrick met her gaze, his eyes wet. "Yeah."

"You thinking of Hannah?" Endelle asked.

At that Marcus's eyes popped open, and as though the men had practiced together for months they bit in unison, "Helena. Her name was Helena."

Endelle smiled, and the tension eased out of her shoulders as she held her hands just above Marcus's neck. "You boys are just too easy to bait."

Parisa stood next to Warrior Medichi. She kept replaying in her head what Madame Endelle had told Warrior Marcus earlier about not being able to find Havily with her *voyeur's eye*. From that point, a terrible feeling of dread had descended on her. What if Endelle asked for her help? What if Endelle wanted her to try to use her special *eye,* to open her voyeur's window and try to locate Havily?

She couldn't do it. She just couldn't.

She stared at the battlefield around her, at Madame Endelle working over Warrior Marcus, at Warrior Kerrick supporting the man's head and upper shoulders on his lap, at the healers clustered around Marcus's almost naked body. Her gaze extended beyond. There were people on the ground everywhere, but dozens of healers were working on the worst of the victims. Most of the moaning had stopped, thank God.

She kept swiping at her cheeks.

Shortly after the attack started, Thorne had called for Medichi. Of course he had to come to the scene, all of the Warriors of the Blood were here, which meant she'd had to come as well.

But oh how she wanted to leave, to be freed from the

sight of so much destruction. People had died here tonight and so many were injured, burned. Most of the fires along both sides of the banks had been put out, but the air smelled torched and rotten.

She'd vomited once but Antony had been so kind. Even now he kept a hand around her waist, very lightly, as though steadying her—and maybe he was. She couldn't exactly feel her knees.

Alison was busy as well. Going from victim to victim and laying her hand upon each forehead. Parisa would watch bodies stiffen then relax, every time. She was a different kind of healer since she'd been a therapist on Mortal Earth, dealing with the mind instead of the body.

Parisa felt useless right now. She wanted to help, but then her stomach kept taking nosedives and it was all she could do to keep from throwing up again.

Besides, she had her own internal battle going on. She had been a librarian most of her adult life; prior to that she had volunteered in the library of whatever school she had been attending. She had lived in a world of books, not in a world made up of *life,* real life. And this life was so very real. It was all about war and battling, trying to stay alive, trying to keep one another alive.

She really didn't want to be part of this.

She wanted to go home and lock herself in her house, maybe nail boards to the inside of every door and window and stay there. Yes, that's exactly what she wanted to do.

What if she started hunting for Havily but found her burned the way Marcus was burned? She could smell him, for God's sake.

"I need to ask you something," Medichi said, his voice almost a whisper. "Do you think you could locate Havily, I mean through your special visions? Endelle has just said she can't, but do you think you could find her?"

This was too much for her to bear.

"I can't," she whispered. "I want to go home. Now."

* * *

Medichi turned toward the ascendiate, released her waist, then took her gently by the shoulders. It had been a long time since his own ascension, and for all that time he had battled as a warrior. He felt her youth and his age, her inexperience and his centuries of living and making war. He had seen worse than this, a thousand times worse than this, but he knew Parisa, her careful world sequestered in a place of books and fairy tales. She had to be in shock.

She lifted her gaze to his, her amethyst eyes drenched with tears. "I don't want this."

He smiled a little. He smoothed back her dark hair. "None of us does. But this is what we've got, at least tonight. This is what we have to deal with, and that includes you."

She shook her head, then she leaned into him and he surrounded her with his arms.

He forgot about everything but her. His body seemed to know this woman, a side effect of the *breh-hedden,* because holding her like this was the most normal thing in the world.

The trouble was, his brother warrior needed his help, needed her help. She had a gift that might enable them to do the impossible, might locate Havily.

"These visions that you have, Parisa," he began.

She sighed against him. "Yes."

"They're not really visions, are they?"

She grew very still. "No. I don't think so." Her voice was muffled because her mouth was pressed into his shoulder.

"They occur in real time, don't they?"

"Yes."

"Now I need to ask you something really hard."

"I won't do it." She gripped his arms, her fingers digging into his biceps.

"How many times did Havily save your life?"

"Don't ask me to do it."

"I'll be right next to you all the way."

After a long moment, she drew back and looked up at him. Her breaths were shallow and fast. Her face was twisted as if in pain. "I don't want to do this. I don't want to be part of this."

"It's not fair to you."

"I never wanted these wings. I never asked to see these things."

"I promise you I'll be right beside you. That's what I'm here for. But Parisa, I need you to have courage right now . . . for Havily . . . just in case she's still alive. If we can find her, get to her, we can save her. Can you at least try for her sake?"

"I'm afraid of what I'll find. I couldn't bear it if she was dead. She was my friend."

Once again, he slid his arms all the way around her and held her fast.

Parisa knew she didn't have a choice, not really. She could protest but in the end she had to do this.

She closed her eyes and focused. She let her mind wrap around all her memories of Havily, of the moment in her Peoria home when she had calmed Parisa enough so that she could retract her wings and escape from that monster, Crace, and later, the next evening, of Havily saving her from a terrible fall when she had first tried to fly. She then thought of Havily teaching her to fly, and later, after she breached the mist and brought death vampires onto the villa property, Havily had taken her to the turret room. She would have died even then, but Havily had drawn her into the darkening.

Because this was her present truth, that Havily was her friend and had saved her life again and again, she focused on her and let the images come.

And come they did.

She drew back and stared at Medichi's chin. "I see a place full of terrible heat, burning coals. A man, a big man, pounds metal near the flames. The man is turning his head." Parisa recognized him. "Oh, God, it's Crace." She panned to follow the direction of his gaze. Off to the side . . . "Oh, dear God . . . I see Havily. I see her."

"Endelle," Medichi called out. "Parisa can see Havily."

"What do you mean, *Parisa can see Havily*?" Endelle called back.

"She says she has visions, but I think it's more like your ability to voyeur. If she thinks of someone, she can see them."

"Well, shit," Endelle cried, but she kept her hands close to Marcus's neck. "Looks like your girl has more power even than me. Parisa, you're a goddamn preternatural voyeur."

Preternatural voyeur. Great.

"Is she alive?" The question came from Marcus, whose voice was still reedy.

Tension flowed toward Parisa from every ascender clustered on the ground and from the Warriors of the Blood walking the perimeter.

"Yes," Parisa said. "She's alive."

"Oh, thank . . . God." Marcus's voice broke on a sob.

Endelle turned and spoke over her shoulder. "Tell us where, Parisa. If we work together we'll have a better chance of finding her. Maybe our combined powers can get a fix on her."

Parisa started to weep and couldn't stop. Her body shook. Medichi held her up by gripping her arms and holding her in place. "He has her . . . manacled to a wall. He has tubes in each of her arms and she looks really pale. She's cloaked in some kind of white gauze."

Endelle again called to her. "Is there blood draining from one of the tubes?"

"No. But there's a bag on the floor full of dark liquid, maybe blood, probably her blood." She broke into a sob.

"Alison," Kerrick called out to his *breh* in a booming voice. "Come to Parisa, now."

Endelle added. "Alison, come! This is too much for a mortal to bear."

Parisa could see Alison through a veil of tears. She rose from a victim at least twenty yards away. She vanished then appeared right in front of Parisa. The next thing she knew, Alison's hands were on her face. Medichi slid his arms around her waist and held her against him. Hot tears tracked her cheeks. She trembled from head to foot.

But the sensation that entered her head was incredible, as though a balm was being poured over her mind.

Her breathing slowed and the tears stopped. Her body calmed down. A cool damp cloth drifted over her face and wiped her tears away.

"Antony, don't let go of her," Alison said.

"I've got her."

Yes, Parisa thought. *He has me.*

"Bring her to me," Endelle called across the space. Medichi dipped and slung his arm behind her knees. He lifted her as though she were a feather but then he was so strong, so powerful, a warrior.

She put her arm around his neck. "I shouldn't be such a child. I feel foolish," she whispered.

He met her gaze. "You're doing just fine. We all understand how hard this is, how impossible this." There was sincerity in his voice, respect in his eyes. She nodded and his lips curved, just a little, just enough. She put her hand on his cheek.

Medichi settled himself on the ground between Endelle and Kerrick but held her close on his lap. Alison went back to tending others. Marcus stayed where he was but his face was completely restored and his color looked better, healthier. Healing was an amazing aspect of ascended life.

Marcus met her gaze. "So . . . Havily is alive?"

She nodded. "I can see her now. Clearly."

"Good. That's good."

Endelle glanced at her. "If the three of us form a telepathic link, we might be able to get this job done. Once I'm in the darkening, I'll use your mind to see her location. With some luck, I might be able to find her that way, but you'll have to be strong. Can you do that for us?"

Parisa nodded.

"I'll need to get inside your head, though. I'll be as gentle as I can but everything about the power you've exhibited tells me you can do this. Okay?"

Again, Parisa dipped her chin.

Endelle's gaze shifted to the healer named Horace, whose brow was covered in sweat, whose hands had never moved from the raw place where Marcus's feet had been burned down to bone. Slowly, flesh had reappeared; the toes looked almost normal now. Parisa could almost breathe.

"Horace," Endelle said. "How long before Marcus is fully restored, ready to fight, hard?"

Horace lifted a weary face to Endelle. "If someone will provide him with food, lots of it, and Gatorade, an hour, I think, so long as we can continue our healing as we are."

Parisa stared at Horace. "Gatorade?" she asked. "Really?" Somehow this was the funniest thing in the world to her, and she started to laugh.

Of course, everyone stared at her as though fearing she'd just lost her mind, so she reined in the amusement but every once in a while a chuckle escaped her. Okay, so she'd lost it. But Gatorade, really?

"So we have an hour," Endelle said quietly, her gaze directed at Marcus.

Parisa glanced at him as well. He really was looking better.

Yeah, she could almost breathe again.

Havily lost track of time.

When she awoke next, or perhaps returned to consciousness, she had no concept of how long she'd been under. Crace was keeping her drugged, that much she knew, but there was something she had to remember to do . . . or not to do, but she couldn't seem to think straight.

She kept her eyes closed because she could hear the rhythmic slam of hammer to metal. So the bastard was still in his forge making more shackles. That much she could remember. She was shackled, she was in Crace's forge, and the bastard had kidnapped her.

She thought about folding the hell out of there but she couldn't. Oh, yeah, she'd tried before. Whatever drug Crace was giving her kept her so weak mentally that she couldn't hold her thoughts together long enough to do what she needed to do. She needed less of the drug in her system if she had any hope of escaping—but what was it she wasn't supposed to do?

She struggled to think, to remember.

She leaned her head against the stone wall. She still sat on the low wooden bench, her legs stretched out in front of her. How long could she survive like this?

The truly horrifying thought shot through her mind. *Indefinitely.* If Crace cared for her body well enough, she could serve as a supplier of her unique blood without end. She could even become the source of experiments if he wanted to go that direction. And why wouldn't he? He was a death vampire. He had no conscience.

She remained very still.

She tried to recall how many times she had awakened and what happened each time. Oh, that's right. Crace would walk over to a machine on her right, punch a button, and tell her nighty-night. Within seconds she'd black out.

That's what she was struggling to remember, not to appear to wake up. She could do that.

She kept her breaths slow and even. Slow and even.

She set what was left of her mind to figuring out how to get herself out of this mess.

From what she had seen, she was in some kind of underground cavern, an enormous space probably blasted out of rock.

She stilled her mind and relaxed. Her body ached fiercely but she had to keep from moaning. If she moaned, more drugs.

Her mind drifted back to Crace's appearance and the bomb.

Her thoughts became fixed on Marcus.

He couldn't have survived that blast. He had turned to run but the bomb had gone off at the same moment that Crace folded her here to this place.

She took a breath. She had to face something here, something horrible—Marcus had probably died in the explosion.

But he had run away from all those people, toward the lake. Her man, her warrior had died saving a host of ascenders.

The awareness that she had undoubtedly lost him sank in deep, taking her mind first, then dipping low to clutch her heart. Only with great effort did she keep from howling like a wounded animal. Tears dripped from her closed eyes. She only hoped Crace didn't notice.

Marcus. Gone.

The words didn't mesh in her mind. She rejected them even if they were probably true. Searing heartache rolled through her. Combined with the drugs in her system and the ache in her body, she must have passed out again.

When she came to, her thoughts immediately returned to Marcus. Again, she kept her breathing slow and even, her eyes closed. She regulated her mind. She ignored the pain.

She thought back on the past several days, then the past four months.

The big questions of life came to her: *Why am I here, what is my purpose, why so much suffering?*

A memory surfaced of her husband. The fever had caught him hard. Their little girls were already buried in the earth and she knew she'd soon have a grave to dig herself. She had wanted to die.

But when his death approached, he had somehow found the strength to clutch her hand and to look at her. "Live, my darling. Live. Live for all of us." The words so faint, the last he had spoken.

An hour later, he was gone.

Live, my darling.

Live.

Live for all of us.

The words echoed through her head, fierce and strong as though something of his wonderful spirit remained within her.

That was a hundred years ago and a million tears later.

She thought of Eric. She had been willing to risk her heart with him, to try to live again, but Eric had died and with his death something in her had died as well, some willingness to press on. Yes, she worked . . . she worked hard. Yes, she was committed to making a difference in Endelle's administration and in the war. But she had not been committed to life, to living. That was what Marcus had been trying to tell her, the reason he believed she couldn't easily do a split-self. The only time she'd succeeded was when he'd held her in thrall and she'd been able to let go.

And now Marcus was dead.

Grief threatened her once more but this time she refused to let it come. It seemed to her that in this dark place, where she was imprisoned deep in the bowels of the earth, where the heat kept her sweating and she was chained to a wall, where she would no doubt be bled frequently for the properties of her blood, she had a choice to make here and now. Would she live or would she disappear behind the safety of her walls, of her half-lived life?

Live, my darling, live.

Sometimes choices came at the oddest times and the most impractical.

While chained to a wall, for the first time in a hundred years, she chose to live, to really live.

And in that choice came a powerful determination to somehow find her way out of this mess, this evil imprisonment. That no one had come before, not Endelle or any of the Warriors of the Blood, told her that Crace's forge was shielded. If she wanted out, she'd have to be the one to get herself out.

Her mind, as weak as it was, flashed over one truth. If she could split into two selves, both parts corporeal, she could find Endelle in the darkening. If she found Endelle, they could work together to figure this out, how to bypass the shields, everything. But it was up to her.

Marcus was going out of his mind.

He had recovered fully. Three hours had passed from the time Horace had declared him healed. *Three hours* and they still hadn't located Havily. He was pissed as hell! He'd eaten a whole cheese pizza and drunk a quart of fucking Gatorade, but Endelle, even with Parisa's help, had been unable to get to Havily.

He moved restlessly, pacing the ground, his hand at his side as though clutching the hilt of a sword. The blast had destroyed his battle gear but he had backups, plenty of backups, and wore one now.

He was still surrounded by his warrior brothers, each armed with sword and dagger and patrolling the perimeter. Endelle was nearby, in a meditative state and hunting through the darkening, but his nerves were raw. She was convinced that all of Greaves's underground military sites were cloaked with heavy shields so that even though Parisa sent a continuous stream of Havily's location, Endelle still couldn't get to her, still couldn't find her.

At least Parisa kept letting him know that Havily was still alive.

Small fucking comfort.

At one point, Marcus had insisted that Parisa *show* him the voyeuristic vision, thinking perhaps his more profound connection to Havily would allow him to see her, then fold to her position. The sight of her had almost brought him to his knees. She was shackled to the wall just as Parisa had described, pale and unconscious. But as hard as he tried, as determined as he was, he found it impossible to fold to her.

So he relied on Endelle, and her haphazard hunt through the darkening. She was confident that once she found Havily by this means, she could bypass whatever shields were blocking the location and if nothing else pull Havily out of danger and into the darkening. She could keep Havily in the darkening indefinitely, but there was one problem: An individual had to exit the darkening at the point of entrance, which meant Havily would have to return to her place of incarceration before she could leave it.

The hope was that once Endelle found Havily in the darkening, she could bring Marcus in as well. In turn, Marcus could create a telepathic link with Havily and fold directly to her position in Crace's forge. At least, that was the current plan.

Of course, if Havily hadn't been drugged out of her mind she could have taken herself into the darkening, something Crace apparently knew, hence the drugs. Parisa had told him that more than once in the past three hours, anytime Havily appeared to be waking up, Crace would cross to her and push a button on the hospital equipment hooked up to her IV.

Too many moving pieces.

Whatever.

"Report," he barked, pausing in his march to stare at Parisa, who remained sitting on Medichi's lap. She was pale and obviously frightened but she kept her voyeur's window open and for that he was grateful.

"She's still unconscious," Parisa said. "She's still sitting on the low bench. She's breathing and Crace isn't near her."

"Good," he said, but, yeah, he was going out of his mind. He started pacing again. "We have to move this along. He won't stay away from her."

He felt helpless. He stared at Endelle and engaged the link he had with her. *Anything?* he sent.

Sorry, Warrior, but the darkening has limitations. If Havily could find a way to call to me, if she could do a split-self, I think I could get to her. She's just so out of it. But we won't stop till we bring our girl home. I promise you that.

He sighed. *I know.*

And that was why he loved Endelle. Why all the warriors loved her. She was a piece of work but at her core, she was all heart.

The droplet of sweat soaked into the gauze draped over Havily's chest. She had been sweating profusely from the time she'd realized her only way out was to do a split-self and move her second self into the darkening. That had been *hours* ago. Creator help her!

Let go.

She was trying . . . so hard.

Let go.

She heard Crace moving around. He even hummed at times and occasionally laughed.

She had worked the problem of splitting-self in many different ways: relaxing her mind, trying to remember what Endelle had taught her, what it had felt like to complete the process when Marcus had held her in thrall.

She focused on that experience once more. When he'd put her there, what had been the truest part of her condition? She'd had no will, that much was true, but there was something else.

When the light came on, a single word shot through her head.

Shields.

The word hit her mind like a sudden wind shear.

She grew dizzy. She knew now exactly what needed to be done.

But a pair of heavy battle sandals appeared below her nose and a hand grabbed her hair and lifted her head up. "So you're awake. Good. I have need of you and I'm not referring to just your blood."

He unwrapped the waist strap that kept her tied to the wall then popped her manacles. She was so weak that she tumbled forward right off the bench. Fear rippled over her as he tore both needles from her arms. He then rolled her onto her back, her head striking the stone. She was little more than a rag doll given the drugs still in her system.

"What can I say," he cried. "Your blood fires me."

Havily was too weak to do more than remain inert. But she closed her eyes and as he pushed her legs apart, she dropped her mental shields 100 percent . . . and what do you know, she split herself and found herself lying in a similar position in the darkening. Alone. In that space, however, her mind was perfectly clear. She could feel her primary self and Crace's muscled knees that kept shoving at her inner thighs.

Oh, God.

She screamed Endelle's name.

Three seconds later Endelle was right there, standing in front of her, almost blinding in the golden glow of her aura.

"Marcus," Endelle cried. She waved a hand and there he was. Alive. Marcus was alive? *He was alive!*

He grabbed hold of her arms.

She had to act fast. "The manacles are off but Crace has me pinned on the floor. I'm still drugged." How easily she could move and talk in her split-self.

He drew in a ragged breath. He put his hands on her face. "Show me." She closed her eyes and focused. She streamed the location to him, the visceral heat of the forge, the hard stone floor, the humid air.

He kissed her. "I will be with you in seconds now." He turned to Endelle. "Send me back to the Festival grounds. From there, I can fold to her."

Endelle nodded and he was gone.

Endelle stared at her. "Return to your primary self. Do all that you can to stay alive, to get both of you out alive when Marcus shows up. Crace is powerful. Marcus will need you, otherwise I'd bring you back into the darkening. Do you understand?"

"Yes." Havily closed her eyes and returned to her body.

She opened her eyes and Marcus stood god-like over Crace, a hand reaching down to grab the monster by his long hair and haul him to his feet.

Marcus didn't have time to fold his sword to him. Instead he jerked the bastard away from Havily. Marcus pulled back his fist and struck him as hard as he could, one heavy right hook that connected with Crace's jaw. Crace's head snapped back. Though he stumbled, he caught himself and sent his own fist flying in Marcus's direction.

Marcus shifted just enough so that the blow glanced off his shoulder, which took Crace and all his momentum forward a few more stumbling steps.

Marcus caught him by the arm and once more drew him upright. He slammed a fist into his ribs and heard a nice crack, but Crace only grunted a little. He had blood around his mouth. Marcus could guess the source, especially since Crace had a maniacal light in his eye and apparently was *feeling no pain*.

Shit. Crace had taken Havily's blood. Shit.

Havily watched the battle. She rolled on her side and worked at dragging herself backward, toward the wall, toward the bench and the shackles, trying to get out of the way. She was so weak and had a hard time focusing.

She wanted to help but what could she do? She couldn't even lift her arm and the effort it had taken her to do a split-self had left her even more lethargic than before.

She tracked the battle in front of her, but they were just two large shapes moving back and forth. She heard deep grunts and the sounds of fists hitting flesh.

The men landed close to her.

Crace was on top and throwing punches into Marcus's face. She could hear them, one after the other, like wet sliding slaps without end.

She blinked. The hitting had stopped and Marcus was flat on his back, pinned down with Crace on top of him. The bastard was smiling, sweat pouring off his porcelain complexion, his muscles flexing, his fangs long and sharp.

Reality finally toughened her mind.

Marcus was going to die.

Crace slapped him across the face. Marcus's eyes were swollen and bleeding. "Havily," he whispered through thick bloody lips. "I'm . . . sorry."

Havily knew what she had to do and she had to do it fast.

She let go once more, lowering her shields all the way. She swished into the darkening and called again for Endelle.

Endelle and her brilliant golden aura reached her within two seconds. Havily explained the situation. Endelle told her to wait. A few more seconds and Luken appeared in the darkening.

"Show me," he cried, his blue eyes glowing.

Havily put her hands on Luken's face and, as she had done with Marcus, streamed the location of the forge. He smiled. "I've got him. Don't worry. Now get back to your primary self and let's get you out of there."

Havily swished back into her primary self, dizziness engulfing her mind. Crace still had Marcus pinned down, still smiling.

But a second later, behind him, Luken appeared, sword in hand. She had never seen such a beautiful sight.

This time, Havily smiled.

"Hey, asshole," Luken called out.

Crace rose off Marcus as though he were floating. Marcus rose up as well, at least to a sitting position. He shifted toward her. "Havily," he croaked.

But Havily couldn't turn away from the other sight of Luken as he faced off with Crace.

Luken's sword began to whirl almost magically. He was the biggest of the warriors and a good match for Crace. Luken's face flamed as his sword whipped in circles. How was Luken doing that?

Crace lowered his head and shoulders. He folded a sword into his hand as well. He even laughed, but he misjudged his opponent. Luken moved with preternatural speed and the whirling sword flew in an arc and glided through Crace's neck as though he'd been cutting through air.

Havily looked away. She didn't need to see the rest. It was bad enough she heard the thump of Crace's head as it struck the stone floor.

Marcus rose unsteadily to his feet in front of her. The next moment, arms embraced her and she was lifted up. She smelled fennel, wonderful, glorious fennel. "I've got you," he said. He turned her toward his brother warrior. "*We've* got you."

She felt the fold. The next moment she was back at the

spectacle site. Luken appeared to the right of Marcus. She reached her hand out to him. "Thank you," she murmured. He caught her hand. Tears tracked down his cheeks.

She heard sobbing and turned to her left. Parisa, held in Medichi's arms, was weeping against his chest. Alison had her hand on Parisa's head. Kerrick stood nearby, sword in hand, guarding all three of them. The rest of the Warriors of the Blood were stationed all around the perimeter, swords still in hand. Endelle steadied herself with a hand on Kerrick. Darkening work took a toll.

"There's just one thing I want to know," Endelle cried. "Is that bastard dead? Did you get him?" Her gaze shifted between Marcus and Luken, back and forth.

Marcus jerked his head in Luken's direction. "He got him. Crace won't be causing any more problems." Marcus drew in a deep breath. "Thank you, Luken."

"Good," Endelle barked. She looked around. "Okay. Enough of this shit. We're getting the hell out of here." She lifted an arm and the next thing Havily knew, the entire group was on Medichi's front lawn beneath the ever-present dome of mist.

Havily felt Marcus's arms lower her to the grass, but she wasn't certain why. Her mind swam left, then right. In some vague recess of her head, she knew she was clothed only in a thin covering of gauzy fabric but somehow she didn't care.

Marcus knelt beside her and held her up with one arm around her shoulders. Using his free hand he felt down her arms and over her wrists. He worked down her thighs, her calves, over her feet. He put his hands on her head, her cheeks, her jaw, her neck. "You're okay. You're alive. You're recovering. You're okay. Did he—?"

Marcus had done something similar before. He'd come to her the day after Crace had attacked her in her town house and fired a bunch of questions at her, *Are you all right, are you hurt, did he touch you.* That moment had been the beginning for them. She had gone to him willingly, now he was here . . . again. And he was alive! God, how she loved him.

"I'm fine," she murmured, her tongue dry and thick in her mouth. He took her in his arms and pulled her against him once more. He rocked her back and forth. His arms trembled.

"I thought . . . you were dead," she whispered against his neck. Her arms were so weak. She wanted to put them around his neck but couldn't make them move.

"I'm not." He drew in a shuddering breath.

"You came for me."

"Yes, all of us. We all came for you."

Havily looked around, her head wagging when she didn't want it to. They were all there, Endelle, Parisa and Alison, and the Warriors of the Blood, every last one of them. Medichi still held Parisa close. Kerrick had his arms around his *breh*. Luken stared at Havily with such affection yet sorrow in his eyes. The rest of the warriors remained at a distance, probably because she was almost naked, in just the strips of gauze fabric. She didn't care about her nakedness, though, not even a little. She was just grateful, so grateful to be alive, to be unharmed.

Marcus pulled away from. "How did you do it, Havily? How did you manage a split-self?"

She smiled . . . crookedly . . . and finally managed to lift her hand enough to touch his cheek. His face was swollen, bruised, bleeding in places, but he'd never looked more handsome. "It was my shields," she said, her tongue still way too thick and unwieldy from the drugs. She spoke slowly. "My greatest strength . . . was my greatest weakness. I had to let . . . my guard down completely . . . in order to find my way into the darkening." She drew a breath. "How's that . . . for irony?"

"Beautiful," he said, one hand pressed to his chest, the other tightening around her shoulder. "I think it's goddamn beautiful."

Love defies our deepest fears.

—*Collected Proverbs*, Beatrice of Fourth

CHAPTER 23

Havily stared up at the ceiling in the bedroom she shared with Marcus, the coffered ceiling with the beautiful wood beams. She sighed. Three days had passed at Medichi's villa. Between the drugs in her system and her loss of blood, she had been in a weakened state and recovery had been slow, even for a vampire.

Right now she wore one of Marcus's soft T-shirts, something he said he only wore on Bainbridge. Nothing else would do, not even her La Perla nightgowns, not because they weren't soft but because they didn't carry Marcus's fennel scent embedded in every thread.

For the first two days she had slept around the clock, waking only at intervals and crying out. But each time, Marcus pulled her close, stroked her back, and whispered his comfort to her.

So she slept, then slept some more.

When she finally knew she wouldn't be going back to sleep, that she was up for the day, Marcus had kissed her once and promised her a meal. If she understood correctly, he was doing the cooking himself. She wasn't sure what to think about that.

She smiled at the thought that Marcus, *Warrior* Marcus, head of a multibillion-dollar Mortal Earth financial empire and former Warrior of the Blood, was preparing dinner for her, Havily Morgan. Who was she—an occasional Liaison Officer, a current executive in Endelle's administration, a vampire whose blood had some of the qualities of dying blood, and an ascender with the ability to split-self and move a second corporeal self into the darkening.

She was calmer now. Sleep had helped, and the heavy sedative had finally left her system. Her mind had therefore started making sense of all that had happened.

She could feel that she had changed but she couldn't seem to define the next step in her life. Something needed to be different, but what?

Some part of her, an old useless part of her, had died in Crace's forge.

She was made new, but in what way and which direction should she go now?

She had never expected to see Marcus again. She had been so sure he had perished that none of her new thoughts had included him and yet her life, in some bizarre, *breh-hedden,* elemental way, belonged to Marcus.

But to continue as they had been seemed impossible.

Tears dampened her hair and trickled into her ears. She didn't even know why she was crying.

The door opened and Marcus appeared with a tray in hand. Her eye was drawn to a really tall red rose standing in a short bud vase. The flower flopped around as he moved. The whole thing looked ready to fall over.

She smiled and her heart swelled.

Then love swallowed her whole. She couldn't speak as

she looked at him. Mostly she was afraid she was glowing with the sensations passing through her, over her, around her. She loved him. Oh, my God, how she loved him.

Then she understood what had changed, what had transformed within her . . . her ability to love had just expanded to embrace the entire universe. She no longer feared losing Marcus. She had already lost him. But that wasn't even the point. Life required this kind of love, from the heart, from the soul, from every molecule of the body, fully present, 100 percent engaged, willing to risk, even if that love would never be returned.

"Are you all right?" he asked, rounding the bed. "Your skin looks flushed. Do you have a fever?" Fevers were rare in ascended life so he looked astonished as he asked the question.

She pushed herself up to a sitting position and shoved a pillow behind her back. "I'm fine," she said, the words a miracle of understatement. Yet she had no other words to speak, even though her heart felt full to overflowing.

He looked like a million bucks since he was dressed in a business suit, black wool, tailored to every muscular curve. But then no one dressed like that in June in Phoenix. Her heart sank. Where was he going? Was it possible he was leaving Second Earth?

She sighed as he settled the tray over her lap. Funny little odors reached her nose and she worked not to grimace. The toast was badly burned on one side and the coffee—grainy looking—had sloshed onto the saucer. The eggs had brown streaks. "This looks wonderful," she said, her gaze again skating over the suit. She knew he preferred Tom Ford and she could see why. But . . . where was he going, when, and why? Her heart ached.

He glanced down at the tray and grimaced. "I made everything myself and for that I apologize."

She looked up at him. She reached for his hand. "Thank you, but you'll stay, won't you, right now, and talk to me?"

"Actually, I have to leave."

So, there it was. Havily's heart constricted and she only barely restrained a gasp. "So soon?" Over before it had really begun?

He dropped to his knees beside the bed and took her hand. "I should be back within a day or two. Don't worry."

Why did two days suddenly seem like the razor edge of eternity? She nodded.

He pushed his longish hair away from his face. "I have business to take care of on Mortal Earth. My CEO has been blasting me with urgent texts. Decisions have to be made. A lot of decisions."

She nodded. "Absolutely." Decisions had to be made. Choices. More of them. Big choices.

She piled some egg on the toast and crunched a bite. She took a sip of gritty lukewarm coffee to wash it down. She smiled. It was the best dinner-breakfast she'd ever eaten.

"Havily, I'm coming back," he said. "Permanently. I need you to know that."

Tears rushed to her eyes. She crunched another bite and nodded over her breakfast. "Uh-huh," she said, blowing bits of dry crust out of her mouth. She sipped more coffee. She chewed and swallowed. Okay, a little more coffee.

She looked at him again. He was frowning at the breakfast. "I can't cook worth shit. You should know that about me."

"I do all right but I'm very fond of restaurants."

At that he looked at her and smiled. He took her hand, drew the fork from her grip, then kissed her fingers. "I have many things I want to say to you, but not today, not like this, and certainly not over burned toast."

"You should go," she said. She drank more coffee until the crumbs got swept down her throat.

He touched a tear that rolled down her cheek. He nodded then leaned close and kissed her on the mouth. He kissed her for a very long time, not penetrating, just his lips to her lips. She felt his promise in that kiss, everything that he was, and her heart swelled all over again.

She breathed his fennel scent and savored. Part of her feared that this would be the last time she ever saw him, but the new part, the part that seemed to understand, let it all go, every damn expectation that life would turn out the way she wanted.

So, yeah, she let him go.

He drew back and stood up. "I've asked Alison to check in on you. She also said to call her day or night if you needed her. Parisa's also staying in the villa until Endelle figures out what to do with her. Medichi will be checking on you as well.

"Parisa hasn't said anything, but I think she's hoping for another flying lesson." His expression softened. "You'll call Alison if you need her, right? Because I'm not happy about leaving you like this."

"I'll be fine. You need to go so you should go."

He leaned down and kissed her once more. He held her gaze for a good long moment. Then he rose back up to his considerable height. He smiled, lifted his arm, and he was gone.

She brushed another tear away then looked at the meal, at the cold brown eggs and black toast. She chuckled. Well, protein was protein and whatever else this experience had been, she needed to eat. Besides, eggs had iron and she still felt weak, dizzy. That bastard had taken *a lot* of her blood.

Marcus folded to his home on Bainbridge Island. The house seemed dark. Of course. Phoenix had brighter sunlight and lots of it. Although June in the Seattle area was a beautiful month, still, he missed all that light.

He walked through the rooms. He wanted Havily here, if he could make it safe enough for her. Yeah, he wanted her here. He'd talk to Endelle and see if she'd lend him one of her mist domes for at least one night. But would Havily come with him? He was pretty sure she would, but shit, anything could happen and he didn't know if her low opinion of him had altered sufficiently yet, or if she could ever really trust him.

To that end, he'd come back to Mortal Earth. If Havily was going to go the distance with him, then he had some proving to do.

He went to the safe in his library and spun the combination until the right tumblers fell into place. He opened the door. He'd had the safe for fifty years. They were old friends.

He pulled out the folder containing the transfer documents, everything Ennis would need to take over Sumer Enterprises. Funny. He'd had these documents drawn up about three and a half months ago, as though he'd known even then that the moment he'd caught Havily's scent his life had changed, permanently.

He closed the safe and spun the dial.

He had jewels in the safe, beautiful necklaces and bracelets he'd bought for the future women he'd screw. He wouldn't think of offering even one of them to Havily. At some point, he'd donate them to a charity auction, raise money for a good cause.

For Havily, he had something very different in mind.

He gave Ennis a call and arranged to meet him in Seattle.

An hour later, he said hi to Jane then walked into his office.

Ennis sat in the big executive chair behind the enormous glass desk. His legs were crossed at the knees, his elbows planted on the arms of the chair, and his fingers steepled over his lap. He swiveled lazily back and forth. He smirked and wore a crooked smile that reached to his eyes. Ennis always laughed with his eyes.

"Bastard," Marcus said, also smiling.

"Well, have you got something for me to sign, or what?"

Marcus threw the documents on the four-inch-thick glass. "You sure you want this?"

"Hell, yeah. I have for the last century or didn't you notice?"

"I noticed."

Ennis spread the documents out and started to sign. He didn't pause. He didn't even read.

"You're not going over these with the usual magnifying glass?"

At that, his pen froze and he looked up at his new business partner. "Marcus, of all the vampires I've known in the last five hundred years, I know your fucked-up soul the best. So the day I need to read your agreements, when we've already discussed the details, is the day I drink dying blood. Got it?"

Marcus smiled then grinned. "Sumer is yours. I'll see you in six months."

It wasn't a sale, just a shift in responsibility and an increased percentage of profit. Marcus would see enough wealth from the empire he'd built to last him a few millennia. He'd check in every six months just to see if Ennis needed him for any reason. But knowing Ennis, they'd share a drink, play a game of who-has-the-bigger-dick, then he'd head back to Second Earth.

"Where do you go from here?" Ennis asked. "You going to marry her?"

"Oh, I think I can do better than marriage."

Ennis raised his brows, but Marcus knew there was nothing more to be said.

"You'll need to tweak Jane's memory of this visit," he said, as he lifted his arm and dematerialized.

For himself, next stop, Vancouver Island.

The next day Havily stood in front of Endelle's desk, and for the first time in her ascended vampire life, from the time she had first met Her Supremeness, she didn't fear the woman. She was, however, uneasy, as though something wasn't quite right, but she couldn't place it.

For one thing, for Havily, everything had changed.

"You still dizzy?"

Havily shook her head. "No, not at all."

Endelle glanced behind her. "Where the fuck is Marcus?"

"Not sure. He left yesterday."

"What?" Endelle was on her feet, her eyes blazing as she planted her fists on the marble-topped desk in front of her. She leaned toward her. "So he returned to Mortal Earth? Are you telling me you couldn't keep your goddamn man? What the fuck is wrong with you?"

Havily smiled then laughed. "You know, you have about as much charm as a water moccasin."

Endelle drew back, left the power position of her desk, and moved to the windows to pace. She wore a yellow mini skirt and halter of what looked like banana python skin. Havily shuddered.

In some ways she was like Endelle, but in others, especially when it came to fashion choices, they went their separate ways. Havily glanced down at her own zebra-striped shoes and white linen pants. She wore a black silk blouse smocked at the hips. Yep, totally separate ways.

After a long tense moment, Endelle said, "We need Marcus here."

"I know that. But more important, he knows that."

"Then why the hell did you let him go? He *smells* you, for fuck's sake."

"Yeah, he does."

Endelle glared at her over her shoulder. "And would you stop with all this Zen-like bullshit that you're at peace with the fucking world? It's giving me the scratch."

"I am at peace, for the moment, anyway. If it's any help, he said he was coming back . . . permanently."

At that, Endelle turned to face her. She scowled. "Why the hell didn't you just say so? Aw, who the fuck cares. Marcus is coming back!" She clapped her hands together. "I'll have eight Warriors of the Blood in the field. Now maybe we can get something done." She glanced at Havily's heels. "I like your shoes, by the way."

Havily would have smiled since she stood next to one of the zebra-skin throw rugs that littered Endelle's office floor, but the uneasiness she had felt earlier descended on her and now she knew why.

She took a deep breath. Endelle was really not going to like what she had to say next. "I don't think Marcus should go back in the field, and I think it would be a huge mistake on your part if you forced the issue."

Well . . . she might as well have detonated an atomic bomb.

If Havily had ever thought that Endelle raged before, she now witnessed some of the farthest reaches of the woman's fierce temper.

Endelle moved around Havily like a tornado, pacing, fuming, screaming at her as though she'd just told her she had decided to defect to Greaves's forces.

"We need him in the field and if you think just because you're his goddamn fucking *breh,* you have the right to come in here and tell me how things are going to be, and if you think Warrior Marcus, yeah goddamn fucking *Warrior* Marcus, will be content not to go out every night and battle, then you are just plain out of your ever-loving fucking mind." The woman's eyes bulged.

Despite the tempest, Havily still wasn't afraid. Maybe because she knew, *she knew,* in this one thing, she was right. "That's just it, Madame Endelle. If you order Marcus to go, he'll go."

"Then what the fuck are you saying to me? Never mind. Marcus is rejoining the Warriors of the Blood and that's final. We're at war, Morgan, and we need him. EOS, goddammit."

Havily felt so certain about what she needed to say that she didn't even flinch as she straightened her shoulders and said, "Madame Endelle, you *suck* as an administrator."

Well . . . Havily had been wrong. *Now* she'd detonated the atomic bomb.

Endelle moved with preternatural speed and built resonance upon resonance into her voice as she screamed.

Havily stood in the middle of the rising energy and

simply strengthened her shields, the same shields that kept her from splitting-self. For a moment she did consider just slipping into the darkening until the rage-fest was over, but there was a good chance Endelle would follow her in.

So, she waited.

When at last Endelle stood panting an inch away from her face, Havily smiled. "Can I finish?"

Both of Endelle's hands formed wicked cat's claws, but she clenched her teeth and muttered, "Fine, but this had better be good."

"As I was saying, you suck as an administrator. Will you at least admit that much . . . to me?"

"What the fuck is your point, Morgan? You know, you've always pissed the hell out of me."

"I used to think it was because I disappointed you. Now I know differently. We're similar in temperament. I learned that the day you tried to teach me how to split-self. I've never used profanity like that in my entire life."

Endelle rolled her eyes. "This is the most useless conversation I've ever had." She turned away and huffed a sigh. "We need Marcus in the field. An idiot could see that."

Havily thought about how to explain her position. Finally, she said, "Do you know what it is Marcus does on Mortal Earth?"

"He has a successful import business."

"Not exactly."

"So exactly what does he do? Enlighten me." Ooooh. *Sarcasm.*

"He runs an empire. He has nineteen or maybe twenty corporations that he manages personally, as in he heads the boards and generally directs operations. I'd say he functions at genius level, probably in part because he's ascended. Does this give you any ideas?"

"You know damn well I don't do cryptic."

"You want me to spell it out?"

"Yes."

So Havily did. "You need to turn your administration over to Marcus."

Endelle stared at her for a long time and for the longest time she didn't even blink. After maybe three minutes, she moved behind her desk and sat down in her chair. Slumped, more like it, and Endelle never slumped.

Her head fell to the marble desk with a loud crack.

Havily moved closer to the desk. "You know, if you did this, you might even be able to get some sleep once in a while."

Endelle, with her chin still fixed to the desk, looked up at her. Her ancient lined eyes looked so sad. "Sleep? What would that be like?"

Havily nodded. "Exactly."

Marcus had all the legalities taken care of, and after three long days of working his way through the bureaucracies of two different dimensions, he finally changed into his business casual of short-sleeved silk shirt, medium gray this time, and tailored slacks. He folded back to Second Earth, not to Medichi's villa, but to Kerrick's mansion in Scottsdale Two.

His business with Havily wasn't the only thing he needed settled.

If he was coming back, he had hatchets that needed burying.

He stood on the porch, his heart weighed down with guilt and remembered loss. He strove to shape the right words together to form an apology but God, how small that word sounded, not nearly large enough to encompass what he needed to say to Kerrick.

For a long time, he couldn't bring himself to give the old-fashioned rapper a solid strike. So he waited as he rehearsed his speech. He would tell Kerrick of the suffering that had led him to speak so many unspeakable things to him two hundred years ago, he would talk about his love for Helena and the children, how his heart hadn't been so much crushed as vaporized by their deaths, he would try to offer some form of apology. At least that was his intention, but his mind was mush.

Fuck. He didn't know what he was going to say.

Finally, he just pounded on the door and closed his eyes. He ushered up a swift prayer to the Creator for wisdom and the right words. God help him.

But when Kerrick opened the door, wearing jeans and a damp T-shirt, his wet warrior hair hanging past his shoulders, his head shrouded in white terry cloth, words failed Marcus.

In a flash, the kind rumored to occur at the point of death, images flew through his mind, of meeting Kerrick some twelve hundred years ago when Kerrick was inducted into the Warriors of the Blood, of battling death vampires side by side with the brother, of a thousand conversations on every possible subject, of Kerrick having his back at the Blood and Bite and the other way around, of having stood up for him at his marriage to Helena, of having loved Kerrick like a brother, of having trusted him implicitly.

For all those reasons, yeah, words failed.

But his emotions didn't. His goddamn eyes burned as he just stared at the man. He felt as though someone had driven a stake through his heart.

Kerrick pulled the towel from his head and the terry slipped to the floor. "Marcus." His shoulders dropped. His head wagged from side to side. "Marcus," he said again. And finally, "My brother."

How he ended up in a powerful embrace with Kerrick, he didn't know, nor did a single word of apology rise to his lips. All he could think to say was, "I loved my sister."

"I loved her, too," came back at him.

This was what had always bound them together. Helena.

"I was too angry to think straight," Kerrick confessed. "And just as you blamed me, I blamed myself."

Marcus nodded. "I loved her and losing her and the kids, it was too much. The fighting, too."

Kerrick put his hand on Marcus's shoulder. "You don't have to explain anything to me ever. What you said to me, believe me, I said worse things to myself."

"I shouldn't have."

"It doesn't matter. Living is what matters."

Marcus nodded. "Then we're okay?"

"Absolutely."

Marcus nodded again. "Good. That's good."

He looked behind him, to the west, in the direction of the White Tank Mountains. He turned back to Kerrick. "I have things to take care of."

At that Kerrick smiled; he even chuckled. "Yeah. You do. I'd offer some advice but . . . wouldn't do any good."

Marcus nodded. "Probably not." Then he laughed as well. "Shit, the *breh-hedden*. I thought it was a myth."

"It's one helluva ride, though," Kerrick said.

The conversation was about to fall into the foot-shuffling stage, so he straightened his shoulders. "Later, Kerrick."

"Later, my brother."

Marcus nodded, lifted his hand, and dematerialized. As he landed in the foyer of Medichi's villa, he put a hand to his chest. Shit he hurt. It was a good kind of hurt, but still, he hurt.

He took a couple of deep breaths, which helped. But what helped more was hearing the laughter of two women in the distance, coming from the direction of the kitchen.

Havily's scent, her beautiful honeysuckle reached him at the same time. He closed his eyes and breathed in. As long as he lived he vowed the smell of that flower would forever remind him of the feeling of *coming home*. Because that's what he felt like right now, as though he was coming home.

He found the women in the dining room, both perched at the top of ladders that were situated at opposite ends of the long formal dining table. They taped twisted red streamers to the fifteen-foot-high ceiling.

"What's going on?" he asked. "Are we having a party or something?"

Havily turned and looked at him. She gave a cry, let her end of the streamer drop, and literally dove from the height of the ladder into his arms. He smiled and caught her easily enough, but said, "You sure trust me. What if I'd stepped back a few inches?"

"You'd never do that." Her lips were on his and her very sweet honeysuckle tongue was suddenly in his mouth. Oh, shit, she felt good, but if she kept this up he'd have to excuse them both and take her straight to their bedroom.

He pulled back and smiled at her. "Wait," he said. He'd added a little resonance so that her peachy-red brows lifted.

"You sure?" she asked. She waggled her brows, growled, and a wave of honeysuckle shrank the fine tailoring of his pants.

He took more deep breaths, nodded, then lowered her to her feet. He glanced up at Parisa, who now sat on the top step of her ladder working not to look at them. "How are you doing, Parisa?" he asked.

She glanced down at him and smiled. "Really good, thank you." She glanced at Havily. "We've been flying."

Havily turned back to him, her arms still around his neck. "You should see her," she cried. "She can do a front flip then float down to land on her feet. I couldn't even do that for the entire first year. She has amazing flight capabilities. She could perform in the spectacle circuits, if she wanted."

Marcus thought he might suggest to Havily that she keep that particular idea to herself. He knew how the *breh-hedden* affected him, and the sheer logistics that would be involved trying to protect his woman during a spectacle performance made his head spin. He didn't think Medichi needed those images right now.

He kept his counsel and instead smiled up at Parisa. "Flying's great. So, this looks like a party. What are we celebrating?"

"Zach's birthday."

"That's terrific but Parisa, why are you suddenly frowning?"

Parisa sighed. "Because Endelle's coming to the party."

"No shit. Well, that has to be a first."

"Hey," Havily said. "I invited her. Besides, her bark is worse than her bite."

"This from you?" Marcus cried.

She shrugged. "We've kind of made up, at least for now."

Marcus could only laugh but he took the opportunity to kiss her again . . . briefly. "And how are *you* doing?"

"Perfect," she said. She looked and sounded as though she meant it. "I had a long talk with Endelle and we got a lot of things settled. So yeah, I'm good."

He nodded. "Okay, that's fine, but what I want to know is if you have any dizziness, any ill effects from the forge."

She shook her head. "Really, I'm okay. No dizziness. I'm just so glad you're home."

"Me, too. So what time is the party?"

Havily glanced at her watch. "In half an hour. The warriors won't be going out till seven or so, which means we get them here until then."

Marcus saw movement in the kitchen; then Medichi appeared in the doorway. His expression was tight around the eyes as he glanced first at Parisa. He looked her over from head to foot then said, "You okay up there? Is the ladder steady? You want me to finish up?"

Parisa's expression also grew very tight, her lips pinched. "I'm fine. Really. You have nothing to be concerned about."

The tension in the air stretched to just this side of breaking.

Marcus looked back at Medichi. The vampire was in hell, 100 percent flaming hell. Oh, he looked normal, but Marcus knew exactly where he was at right now—the need to be close, to have his arms around his woman, but no possible right to get within fifty feet of her.

"We need to get changed," Havily said. "How about you men finish this last streamer." She held her hand out in Parisa's direction.

So that's the way it was. Havily had placed herself between the couple, probably on Parisa's request.

Marcus sent, *Was this Parisa's idea? You playing go-between?*

Havily didn't look at him as she returned, *Antony's. He's in agony on many fronts and Endelle put him on guardian duty . . . indefinitely.*

Jesus.

Exactly. No one knows what do with Parisa and she's lost here.

Parisa climbed down the ladder.

"Ready?" Havily asked as Parisa slid off the table.

"Ready. Are you going to wear the new dress you bought?"

"Absolutely."

Marcus watched Havily leave the room. It took considerable willpower not to follow after her. Her honeysuckle tugged at his soul. He had so much to say to her. Everything seemed settled but he knew he walked a fine line here and she seemed somehow different to him, as though she'd made a decision or two herself.

Maybe words would help but he hoped, *he hoped,* that what he'd brought her from Vancouver Island would show her the intention of his heart. The real question kicked his anxiety up a couple of notches—would she go for it, all of it? Because that's what he needed from her now, everything, the whole damn enchilada. For him, from this point forward, it was all or nothing.

He turned to Medichi, who had moved to stand next to him, so that he, too, could watch the women, arm in arm, head to their respective rooms. His eyes blazed, and his body gave off heat in waves.

Marcus laughed. "Need a cold shower?"

"The waters would have to be arctic to calm this down. Jesus H. Christ." In a voice that sounded ruined, he added, "She won't even talk to me. I mean *talk,* as in *talk.*"

Marcus slapped him on the shoulder, "I feel you, brother."

Havily dressed slowly, but her mind whirled.

Marcus seemed so different, and he stopped the kiss. *He stopped the kiss.* Usually he initiated, then complained if she even so much as tapped the brakes.

She had expected him to take her straight to the bedroom and get her good and naked. Instead, he'd basically told her to back off. Had the fierce driving need of the *breh-hedden* lessened in him? Did he no longer want her as desperately as she wanted him, needed him, *craved* him?

Her body melted into a weak puddle as she thought of just how much she craved him. His absence for the last three days had been like fire on her skin and in her belly. She had picked up her iPhone to call him, oh, about a hundred times. But she was the one who had told him to go, even though she hadn't wanted him to. He said he would return and he had, but he seemed so different now and she just didn't understand. Although he did shed enough fennel to set her heart on fire, but maybe for him that no longer mattered.

Oh. God.

Well, maybe her dress would help. She had bought it yesterday because he hadn't called her and she intended to wear it for him to remind him she had certain assets he valued. The V of the dress was low, very low, and gave full expression to her cleavage, which she knew he enjoyed . . . a lot.

The length was short as well and she'd bought stilettos, five inches tall, which would put her almost at eye level with her man when he kissed her. She would be able to slide her arms around his neck and hook him hard, hold him plastered against her mouth . . . she groaned at the thought.

If that was even what he wanted anymore . . .

Marcus stood outside the door of the bedroom he shared with Havily. He didn't know whether to knock or walk in, but when a wave of honeysuckle punched at him through the narrow spaces between the door and the frame, he took a step back.

Damn, that scent got to him, as it had from the first, tingling in his nose then working like lightning down his chest and abdomen to strike straight into his groin. This was his woman, his mate, his *breh*. He needed her, wanted her, craved her.

But they had some stuff to get settled. So instead of joining her in their shared bedroom, he turned away from the door and went south to the next wing. He folded a Tom Ford suit from his Bainbridge house then he took a shower, a goddamn, ball-and-dick-shrinking shower until even his teeth were chattering.

But if all went as planned, he'd suit up in flight gear this very night, rejoin the Warriors of the Blood, and begin his new life battling death vampires.

However, as he soaped up, the thought of resuming that part of his life emptied his chest of all feeling. He knew he was needed, but fighting like that was going to be hard for him, *very* hard.

He straightened his shoulders. But he would do it. Just as Endelle served in ways she hated, so would he.

Change rides in
On the galloping back of wisdom.

—*Collected Proverbs,* Beatrice of Fourth

CHAPTER 24

Havily really did want to raise her glass to Warrior Zacharius, since Thorne was making a toast in his honor, but she was trapped. "Marcus," she whispered. "Can you let go of my arm?"

She heard the faint growl, a sound that pleased her much more than it should have, as he lessened his grip.

The moment he'd seen her dress, his gaze had landed on her cleavage and stayed there. Since then, he'd been in a state, caught between a rock and a hard place called desire and jealousy and . . . she loved it.

She'd definitely gotten the response she'd been looking for—Marcus had released a roll of fennel that caused her knees to shake. So at least in this she was reassured that his need for her hadn't changed.

As for Marcus, he was the only vampire present who wore a tie. He looked sexy as hell and his clothes, so at odds with the warriors present, so much a reflection of how he'd spent the last two hundred years, gave her a measure of confidence that her conversation with Endelle had been the right one.

"To Zach," Thorne said. "A millennium of happy returns."

The warriors rose in his honor as well. "To Zach" reverberated around the room.

Warrior Zacharius hadn't bound his hair but let his mass of black curls flow from his shoulders in waves. He was as tall as Marcus and heavily muscled—all the warriors were—but he had an exotic appearance that always made the ladies do a double take. Most women stared at him, trying to balance all that hair, with the body, with the large brilliant blue eyes. He had a determined wildness about him that begged a woman to just try and tame *that*.

As everyone sat down, he rose from his chair.

He thanked Parisa and Havily for their efforts in making his birthday special, but in his deep voice, he lifted a glass in Marcus's direction and said, "From the brothers. We wanted to say thank you for protecting our beloved Havily. She's been a sister to us this past century. She blesses our mornings after a night of battle, she lightens our spirits, she means the world to us. Thank you for bringing her home." He nodded, dipped his chin, cast his gaze around the table. "To Marcus."

Havily's eyes burned as the warriors once more rose to their feet and lifted goblets of Medichi's fine Cabernet. "To Marcus" went around the room.

Havily turned toward Marcus, leaned close, and kissed his cheek, which of course set the men to hooting as they took up their seats again.

Marcus stood up and settled his gaze on Luken. He raised his glass. "But neither of us would be here if it weren't for you, Luken. You saved us both and you finished Crace off. We all owe you a debt for that. To Luken."

Another rousing cheer went around the table.

Luken nodded but he blushed. He didn't handle compliments all that well.

Thorne once more gained his feet and addressed Marcus. "We do have one issue we need to resolve, and here it is. We want you back, brother. Will you rejoin?"

Havily glanced at Endelle, who met her gaze. This wasn't the timing she would have planned, but Endelle gave her a short I'll-handle-this nod. Havily inclined her head in response but her heart rate picked up. Would Marcus understand the what and why of it?

She looked up at him, her heart in her throat. "I accept," he said. "And of course, I'll start tonight."

A cheer rang through the room all over again.

This time Endelle took the floor and patted the air, indicating she wanted Thorne and Marcus to sit back down, which of course they did.

She was an amazing woman, powerful, absurdly tall in her stilettos, almost seven feet, a real Amazon. She had even toned it down for the party and wore a simple black leather vest and leather pants. The only decorations were some small red feathers that lined the low-cut V. "As for Marcus rejoining, don't I get a say in this?"

Almost as one, they shouted, "No." But laughter ensued.

For just this moment, Havily's gaze rested on each warrior, astonished as she had been from the first at not just the size and musculature of the men but at the lethal quality each carried in the movements of arm and leg, of torso, even the turn of head and shift of feet. Individually, they were stunning. As a group, overwhelming.

And Endelle ruled them.

She stood at the head of the table and waited for the men to settle and for all attention to turn in her direction. At last she drew a deep breath and began, "I had it brought to my attention a couple of days ago that I was wholly and completely incompetent in my position as Supreme High

Administrator. In fact the person who said this to me had the audacity to say I *sucked* at being an administrator."

Though Endelle spoke with a half smile, and her words were meant to be a sort of joke, a deadly silence fell over the room. The warriors tensed. Even Marcus leaned forward.

Havily glanced at Alison, whose empathic skills were at third dimension level, but even she frowned and appeared confused, which confirmed Havily's belief that the warriors all agreed with Endelle's statement but were at the same time ready to go to war on her behalf against anyone disparaging her service.

Havily loved them for that. She slid her arm around Marcus's and squeezed. He glanced at her and scowled. *You're not upset about this,* he sent, almost like an accusation.

She shook her head at him.

Santiago rose to his feet, his ruby-encrusted dagger suddenly in his hand. "Name the bastard who would say this to you."

"Well," Endelle said. "Thank you for the warm gesture of loyalty but it isn't necessary." She nodded in some satisfaction. "Actually, the bastard is a she and *she* is sitting next to Marcus fondling his bicep."

Havily blushed as she glanced down at her hand. Endelle was right. She had been playing with Marcus's arm without even knowing it.

But it was the gasp among the warriors that made her pull away from him.

"Oh, for fuck's sake," Endelle cried. "You know I suck at my job." She huffed a sigh. "I do, but I still needed to hear it said aloud. And I would never have considered this next course of action had it not been for Havily but she's right. I know it in my gut. And if I'm freed up from some of the administrative work, I can start strategizing against Greaves, find some way to stop him from turning my High Administrators. As it is right now, I don't get enough sleep and I'm so sunk in reports that I can't see the war clear enough to figure out what we need to do next. And the Creator knows we need to do something fast. That bastard has been gaining ground steadily for the past fifteen years."

Thorne cried out, "What the hell is this all about? What the fuck are you trying to say?"

Endelle looked straight at Marcus. "I am appointing, without reservation, Warrior Marcus as High Administrator of the Southwest Desert Territory and at the same time granting him Guardian of Ascension status."

Silence filled the dining room for a long tense moment.

"Merde," Jean-Pierre muttered, the first to speak.

"Holy mother of God," Santiago cried.

Thorne turned to Marcus. "Did you know about this?"

"No," he stated, shaking his head. He turned to Havily his eyes narrowing, his jaw rigid. "Was this your doing? Because you don't want me fighting? I have to fight. I'm needed at the Borderlands. You know that."

Havily knew for certain in this moment that she had erred, so gravely that she wondered if she would ever recover Marcus's trust. She hadn't meant for her discussion with Endelle to seem as though she was going behind his back and manipulating things just to keep her man out of the war, but so it appeared.

Her panic rose to chest level and her mind bent straight back to being in Crace's forge. She felt trapped and weak all over again, as though she was one down in this setting and had nothing worthy to contribute.

However, as she met Marcus's accusing gaze, as she saw the anger in his light brown eyes, that he believed she'd overstepped her bounds, she took a deep breath and lifted her chin.

Newer, stronger thoughts flowed through her mind, of the courage she had displayed over the past several days, of her mettle tested in horrific ways, of her absolute certainty that she was right in this situation. Nor was she a simple woman with selfish designs. She knew her man, she knew his abilities, and she understood the situation from an administrative point of view. If the macho warrior strain in this room wasn't countered with rationality, the war would continue on just as it had, with determination, yes, but with Greaves gaining ground each and every day.

So she lifted a brow to him in response, rose to her feet, and met the scowls of all the warriors present. "I have something to say, and by God you're all going to listen to me." She turned to Marcus. "Especially you."

Marcus crossed his arms over his chest and glared, but he gave her the courtesy of remaining silent.

Havily nodded to Endelle, and Her Supremeness returned the favor and resumed her seat.

Havily shifted to face the warriors once more. "First of all, if Warrior Marcus chooses to fight, that's up to him. I am not nor will I ever be his keeper and I would never stand in the way of his rejoining the Warriors of the Blood if he believed he would best serve Second Earth by taking up his sword.

"But I want to remind you that war isn't fought only with the sword, and Greaves has been undermining Madame Endelle's administration in a host of ways. He's steadily increased shipments of death vampires to Metro Phoenix to wear you men down, he's seduced High Administrators around the globe into his camps because he has significant wealth at his disposal, and he knows how to work propaganda on behalf of his Coming Order like nobody's business. And we all know the travesty that COPASS has become—and that if Greaves turns a majority of the committee members, Madame Endelle's administration will sink."

The truth of her words was visible in every expression of clenched jaw, exasperated sigh, or flexing of sword arm at the table.

She continued, "When I spoke with Madame Endelle two days ago about Warrior Marcus's future, when I suggested that Warrior Marcus should do anything other than serve as a Warrior of the Blood, only my mental shields kept me from being consumed by the blast of her fury."

Luken shifted in his seat and glanced at Endelle. Thorne grunted. Kerrick nodded.

"Fuck," Jean-Pierre murmured.

Havily continued, "So you were not alone in your initial reactions to what essentially was my proposal to Madame Endelle.

"I'd also like to say that I resented the hell out of the *breh-hedden* when it hit me as it did four months ago. I despised the man sitting next to me for having deserted the Warriors of the Blood two hundred years ago. For that, I considered him less than a man because . . . because of my love for all of you and for the terrible sacrifices you have made, especially in your personal lives." She put a hand to her chest and took a couple of deep breaths. "But sometimes the incomprehensible decisions we make in earlier parts of our lives come forward to show us the way to the future. Marcus built an empire on Second Earth during the last two centuries and knows more about waging an administrative and propaganda war, one that involves building loyalty and service among employees, than anyone sitting at this table."

"Except for you, Hav," Zacharius called out. "Look at what you've accomplished in the last four months. Look at the success of the Ambassadors Festival. You could serve as High Administrator. I'd give you my vote."

Havily smiled. "Thank you, Zach, that means a lot to me. However—" She paused and met Endelle's gaze. Once more Her Supremeness surprised her with an ancient, knowing look of sympathy and support.

Havily continued, "Actually, I'll be taking up a new position soon, a very different kind of work." Oh, God. The words she was about to speak had weight, heavy, burdensome, shoulder-sagging weight. She felt her future blast in her direction so powerfully that she staggered a little on her feet. Tears flashed to her eyes and for a moment she could only swallow hard, her gaze fixed to the table.

When at last she composed herself, she said, "I've

agreed to become apprenticed to Madame Endelle in darkening work, to assist her nightly efforts as best I can in order to prevent Commander Greaves from overloading the Valley with death vampires."

Once again, momentous silence captured the room.

"*Darkening* work," Santiago whispered, penetrating the awful quiet. He flipped his dagger in his hand.

"Holy fuck," Kerrick murmured.

Luken shook his head back and forth. "Havily, this is some crazy-ass shit."

Havily suddenly felt uncomfortable. "I have a lot to learn, of course," came out in a rush. "But I've told you this by way of answering Zach's question. I have other duties now. As for Warrior Marcus, what I wanted to say is that we need *someone* to begin waging war as Greaves has been waging war, attacking his efforts where the High Administrators are concerned as well as the ongoing propaganda war. For all these reasons, I asked Madame Endelle to consider the possibility that Marcus would be of greater value and use to the war effort in an administrative position rather than in the field."

She looked down at Marcus. "I believe with all my heart, knowing you as well as I do, that Second Earth needs you to serve in this capacity. But the decision must be yours and"—here she met the gaze of each of the warriors one by one—"the decision of the warriors as well."

Lastly, she met Endelle's gaze. There was approval in the Amazon's eyes. Havily gave a curt nod then sat down.

Endelle rose to her feet. "I agree with everything Havily has just said. Most particularly, that the Warriors of the Blood must have a say. This should be a joint decision and Marcus, I say this to you most of all, whatever you decide will be perfectly acceptable to me as I know it will be to Havily." Endelle glanced at her once more. "And as much as I've given you shit, I admire you, Morgan. You've got balls, that's for sure. And I know that if Marcus decides he must fight, you won't stop him."

"No, of course not. Never." A murmur of approval went around the table.

When Endelle sat down, Thorne stood up and addressed his men, his gravel voice restating both cases, the need for another warrior and yet the critical need for someone with executive ability to combat all the other fronts on which Greaves operated, all those ways he was currently winning his bid for world domination.

The discussion lasted a good long hour as Marcus answered numerous questions about his financial empire, how he'd built it, his basic philosophies, and if he felt he could make a significant contribution as a High Administrator. The second hour involved even more discussion about just what kinds of measures Marcus would take if he were to become a High Administrator.

When the subject wore itself out, when there were no more comments to be made, pro or con, Medichi served up a massive strawberry cake as well as glasses of Dom Perignon.

When the last of the cake had been devoured and the last drop of champagne swallowed, Endelle rose to her feet once more. "Well, boys, I have darkening work to get to. As for you, Marcus, don't wear your woman out tonight. Come to my offices tomorrow about nine. Thorne, you as well. We'll discuss this situation further. Agreed?"

Both men nodded.

She wasn't an easy woman, Madame Supreme High Administrator, but she was the right woman to command the Warriors of the Blood. She lifted a hand, flipped them all off, then dematerialized. Laughter and a shaking of heads traveled around the table.

Thorne called the meeting and birthday celebration to a conclusion by saying, "Well, men, we have some blue skin to off. Everyone to the Blood and Bite . . . at will."

One by one, the warriors came to Marcus and clapped him on the shoulder, or grabbed his palm, afterward folding away.

Luken was next to last and shoved Marcus's palm away in order to torment him by grabbing Havily up in a hug. Havily laughed. She held on to Luken a little longer than she normally would have. She felt sad suddenly, knowing how Luken felt. The warrior was so deserving.

He let her go first, met her gaze for a long meaningful moment, then lifted his arm. He offered a wink as he disappeared. She had the strangest thought that she would miss him, really miss him, and not just because she was now with Marcus or because a lot of her time would be spent with Endelle in the darkening. The future blew over her, chilling her. She shivered, but then a moment later, the sensation disappeared.

Okay, that was weird.

Marcus leaned close. "You okay?"

She nodded and smiled. She gave herself a shake. "I'm fine. Really."

"Good."

Kerrick approached last, with Alison on his arm. The two men just stared at each other for a long hard moment. Simultaneously, as Marcus raised his hand, Kerrick's palm slapped hard against his, then he drew him in for a tight man-hug. "Welcome home, my brother."

Marcus nodded as though everything had already been settled between them, but when and how?

Alison met Havily's gaze, and her eyes were misty as she smiled. "Marcus stopped by earlier," she explained.

"Oh," Havily whispered. She glanced at Marcus and couldn't help the tears that filled her eyes as well.

Kerrick released Marcus. "Come over in a week or so, to the house. There's something I'd like to show you." He shifted his gaze to Havily. "We'd love it if you both came."

The time and date were set. Alison settled her head on Kerrick's shoulder and, as he slung an arm around his *breh*, the pair vanished.

Only Parisa and Medichi remained. They stood at opposite corners of the table not looking at each other. Parisa stared at the table and ran her finger around the rim of her champagne glass. Medichi had his back to her, looking out the window to the front yard, his expression resolute.

Marcus slid an arm around Havily's waist. In a quiet voice, he asked, "Will you come with me to Bainbridge? I asked Madame Endelle to prep the house for us."

Havily met his gaze. He seemed . . . strained, even uneasy. "Prepped?" she asked.

"Misted."

"Oh." She tilted her head and leaned close. She whispered, "That's where we . . ."

His smile was crooked as he nodded. "Yeah. For four months."

Her cheeks warmed up.

"There's something I need to say to you, Havily, and I want to say it there, where so much of this, between us, began. Will you come with me?"

There was no question in her mind. "Of course."

He nodded, and his smiled broadened. "Good." He turned to Medichi and asked, "You okay with us taking off tonight?"

The tall warrior turned to look at him. His eyes had a haunted look, which sliced to Parisa then back. "Go," he said. "I've got things here."

Parisa stepped forward, her hips hitting the table. "When will you come back?" she asked quickly.

Havily glanced at Marcus, but she made the decision by herself. She could see the panic rising in Parisa's eyes. "I'll be here by eight in the morning. Would you like to come to the office with me? We have a library on the second floor of the admin building you might be interested in seeing."

Parisa smiled, but her lips trembled. "That would be great. Yes. Yes. I would like that."

Havily knew exactly what she was feeling right now because she'd been in that place four months ago, overwhelmed with all these new, improbable sensations and yearnings. All of it made worse, of course, because Parisa had arrived on Second Earth only a handful of days ago, so, yeah, the *breh-hedden* was taking one heavy toll.

Parisa then turned to Medichi and, with her shoulders squared and her chin up, she said, "If it would be all right with you, I'd like to study in your library again."

"Of course."

Once more the tension between the ascendiate and Medichi thickened as she left the room. Medichi waited for a count of five, cursed, then followed in her wake. Havily had never seen him look more determined, nor more miserable.

"It will all work out," Marcus said quietly as they disappeared into the adjoining sitting room.

"I know," Havily whispered.

When their footsteps echoed across the planked floor of the foyer, Marcus squeezed her waist. "Ready?" he asked.

Havily felt the weight of the world in that one question. Was she ready?

Oh, God. Was this it? Was it possible they would decide right now to complete the *breh-hedden*?

She nodded, and the vibration began.

Marcus couldn't let go of her hand. He had folded Havily to the tall glass entrance of his Bainbridge home, which faced the wooded part of the island. The hour, just half past seven so far north, in the state of Washington, meant that the sky would be held in a fading twilight for hours yet.

He glanced up through the skylight. "There," he murmured. "Do you see it?"

Havily looked up as well and smiled. "Endelle may be a pain in the ass, but she makes the most beautiful mist."

"Yes, she does, and you'll be safe here, which is all I care about."

He turned her toward him and took her in his arms. She fell against him with a whimper, her arms encircling his neck, her need apparently as great as his. He kissed her deeply, his tongue making a full sweep and tangling with hers. His chest was filled with fire.

Everything had changed. Every goddamn thing.

He had never expected to be in this place again because he could never for the life of him picture how it could work, how he could give himself to another woman and not be strangled by the fear of losing her.

Yet here he was, ready and willing, the events of the last few days having turned his soul inside out and forced him to accept one certain fact—he would rather be with Havily and risk losing her than face living his life without her. The process hadn't been simple. Falling in love with her had been a necessary opener to the transformation of his closely held self. But he was ready now to make a commitment.

He drew back and took a deep breath. "I have something for you."

"You do?"

He slid his arm down her back and took her hand in his once more. He led her past the open staircase and down a small set of stairs into the expansive living room. The windows offered a view of the sound and the emerging lights of Seattle across the broad stretch of water in between.

"Marcus, it's so beautiful here," she said, her gaze fixed toward the windows. "Only when I come back to the ocean, even to the sound, do I remember how much I loved the water, the smell of it, the humidity in the air, the solid weighty presence of it."

"The light is different here as well."

"Yes, but I've always loved this part of the world. I lived north of here, remember? I was born in Victoria."

"I do remember. Vancouver Island." His nerves hit him. Would she understand what he had done? Or would she think his gift invasive or insensitive?

"Havily."

She turned toward him. "What is it?"

"I'm not sure. I . . . well . . . here it is. If . . . if for some reason what I've done offends you, I'll apologize right now. My motives were . . . well, I was thinking only of you." He gestured to the coffee table.

She glanced down where he'd placed the long, silver-foil box, wrapped with a burgundy ribbon. She reached down and picked it up. "Should I open it?"

He nodded. "Please." Were her hands trembling?

She pulled the ribbon apart and lifted the lid. She pushed back the dark gray tissue paper and stared at the photographs.

He felt sick, worried. Jesus, maybe he shouldn't have done this.

She took the photos from the box. She blinked and the box tumbled to the floor. "This is . . . the farm . . . our farm . . . on Mortal Earth." Tears welled in her eyes. She touched the photo. "My family is buried back there, all of them." She gave a little cry and the tears flowed down her cheeks.

"Havily, I'm sorry." He rushed his words. "I've made a mistake. I shouldn't have done it. I meant well."

She looked at him. "You went to Vancouver Island and took pictures of my farm? Why?"

"No. I mean yes. No, I didn't just take pictures. I . . . I bought the property. I bought it for you. And then I went to Second Earth and bought the same piece of land, same exact acreage. It's in a much more rustic form on Second, but I thought, maybe, if you wanted to, we could build a house there, together, you and me. Oh . . . shit . . . I have so fucked up." He dropped to the leather sofa and buried his face in his hands. "I'm sorry. This was wrong. All wrong." He had meant it for good but now it seemed so harsh, invasive, even cruel. Her daughters were buried there, for Christ's sake. Her three little girls, all with red hair and ringlets. He'd seen them in her mind. Jesus H. Christ, could a man be more of an idiot?

He felt the sofa dip beside him. He felt her fingers on his

as she pried his hands away from his face, the photos now on the coffee table, one teetering on the edge.

"Marcus," she whispered. She kissed his cheek, but her lips were wet. Dammit, he'd made her cry. "Marcus. You're wrong. This is the sweetest gift I've ever received, in my whole short one hundred years. I can't even begin to tell you how much this means to me."

He turned toward her and met her gaze, her green eyes full of light and warmth, even as tears poured from them. She shook her head back and forth. "You see, I've been saving for decades now to buy back my farm. That's why I live in my little town house. I couldn't save much each year, and then inflation would drive the Mortal Earth prices up and I would fall behind. I was so afraid someone would buy the property then dig up the graves. I . . ." She wept hard now, her own face buried in her hands.

He put his arms around her and held her close. His heart ached for her, with her. Then he'd done the right thing? "You're not upset with me?" he asked.

"Upset? Oh, no, how could I be?" She looked up at him, wiping her face with her fingers. "Oh, Marcus. Thank you. Somehow you saw into my heart and gave me exactly what I desired most. Thank you."

Still holding her in his arms, he pulled her onto his lap, turning her to lean against him so that his arms were around her shoulders. He smoothed back her hair and kissed her. He folded a tissue from the bathroom and wiped her face.

She smiled at him and searched his eyes. "I didn't know how this would be between us, if this would become more than just an insane attraction. Marcus, are we completing the *breh-hedden*? Is that why you brought me here?"

"I want to, Havily, more than anything. I never expected to feel this way, to feel like I could make a commitment again. I didn't think it was possible, especially after Helena died. She and her children were as much my world as they were Kerrick's. When she died, I lost my mind. I lost my soul."

She nodded. "Eric's death had settled everything for me as well. I knew I would be alone forever. I wasn't just resigned, I was resolved. I never wanted to hurt like that again, the same way I'd hurt when my babies died, my husband.

"Then you came along." She stroked his face with her palm and ran her thumb over his lips. He kissed her thumb. "And even then, not until I was manacled in Crace's forge, when I believed I had lost you forever, did my heart open enough to embrace love. Don't you think that's strange—because I truly believed you were dead? I didn't think you could have survived that blast."

"What are you saying?"

She drew in a breath and huffed a sigh. "I'm not explaining this well. I'm not even certain I understand all the meanings myself. Do you remember when we made love the last time and you took me to a place of really letting go because you enthralled me?"

He drew her closer. She was still seated on his lap and he loved it. He nuzzled her neck. "Yes."

"Do you remember how you kept saying, *Let go, let go*?"

He drew back and looked into her eyes. He nodded.

"That's what went through my mind when I was struggling to find a way out of the forge. I needed to let go, really let go. Everything changed for me in that moment. Everything. I knew you were dead and I was okay with it. I let go. I let go of all this grief that has held me as captive as I was manacled to that wall. I let go. That's when I figured out how to split myself into two parts. I let go . . . of my shields, my mental shields. Within a whisper of a thought, I was in the darkening, found Endelle, then like this miracle, there you were, alive and ready to do battle.

"I'm still astonished when I think about it. And now here you are, alive, holding me, having given me a gift that my heart cried out for. Oh, Marcus, yes, I want to complete the *breh-hedden* with you, whatever that will mean for you and for me, whatever new barriers will need to be broken down. Yes, I want this."

He stroked her hair, then kissed her hard, driving his tongue inside. She suckled and turned the heat up a notch.

But his soul was on fire as much as his body and like hell he was going to push this to a furious pace. There were things yet to be said.

He pulled back.

But she closed her eyes and her nostrils flared as she drew in a deep breath. "You smell like licorice and I swear I could lick you from the top of your head to the bottom of your feet and everywhere in between."

Okay. That visual didn't help at all.

He kissed her again, one full heavy kiss on her lips. "Hold that thought."

She nodded but she was shedding honeysuckle from every pore of her body and his body thrummed with his need for her. He trembled then struggled to remember exactly what it was he wanted to say. He closed his eyes. Fortunately she remained very still.

After a moment, he opened his eyes, met her gaze, and said, "Being burned like that was nothing to what I felt when I realized you'd been taken by that monster. I was in and out of consciousness but every time I came to, you were what I thought of and I knew what would happen to you if he kept you for any length of time.

"The *breh-hedden* hooked me in deep in all the ways that men get hooked in with their women, a burning need to stick close, to protect you, to make sure no other man got to you. Damn, the possessiveness and jealousy alone—" He stopped for a moment and dipped low, kissing down the length of her cleavage, then licking his way back up. He ignored her whimpers. "Like this dress . . . I love it and I hate it, because every warrior there tonight could see what only I should be allowed to see and yet I loved showing you off . . . see how twisted it all is . . . because I wanted them to know that this was mine, you are mine." He buried his face between her breasts. He used his tongue, his lips, his teeth.

She moaned softly and he felt her arm move, then her hand. Oh, shit, she'd slipped her finger into his mouth. He nearly lost it as her finger stroked his tongue.

He wanted to rip the dress off her and take her then and there, but his soul still cried out to speak the words that had to be spoken.

It killed him, but he drew away from her breasts and lifted his gaze to her once more. Her finger followed and slid down his cheek. "You're mine," he said. "And I want to make you mine in every possible way.

"But I have to try to help you see what you did for me this evening, when I realized you were the one who instigated a change of administration. Yes, I was shocked at first that you or anyone would suggest that I not return to the Warriors of the Blood. I owed them for the two centuries they'd fought on without me.

"But you called it. Dammit, you called it exactly right. As soon as you started talking about what was needed I realized I'd just spent the last two hundred years preparing to take over. That you saw it in me first, and matched my skills with the current need . . . Havily, that was pure fucking genius."

Havily smiled. "You should have seen how furious Endelle was when I first mentioned it. Tonight she was all poise, but back then she sprouted horns, big, thick, heavy, twisted horns. I thought she would jump out of her skin. I was just afraid you would misunderstand and think I was trying to keep you safe."

He shook his head. "I took it that way at first. I shouldn't have but damn, you gave a good accounting of yourself, of your reasoning. You've got some serious administrative chops."

"Thank you," she said, her head tilted.

He kissed her. She drew a breath, and a little puff of nervous air returned. "So we're doing this, you and me?"

He nodded slowly. "If you'll have me, I want nothing more than to complete the *breh-hedden* with you. But what about you?"

"I want to but I'm so nervous. What do you think will happen? Did you ever know anyone who completed the ritual, I mean before Kerrick and Alison? All the warriors kept saying they believed it was a myth."

"Over the four millennia that I served as a warrior, I only knew of one case, but it was so long ago I don't remember the details. Although I think once the bond was sealed, I saw very little of my fellow warrior except during battle and he didn't speak of his *breh,* out of respect. Besides, the subject would have been too damn personal."

"Are you anxious about this?"

"I need you too much to be worried. Whatever this ritual is, whatever it's meant to be, I want it, with you, now."

She looked around. "So where do you want to do this? Right here? On this couch?"

He smiled. "Actually, I'd like to be in the place where you came to me every night in what we both thought was a dream."

She smiled but a blush suffused her cheeks. "Your bed."

"My bed. You don't know how much I've wanted you there and Havily, I want you to know that I've never brought a woman to this house before. This place for me was, *is,* sacred."

She smiled and once more put her hand on his face. She leaned forward and kissed him.

When she drew back, he slid her off his lap, and as he stood up he lifted her to her feet at the same time. He could have folded her to the bedroom but for some reason he wanted to lead her there. He turned in the direction of the stairs by the entry. She followed him, her free hand on his forearm. She stroked her fingers lightly over the muscle. His heart swelled again, that strange sensation he knew now to be his yearning for her, his love for her.

Yes, he loved her.

That which hides in the heart
Must be brought to light
And Forgiven

—*Collected Proverbs,* Beatrice of Fourth

CHAPTER 25

Havily held on to Marcus, her right hand in his, her left hand latched onto his muscled forearm. He was her tether right now as she followed him up the stairs. The skylight above was a mixture of light and emerging stars. She remembered the summer nights, the twilights that lasted for hours in the Pacific Northwest.

When she entered his bedroom, she knew she'd been here before if only in the darkening. The room was exactly as she remembered it.

"Havily, there's one thing I have to do first." He released her hand, turned into her, and planted his hands on her waist. She watched his gaze fall to her cleavage. "Your dress has been tormenting me for hours."

She gasped at the wild, intent look in his eyes. Fennel rushed at her. He slid his hands low around her hips, dipped down, and put his mouth in a warm wet assault on the well of her breasts.

Oh. My. God.

She drew a deep breath through her nose, which sent all that rich fennel straight into her brain. Desire cascaded over her body, tingling the tips of her fingers, sending chills down her arms and her back, making her feet arch even in her stilettos. She moaned as he pushed her back—his favorite move—only this time in the direction of the bed until her legs touched the mattress. He lowered her down, one hand supporting her across her shoulders, until the upper half of her body was on the bed. The lower half she supported with her heels square on the carpet, the tips of her stilettos digging in.

He pulled at the shoulders of her dress until the straps were hanging down her arms. In quick, practiced, but almost desperate maneuvers, he freed both breasts from her dress then her bra. He settled onto her left breast, his hands molding the flesh as he devoured her with his mouth, kissing, licking, suckling hard. At the same time, he plucked and pulled and rubbed the other.

She arched off the bed, which encouraged him to take more of her breast into his mouth. She whimpered and buried her hands in his hair. "Marcus" left her lips in a moan.

He drew back suddenly, his eyes fierce. "Turn over," he barked.

She leaned up on her elbows. "Why?"

His eyes once more fell to half-mast and he murmured. "Does it matter? Have you ever disliked anything I've done to you?"

She gasped and without demur flipped over so that she was facedown. Why wasn't she surprised that, before she could protest, he ripped her gown straight down the middle of the back, ignoring the zipper that was right there.

"You didn't like this dress?" she asked, smiling, her cheek pressed into the comforter. She knew what his answer would be.

He growled. "I liked this dress *too much* and so did all the other men in that room. Every time one of them looked at your chest, I was ready to draw my sword."

Havily shouldn't have enjoyed the sensation so much but she trembled all over at this absurd demonstration of testosterone. He kept tugging the dress until he had jerked it off her arms, down her abdomen, and pulled it from her hips. She now lay facedown in a black silk thong and thigh-high black stockings, the tops laced with red ribbon. He unclasped her bra and that, too, got tugged off her body until she rocked from side to side and was laughing.

She heard another displacement of clothing. His. Oh God.

She wrenched her head around and watched as he shucked his shirt, slacks, shoes, and socks. His briefs were tented, which of course made her groan. He caught the angle of her gaze and slowly slid the Calvins down until what she wanted most sprang free. He stepped out of his briefs and moved in behind her.

Spread your legs, he sent.

How wicked to be so on display for him. She felt his warm fleshy hand on her thong and with a whisper of thought folded her panties away. Now he could see every bit of her. She moved her hips from side to side.

He groaned then moved between her legs, and the hardest part of him teased the opening to her core. *You're wet* drifted through her mind, his voice in her head an erotic thrill.

You're here, she responded. *What else would I be?*

He planted his hands on her waist then smoothed his palms over her buttocks, up her hips, over her back. She writhed as his fingers played over the sensitive wing-locks. She cried out. Each touch sent shards of pleasure straight to her core. She clenched.

His hands moved off her back until he had one planted to each side of her. She felt his hips on her buttocks first then his mouth, as he kissed one of her wing-locks. She jerked at the sensation.

You like? he asked. He licked the delicate aperture.

Oh, God, was the only response she could think to send. He settled in with his tongue and little cries erupted from her throat. Her body undulated. A wave of fennel wafted over her. He teased her opening with the crown of his cock, but never quite made his way inside even though she pushed back with her hips, inviting him. What a tease he was.

He shifted his body to the side just a little. She felt the weight of his arm across her upper back as his free hand drifted down her buttocks. His fingers teased all the fully exposed, sensitive flesh. He played at her opening and when she groaned, he thrust two fingers inside hard. She cried out and he became a machine of movement as his arm worked her body like a piston, shoving his fingers inside and pulling them out, over and over, until she was clenching hard. At the same time, *at the same time,* his mouth moved over the same wing-lock, teasing, tasting. He suckled and bit. Moans left her mouth. Her body was on fire.

The orgasm hit her like a rocket and she was screaming into the comforter, her body undulating as his fingers kept working her. When her body settled down, he removed his fingers then leaned over her to smooth back her hair. He kissed the back of her neck then kissed his way up to her ear and murmured, "We're just getting started."

"Oh, God," she said aloud. She shuddered and moaned. She drew her arms up close to her body. She breathed in and let his scent envelop her once more. Fennel was thick in the air.

Do you like the view? she sent.

A growl returned and once again she felt his cock poised at her core.

She closed her eyes and savored. She was so happy.

Havily was right where Marcus wanted her, on her stomach and vulnerable, her legs spread. He wanted her from behind, then on her front, maybe sideways, against the wall, in the shower, on the sandy beach, in the arctic water, the hell if he cared. He would have her tonight over and over.

It was such a turn-on to see a naked woman, naked except of course for the ridiculous sexy stilettos that showed every gorgeous curve of her legs and the thigh-high stockings trimmed with red ribbon. She was a feast for him, a honeysuckle-drenched feast. He dragged air through his nose and let her erotic scent drift straight into his brain. He got up close to her.

He pushed at her entrance with the tip of his cock but he wasn't ready to enter her, not yet. He breathed in again and, because her hips flexed, she released a wave of honeysuckle that brought him straight to his knees, which was exactly where he wanted to be.

He pushed her legs farther apart, held her thighs wide, and licked, a long slow lick so that he could take into his mouth what she was giving.

He groaned, his cock throbbing, his mouth tingling.

He licked again. She whimpered and her pelvis bucked. In the same way he had held her shoulders down, he held her buttocks down, pinning her in place so that he could do to her what he needed to do. He drove his tongue deep and for the next several minutes, he tongue-fucked her, hard thrusts, his jaw pressing into the tender flesh around her opening as he went as deep as he could get.

Marcus. Oh, God.

Her voice in his head made him thrust harder, faster.

Marcus.

Each time she said his name, he rewarded her until he was punching into her and she was screaming once more.

Oh. Oh. Oh, bounced through his mind and made him smile as he tongued what belonged to him. He kept punching into her until the wild shudders of her body eased and her hips once more relaxed on the bed.

I love you, he sent.

She rolled slightly so that she could look at him. "You are taking such beautiful care of me. Is there anything I can do for you?" She licked her lips, which caused him to shudder. Several images pounded through his head, each one causing his cock to jerk. He massaged her buttocks, savoring the softness of her flesh, the womanliness of her body.

"You're here. That's enough." He knew what he wanted next, but first he had to feel her in just this position, take her just like this. He rose up and settled his hips between her legs. He positioned himself and with his hands on her hips he began easing his cock inside.

He hissed. She was so damn tight.

Marcus, she sent. *Heaven. Just heaven. The feel of you. God, yes.*

He thrust into her, his hands creeping up her waist, her back, spreading in ownership over her wing-locks and over her shoulders as he flexed his hips and set up a rhythm. He possessed her now. Again, he was where he wanted to be. Honeysuckle floated all around him. He leaned over and kissed the nape of her neck, his thrusts not too forceful. If he went any faster, he'd come and he didn't want to.

Heaven came back to him again.

He didn't want to leave the well of her body, but his chest was full of longing, that peculiar call of Second Earth. They needed to finish what had begun four months ago. It wouldn't take much to complete the *breh-hedden* now; his cock buried inside her, each of them taking blood at the same time, and the mutual sharing of deep mind-engagement.

Damn, his chest burned. He withdrew and she gave a cry of protest. He leaned over her and kissed her cheek. "It's time." He stroked the side of her neck with two fingers.

She groaned. She met his gaze. He stroked her neck again and a heavy wave of honeysuckle flowed over him. His nostrils flared as he squeezed his eyes shut and drank in her scent.

"Yes," she whispered.

He stepped away from her just enough to allow her to roll onto her back. "We need to get rid of the comforter."

When she sat up, he scooped her up in his arms then

carried her to the side of the bed. With a single thought, he folded the comforter to the chair in the corner. He kissed her and she licked his lips. "I taste some of me on you."

He kissed her again. "I love how you taste."

She smiled and put her arms around his neck. "I'm so grateful you're here."

"Me, too." He laid her back on the bed, on the black silk sheets. He stated his case plainly as only a vampire could do. "I want your blood."

She smiled. "And I want you to have my blood, now and forever."

His smile eased into a grin. "At the very least it will give me stamina."

She glanced down at his cock, shuddered, then tilted her head to expose her neck, "By all means then."

He laughed. He was loving this. He had forgotten how wonderful this could be, the closeness, the intimacy, the sex when love was on the menu.

He stretched out on top of her, pushing her thighs apart with his knees, making room for his big warrior body between her legs. But he felt her tense suddenly. "What is it?" he asked.

"This is it, isn't it? The *breh-hedden*."

"Yeah," he said, petting her peachy-red waves with his hands. "Once I have your blood in me, there will be no stopping, no going back."

"And I'll take your wrist?"

"Oh . . . yeah." His voice dropped an octave.

She tilted her neck and exposed her throat for him.

His cock throbbed all over again and, just to appease it a little, he connected with her entrance and thrust in about an inch. She moaned.

More, she sent.

Wait. But he groaned. His body wanted more, a helluva lot more, but he needed to hold back. He held steady as he dipped down and licked her throat. His fangs emerged, the scent of her rich in his nose.

Now was the time. He took a deep breath and eased his cock into her core, pushing and pushing until he was seated deep. Her arms slid around his shoulders and tightened. He began to drive into her and set a slow steady rhythm. But now his fangs throbbed. He feared, however, what would happen to his body once her blood hit his stomach and fired through his bloodstream. Even thinking about it made his lower back tense. Again he breathed, keeping his control tight for all that needed to happen first.

Oh, Marcus, she whimpered inside his head. *I'm on fire. Take me.*

He drew in a deep breath. With his fangs, he struck quick and deep, just to the right depth, and began to draw her nectar into his mouth. Oh. God.

Sensations rolled through Havily, of the penetration at her neck and the invasion down deep as he thrust his cock into her in quick erotic jabs, that which was so essentially masculine and so welcome. Her internal muscles pulled on him the way he pulled on her neck. She drew him into her and he groaned.

Because he pinned her at her throat, she didn't have the freedom to use her hands the way she wanted to, which was *all over him*.

Instead, her fingers were a light fluttery touch over his shoulders and up his neck, through his hair. She loved the feel of his hair through her fingers.

A groan flowed from his mouth even as he took her blood.

She was aroused, an inferno.

His thrusts grew heavier, his hips pumping hard.

Take ... my ... wrist, he said, his telepathic voice nothing more than a pant inside her head.

She reached for his arm and brought his wrist to her mouth. She felt the veins, stroked them as he pummeled her body low, his mouth still dragging against her neck. Fire traveled in streaks where he drank from her, ignited over the tender flesh between her legs and deep inside her body.

Her fangs emerged. She positioned his wrist over her lips. She licked his skin, drawing the veins forth. He groaned and she struck, swift and clean.

His blood hit her mouth in the most exotic elixir. *Fennel,* she sent.

Honeysuckle, he responded, groaning again.

For a long moment, she drank, savoring this part of him, wet, warm, and tasting of him. Oh. God. She clenched deep and her pelvis rolled.

He grunted, pushing harder into her.

Marcus, we'd better move this along. I'm so close.

You ready?

Yes.

I'll enter your mind, then you'll return the favor and after that just hold on.

Got it. She didn't know how much more she could take. Her body was on the edge of orgasm as it was.

She felt him push against her mental shields and she lowered them, all the way down, so that his mind flowed into hers, not in the simple way words could be layered telepathically over a mind, but in deep possession. She felt penetrated and taken all over again as she continued to drink from his wrist. She loved being a vampire and now he was in her head.

Havily, how beautiful you are. My heart is so full. Now . . . flow into my mind. Just . . . be ready and . . . let go.

Havily didn't wait. She moved to his mental shields and pushed. His shields gave way and he groaned as she slid into his head. Once there, his life was laid out before her like a feast. She saw his life, his memories like swiftly flowing images. Mostly, she felt the level of his pleasure, that he was poised on the threshold of ecstasy and barely holding back. She was struck overall with the intensity of his character, the willfulness of his life, his determination as he'd built his empire, the passion with which he'd fought as a warrior. All this came forward and swelled her heart, because this was the man who had met her in the darkening, not just to make love with her but to come to her when she needed him, to battle Crace, to get her to safety.

Then the *breh-hedden* changed the dynamic.

At first, all she felt was a tightening, everywhere, as though each sensation she experienced had been given a hard shove. She felt Marcus deep inside her, then she realized she was also feeling what he was feeling, the sensation of his powerful male muscles pushing into her and the feeling of her very wet sheath dragging against his cock.

Feeling his pleasure intensified her own and she clenched.

I can feel what you're feeling, he sent. *Oh, God!*

Same here. So . . . arousing.

Shit, yes. He groaned as he pulled on her vein. *Havily, I can't last much longer.*

Me, neither. Just . . . let go.

The orgasm when it streaked through her was doubled in intensity because she could feel his orgasm as well, pleasure stacked on pleasure. She gasped, releasing his wrist. She cried out. She wrapped her legs around his buttocks. His release kept coming and she cried out all over again at the pleasure she felt because it was his pleasure, his groans, her groans, his thrusts, her thrusts . . . and she loved it. He released her vein and arched back, his beautiful warrior body on display for her as he cried out again and again. His muscles looked pumped . . . everywhere.

By the time he had released the last of his seed she was panting hard and he was gasping for air. He looked down at her and met her gaze. "That was incredible."

She nodded, laughing and clutching air.

"We're one," he said, his words a quiet hush in the bedroom.

She nodded. She tried to understand what she was feeling. His hips had slowed and she was still inside his mind and . . . he was inside hers. She felt his blood in her body, warming her, swirling through her veins, like tendrils. His lips were parted and she saw her blood on his mouth. He planted his hands on either side of her shoulders.

She had the sense something was coming but she couldn't imagine what.

She waited.

He waited.

The sensation when it struck was like having a bolt of lightning pass through the chest. Havily's body arched as Marcus arched away from her.

Power flooded the space between them, arcing from chest to chest. The physical connection was profound, a bond forged that felt like steel connecting them.

A second later Havily lifted her hand and planted it on his shoulder. "Come with me," she said, her resonance split into a dozen vibrations.

He nodded, sweeping his arm around her waist.

She took him in a rush into the darkening, not to remain still but to move at light speed. Side by side they flew, without wings, through nether-space, neither of them clothed. A second passed—Crace's empty forge. Another second—Endelle in her secret meditation chamber. Another second—Thorne battling death vampires alongside Luken at the Superstitions. Another second—Leto in the war room as he surreptitiously deleted files. Another second and they overlooked the High Administrator of Brazil wearing rubies on her fingers and a blank expression on her face while the Commander serviced her and took her vein. Another second—the Eiffel Tower . . . then the ruins of the Parthenon . . . the Nile . . . the Great Barrier Reef . . . Mount Kilimanjaro, back to the Grand Canyon, then the deep rain forest of the Olympic Peninsula, then back to Bainbridge Island.

Havily thought the thought and they were back in bed together and he was on top of her again.

"Jesus," he murmured. "That was amazing."

She released a deep breath. "Is it because we're together, you and me?"

"I think so. I'm not sure." He glanced down at his chest. "I feel something between us, here." He leaned on his left elbow and rubbed his free hand over his heart. He then shifted his hand to her chest. "And here. Do you feel it?"

"Like we're connected. It feels almost physical." She couldn't help the smile. "Like binding tendrils of euphoria."

He nodded. "Yes, *binding tendrils of euphoria.*"

She nodded but her smile dimmed. "The bastard enthralls the High Administrators."

"We have work to do."

She dipped her chin then slipped her arms around his neck. "But right now, we have love to make. Yes?"

He growled low and also dipped his chin. "Your blood strengthens me. I may just keep you up all night."

"You forget. I've had your blood as well, so if that's a promise you're making, I can take it."

He chuckled, kissed her on the lips, and once more moved inside her.

A week after the Ambassadors Festival, Rith Do'onwa moved down the main hallway of his home in Burma outside of Mandalay, Second Earth. This was one of the homes he owned, but perhaps his favorite. It was a British Colonial replica constructed of the finest mahogany and modeled on the British homes from the 1800s, Mortal Earth.

Three women kept his home in perfect condition, three Burmese slaves he'd had for a very long time, centuries in fact. They were well trained, as they should be after so many decades of obedient service.

When he reached the first bedroom, the largest of all the bedrooms, he paused in the doorway. He felt a familiar rush of pleasure, a kind of dizzy euphoria that he'd first experienced a year ago when he'd come across the mortal-with-wings in the future streams.

In recent weeks, he had seen her here, in this very room, in this massive four-poster bed, tucked beneath lavender silk sheets and a coverlet of silk in a patchwork of elegant jewel tones. Of course, he'd purchased everything in this chamber because of what he'd seen in the future streams, including the antique Burmese Buddha, a lovely bronze piece settled on a small table to the right of the bed.

She would find peace in seeing the Buddha.

Rith smiled.

He could hardly wait to bring her here, to keep her here. His master would have need of her, though in exactly what way had been unclear to him in the future streams. But the why of the situation did not matter to Rith, only that he fulfilled his role in the Commander's magnificent destiny.

He believed in the Oriental state of mind, in patience and in getting all the pawns lined up before making a move.

The death of High Administrator Crace had simplified his future—but then he'd already foreseen Crace's death.

Rith knew things that he was pretty sure even Greaves didn't know. He knew things because he was able to ride the future streams, to pluck phenomenal amounts of critical information from those glorious ribbons of light, usually far in advance of most Seers around the world. He had therefore already *seen* that Crace would die in his forge, even though the details of his death had been unclear at the time. He'd also foreseen that Havily Morgan would complete the *breh-hedden* with Warrior Marcus and upon that completion would weld a bond of power that put her beyond his reach or even Greaves's. From that point in time, no matter where the woman was, her warrior guardian could get to her. No tricks, just a massive amount of newly created preternatural power.

Rith left the prepared bedroom and went to his little sanctuary off his formal study. In his meditation chamber, a room only nine feet square, sat a single piece of furniture, a chaise-longue covered in soft dark blue velvet. He closed and locked the door. He stretched out on the well-cushioned chaise, folded his hands over his abdomen, and closed his eyes. He took a deep breath and employed a form of deep relaxation that permitted him to enter the streams of rainbow-hued light. From those streams he could map the future.

Havily Morgan's stream of light had always been powerful, but it shone now with a soft green aura. Beautiful. If she hadn't been the enemy, he would have reveled in the sight. The ribbon expanded and the vision came. Rith saw her in a future stream, flying above White Lake, her hand linked with Guardian Alison Wells. Above them, as they flew, the portal to Third Earth began to open, just a little. He knew of this prophecy, that Alison Wells would open the dimensional gateway to Third Earth even though none of the Seers' reports spoke of it. But then he was no ordinary Seer. He made a mental note of the vision, filing it away for later use.

For now, he sought another ribbon of light, one that was gold and amethyst in color. The ribbon belonging to the mortal-with-wings, the one the Seers all over the world had assigned great value to, the one belonging to Parisa Lovejoy.

Yes, ascendiate Lovejoy was now the key, and Rith would do what he must to define the exact point in time at which he would take possession of the woman and lay her at Greaves's feet. She was the real prize since she had a gift, an unparalleled power that would tip the war in the Commander's direction. She was a preternatural voyeur, but that wasn't the power that interested him. Her real value lay in the composition and meaning of her *royle* wings, even though he still didn't understand how the possession of such wings constituted a power that could be used for Greaves's war effort. However, he was a man of faith and he believed that all would be made known to him in due course. For now he began putting his plans in place to secure her.

Rith was a simple man. He had but one overriding need, to be of use to his master. From the moment he had partaken of dying blood, he had belonged heart and soul to Darian Greaves. He could not explain the phenomenon;

nor did he care the cause or the reason. He was a man who accepted his lot.

He had always had one thing in common with Crace. Rith, like Crace, wanted to be seated at the right hand of God when Greaves finally brought his plans into the fullness of time and won two worlds. He wanted to be there not because of a need to rule, nor for a need for power, but because he lived for Greaves, to serve him, to please him, to be near him. His was a love that transcended gender, transcended levels of power, transcended all rational thought. He had been born to serve, he had chosen his master, and he would do everything in his power to see a light of approval in the Commander's beautiful ascended eye.

When he released Parisa's ribbon of light, he searched for the dark blue ribbon he had been familiar with from the day of his ascension so many centuries ago. The ribbon was his.

He entered the stream of light and to his surprise found an image that swelled his heart. He was donning a uniform that belonged to Second Earth Merry Ascenders, a household cleaning service. How quaint. In this vision, he rode in a van belonging to the cleaning service. The van stopped a few yards away from a gas station near the I-10 and Litchfield Road, Second Earth, a Mobil Oil station. The driver of the van made a call to Central. A moment later an archway appeared and beyond Rith could see an olive grove and a long drive set with terra-cotta cement-formed pavers.

Rith knew the property well. It belonged to Warrior Medichi.

He drew out of the future streams. His heart beat rapidly. The time was nearing in which he would play a critical role for the Coming Order, and apparently he needed to apply for employment at Second Earth Merry Ascenders.

More than a week had passed since the Ambassadors Festival. Parisa struggled to find the right words to tell Medichi of her decision. She would make him unhappy, but it must be done.

Life had settled down at the villa so much so that a cleaning crew had arrived and ejected both Parisa and Medichi from the main house.

So she walked the olive grove now, but with a heavy heart. Warrior Medichi stood thirty yards away, watching her, always watching her, *guarding* her, even though a dome of mist shielded the property from powerful intruders.

He was so tall and so handsome and even at that distance a faint trace of sage touched the air. He wore jeans and his black T-shirt pulled across his muscular shoulders, shoulders she had leaned on at the spectacle disaster. His long black hair was still damp from a recent shower and drawn back in the ritual *cadroen*.

Her heart hurt as she watched him, his head lowered as he spoke into his phone. It was strange to think of him as a vampire, a creature with fangs who could take her blood. Yet how many times had she fantasized that very thing?

None of those fantasies would happen now. She'd made her decision.

Second Earth was not for her and she would not be ascending. She'd seen too much, been through too much, and despite the fact that she was more normal in this world than in her birth-world, she'd had enough.

She might have wings, the ability to throw a hand-blast, and she might even be a preternatural voyeur, but she was not built for war. She knew that. She wanted the world of her library back. She'd called in sick for over a week now so she was due back at work. Besides, she longed for the quiet and order of books and computers and a building that smelled of ink and print.

When Medichi turned away from her slightly, still talking into his phone, she caught sight of one of the estate workers waving to her, a pleasant-looking man with somewhat Asian features. He had a wide forehead and a broad nose. He wore white cotton trousers and a loose white cotton shirt. He must work in the olive press. He smiled and waved her forward.

A sense of ease came over her, even happiness as she moved toward him. "Do you work in the press?" she called out.

He shrugged and shook his head. It was possible he didn't speak English. With the ability to dematerialize, she supposed he could have come from anywhere on Second Earth to work on the estate.

Only when she drew within two yards of him did the hairs on the nape of her neck rise and give warning, but she didn't know what it meant. She thought perhaps this poor man was in danger. She looked around, hunting for a death vampire that somehow had made its way onto the property. But that was when a lean arm surrounded her, choking her, and she felt the needle prick her neck.

She had just enough consciousness to turn her head and see that the only adversary present was the man with the wide forehead and broad nose.

How strange . . .

Antony, she called out softly within her mind, something she did when she needed comfort.

Antony. Then . . . nothing.

Medichi heard his name within his head, *Antony.* Parisa? She must have telepathic abilities and still not know it. He turned toward her, sliding his phone back into the pocket of his black cargoes.

The hour was one in the afternoon and Parisa was some twenty or so yards away, not far from the building that housed the olive press. Had she spoken his name within his mind? Or had he imagined it?

She was turned away from him as though she was watching something very intently. She was even smiling.

She looked so pretty today in a pink-flowered sundress.

She wore her dark brown hair in loose curls on top of her head against the climbing June heat. He ached to go to her and take her in his arms.

Then the hairs on the nape of his neck rose.

Oh, shit.

He didn't wait, but folded his sword into his hand.

He turned in a circle and looked for the enemy but found nothing. The cleaning service was in his home doing the usual. This particular service had careful employment screening procedures.

He scanned his property carefully, turning, turning.

Still nothing.

Huh.

He'd just gotten off the phone with Thorne, who informed him that Marcus intended to serve in the field with the warriors two nights a week, in addition to taking on the duties of High Administrator of Desert Southwest Two. Medichi liked the arrangement. The moment Havily had stood up during Zach's birthday celebration and made her plea for the shift in Marcus's duties, he'd been on board. Marcus had what it took to administer a Territory and yeah, Endelle *sucked* at it.

He started moving in Parisa's direction. He was about to fold his sword away when the hairs on his nape fluttered once more. Something *was* wrong. He could *feel* it. Parisa remained in the same position, standing very still, which suddenly struck him as odd.

"Parisa?" he called out, his feet moving faster.

When she didn't respond, he called out her name again. She didn't turn toward him or in any way indicate that she'd even heard him. What the hell was going on?

He started running. A dust devil kicked up and moved through the grove, passing near her. Leaves blew in circles, but the summery pink-flowered sundress didn't move, not even a little around the hem.

Then he understood.

"No," he cried out.

What he had thought was Parisa rippled then disappeared . . . a time-delayed hologram.

She was gone. His woman was gone.

He fell to his knees and roared to the heavens.

Two hours later, with a hundred Militia Warriors combing his estate, with all the Warriors of the Blood surrounding him, with his villa and the guesthouse turned upside down, he had to accept the fact that Parisa was gone. Taken. But how and by whom?

He sat on the ground where Parisa had disappeared.

Marcus and Havily materialized in front of him. Marcus had his arm around Havily's waist. She extended a sheet of paper to him.

"We had the cleaning service investigated," Marcus said. "This man was new, the one pictured here. The service checked him out thoroughly. He passed all their stringent tests, but Colonel Seriffe knows him as a servant of Greaves's by the name of Rith Do'onwa."

Antony stared at the face of his enemy. The rage he felt was too powerful to give expression to. It lived in him now, a reflection of the day when he had first learned of his preternatural powers and had slain his enemies. He had raged then. He raged now. The woman meant for him was gone, taken by a man who he vowed would one day die by his hands.

A week later, Havily dressed with care and as quietly as she could. She didn't want to disturb Marcus. He had fallen asleep after making love to her, but he was exhausted. He had battled through the night, beside Warrior Medichi, slaying death vampires at the Superstitions.

His routine was demanding but he could handle it. She'd given him some of her blood, which always strengthened him, so he would rest until about one, then come into the administration building to fulfill his new duties.

Endelle had begun the process of having him confirmed

as her High Administrator of the Southwest Desert Territory. The committee wouldn't oppose Marcus because Endelle had agreed to accept the surrender of four death vampires as payment for the incendiary bomb attack at the Ambassadors Festival. Everyone knew that other, more powerful vampires were to blame, but without proof, pursuing the matter was useless.

Wearing a light green cotton skirt, white ruffled blouse, and four-inch heels, she crossed the room to Marcus and, as was her habit, she put her hand on his forehead. *I love you,* she sent.

Usually he offered a smile but didn't wake up. This morning his eyes opened and he released a heavy sigh. "Tend to Medichi, please."

"You know I will." She leaned down and kissed him on the lips.

"I love you," he said.

"I love you, too, sooo much."

He nodded, smiled, then closed his eyes. He released a deep sigh.

She smiled at the expression, kissed him again, then went in search of Medichi.

She found him in the olive grove. She crossed to him and slid her arm around his waist. He accepted her presence and rested his muscled arm loosely across her shoulders. He had showered and wore white cotton against the oppressive summer heat. It was now July and the humidity was rising, a promise of the forthcoming summer monsoons. His damp hair hung halfway down his back.

"She was here, in this very spot," he said. "Now she's gone."

"Antony," she said softly. She was not going to cry.

He released a ragged sigh. "What am I going to do? I failed her, just as I failed my wife, and our unborn son, all those centuries ago. How could I have let this happen? Dammit, I know better."

She hugged him. There was nothing she could say. The

enemy was powerful and for whatever reason, in this situation, he'd gotten the upper hand. So now Medichi suffered as all the warriors suffered when their loved ones were impacted by the war. "We'll find her. We're all looking for her. We'll find her. Endelle has permitted me to hunt for her in the darkening."

He uttered no response except the lengthening of his breaths as he strove to contain himself.

If she could undo this, she would. If she could spare him, she would. "Tell me, what can I do for you, my friend?" she asked.

He looked down at her and his expression softened. "Love your warrior, while you can. Love him with all your heart. Be with him because in a breath it can all disappear."

"I know," she whispered. "I know."

Marcus held Havily's hand in too firm a grasp, but he couldn't seem to do less than that right now. He walked with his *breh* beside Kerrick and Alison. As a group, they were crossing the rolling lawn of Kerrick's mansion in Scottsdale Two, heading in the direction of the great mounds of honeysuckle that topped the stone walls at the back of his property.

Kerrick had already told him what was back there and his heart ached, which was why he had a hard grip on Havily's hand. She didn't complain, however, but pressed his hand in response every now and then. He glanced at her as they walked.

"It'll be all right," she said.

"How can it be all right?" he asked. "All I can think about is Parisa and Medichi."

"I know."

Kerrick called a halt to the march. He drew Alison close to him on his left. "Marcus, we don't have to do this right now. We can do it another time."

Marcus met his anguished green eyes. Goddamn, they

were all in turmoil because of the kidnapping, all of them reminded of past losses and present dangers.

He took a deep breath. He strove to remember his sister and her wisdom, the serenity of her nature, her acceptance of life on Second Earth, of the profound impermanence of ascension despite their relatively immortal self-healing state. As he thought of Helena, peace descended on him. *Life is for the living,* she had said.

But something more, he thought: *Life is for the battling.* They were battling now, to find Parisa, and somehow they would. And if in their pursuit they discovered she no longer lived, then he and the warriors, as well as Endelle, Alison, and Havily would all work to get Medichi through. They would rally around him, support him, carry him on their backs every step of the way until he could overcome this loss.

He looked at Havily, and released her hand so that he could slide his arm around her waist and draw her close. He searched her eyes. *I love you,* he sent.

She nodded, more than once. He brushed away the tears that rolled down her cheeks. He felt her sadness as his own; he could feel the warmth of the sun on her bare shoulders, that her left heel had sunk into the lawn—she moved it now—that her thong was causing her trouble, which she ignored, all evidence of their connection, results of the *breh-hedden.* He loved her so much.

He turned back to Kerrick. "I think it's appropriate we do this today. I want to do this."

Kerrick nodded, but his jaw was tight and his breathing harsh. "Let's do it then."

He led the way to the fiery red honeysuckle and stepped between an overlap in what was actually two walls. From a distance the breach could not be detected. The honeysuckle had long since formed an arch overhead. Sparrows chattered madly, disliking the intrusion. A few wasps moved here and there. A green-throated hummingbird made a whirring appearance then darted away.

Marcus dipped his head in those places where the honey-suckle had sunk under its own weight. A few more steps and he arrived at an opening. Shit, his knees felt weak and his head spun for there were five gravestones, old weathered stones, lined up in a row. Three belonged to his loved ones, Helena, Christine, and Kerr; the other two had been placed in honor of the servants who had died in the explosion that same night so long ago.

He moved to stand in front of Helena's grave and yep, his knees quit on him and he fell to a kneeling position, his heart in his throat. He wasn't surprised that Havily joined him, also on her knees despite the fact that the grass would probably leave stains on her sundress. But he knew her. She wouldn't care about that. He put an arm around her shoulders and held her close.

The funny thing was, Kerrick joined him, on his knees, Alison as well. How long they remained there, he couldn't say, but it felt right.

At long last, Marcus bowed his head and murmured prayers to the Creator for his sister, his niece, his nephew, and finally it was enough. The burden of his grief, the rage of his loss dissipated. With Havily by his side, her head leaning on his shoulder, with Kerrick's hand resting on his opposite shoulder, it was enough. Helena would always be the greatest loss of his life, but her legacy continued, in the child Alison carried who already bore her name, in the words Helena had spoken to him that had allowed him to give his heart to Havily, in the love he would always bear for his beautiful wise sister.

Yes, it was enough.

ASCENSION TERMINOLOGY

ascender n. A mortal human of earth who has moved permanently to the second dimension.

ascendiate n. A mortal human who has answered the *call to ascension* and thereby commences his or her *rite of ascension.*

ascension n. The act of moving permanently from one dimension to a higher dimension.

ascension ceremony n. Upon the completion of the *rite of ascension,* the mortal undergoes a ceremony in which loyalty to the laws of Second Society is professed and the attributes of the vampire mantle along with immortality are bestowed.

the Borderlands pr. n. Those geographic areas that form dimensional borders at both ends of a dimensional pathway. The dimensional pathway is an access point through which travel can take place from one dimension to the next.

***breh-hedden* n.** (Term from an ancient language.) A mate-bonding ritual that can only be experienced by the most powerful warriors and the most powerful preternaturally gifted women. Effects of the *breh-hedden* can include but are not limited to: specific scent experience, extreme physical/sexual attraction, loss of rational thought, primal sexual drives, inexplicable need to bond, powerful need to experience deep *mind-engagement,* et cetera.

***cadroen* n.** (Term from an ancient language.) The name for the hair clasp that holds back the ritual long hair of a *Warrior of the Blood.*

call to ascension n. A period of time, usually involving several weeks, in which the mortal human has experienced some or all of, but not limited to, the following: specific dreams about the next dimension, deep yearnings and longings of a soulful and inexplicable nature, visions of and possibly visits to any of the dimensional *Borderlands,* et cetera. The mortal human who experiences the hallmarks of the call to ascension will at some point feel compelled to answer, usually by demonstrating significant preternatural power.

Central pr. n. The office of the current administration that tracks movement of *death vampires* in both the second dimension and on *Mortal Earth* for the purpose of alerting the *Warriors of the Blood* and the *Militia Warriors* to illegal activities.

the darkening n. An area of *nether-space* that can be found during meditations and/or with strong preternatural darkening capabilities. Such abilities enable the *ascender* to move into nether-space and remain there or to use nether-space in order to be two places at once.

death vampire n. Any *vampire,* male or female, who partakes of *dying blood* automatically becomes a death vampire. Death vampires can have, but are not limited to, the following characteristics: remarkably increased physical strength, an increasingly porcelain complexion true of all ethnicities so that death vampires have a long-term reputation of looking very similar, a faint bluing of the porcelain complexion, increasing beauty of face, the ability to enthrall, the blackening of *wings* over a period of time. Though death vampires are not gender-specific, most are male. See *vampire.*

dimensional worlds n. Eleven thousand years ago the first *ascender,* Luchianne, made the difficult transition from *Mortal Earth* to what became known as Second Earth. In the early millennia four more dimensions were discovered, Luchianne always leading the way. Each dimension's ascenders exhibited expanding preternatural power before ascension. Upper dimensions are generally closed off to the dimension or dimensions below.

duhuro **n.** (Term from an ancient language.) A word of respect that in the old language combines the spiritual offices of both servant and master. To call someone *duhuro* is to offer a profound compliment suggesting great worth.

dying blood n. Blood extracted from a mortal or an *ascender* at the point of death. This blood is highly addictive in nature. There is no known treatment for anyone who partakes of dying blood. The results of ingesting dying blood include but are not limited to: increased physical, mental, or preternatural power; a sense of extreme euphoria; a deep sense of well-being; a sense of omnipotence and fearlessness; the taking in of the preternatural powers of the host body; et cetera. If dying blood is not taken on a regular basis, extreme abdominal cramps result without ceasing. Note: Currently there is an antidote not for the addiction to dying blood itself but for the various results of ingesting dying blood. This means that a *death vampire* who drinks dying blood and then partakes of the antidote will not show the usual physical side effects of ingesting dying blood; no whitening or faint bluing of the skin, no beautifying of features, no blackening of the *wings,* et cetera.

folding v. Slang for "dematerialization," since some believe that one does not actually dematerialize self or objects but rather one "folds space" to move self or objects from one place to another. There is much scientific debate on this subject since at present neither theory can be proved.

grid n. The technology used by *Central* that allows for the tracking of *death vampires* primarily at the *Borderlands* on both *Mortal Earth* and *Second Earth*. Death vampires by nature carry a strong, trackable signal, unlike normal *vampires*.

Guardian of Ascension pr. n. A prestigious title and rank at present given only to those *Warriors of the Blood* who also serve to guard powerful *ascendiates* during their *rite of ascension*. In millennia past Guardians of Ascension were also those powerful ascenders who offered themselves in unique and powerful service to Second Society.

High Administrator pr. n. The designation given to a leader of a Second Earth *Territory*.

identified sword n. A sword made by Second Earth metallurgy that has the preternatural capacity to become identified to a single *ascender*. The identification process involves holding the sword by the grip for several continuous seconds. The identification of a sword to a single ascender means that only that person can touch or hold the sword. If anyone tries to take possession other than the owner, that person will die.

Militia Warrior pr. n. One of hundreds of thousands of warriors who serve Second Earth society as a policing force for the usual civic crimes and as a battling force, in squads only, to fight against the continual depredations of *death vampires* on both *Mortal Earth* and Second Earth.

mind-engagement n. The ability to penetrate another mind and experience the thoughts and memories of the other person. The ability to receive another mind and allow that person to experience one's thoughts and memories. These abilities must be present in order to complete the *breh-hedden.*

mist n. A preternatural creation designed to confuse the mind and thereby hide things or people. Most mortals and *ascenders* are unable to see mist. The powerful ascender, however, is capable of seeing mist, which usually appears as an intricate mesh, a cloud, or a web-like covering.

Mortal Earth pr. n The name for First Earth or the current modern world known simply as earth.

nether-space n. The unknowable, unmappable regions of space. The space between dimensions is considered nether-space as well as the space found in *the darkening.*

preternatural voyeurism n. The ability to "open a window" with the power of the mind in order to see people and events happening elsewhere in real time. Two of the limits of preternatural voyeurism are: The voyeur must usually know the person or place, and if the voyeur is engaged in *darkening* work, it is very difficult to make use of preternatural voyeurism at the same time.

pretty-boy n. Slang for *death vampire,* since most death vampires are male.

rite of ascension n. A three-day period during which time an *ascendiate* contemplates ascending to the next higher dimension.

royle **n.** (Term from an ancient language.) The literal translation is "a benevolent wind." More loosely translated, *royle* refers to the specific quality of having the capacity to create a state of benevolence, of goodwill, within an entire people or culture.

royle **adj.** (Term from an ancient language.) This term is generally used to describe a specific coloration of *wings:* cream with three narrow bands at the outer tips of the wings when in full span. The bands are always burnished gold, amethyst, and black. Because Luchianne, the first *ascender* and first *vampire,* had this coloration on her wings, anyone, therefore, whose wings matched Luchianne's is said to have *royle* wings. Having *royle* wings is considered a tremendous gift, holding great promise for the world.

Seer pr. n. An *ascender* gifted with the preternatural ability to ride the future streams and report on future events.

Seers Fortress pr. n. *Seers* have traditionally been gathered into compounds designed to provide a highly peaceful environment, thereby enhancing the Seer's ability to ride the future streams. The information gathered at a Seers Fortress benefits the local *High Administrator.* Some believe that the term *fortress* emerged as a protest to the prison-like conditions the Seers often have to endure.

spectacle n. The name given to events of gigantic proportion that include but are not limited to: trained squadrons of DNA-altered geese, swans, and ducks; *ascenders* with the specialized and dangerous skills of flight performance; intricate and often massive light and fireworks displays; as well as various forms of music.

Supreme High Administrator pr. n. The ruler of Second Earth. See *High Administrator.*

Territory pr. n. For the purpose of governance, Second Earth is divided up into groups of countries called Territories. Because the total population of Second Earth is only 1 percent of *Mortal Earth,* Territories were established as a simpler means of administering Second Society law. See *High Administrator.*

Trough pr. n. A slang term for a dimensional pathway. See *Borderlands.*

Twoling pr. n. Anyone born on Second Earth is a Twoling.

vampire n. The natural state of the *ascended* human. Every ascender is a vampire. The qualities of being a vampire include but are not limited to: immortality, the use of fangs to take blood, the use of fangs to release potent chemicals, increased physical power, increased preternatural ability, et cetera. Luchianne created the word *vampire* upon her *ascension* to Second Earth to identify in one word the totality of the changes she experienced upon that ascension. From the first, the taking of blood was viewed as an act of reverence and bonding, not as a means of death. The *Mortal Earth* myths surrounding the word *vampire* for the most part personify the Second Earth *death vampire.*

Warriors of the Blood pr. n. An elite fighting unit of usually seven powerful warriors, each with phenomenal preternatural ability and capable of battling several *death vampires* at any one time.

wings n. All *ascenders* eventually produce wings from wing-locks. *Wing-lock* is the term used to describe the apertures on the ascender's back from which the feathers and attending mesh-like superstructure emerge. Mounting wings involves a hormonal rush that some liken to sexual release. Flight is one of the finest experiences of ascended life. Wings can be held in a variety of positions, including but not limited to: full-mount, close-mount, aggressive mount, et cetera. Wings emerge over a period of time from one year to several hundred years. Wings can, but do not always, begin small in one decade, then grow larger in later decades.

Don't miss the first novel in this
spectacular new series from Caris Roane

ASCENSION

ISBN: 978-0-312-53371-7

Available from St. Martin's Paperbacks

. . . and look for

WINGS OF FIRE

ISBN: 978-0-312-53373-1

Coming in September 2011 from St. Martin's Paperbacks